MUCH

Rubbing away ━━━━━━━━━━ lling, Georgie came bac━━━━━━━━━ in front of Rob. "When my father sent for me and said he'd take me back if I agreed to marry Travers, I had no choice but to say yes. My mother's inheritance does not come to me until I am thirty. Do you know a gentleman who would wish to wait so long, who would take me with nothing to my name?"

He took her hands, which made her want to cry all the harder. "Georgina, they would line the streets of London if only you would say the word. And I would be at the head of the line."

"What?"

"Do you think your father would change his mind if someone else offered for your hand?" He grinned down at her like a lunatic. "Someone with more wealth and better social position than Travers could ever hope to have." Loosening his hands from hers, he stroked his thumb down her cheek, leaving a trail of fire in its wake. "Someone you would prefer to marry."

Scarcely able to make sense of his words, Georgie gasped as Rob tilted her face up to his and pressed his mouth to hers. As though the world around her had stopped, she knew only the touch of his lips and the fierce longing that their gentle touch awakened in her. She slid her hands up to cup his face, to keep them together as long as she possibly could.

He must have taken that as a signal, for he immediately deepened the kiss . . .

Books by Jenna Jaxon

The Widows' Club

TO WOO A WICKED WIDOW

WEDDING THE WIDOW

WHAT A WIDOW WANTS

MUCH ADO ABOUT A WIDOW

The House of Pleasure Series

ONLY SEDUCTION WILL DO

ONLY A MISTRESS WILL DO

ONLY MARRIAGE WILL DO

ONLY SCANDAL WILL DO

Published by Kensington Publishing Corporation

MUCH ADO
ABOUT
A WIDOW

JENNA
JAXON

ZEBRA BOOKS
KENSINGTON PUBLISHING CORP.
www.kensingtonbooks.com

ZEBRA BOOKS are published by

Kensington Publishing Corp.
119 West 40th Street
New York, NY 10018

All Kensington titles, imprints, and distributed lines are available at special quantity discounts for bulk purchases for sales promotion, premiums, fund-raising, educational, or institutional use.

Special book excerpts or customized printings can also be created to fit specific needs. For details, write or phone the office of the Kensington Sales Manager: Attn.: Sales Department. Kensington Publishing Corp., 119 West 40th Street, New York, NY 10018. Phone: 1-800-221-2647.

Zebra and the Z logo Reg. U.S. Pat. & TM Off.

First Printing: January 2020
ISBN-13: 978-1-4201-4973-9
ISBN-10: 1-4201-4973-3

ISBN-13: 978-1-4201-4974-6 (eBook)
ISBN-10: 1-4201-4974-1 (eBook)

10 9 8 7 6 5 4 3 2 1

Printed in the United States of America

For my very best friend, Wayne,
whose friendship and love
has been my best adventure ever

ACKNOWLEDGMENTS

I wish to thank, as always, my agent, Kathy Green and my editor, John Scognamiglio, for all your help, support, and guidance with the writing of this book. I also, as usual, wish to thank my wonderful beta readers, Alexandra Christle and Ella Quinn, for all their help with pointing out the faulty grammar and Regency blunders. Special thanks to Ella for helping with all things nautical in the book, of which I was particularly unschooled. This book is all the richer because of you all.

Chapter One

Late January 1817

Staring out at the bleak winter landscape of frozen grass and lifeless trees, Lady Georgina Kirkpatrick decided that the infernal bumping of the carriage taking her back to her father's estate in East Sussex had been substantially less annoying to her yesterday. Of course, then Georgie had not spent eight hours the previous day being bounced about, plagued by roads that seemed to conjure up every rock, good-sized boulder, and deep rut possible just to shatter her spine. Now, though she was determined to face the rest of the drive with the steely fortitude passed down by generations of her family's ancestors, she couldn't help but sigh over the fact that the arduous ride was rather symbolic of the onerous marriage she faced at journey's end.

The carriage hit a particularly deep rut, tossing Georgie into the lap of her lady's maid, Clara, and making Lulu, Georgie's King Charles spaniel, yip vigorously.

"Goodness gracious." Georgie picked herself up off of Clara's ample lap and gathered the protesting Lulu into her arms. "There, there, my girl. Are you quite all right?"

Lulu yipped again and sneezed.

Inspecting the dog's paws and legs, Georgie gave a nod

and placed the little animal on the soft, black leather seat beside her once more. "Folger. Folger, I say." She stood up, swaying with the rocking motion of the carriage, and rapped on the trap with her bare knuckles. A little too smartly from the sting of them.

The trap door opened, and one of her father's coachmen peered down at her. "Something the matter, my lady?"

"Is it at all possible to avoid at least some of the ruts in the road, Folger?" She grabbed hold of the lip of the trap as the conveyance hit another bump. "I'm being tossed about like a leaf in a high wind." If this ghastly motion continued she might even cast up her accounts, though that was something she could not tell her coachman. "Poor Lulu cannot stay on the seat."

Folger sent a sharp look toward the spaniel, who bared her teeth at him in return. "I'll do what I can, my lady. This road's a bad 'un, especially this time of year. I'll slow the team down a mite. That should help."

"Thank you, Folger. You are a prince among coachmen."

The elderly servant ducked his head, his cheeks turning even redder than the cold had already made them.

Georgie beamed at him and lowered the trap. "He's one of Father's more reasonable servants." She sat down and pulled Lulu into her lap, completely disregarding possible damage to her new blue-striped pelisse. "I'm surprised he's lasted this long in my father's employ."

"Why's that, my lady?" Clara's head tilted to the side like that of an inquisitive finch. She'd only been with Georgie for two months and still had a lot to learn about the household.

"Because my father prefers his servants to do exactly as they're told, no questions and no deviations. Folger should have just told me that he had his orders to deliver me to Blackham Castle by sundown this evening, and that should have been that. No slowing down suggested at all." Georgie grinned at her maid. "If it had been Dobson on the seat, he'd have sped the horses up."

Clara chuckled, then remembered herself and cleared her throat. "When you're married you can hire a coachman who will take your orders and no others."

As if Clara had waved a magic wand, Georgie's good mood turned to dust, and she frowned, twisting around in her seat to stare out the window. "My husband will be the one to hire the coachmen, Clara. Hire all the outside servants." She turned her gaze on her maid—her hard-won lady's maid—and all the joy Georgie had known during the past weeks with her friends and brother at Hunter's Cross attending Fanny's wedding drained slowly out of her, leaving her as empty as a husk.

"I'm ever so sorry, my lady." Clara eased back in her seat, trying to disappear it seemed. Glancing at Georgie and away, she picked at the hem of her handkerchief. "Perhaps Lord Travers will—"

"Never mind, Clara. From what I know of Lord Travers he is a man, much like my father, who will wish to bend all his servants to his will alone. Perhaps that is why Father agreed to his original suit and to its renewal since I became a widow. Like always fancies like from my experience." Georgie wrinkled her nose. The idea of being married to a man like her father almost succeeded in swaying her from her resolve to marry Lord Travers.

"Your father is not like you at all, is he?"

"Hardly." Georgie sniffed. To think she bore any resemblance to her father made her cringe. "If Father had tried to find a suitor who would be more offensive to me, I don't think he would have succeeded." She shivered. "Lord Travers managed to make my second Season sheer torture with his excessive attentions to me. I could not attend any party, rout, ball, soiree, or entertainment without seeing him leering in my face, fawning over me, and constantly asking me to dance."

"Did you have to accept every one of his requests? Could you not turn him down a time or two?"

"Only if I didn't want to dance very much that night." As though she'd bitten into a sour lemon, Georgie puckered her mouth at the memory. "He always managed to be the first gentleman to ask me to stand up with him at the ball. Unless some other gentleman had asked for a dance beforehand, if I refused Travers, I could not have danced with anyone else who asked me for that dance. It would probably have been remarked upon, too—to my detriment instead of his, of course." She sighed heavily. That second Season had been trying to say the least. "So inevitably I'd accept him, and he would smirk and saunter off, very proud of himself, and wait for our dance." Recalling the naked hunger in his black-eyed gaze, she shivered. Even when dancing with other gentlemen she'd been uncomfortably aware of him watching her—like a thousand dirty fingers poking her bare flesh.

"He sounds like a very undesirable gentleman to be sure."

"Undesired by me, certainly. Other ladies, apparently, were not so discerning. There was much gossip about him and Lady Osbourne that Season, and one of my cousins who had come out that same year as well said her mama had stricken his name from her list of eligible suitors for just such behavior." If only Georgie's own mother had been alive then, perhaps she could have made a stand against Father.

Instead, Georgie's father's sister, Aunt Augusta, had brought Georgie out, but under strict instructions about chaperonage from her father and the decree that she would not marry during her first Season so that he could turn to arranging the marriage himself. At that time he'd been busy with arranging marriages for her older twin sisters, Emma and Mary. That distraction had lasted two years and had been a godsend for Georgie because it had allowed her to circulate throughout the *ton*, making the acquaintance of many gentlemen without fear of making an alliance with any of them. Which was just as well. She'd not been out a month before she'd known without a doubt she could never marry anyone other than Mr. Isaac Kirkpatrick, their parish vicar's son.

"Lord Travers must have behaved scandalously for a mother to have stricken an earl from her list." The horror in Clara's voice brought Georgie back to the swaying carriage.

"My cousin didn't know all the particulars at the time—her mother would not tell her everything and for good reason. Such things are not spoken of to virginal young ladies. But after I married Mr. Kirkpatrick, I was able to find out more about Lord Travers's escapades." She leaned forward and lowered her voice, even though no one else was there to hear. "He had ruined at least one girl on one of his outlying estates, leaving her with a child to raise. And he dallied with a young lady of good family."

Clara's eyes widened. "They didn't force him to marry her?"

Shaking her head, Georgie sat back. "The young lady was too distraught to tell anyone when she discovered her predicament. Then when she had to admit their transgression, Travers denied it had been him." Poor wretched thing. "She was sent into the country as they scrambled to find a decent man who would wed her. I believe they found one in time, but of course everyone knew about it. She hasn't been seen in Society since. She may never be again."

And the rake who had ruined her reputation was the gentleman Georgie was supposed to marry.

"I had not realized Lord Travers was such a . . . a disreputable man." Clara bowed her head. "I wonder that you have decided to go through with the marriage, my lady."

Georgie peered at her maid, her spirits plummeting. "Are

you beginning to think differently about accompanying me to his household when I marry him, Clara? I would not think less of you if you did. Living with him will be quite a change in circumstances." For both of them.

"Oh, no, my lady." Clara straightened and looked Georgie in the eyes defiantly. "I could never abandon you to go to him alone. Not and call myself a Christian woman." A grim smile crossed her face. "I'll be right there by your side when you go to his household. I suspect you'll have need for a loyal servant then." The maid bit her lips. "No, my lady, I simply wondered why you decided to marry him if he has such a scandalous reputation."

That had been the question Georgie had been asked constantly for the past two weeks at Hunter's Cross. "Because my father has commanded it, and if I do not accede to his wishes he will disown me once more, and forever, he assures me." As untenable a position as a ship sailing between Scylla and Charybdis. "As I have no means to support myself if he does, I will be truly destitute. Neither is my late husband's family able to support me at this time." Inquiries to her father-in-law had yielded this information shortly after her father had informed her of his choice for her second marriage. "And although my brother and his wife would surely welcome me, they are currently dependent on our father's good will as well."

Her other friends had offered her assistance, but she could not countenance being the burden on them she must be for the six years before she received her mother's inheritance. Georgie straightened her shoulders and raised her chin. "So I am resolved to marry Lord Travers and try to make the best life possible with him." She smiled at her maid, whose eyes glistened with tears. "So thank you very much for coming with me, Clara. I value your loyalty to me above all. You and Lulu will be the only friendly faces I will have. At least until I get my bearings and begin to know my neighbors." Surely the people in Essex wouldn't be very different from those she knew already. "And as I will be scarcely half a day's ride from Lord and Lady Wrotham, perhaps they will visit me once their baby arrives."

"Your brother too, my lady. He and his wife won't abandon you, I'm certain."

"Of course." Georgie smiled at the prospect of Jemmy and Elizabeth settled in London with her family until their child would be born. They would be close enough for her to visit. If Travers allowed it. "I shall not be completely bereft of company. Indeed, I shall get along quite well in my new life."

If only she believed it.

The pitching of the carriage lessened as the team veered into the yard of a coaching inn called The Running Horse. Glancing out the window, Georgie discovered a bustling scene with grooms hustling to and fro leading horses here and there, all types of people disembarking from a mail coach, children crying, hostlers shouting, bridles clinking. The panorama teeming with life chased away her somber mood.

"Let us stretch our legs, Clara, and get something hot to drink. Come, Lulu." Georgie held the lead in one hand and gathered the little dog under her other arm.

Lulu yipped and struggled to get down.

"You know you cannot leap down from the carriage, so I do not know why you put up such a fuss each time I carry you." Sighing, she took the coachman's hand. "Thank you, Folger. We will require hot tea and a moment's rest."

"Very good, my lady." He turned to a groom who was already unharnessing the team.

Putting Lulu on the ground, Georgie gave her a pat and tried to untangle the leash. Lulu shook herself, sniffed the air, growled, then bolted toward the center of the inn yard.

"Lulu!" The leather lead slipped through her fingers and

Georgie stopped, paralyzed. A party of riders thundered into the yard, their horses' hooves slashing the frozen mud mere feet away from the little dog. Lulu backed up, barking as though she would attack the giants.

Heart beating almost out of her chest, Georgie raced forward and grabbed the lead. She pulled with all her might, and Lulu slid back toward her, out of danger. Gathering the dog into her arms and thanking heaven for her salvation, Georgie glanced up at the riders who had just missed her pet. The party of four rather rugged-looking men was dismounting. Grooms bespeaking lodging for their master, perhaps, for she could see their mounts were costly. One fellow with a round, jowly face and a flattened nose glanced at her and nodded.

Too distraught to even acknowledge him, she turned away, holding Lulu tight against her chest.

"My lady, are you all right?" Face pale as snow, Clara ran up to her.

"Perfectly fine." Georgie's shaken voice belied her words, but she couldn't help it. Trying to breathe normally, she headed for the inn, relieved the incident had ended with no harm to her save some mud on the hem of her pelisse. Once they were free of the inn yard, she put Lulu down again, and the dog trotted happily in front of her, tail waving like a fringed white flag.

The innkeeper was a pleasant red-faced man who took them to a private parlor where they enjoyed hot tea and biscuits, while Lulu relished a bowl of chopped chicken. When they were through, Georgie handed the leash to Clara. "Will you take Lulu into the yard? I must use the necessary, and then I'll join you in the carriage."

Some little time later, Georgie emerged from the inn then stood in the doorway, looking for Clara and Lulu. The yard hummed with activity, but her maid was nowhere to be seen. A glance told her they were not in the carriage. Had Clara gone around to the stable to let Lulu relieve herself? Surely any patch of ground would do. She started toward the stable when, out of the corner of her eye, she caught sight of the man with the jowly face who had almost trampled Lulu; he was watching as she strode across the yard. Normally, she would have paid him no mind, but something about his intent gaze, turning his head to follow her as she crossed the yard, made the hair on the nape of her neck prickle. What had sparked such interest in her? The fellow had almost killed Lulu, so she certainly wanted nothing else to do with him.

Suddenly Clara appeared, Lulu at her heels, tail still proudly wagging.

Thank goodness. Georgie hurried toward her maid, who smiled and handed over the leash.

"Here you go, my lady." She nodded toward Lulu. "She needed a bit of encouragement as she couldn't decide just where she wanted to squat." Clara stopped and frowned. "What's wrong? Your face is all in a knot."

"It's nothing, I suppose. That man over there—" Georgie pointed surreptitiously toward the place where the man was sitting. Had been sitting, for now he had vanished. "He's gone."

"Who's gone?" Face puckered, Clara looked around the inn yard.

"The man who almost rode over Lulu." Georgie shook her head. Had she imagined the man's interest? "I could swear he was watching me when I was searching for you."

"I'm sure most gentlemen do."

Heat rose in Georgie's cheeks. "He wasn't a gentleman. I think he's a groom. And it wasn't that kind of watching." Although perhaps that's all it was. An insolent servant ogling a lady and nothing more. She shrugged it off and put Lulu in the carriage then clambered in after her. Clara followed, and a groom shut the door. The carriage started with a jerk, and they were off on the next part of the journey. In several hours they would stop at Horley for luncheon.

Georgie settled herself in the forward-facing seat, drew Lulu across her lap, and stroked the long silky fur. That always had a calming effect on both her and her pet. The soothing motion together with the slight swaying of the carriage relaxed her until she fell into a doze, not quite sleeping, not quite awake. Just peaceful and warm.

A low whimpering slowly brought Georgie back to the edge of consciousness. Blinking, she gazed about the carriage. Clara had fallen asleep as well, but Lulu had her ears raised. Growling softly, the spaniel padded across the tufted leather seat and raised her paws to rest on the edge of the window. Her growls changed to barking, and Georgie yawned, then slid over to her.

"What is all this fuss about, Lulu? You can't need to go out again so soon." Peering over the dog's head, Georgie looked at her father's outrider cantering beside the carriage.

"Goodness." The maid stretched and stifled a yawn. "I must have fallen asleep."

"That's quite all right." Georgie's attention was fixed on the rider. "Look at the man riding alongside us, Clara."

The maid glanced out the window and shrugged. "What about him?"

"He's not one of my father's outriders." Frowning as she pressed her face against the cold window pane, Georgie moved her head this way and that, seeking a better look.

"He's not?" Clara slid over to gaze out the window as well. "Then who is he?"

"He's the man I told you about, the one with the flattened nose who was watching me in the inn yard." Georgie bounced over to the other side of the carriage, panic rising at the sight of another unfamiliar outrider. "This one too. Folger!" She leaped to her feet and banged on the trap. "Folger! Who are these men? What is going on?"

The chilling silence that ensued was punctuated by the high crack of a whip. The carriage shot forward, throwing Georgie back into her seat, where she narrowly missed Lulu, who was barking wildly.

"What's happening, my lady?" Eyes wide and wild, Clara clutched her arm.

Georgie's composure slipped, and dread threatened to engulf her, but she took a deep breath to steady herself and announced, "I am very much afraid we are being kidnapped."

Chapter Two

Whistling a rather bawdy drinking song, Robin Kerr, Marquess of St. Just, smiled as he strode down the crowded streets of Portsmouth. It had been good to be out on the water again after all this time. The last day of his journey had dawned clear and cold, wonderfully bracing as his ship cut through the choppy waves just off the shore. The brisk air did a man's heart good. He'd made the run from Cornwall to Portsmouth countless times during his life, more since his grandfather's death two years ago. Not that he had to captain the ship, but he liked to. Fetching equipment and supplies for the family's tin mining business wasn't strictly the duty of a marquess, but Rob had always enjoyed sailing the sea, especially with his grandfather when he was a young lad.

He'd taken to sailing like a young hawk takes to the skies. Good thing too, as the remote location of the family's primary seat, St. Just in Cornwall, meant a certain amount of isolation, save for journeys that could be made by ship. His present trip had been of utmost urgency, else he would not have attempted it in the rough January waters of the Channel. But the package he had sent his crew to fetch could not wait.

Turning into a tavern he frequented when in town, Rob

strode to the counter and motioned to a pleasantly plump barmaid. "A pint of your best, mistress."

Her smile growing, the lass gave him a thorough look, taking him in from the top of his tall hat, dark brown unruly hair likely sticking out from beneath the brim, to his well-worn black Hessians, the only footwear he'd wear when shipboard.

"Right away, milord."

Rob smiled, then sent an appreciative look at the retreating figure, her round hips swaying seductively as she headed through the doorway to the kitchen. He sighed and shook his head. Time enough for such distractions after his package arrived.

Waiting for his ale, Rob gazed out the window at the busy docks, then rummaged beneath his frock coat and withdrew a letter from the breast pocket of his blue superfine jacket. A letter he'd read several times since it had arrived at Castle St. Just last week. His great friend, Lord Brack, had asked his opinion in regard to the dilemma facing Brack's youngest sister, Lady Georgina Kirkpatrick.

The lady, a widow he'd met last autumn at a house party given by Lady Cavendish in Kent, had been betrothed by her father to a certain Lord Travers. No one else of Brack's acquaintance liked the match at all, including the lady herself. Nor did Rob, if anyone had asked his views on the subject. Travers was a bad apple, rotten through and through. What the woman's father was thinking passed all understanding.

The barmaid set his tankard before him, and Rob tossed a coin down on the bar. "Much obliged."

"Anything else you'd be wanting, my lord?" The girl's gaze had fastened on his chest, then strayed quickly downward.

"Nothing at the moment, thank you." Another time and

he might have taken her up on the obvious offer. Today, however, he must keep his wits about him.

The maid's downcast expression made him briefly regret his answer, as did the sudden swelling in his groin. But the lass turned and hurried off to her work, allowing him to cool his ardor in the cold ale. He had a duty to perform, and nothing, no matter how tempting, would keep him from it.

"Kidnapped!"

Clara's face turned so pale Georgie feared she would swoon. She opened her reticule in search of her smelling salts.

"Why would you say that, my lady?"

"Because unfortunately that is the only thing that makes sense." Despite an icy trickle of fear down the back of her neck, Georgie managed to keep her voice steady. "Drat it. Are you about to faint, Clara? Because I simply cannot find my vinaigrette."

Wide-eyed, the maid paused as if trying to sense an approaching darkness. "N-no, my lady. I don't think so."

"Good." Georgie tossed her reticule aside. The time for hysterics was not yet. "My father's outriders have been replaced, and the coachman will not answer me. You know Folger would have responded immediately." She stood and pushed against the trap door. It refused to budge. "See? It's locked." Her strength waning, Georgie sat down abruptly. "But why would anyone want to kidnap me?"

"I'm sure I don't know." Wringing her hands, Clara peered out the window. "Are you certain that's what's happening? The new outriders could be more of your father's men, couldn't they?"

"No, I don't think so." Georgie bit her lip, trying to make sense of this extraordinary turn of events. "If Father had sent additional outriders, they or Folger would have informed us when we stopped at The Running Horse. They are very well-trained servants. I only pray they were unharmed when these ruffians accosted them." Unfortunately there seemed to be only one logical conclusion. "I believe the culprit must be Lord Travers."

"Lord Travers?" The confusion on Clara's face was almost comical. "You think Lord Travers is kidnapping you?"

"Nothing else makes sense." Georgie could scarcely contain the disgust in her voice. The man had not one ounce of intelligence that she could determine. "Because I have refused to discuss or agree to anything regarding our marriage, he has most likely taken matters into his own hands. By kidnapping me he thinks he can force me to speak to him." A wave of outrage poured through her. "I will very much like to see him try. I dare to tell you, he will not like what he hears."

"That seems an awfully drastic thing for a gentleman to do." Clara looked askance at her.

Georgie sighed and tried to relax her shoulders. They ached abominably. "The man hasn't got a bit of sense, Clara. I doubt he's managed to think the scheme through completely. He doesn't realize that if he inconveniences my father, or disturbs his plans he's likely to find himself unbetrothed. Father insists that things go his way exactly on schedule. If he has to discommode himself by having to fetch me from Lord Travers, it will go very ill for the man." For the first time since entering the carriage, Georgie grinned. Serve Lord Travers right.

"I take your point, my lady, however—" Clara's alarm didn't seem to have abated. Her ashen face drooped, and her bottom lip almost bled where she'd worried it with her teeth. "What if it's not Lord Travers? What if some stranger's making off with us?"

"Pfft." Georgie dismissed that worry out of hand. "Why would anyone do that?"

"For ransom, my lady." Clara nodded so vehemently the bows on her cap waggled. "Highwaymen used to do that all the time."

"Highwaymen used to stop carriages and steal the passengers' money and jewelry. They didn't kidnap anyone." At least Georgie didn't think they did that. Not these days anyway. "Besides, who would pay to ransom me?" Glancing out the window, Georgie gasped, her heart racing anew. Riding close enough to the carriage to leer at her was the odd man from the inn yard.

"Your father, of course, my lady. A marquess with all his wealth could pay a pretty sum to get his daughter back."

Georgie laughed, a sharp, bitter sound. "If they are counting on that, I fear they have seriously mistaken their game. My father wouldn't pay a farthing to get me back." Absently, she pulled Lulu into her lap, stroking the silky fur. Holding her pet gave her a modicum of courage.

"But the kidnappers won't know that, will they?"

That brought Georgie up short. Clara had a point. "Perhaps not. They may just assume that since he is my father he will pay. Or if he doesn't, then Jemmy will pay."

"Or that Lord Travers will pay, because you are betrothed to him." Clara looked at her expectantly.

It was not a bad plan. Three chances to make money on her. "That does seem possible, but if someone were doing something like this, why wouldn't he have found out the facts first?" Georgie shook her head, both in denial and to dispel the panic that was again rising. Better the devil you knew. "No, I still believe it is Lord Travers, and, I promise you, he will hear quite enough from me on this horrible behavior. I will give him a curtain lecture even before the first banns are read."

"Well, I hope it's nothing more than his lordship wishing to speak with you, then." Drawing her cloak more snugly around her shoulders, Clara settled back, a glum look on her face, and deliberately shut her eyes.

Upsetting her maid was another topic about which Georgie would ring a peal over Lord Travers's head.

The lengthening shadows out the window gave Georgie heart. They must stop at an inn yard soon to change the horses. When they did, she and Clara and Lulu would bolt from the carriage, run to the innkeeper, and inform him of what was happening. Even if they pulled into a smallish coaching inn, there surely would be someone—a groom or ostler at least—who would help her. Thank goodness horses had to be changed at regular intervals.

After what seemed an eternity, the carriage began to slow. Georgie tightened her grip on Lulu's collar and nudged Clara. "When they let us out in the yard, I'll make a run for the inn. You stay close by me. We'll find the innkeeper and tell him the whole story. If I mention my father's name in this part of the world, people will be more willing to help us. He's got a reputation."

"God be praised for that, my lady." Clara sat up, suddenly more alert as she glanced out the window of the slowing carriage. "Do you see an inn?"

Peering out the other window, Georgie frowned, a new foreboding creeping into her mind. They were slowing, but there was no inn in sight. A forest of evergreens lined the road on both sides. No houses, no hedges, no fences even. Nothing to indicate a coaching inn at all. That was very peculiar. She shook her head.

"If there's no inn, why are we stopping?" Twitching her cloak even closer, Clara sank back on the seat, mouth stretched into a tight line.

"Perhaps a wheel has broken, although I didn't feel anything amiss." Georgie sat up straighter, hope beginning to glimmer. "Maybe there is another carriage stopped in the road and we can call for help."

"Oh, no, my lady." Clara grasped her hand. "That sounds too dangerous. Those men won't like if we try to escape."

"I for one do not care what they like or do not like." Didn't Clara understand that they were in desperate straits? They must escape, no matter what. "They cannot kidnap someone and then expect her not to try to get away."

Sinking back even further into the leather seat, Clara seemed ready to give up, which made Georgie's decision even harder. If faced with the choice of escape without Clara or remaining with her, she would have to attempt escape by herself. Once she reached help she could come back for Clara and Lulu. It would be agonizing to leave them, but there was no other way.

The carriage ground to a halt. Georgie gripped Lulu with a frantic hand. "Be ready to run on my signal, Clara. Toward the other carriage as fast as you can go."

Though fear shone out of her eyes, the maid nodded, gripped her reticule, and set her jaw.

The carriage had not even come to a complete halt when Georgie pushed open the door, flew down the steps, and landed miraculously on her feet. "Help! Help!" She dropped Lulu to the ground, then straightened and turned this way and that. Where was the other carriage? The road in front of the horses was smooth and clear.

Clara jumped down beside her, and Lulu began to bark.

Action was better than no action. Darting toward the front of the carriage, Georgie pelted down the road, her shoes slipping now and then on the rocky surface, until a rider cut her off, coming so close she had to stop and windmill her arms to avoid being run down. She stumbled backward and bumped into Clara, whose feet skidded out from underneath her, landing her in a mound of dead grass.

Still off-balance, Georgie swayed, trying to stay on her feet until she lost the battle and sat down hard, right next to

Clara. Lulu strained at her leash, barking shrilly at the enormous bay horse that loomed over their heads.

The odd-looking stranger grinned down at them. "Thought we'd let you get away that easy, my lady?"

Struggling to stand, Georgie found her annoyance overcame her fear. "I think you have made a terrible mistake, Mr. Whoever-you-are." Fuming, she slapped at the dirt that streaked her pelisse. "I am Lady Georgina Kirkpatrick, daughter of the Marquess of Blackham, and I assure you my father will have you drawn and quartered when he hears of this outrage." She picked up Lulu and stared defiantly at the man. "I demand you take us back to The Running Horse."

"Right high-and-mighty, aren't you?" The kidnapper with the flattened nose chuckled as another outrider rode up beside him. "Is the new team ready, Tanner?"

"Aye. Just coming up now." The new ruffian leered down at her. "It'll only take a few minutes to change 'em. Of course, it wouldn't take much longer if we had a mind to occupy ourselves with these two for a bit."

A sickening lurch in her stomach almost made Georgie cast up her accounts there and then. The deserted clearing where they'd stopped held nothing and no one but them and the kidnappers. She clutched Lulu tighter. No one was coming to help them. She and Clara were completely at the mercy of these dastardly men. Swallowing hard, she blinked back tears and drew herself up to her full five foot two. What could she do if the men decided to attack them? She must think clearly and come up with a plan.

"Are you truly daft, Tanner?" The odd-looking man shot a menacing look at his companion. "The master would skin us alive and dump us in the Thames if we laid a finger on her or her maid. Go see to the team before I shoot you just for being ignorant."

Gravelly voice muttering things Georgie was just as

happy she couldn't hear, Tanner turned his horse and jogged toward the tree line where a team of four horses was emerging from the forest.

Georgie's mouth dropped open. "Where did they come from?"

"My master's laid his plans well, don't you think?" The man she now thought of as Odd Fellow chuckled. "He's had this whole scheme planned for days, including stashing a team in an abandoned barn half a mile from here. He said if we didn't have to go to an inn to change horses, you wouldn't have a chance to escape."

Incensed, Georgie straightened and looked Odd Fellow in the eyes. "And just who is this master planner you work for? I demand to know who he is."

A loud laugh filled the clearing. "You are a spitfire, aren't you, my lady? The master warned us of that." The man's gaze grew cold. "He gave instructions that I tell you nothing, so nothing is what you'll get out of me." He glanced toward the approaching team and quickly dismounted. "Best move out of the road now." Drawing a pistol, he motioned her and Clara onto the brown grass on the opposite side of the woods.

With a glance at her maid, whose eyes looked ready to start from their sockets, Georgie strode onto the crackling grass, thinking furiously. There must be some way to escape. "While you change the team my maid and I will need to use the necessary. We usually do at the inn when we stop. Come, Clara." She nodded toward a series of thick bushes not five yards away. If they could make it to those and duck behind them, perhaps they could evade the men long enough to get away.

"Very well, my lady. You can go." Odd Fellow nodded, then seized Clara by the arm. She shrieked, and he pressed the pistol to her head. "But if you don't return, I put a ball in her head."

Narrowing her eyes, Georgie wanted very badly to open her mouth and berate the man as he deserved. However, one look at Clara's face—tears trickling down her cheeks, eyes filled with terror—made Georgie bite her tongue and say nothing. No need to antagonize him and make him hurt poor Clara.

Odd Fellow nodded toward the bushes. "Get on with it, then."

"Come, Lulu." Georgie started for the makeshift necessary.

"Leave the dog here." Odd Fellow didn't move his pistol, but nodded toward Lulu, who growled deep in her throat. "If you run I'll shoot it too."

Georgie stopped, clenching her fists. This man would pay dearly for his treatment of them. Without a word, she passed the leash to Clara, who seized it as though it were a lifeline, then stalked toward the bushes, thinking furiously. She'd been in difficult circumstances before and gotten out of them, although never quite as horrible as this. Still she was confident that she could thwart this elusive "master" and escape his men. It was merely a question of when she could make her move.

Chapter Three

When several minutes had passed and no inspiration had presented itself, Georgie reluctantly made her way from behind the bushes. Clara stood stock-still, her eyes straining to see the pistol pressed to her temple. Lulu barked a short yip and darted to Georgie, pulling her leash from Clara's nerveless fingers.

"You'd better go now, Clara." Georgie indicated the bushes. "No telling when we'll have the chance again." She turned a furious gaze on Odd Fellow. "Put that silly pistol away. Stop terrorizing my maid, or I'll make certain your master hears of it."

The man sneered, but uncocked the pistol and pushed Clara forward. "What makes you think the master cares what I do to your maid?"

Sobbing, Clara picked up her skirts and fled behind the bushes.

"He may not care about that, but he obviously cares about me if he's going to such lengths to kidnap me." She scowled at the man until he looked away from her. "He may be perturbed to find that I was upset by your mistreatment of me and my servant. If he wants me to cooperate with him, I might do so if he agreed to dismiss you."

The ruffian scarcely seemed to hear her, his attention fixed on the rustling behind them in the bushes.

"Or I could tell him to shoot you."

Odd Fellow jerked his head back to her, eyes wide, a snarl on his lips. "What?"

Georgie smiled serenely. "I think that would be simpler for him in the long run. Dead men tell no tales."

A snarl on his lips, Odd Fellow gripped his pistol tighter and motioned her toward the carriage. "Get in."

"I'll wait until my maid returns, thank you." Gathering Lulu into her arms, Georgie faced the ruffian. "I wouldn't want anyone to get left behind."

As if to punctuate her mistress's words, Lulu growled at Odd Fellow and bared her teeth.

Odd Fellow drew back. "Keep that mongrel away from me."

"Mongrel?" How dare he disparage Lulu's ancestry? "We have traced Lulu's lineage back to the original spaniels bred by King Charles I. I daresay her pedigree is much more illustrious than your own."

Red-faced, Odd Fellow dipped his brows down in a frown. He had started to raise the pistol at Georgie when Clara stumbled from behind the bushes, and he swung it around, training it on her instead. "About time." He shoved the gun into the waist of his rough breeches and grabbed Georgie's shoulder, making her wince. "Now get in that carriage before I make you wish you had."

Shoving Lulu in before her, Georgie climbed in and settled in the forward-facing seat. When Clara followed her, she patted the seat next to her. Odd Fellow slammed the door, and moments later there was the clinking of harness as the horses started.

"What are we going to do, my lady?" Clara whispered despite their relative seclusion.

Her bravado ebbing as soon as the door shut, Georgie

slumped against the seat, blinking back tears of fear and outrage. How could this be happening to her?

More in need of comfort than ever before, she grasped the maid's hands, trying to draw strength from the simple human contact. She couldn't admit to Clara she didn't know what to do. She had to be strong for both of them. "Give me some time, and I'll come up with a plan. I always do." Forcing a smile, she patted the servant's hands. "I helped my brother escape from my father's castle when he'd locked us both in. Surely I can devise a way to get us out of this scrape."

Inns flashed past at intervals, but they had no hope of stopping and so no possibility of rescue. They'd obviously have to wait until they reached journey's end—and her true kidnapper—to put a plan into action. But what plan?

In the event the kidnappers took them to a private estate, their options were grim. The only people likely present at such an establishment would be servants or tenants of the "master." Not the sort of folk who would put themselves out to rescue a woman their master had kidnapped.

Georgie clenched her jaw until her teeth ached. If that were the case, they would have to split up and simply run for it, back up the road they had come down, and pray they found either a village or a passerby who would assist them.

If their destination turned out to be an inn and if she, Clara, and Lulu could get free, they could shriek, run, and take refuge in the inn and pour out the story to the innkeeper or any other kind soul who would listen. Georgie could mention her father and a sizeable reward for helping them. Getting free from the kidnappers was the sticking point. Unless . . .

"Clara." She leaned toward her maid and spoke low. "I've come up with a plan."

"Saints be praised!"

"Shhh. Listen."

After Georgie had explained everything twice, Clara wrung her hands and said, "I don't know that I can run fast enough, my lady."

"You'll be fine." Georgie squeezed Clara's cold hands. The maid must try, or they would be lost. "I have every confidence in you."

"I'll try my best." Clara nodded, though her puckered brow said she was still unconvinced.

The carriage rolled on until at last Georgie spied clusters of small houses, as if they were on the edge of a town or city. Scattered cottages gave way to larger dwellings, although they too were spaced well apart. Not a very large town, then. Despite the closed carriage, Georgie detected a bit of salt and fish on the air. Were they being taken to a seaside town? Brighton came first to mind, but there would have been more houses by now. She must think of a smaller town.

Summoning to mind a map of England, Georgie tried to recall all the cities and towns near the seacoast, but gave up. There must be hundreds of small or middling ones. They could be anywhere on the southern coast of England.

The thought of Brighton, however, took her back several years, to the days immediately after her marriage to Isaac. They had managed a brief wedding trip to Brighton, less than a week, yet she had very vivid memories of that time. Her throat thickened with tears as it often did when she thought of her late husband. Oh, how she wished he were here.

No, she could not be weak now. If anyone was going to rescue her, it would have to *be* her. Pulling her mind away from the sweet thoughts of her husband, Georgie recalled her plan. At least the destination seemed to be a town rather than an estate. That would make escape easier, though not by much.

"My lady." Clara leaned over to her. "Do you smell that?"

"What?" Georgie sniffed again. The smell of fish had gotten stronger.

"That fishy smell. We're near the water, I'll be bound." The wide blue eyes had a panicked look about them, like those of a horse about to buck its rider.

"I noticed that a few moments ago. Is that troubling to you?" Perhaps the scent was making Clara ill. "Are you feeling unwell?"

"Oh, no, my lady. But I thought if they've brought us to the water they may plan to make away with us, over the ocean, to sell us as slaves in some heathen country." Clara burst into tears. "I've read about such horrible things happening to good Christian women." A high keening filled the carriage.

"Hush, Clara." Good Lord. Of all the times for her maid to have hysterics. "Of course they won't do that. They're going to ransom us is all, just like you said."

"But Lady Georgina, what if that's not this master's plan at all? He may want the money, but knows your father won't pay." Clara dug into her reticule, pulled out a handkerchief, and wiped her streaming eyes. "He could send us somewhere horrible, like Turkey, and sell us to a Pasha for his harem!"

"What?" Georgie's mouth dropped open. What could have given Clara such a fanciful idea as that? "Whatever gave you such a wicked idea, Clara? And where did you even hear the word 'harem'?"

"Did you never read any of Lord Byron's poems, my lady?" The maid's indignant tone almost surprised a laugh out of Georgie. "I've read many of his tales, and learned a thing or two about those awful heathens. *The Giaour* and *The Bride of Abydos* both tell of these harems where the Pasha has many, many women held there just to"—Clara's cheeks turned apple red—"serve his needs."

"Well, no, I cannot say I have read many of Lord Byron's works." Perhaps she should have done. "*The Corsair*, of course, but nothing else. I have, however, heard of harems, and wondered what the women did with all their time."

Clara blinked. "You wondered what they did, my lady?" She sounded scandalized. "You were married once. I'd think you'd know what they did."

"I don't mean *that*. Of course, I know what they did with the Pasha." Or Georgie suspected she did. "But that would only be one at a time, unless he was a truly depraved man. And he wouldn't likely be with his . . . wives all of the time every day." Georgie shrugged. "So I wondered what they did all the rest of the time. I don't think they are allowed to go out, so no shopping, or visiting, or going for ices. And I daresay they have their own servants, so they wouldn't cook or clean. They would be waited on, I suspect." She frowned, still perplexed by the question. "So I do wonder what they do."

Clara's face had gone from white and stretched to red and puckered. "Well, if my guess is correct, you may have cause to find out, my lady. And soon."

"If my plan works, neither of us will ever know." Georgie peered out the window. The carriage had slowed a bit, but was still moving forward. Another few minutes and more houses had appeared along the road.

"Be ready and follow my lead."

"Yes, my lady." Tensed, Clara glanced from window to window, clutching the edge of the leather seat.

"Lulu." The little dog woke with a yip and jumped to the floor, tail waving like a battle flag. "Get ready. I'll let you know when to bite them." Georgie turned her attention to the street outside. They were closer to the town's center to judge by the traffic and the busy nature of the street. Closer to the water too, from the all-but-overpowering smell of fish.

At last the carriage rocked to a halt.

* * *

Walter Endicott, Lord Travers, glanced at his pocket watch for what must have been the fortieth time that day. Had blasted time stopped altogether? The hands read a quarter past two o'clock, just five minutes since the last time he'd looked. The watch must be running slow. Perhaps he'd forgotten to wind it. He grasped the stem between his thumb and forefinger and gave it a vicious twist, although winding it now would do no good if the time was already wrong.

His grip was so tight the stem popped off and went flying across the table, skittering between his glass and the bottle of brandy he'd ordered at noon, and rolled off the edge and out of sight. Disgusted, Travers slammed the watch onto the table. Worthless piece of metal. He grabbed his glass again. Nothing had gone right with this venture, but he'd be damned if he'd give up yet. He trusted his men. They'd be here soon. With Lady Georgina.

Abandoning the broken watch, Travers raised his glass and downed the two fingers worth of spirits left in it. He shouldn't drink any more at present. His fuzzy head and blurry sight told him he was dangerously close to passing out, and he wanted to be quite clearheaded when his men arrived with his future wife. Lady Georgina. Despite his prodigious consumption of brandy, his shaft hardened at the mere thought of her name. After five long years of lust and longing, she was almost his.

He still didn't know what it was about the red-haired little wench that had captivated him for so long, but he had craved the sight of her ever since he'd first been introduced to her, the year after she'd come out. He'd tried to initiate a marriage arrangement with the Marquess of Blackham immediately after that initial meeting, but the man had quashed his suit, citing other arrangements he was making with the eldest son of the Duke of Carford.

For once, Travers had been prudent and bided his time, and, when those negotiations had fallen through, he'd quietly renewed his suit. And that time, for whatever reason, Blackham had agreed. Travers had walked around his London townhouse in a perpetual state of arousal for weeks, thinking about nothing but the sight of Georgina, nude and beneath him on their wedding night. He'd had to visit his favorite brothel almost daily, so intense had been his lust for the woman. Then, somehow, it had all fallen apart when the lady in question had married a nobody—a vicar's son— the day after her twenty-first birthday and two weeks before their wedding would have taken place.

Abruptly, Travers seized the bottle and upended it into his glass. The day he'd learned the news had been the blackest of his life. He'd raged about London, drinking and whoring until time ceased to exist. He'd awakened on the fourth day in a stall behind his townhouse, his clothing stinking of spirits and his own essence, his tongue so thick he could barely swallow, and his head exploding with pain every time he moved an inch.

His valet had suggested a change of scenery and had removed them to the continent, to Brussels, where Travers had spent the year drinking and whoring, but in moderation. Then, with the Battle of Waterloo looming, he'd sobered quickly and set out for London. In the days after his return, he'd learned of the death of Georgina's husband and immediately had applied again to Lord Blackham, vowing she'd not slip through his fingers again.

Which was why he'd sent his men to kidnap her today.

He glanced at the shattered watch. Why hadn't they arrived yet?

"Crawford." He bellowed, and his valet, a tall, lanky man

with nervous hands, appeared at a trot. "Fetch me another bottle, and see if Cole has arrived."

"Very good, my lord." The valet hurried out.

Travers rose and tottered over to the window, although the trip was totally in vain. When he'd demanded the best rooms in the inn he hadn't been thinking that meant he'd be lodged at the back of the establishment to spare him the noise of the courtyard. Had he been taken to a front-facing room, he could have seen for himself when Georgina arrived. When he'd finally realized his mistake, the other rooms had already been occupied. Damned nuisance. He peered out the window anyway at the cold, gray Channel. Of course, the back-facing rooms would be to his advantage if the lady put up a struggle. Fewer people to hear her cries, and Travers fully expected she'd not submit to him willingly before the wedding. But he had to ensure that this time there would indeed be a wedding. His entire future depended on it.

"Where the hell is Crawford with that bottle?" he growled to no one. Perhaps he shouldn't drink any more until after Georgina was brought to him. He needed to be sober enough to explain to her that they must anticipate their wedding night because he couldn't be left at the altar again. Quite apart from his raging lust, there simply were bills to pay and no money with which to pay them. At least, not until he had control of his wife's money. And, although the betrothal was signed, he'd heard her brother was actively seeking to break that agreement. Oh, yes, he'd heard that Brack was advocating to Blackham that he allow Georgina to go to London for the Season and let her choose her own husband.

Ludicrous to think Blackham, of all people, would do such a thing. When the marquess gave his word, it was as good as a sacred oath. However, Travers had also heard that Blackham was so delighted that Brack's wife was increasing with what could be his heir, that the man would do anything for his son, including allow the dissolution of the betrothal between him and Georgina.

Such treachery could not happen, of course, if Travers had compromised her irrevocably. And her spending a week or so with him here, at The Ship's Arms, and being seen very publicly with him would squash all attempts to negate the betrothal. Unless they wanted Georgina's reputation in tatters. After Travers informed his friends of this little escapade, and they gossiped about it all over the *ton*, Georgina wouldn't be received by anyone in London unless she married him.

He slumped back into his chair. Not the best way to begin a marriage, perhaps, but completely necessary. His wife-to-be would come around once she realized she had no other choice. And she had agreed to marry him, after all. They could take this time to go about the business of getting them an heir of their own. A thought that always brought a smile to his lips.

"My lord." Panting, Crawford burst into the room. "They've arrived!"

As soon as the carriage stopped, Georgie nodded to Clara, then shrieked at the top of her lungs, "Help! Help! They are kidnapping me!"

"Help us!" Clara screamed, banging on the carriage window.

Barking shrilly, Lulu jumped up on the seat and put her paws on the window.

Georgie knocked loudly on the trap. "Help! Help us! Kidnappers! Thieves!"

Curses erupted from outside. Horses snorted and bits jingled as the outriders pulled up their mounts.

"Now," Georgie whispered to Clara, then they dove to the

floor on opposite sides, so each one's feet faced the doors, and they commenced kicking the panels.

Men shouted, and the carriage rocked. The door jerked open on Georgie's side, revealing Odd Fellow, his face twisted into a demented mask of outrage. "What's all this damned fuss for?"

"Help!" They screamed in unison.

"I'll help you all right." Odd Fellow began to clamber into the carriage.

Georgie lay back, drew her knees up to her chest, and kicked out with all her might. As if she'd practiced it a hundred times, her feet connected squarely with the ruffian's stomach in a thoroughly solid kick.

He let out a startled squawk and flew backward out of the carriage.

Georgie popped up, grabbed the still barking Lulu, and cried, "Come on." Leaping out of the carriage, she glanced at the other men, still milling around on horseback, yelling as they tried to dismount. Odd Fellow lay on his back, unmoving. So far the plan was working perfectly.

A quick sweep of the area showed the street they'd arrived on was blocked by one mounted outrider. The opposite way, however, was clear of their captors.

"This way." Georgie dodged to her right, pounding down the sandy ground as if demons were after her, which they would be in moments. Clara panted behind her, obviously keeping up, so she tucked Lulu tighter against her and darted around two sailors carrying a huge wooden crate. Turning to her right, she narrowly avoided running into an elderly gentleman in a tall black beaver with a skimpily dressed young woman hanging onto his arm.

Entering a wide street right next to the water, Georgie peered at the crowd of people milling around, searching for a lady, an older one for choice, from whom she could request succor. Despite the time of day, however, no ladies of that sort were in sight. Only the ones Georgie understood to be "undesirables" were in evidence. Where on earth were they?

"Stop her! Stop that woman!" Cries behind her sent Georgie's heart leaping into her throat and sped her legs to greater strength. If one of these sailors or unsavory gentlemen apprehended her now, they would likely hand her directly over to Odd Fellow and his crew despite her protests. Gentlemen tended to believe other gentlemen before they would ladies, she'd found in her experience. Especially the type of gentlemen lingering on this street.

Men who had ignored her as she fled were now turning their heads to watch her as she ran past them. It would only take one such person to snare her arm and stop her in her tracks. Well, that man had better learn to live with one hand then, because she wouldn't be stopped no matter what.

Panting for every breath, she swerved around a wooden barrel and ran up a steep staircase that seemed to lead away from the water and the awful inhabitants of the area. The cries of "Stop" behind her had not diminished enough for her to feel safe, but neither she nor Clara could maintain this frantic pace much longer. A painful stitch throbbed in her side, and her lungs burned with every breath. A sharp glance over her shoulder told her Clara had fallen behind her several paces. Too winded to call out to her, Georgie turned back to the boarded walkway she'd been running down and ran directly into a man's very solid chest.

The impact bounced her backward and elicited a pained yip from Lulu. Georgie staggered several paces, certain she would be sprawled across the planks in moments and too exhausted to care.

The man shot his hand out. It closed around her arm with a vice-like grip, steadying her and bringing her to a complete halt.

Lulu bared her teeth, growled, then barked. She lunged at the gentleman, almost jumping out of Georgie's arms.

Gasping for breath, Georgie twisted her arm away. Behind her the sound of halting footsteps and a faint cry of "My lady" assured her that Clara had not fallen back into the hands of the kidnappers.

Pray God the gentleman before her would aid them in returning home to Blackham Castle. Shaking her head to clear it, Georgie backed up a step and raised her head, a thank-you on her lips to be followed by a plea for his assistance.

Instead she stood dumbfounded and gasped, "Lord St. Just?"

Chapter Four

Travers bolted up out of his chair. "You saw them?"

"The carriage just pulled into the yard. I ran back immediately to inform you." Crawford pressed his hand to his side.

"Very good, very good indeed." Travers started for the door, then caught sight of himself in the small tabletop mirror. His cravat was undone, his shirt stained, and his black hair stuck out at odd angles. "Perhaps I should freshen up a bit before meeting my bride."

With face flushed, Travers held out his arms, waiting impatiently while the valet stripped the blue superfine jacket and shirt off him and headed into the bedchamber. They had been fresh when Travers had donned them that morning, but as the day had worn on, and his thirst had increased, he'd spilled more than one drink on them. Must be at his most presentable to meet Lady Georgina, though.

Once the old jacket was removed, he plied the brush to his tangle of thick, curly hair. His ruddy cheeks didn't seem to be subsiding, however. "Cold water, Crawford."

"Right away, my lord." The man entered from the bedroom holding the brown merino, then hurried back into the chamber and emerged once more with basin and cloth.

Bracing for the cold onslaught, Travers dunked the cloth,

wrung it out, and pressed it gingerly to his cheeks. The cool water stung his heated flesh, but only for a moment. After two more applications he convinced himself the red had begun to recede and dropped the cloth into the basin. "My coat. Now."

Crawford slid his master's arms into the sleeves with tremendous care and pulled the brown jacket up over his shoulders, then deftly smoothed out the material.

A glance in the mirror persuaded Travers that he was tolerably presentable. He straightened, raising his chin. He'd greet his bride with the commanding presence she should quickly come to know well. He threw open the door and strode from the chamber, anticipation of the meeting now overpowering his nervousness.

Tottering down the stairs, Travers eagerly envisioned Lady Georgina's terrified or, more likely, outraged face when he made himself known to her. He'd begin calmly by explaining that there had been a change in plans and escort her into the inn. Show her to her room and, once she was inside the door, inform her that the room would actually be theirs for the next several days, while he and she became very, very well acquainted.

He reached the first floor and hurried through the tap room where several travelers were drinking and talking. Middling sorts, no one of the *ton* to be seen. No one for her to beg assistance from. Good.

As he reached the doorway, the sun came from behind the clouds, shining bright light onto what seemed to be a scene from Bedlam.

Bill Cole lay flat on his back beside the black lacquered carriage, his mouth opening and closing like that of a landed carp. Four horses milled around, although John Brown, the coachman, seemed to be trying to control the skittish beasts. None of his other servants were in evidence. The carriage door hung open, but Lady Georgina was nowhere to be seen.

"What the deuce is going on here?" Travers turned from the sight to Crawford, who shrank back from his master. "You said they had arrived. You didn't say she had gotten away."

"I . . . I didn't see that part, my lord." Crawford's face had taken on a pasty look, and he backed away until he bumped into a box of goods and had to stop. "I left to inform you, you see."

Drawing a ragged breath, Travers stomped over to Cole, towering over the downed man who looked white as chalk as he lay gasping for air.

"How in blue blazes did you let her get away?" Travers leaned over, peering directly into the man's face. "You had one job alone. To deliver Lady Georgina to me. And you have failed. Disastrously."

Wheezing, Cole drew in a shuddering breath as he rolled onto his side. Several minutes passed before he regained enough breath to speak, and then the news was every bit as bad as Travers had feared.

"Must 'a been layin' for me, your lordship. Started kicking up a ruckus, and I had to get to 'em quick like so they wouldn't draw no crowd. I climbed in the carriage to shut her mouth, and she kicked me like an ornery mule. I landed on my back, and it drove all the wind out of me." He drew a painful breath. "The others must have gone after her, milord. They'll catch her quick, mark my words."

"Worthless." Travers straightened, glancing at the coachman, who was relinquishing the wild-eyed horses to the inn's grooms. "You had best be right, Cole." He peered into the carriage, then below it. "Are those her trunks?"

"Aye, milord. She didn't have time to take 'em with her." Laboriously, Cole creaked to his feet, his face in a deep scowl.

"Of course she didn't, you imbecile," Travers barked, "but that doesn't mean she won't want them. You and Brown stand guard. She may sneak back to try to retrieve them. When she does, bring her to me, or I'll make tallow out of your hide." Travers spun on his heel and headed back into the inn. Day was getting worse and worse. Skewering the innkeeper with a glare, he growled, "Send another bottle to my room, and be quick about it."

The sight of her brother's tall, handsome friend with the disturbing gray eyes took Georgie completely aback. Mouth gaping, she could only stare at him, trying to determine whether or not he was a ghostly apparition brought about by her panic. The rock-hard chest she had just rebounded off of persuaded her the man was real. Manna from heaven, in fact, in her desperate situation.

"Lady Georgina." His eyes had widened at the recognition, their unusual color reminding her of a stormy day on the water. "What a surprise to find you here." He looked over her head. "Is Brack with you?"

Of course, he would think her with his friend. She shook her head. "Alas, he is not. I am with my maid and Lulu." She set the spaniel on the ground, then glanced over her shoulder. The kidnappers could come into view at any moment. Although she had not held Lord St. Just in high esteem before, beggars could not be choosers about anything, including their champions. She grabbed his arm. "My lord, you need to hide us."

"I beg your pardon. Did you say *hide* you?" His dark, thick eyebrows swooped up, looking like startled birds, while his mouth twitched in an annoying way. "I'm afraid I don't quite understand."

"Let us talk as we walk, please." Speeding down the planked walkway, Georgie held tightly to the strong arm in her grasp. Surely her brother's friend would know of a place they could hide and avoid Odd Fellow and his gang of ruffians. If only she had time and a safe haven, she could devise a way to return to Blackham Castle. The marquess would not be pleased to discover his youngest daughter had been kidnapped. Quite likely he would find a way to blame her for her misfortune. Well, she'd have to cross that bridge when she came to it. First things first. "I need your help, my lord. You see, earlier today, my maid, myself, and Lulu were kidnapped."

"Kidnapped?" St. Just stopped so abruptly Clara plowed into Georgie's back, and Lulu yelped as her collar choked her. "Are you sure? Who would do such a thing?"

"Please, my lord. They were right behind us." Tugging on his arm, Georgie managed to propel him once more down the walkway. "Yes, I am certain they were kidnapping us. Clara can verify it, if you doubt my word."

The marquess cut his gaze toward the maid, raising his eyebrows ever so slightly, which somehow irked Georgie to no end. She had never seen a gentleman with such expressive brows.

"She's right, my lord. Those men overtook his lordship's carriage at the last inn where we changed horses. It was only by God's good will and my lady's quick wits that we managed to escape those villains."

St. Just furrowed his brows and pinched his lips into a tight knot. "Come with me." He turned left, down a narrow path between piles of crates bound in rope and huge casks that reeked of spirits so strongly it overpowered the stink of fish. Georgie's nose twitched, and Lulu sneezed.

After several minutes of twisting and turning the boarded walkways gave onto a sandy trail heading back toward the water. The press of sailors had thinned out so that only a few, here and there, attended to coiling rope or unloading goods onto the sand from small boats. The stench of fish had returned, more potent than ever.

"Ugh." Georgie clamped her hand over her nose.

St. Just grinned. "You'll get used to it."

"I thought I had already." Gingerly she removed her hand and wrinkled her nose.

"This way, my lady." He led them to a small rowboat beached in the sand, large enough for five or six passengers.

"Where are we going?" She had assumed he was taking her to an inn so she and Clara could rest before arranging transportation home.

"To my ship."

She stopped, stunned. "You have a ship?"

"I do. That one there." He pointed to a tall ship with two masts towering high, perhaps fifty yards offshore. On the bow was written the name *Justine*. He gestured to the rowboat. "Let me help you in."

"That is your ship? And we have to row out to it?" The sand seemed to sway beneath her feet.

"That is the accustomed method." He offered his hand first to Clara, who stepped in and headed to the back of the boat, then to her. "My lady?"

"Why must we go to your ship?" A lead balloon sat on her chest, pressing her down until she couldn't move.

"You asked for my assistance. I am offering the only safe place I have available to me." He cocked his head to look at her. "Is there a problem?"

"I thought you were taking us to an inn, somewhere on dry land where we could—"

"I am afraid this is the best I can arrange at such short notice." He waved a hand toward the ship. "If you visit me in St. Just I believe I can oblige you with a suite of rooms. However, in Portsmouth, I am somewhat at a loss for other accommodations."

Beggars cannot be choosers. "Very well, then, my lord." She reminded herself it was only temporary. "We are in Portsmouth, then?"

"Portsmouth Point, to be exact. Take my hand, my lady."

She grasped it and stepped into the boat. If she ever brought Odd Fellow to justice, she would make certain he would swing for making her undergo this ordeal.

"I'd suggest you hold your dog so he doesn't come to mischief." St. Just pushed the craft into the water until it floated, then climbed in and grabbed an oar. He doffed his coat, turned his back to them, sat on a plank, and began to row in long, even strokes.

Fascinated, Georgie stared at the play of muscles across his back as they flexed and moved with the precision of a well-sprung carriage.

Lulu barked and struggled to get down, bringing Georgie out of her daze. "She's a she."

"Ah, and apparently dislikes being misidentified. I beg your pardon, Miss—?"

"Lulu." Drat the man. He was trying to be charming, but only succeeding in annoying her.

"Miss Lulu, then. Here we are." He pulled them alongside the *Justine*, tied a rope to a cleat on the side of the ship, then grabbed a rope ladder that had been left hanging over the side. He looked at them expectantly. "Which of you wants to go first?"

For the second time that day, Georgie's heart thundered as though she were embroiled in a race. "We have to climb up the rope?" She shook her head. Enough was enough. "Ladies do not climb ropes in view of a public beach, Lord St. Just."

"I appreciate that, Lady Georgina. Far be it from me to suggest you are not a lady." His eyes twinkled. He was enjoying her discomfort far too much for a gentleman. "However, the *Justine* has an alternate plan for boarding you, never fear. Cartwright," he called loudly, bringing forth a sudden thumping of feet on the planks of the ship.

Georgie gazed up, and the pale blond head of a sailor appeared over the railing.

"Aye, Captain. You ready to—" Cartwright's words stopped as though cut off with a pair of sharp scissors. His deep blue eyes nearly popped out of their sockets. "Beggin' your pardon, milord, but what is happening?"

"Stand easy, Cartwright. We have new guests who require both our assistance and our discretion. Please lower the rope sling for the ladies."

"Aye, Captain." The lad disappeared as quickly as he had come.

Georgie looked back to shore. No sign of Odd Fellow. However, that did not mean he might not have followed her. As little as she wished to admit it, she would be extremely safe moored out here in the harbor. A glance at Clara found her maid looking expectantly at her, eager to get on board. They were all tired, even Lulu. Georgie closed her eyes, summoning strength. "Very well. What do we do?"

"Once Cartwright lowers the sling, may I suggest you allow your maid to ascend first? That way you can hand Miss Lulu up to her. Then you will ascend, and I will follow up the ladder."

"Here she comes, Captain."

A bundle of ropes dropped into the boat, attached to a thick, single one that led up to one of the ship's masts.

The marquess tugged at the tangled mass, revealing a sling of sorts, and gestured to Clara. "Stand here. Now grasp these ropes here and here and simply sit down."

"Yes, my lord." One terrified glance at Georgie, and Clara deliberately shut her eyes. She grasped the ropes as she had been told and sat. The device swung slightly.

"Ohhh, I don't like this, my lady."

"You are doing fine." Lord St. Just steadied the device. "Don't look down. Keep your eyes closed if that makes you more comfortable, but keep your hands firmly anchored on the ropes, and try to relax."

The maid grimaced, and clung to the ropes.

"Excellent, Clara. Lady Georgina would do well to mark what you are doing. Here we go. Hoist away, Cartwright." St. Just continued a running commentary, offering advice on everything from the best footwear to use onboard to the ratio of flour to mix into biscuit dough. The man seemed to know something about everything, whether or not it applied to the ship. But before she knew it, Clara had reached the deck and was leaning over the rail to take the barking Lulu from Georgie.

Cartwright lowered the sling again, and St. Just turned to Georgie. "Now up you go, my lady. You need to get on board to restrain your wild animal." He held the ropes out to her.

"I will have you know that Lulu is a perfectly behaved King Charles spaniel. She becomes disturbed when in the company of unsavory . . . characters." Georgie fixed him with a bold stare, then grasped the ropes and sat down. "You had better be careful, my lord. She has been known to bite."

"An excellent guard dog, then. *Cave canem*, as the Romans would have said." He laughed, and Georgie gritted her teeth to keep in a retort. Lord St. Just was helping them, she had to remind herself. She could restrain her animosity toward him for the few hours it might take to arrange for lodgings for them for the night and send a letter to her father.

Despite her misgivings, Georgie had reluctantly admitted to the necessity of informing her father of her situation so he could either send more men to rescue the carriage, or send another carriage for her, her maid, and the dog. The *Justine* was the perfect place for them to hide until all the arrangements could be made. Then she could thank Lord St. Just for his assistance, and they could be on their way before the sun set.

Before she quite knew she had begun, Georgie found herself swinging over the side of the railing, her feet on firm ground again. The clever gentleman had distracted her just enough to keep her mind occupied while she was lifted onboard. She pursed her lips. His cleverness irked her.

"I'll show you to the main cabin, ladies." St. Just leaped nimbly over the railing. "Then we can speak in comfort and privacy. Cartwright, you'll need to go ashore and collect the others. I couldn't wait for them, obviously. And . . ." He paused in the act of showing them to a corridor and turned back to the sailor. "Bring tea please, before you go. I am certain the ladies could use a cup after their ordeal."

"Very good, Captain." The sailor bobbed his head and scurried off.

"Thank you, my lord." Clara gave a curtsy. "I could indeed do with a cup. I've never been so frightened in my life as I was today."

"Tea will set you to rights quicker than anything else, Clara. This way, if you please." He led them toward a dim corridor.

As they walked, Georgie took in the ship, her curiosity sharp. The deck planking was spotlessly clean and oddly empty of any goods. The ship was also eerily silent. "If I hadn't seen Mr. Cartwright, I would wonder if this was your ship at all, my lord. Where is the rest of your crew?"

"They have gone ashore to fetch the cargo I came for, my lady. Cartwright was left aboard to man the ship. This way, please. You should be out of the cold as soon as may be." St. Just led them down a flight of steps to a sizeable cabin, paneled in teak and mahogany woods and furnished as a sitting room, with an iron stove that threw off blessed heat.

Like a magnet seeking its mate, Georgie made a beeline for it, holding out her hands to the lovely streams of warmth. Clara followed right behind her, and Lulu sat at her feet, yawning. Georgie stifled one of her own. After so much cold, the heat was making her sleepy. She struggled to keep her eyes open.

"When you're sufficiently thawed, please have a seat over here." St. Just indicated a comfortable-looking wing-backed chair next to him and a smaller chair beside it. "I am most eager to hear of your adventures, Lady Georgina."

Something in his voice, perhaps a touch of sarcasm, irritated Georgie to no end. Apparently, his lordship still didn't believe her story, and that irritated her even more. Straightening her shoulders, she strode to the chair he had indicated and sat primly on the edge, Lulu at her feet. After another moment at the stove to soak up more heat, Clara joined them.

"Now, my lady, tell me how you came to be kidnapped."

There it was again, that supercilious smugness in St. Just's voice that set her teeth on edge and drove her to distraction. She'd banish that tone from his voice forever before she was finished here. He might be Jemmy's good friend, but that didn't mean St. Just could doubt her word—no matter how outlandish those words might be. Even as she itched to ring a peal over his head, an inner voice urged caution. His lordship had helped them evade the kidnappers; however, they still needed his assistance if they were to truly escape. She must let her rancor go, at least for the moment, so she could convince him to help them contact her father. Breathing deeply, she smiled. "Well, my lord, I was returning home from Fanny and Lord Lathbury's wedding in Buckinghamshire, at Hunter's Cross. Jemmy and Elizabeth and I had the most wonderful time. My brother and his wife are there yet."

"Your brother mentioned Lord Lathbury's impending nuptials to me in his latest letter." St. Just peered at her as if to say, "Go on already."

"It was quite a lovely wedding, by the way." Georgie smiled at the memory of Fanny standing at the altar of the All Saints Church, near the estate. "I believe she and Lord Lathbury will be supremely happy."

"I do hope so. They didn't seem particularly blissful when last I saw them." St. Just leaned back in his chair, arms crossed.

"When was that?"

"At that very exciting house party in Kent, last October."

"Oh." Georgie waved his concerns away. "Heaps of things have happened since then. Fanny was kidnapped and almost murdered. But Lord Lathbury saved her, and now they are very much in love."

"So Lady Lathbury was kidnapped also?" His brows rose to an impossible height.

As did Georgie's hackles. "Her kidnaping had nothing whatsoever to do with mine. That was all Lord Theale."

"So who kidnapped you?"

"I don't know."

A look of pained patience, such as one would have if talking to a small child or a lunatic came over St. Just's face. "Then how do you know—"

"I have begun badly, my lord. Please forgive me and let me start again."

The door opened, bringing in Cartwright with the tea tray. Once he deposited it and left, St. Just poured cups for them all and passed them around the little circle as deftly as any London hostess. "You were going to begin again, Lady Georgina."

"I will, my lord, although it would help us both if you would listen to me as if you intend to believe what I'm saying rather than presupposing that I'm making all of this up. On my oath, I am not."

The gentleman opposite her sighed, then nodded. "I beg your pardon. I promise you I will listen with a completely open mind to your tale." He smiled, making his handsome features—his firm jaw, his high cheekbones, and his devastatingly different gray eyes—even more irresistible.

Her stomach fluttered, as if butterflies fought to get out.

"Please begin again. You have my complete attention."

Flustered, but determined to continue, Georgie proceeded to tell the marquess, with absolutely as little embellishment as possible, what had occurred earlier today, up until the point they met. Settling back in the seat, sipping the almost cold tea, Georgie congratulated herself on delivering a coherent and rather moving rendition of the tale. "So there you have it, my lord." Surely he must believe her now. If he did not, she, Clara, and Lulu would be in a fix.

Lord St. Just sat still, his fingers from both hands lightly touching one another at the tips, his face a study.

"If you could loan us your carriage, we will be on our way to Blackham Castle before the sun has traveled another hour. Once we are out of Portsmouth, we can stop at an inn for tonight and complete our journey tomorrow. My father will, of course, arrange to have your carriage returned."

"I am sorry to put a damper on your plans, but I am afraid I have no vehicle to loan you." His grave countenance affirmed that he spoke the truth.

"Whyever not?" The words made no sense. Why would a gentleman of means not keep some sort of vehicle? Oh. "I see. You mean you do not have a *carriage*. Allow me to assure you, a curricle, while not as comfortable for a long drive, will certainly do under the circumstances."

A gentle smile spread over his face. "I fear I must truly disappoint you, Lady Georgina, but I have no means of transportation of any kind here in Portsmouth, save the *Justine*."

"You don't?" How singular of him. "Do you prefer to walk everywhere?"

A deep chuckle erupted as his chest shook with laughter.

"Not at all. I simply don't keep a carriage in a small port town, such as Portsmouth. I arrived here this morning to procure equipment for our mining operation in Cornwall. My carriage is there, in St. Just."

"Oh." The unsettling feeling of falling but with no ground to land upon swept through her. "I beg your pardon." Heat to rival the stove rose in her cheeks. "I did not know this was not your home, although I should have realized it because you had told me at Charlotte's party that you were intimate with a smugglers' gang." In fact, she'd remarked to Jemmy at the time that Lord St. Just was a wild young gentleman who seemed to fancy himself a pirate. "I suppose smugglers wouldn't choose such a civilized place as Portsmouth for their lair."

"And Cornwall is less civilized, and therefore a much more perfect place for all sorts of nefarious characters." The twinkle in St. Just's eyes belied his arch tone, but Georgie had had enough.

"Perhaps it is, my lord. I would not know, because I have never journeyed there. However, if I were to judge by what I know about it from you, I might have to agree." Why did the man annoy her so much? She always got along famously with the gentlemen of her and her brother's acquaintance. This one, however, always seemed to cut up her peace.

Surprisingly, the gentleman did not take offense. "I hope to change your opinion of Cornwall someday, my lady, if not your opinion of me." He sobered. "As I have no carriage to offer you, we must produce an alternate plan, *post haste*."

Georgie was getting tired of all the subterfuge. "Can you not simply hire a carriage in the town to take us to Blackham?" The easiest solution seemed obvious even to Georgie.

"I could, my lady," he said slowly, pouring another cup for himself. "The question is, should I? This late in the day I do not think it wise." St. Just sipped his tea and shook his head, his curly dark hair catching rays of the afternoon sun as if to point out the lateness of the hour. "You would not be able to travel very far. And where, pray tell, would you spend the night? Who would accompany you? Previously you had the protection of your father's servants. Now you would be traveling only with your maid. Far too dangerous by half, especially with kidnappers after you."

Georgie pursed her lips, itching to decry his estimation of the scheme, but drat it, she could not. He was probably right about Odd Fellow and the other kidnappers. They would be searching for her in every nook and cranny in the area. And checking every carriage that left the city heading east toward Sussex. It would be more prudent to stop here, retire to an inn, and send to her father. "As you say." She rose and pulled on her gloves. "Then Clara and Lulu and I will retire to an inn and await the morning. If you will be so kind as to escort us to a decent inn—you do know of a well-run inn hereabouts, I hope?" The question was only half in jest. St. Just might know very little about the city, even though he visited it frequently.

"I do know of such, however, I do not think it wise for you to go there either."

Georgie's mouth dropped open. "Why not? Why should we all not go to an inn?"

"Because—again—your kidnappers will be looking for you in all the inns. There are not many a lady would go to by herself with her maid. And even a small number of men could search thoroughly throughout the night and find you." He glanced at Lulu, who had nestled at Georgie's feet. The dog raised her head, bared her teeth at him, then settled back down. "It would be more than easy to ask for a woman, her maid, and such a distinguishable dog."

Again, Georgie wanted to argue, but St. Just's logic simply got the better of her. If the kidnappers were still looking for her, they likely would find her. And take her to their "Master."

"I must say, Lady Georgina, even if it seemed safe to send you back to Blackham Castle, I am not convinced such a journey would be in your best interests."

That took her aback. She cocked her head. "Why?"

"The kidnappers must guess that is where you will try to go when you leave Portsmouth. It will be child's play for them to lie in wait along the post road for you and simply capture you again."

Drat! She might not like the man, but she had to admit he had some wits about him. Odd Fellow would take her easily if she headed for home. But where else could she go to put them off the scent? She could go to Jemmy and Elizabeth in London, except that they would not be there for likely another week. She had no other friends or relatives in Town this time of year. They were all on their estates, waiting for the beginning of Parliament and the Season. All of her Widows' Club friends were still at Hunter's Cross. There was no one she could turn to. She raised her head. "Do you have another suggestion, my lord? I seem to have no safe harbor to turn to at the moment."

An eager light gleamed in his eyes. "I believe I do, Lady Georgina. An idea that will confound the kidnappers and take care of your other problem as well."

"My other problem?" She had no other problem, save to avoid capture again by the plaguey kidnappers.

"I am referring to your unwanted marriage to Lord Travers."

Stunned, Georgie stared at him until her vision almost went dark. Finally, she took a breath. "You know about that?"

"Yes." He grinned like an idiot. "Your brother wrote me about the situation, asking if I could come up with a plan to save you from it. And I believe I have done. Two birds with one stone, so to speak."

The last thing Georgie wanted was for this wild young buck to be meddling in her personal affairs. She should plant Jemmy a facer for involving him at all. "What plan is that, my lord?"

"Sail to Cornwall with me."

Chapter Five

A fierce excitement coursed through Rob's veins as he made that pronouncement. Ever since Brack had written him about his sister's predicament, Rob had wracked his brain for some way to help prevent the marriage of Lady Georgina to the odious Travers. With this God-given opportunity before him, how could he resist? "Will you come with me?"

Aghast, Lady Georgina stared at him, mouth slightly agape. "I most certainly will not go with you." She darted her wide-eyed gaze toward her maid, as if to ask if he'd run mad. "As I have already informed you, Lord St. Just, I must go to my father's estate at Blackham Castle in East Sussex. One does not make that journey by way of Cornwall unless someone has a very odd sense of direction indeed." The lady puckered her brows. "Well, I suppose it could be done, but it would take a frightfully long time. Weeks and weeks in a carriage. And I am to be married within the month, so you see that suggestion will simply not do."

"Do you truly wish to marry Lord Travers then?" Perhaps Brack had been mistaken about his sister's affection for the man. The fire in the lady's eyes when she spoke of her wedding had been truly fierce. Although hard to imagine, considering Travers's reputation, he supposed Lady Georgina could hold some regard for the fellow. Or wished to make an advantageous match. Travers was rumored to be fairly flush in the pockets, although Rob's own wealth was as substantial, certainly. As was that of dozens of other more reputable gentlemen of the *ton*.

"You are impertinent, my lord." Lady Georgina's cheeks were tinged with pink, making her whole countenance glow. She turned abruptly on her heel and stalked over to the stove. Holding her hands out to the warmth pouring off the cast iron, she rubbed and chaffed them. Still, she could not disguise that they were shaking. He doubted it was from the cold.

"I may be at that." With measured steps, he came to stand beside her and held his hands out to the blaze as well. "But I would like to know the answer all the same."

The petite woman—the top of her head scarcely reached his chest—glanced at her maid, who shrugged. That must have been the deciding vote because Lady Georgina brought her gaze back to him, pinning him with a heated glare. "Of course I do not wish to marry Lord Travers. He is without a doubt the most loathsome creature to whom I have ever been introduced, and that includes Lord Fernley, who is loathsome, but who does seem to have a few redeeming qualities. He plays whist very well. Anyway"—Lady Georgina shook her head and her straggling curls bobbed—"Lord Travers has made me uncomfortable ever since I met him." She looked Rob squarely in the face. "That does not, however, mean that I will not marry him."

Hmm. A far cry from the answer he'd expected. Lady Georgina was not a predictable lady at all. "But if you have no affection for him, why marry him? Surely there are other gentlemen of the *ton* who are just as eligible and not as disagreeable as Travers."

"You know Lord Travers then, my lord?"

"I do, although mostly by reputation. I do not run in the same circles as he." Rob wouldn't give a hot ha'penny for

Travers's usual companions. Not since the Hellfire Club had a more profligate group of gentlemen assembled. "I daresay he would not have been the choice most fathers would arrange for their daughters."

"My father is definitely not as most fathers are." The lady bit her lips, then shrugged. "I have no idea why he chose Lord Travers as my favored suitor, but I do know how incensed he was when I instead married Mr. Kirkpatrick. Had my husband not died, my lord"—she paused and swallowed hard—"I should have been the happiest woman in all of England at this moment. Possibly in all the world. Because I would have had my dearest companion by my side. But when I married against Father's wishes he cast me out of the family, withdrew all of my financial support, and even forbade all my brothers and sisters from so much as speaking to me on the street if I happened to pass them by. After my husband's death, that decree remained until a month or so ago, when he suddenly sent for me and announced my betrothal to Lord Travers." Lady Georgina dropped her hands and backed away. "If I refuse to marry him, my father will cast me off again, and for good this time."

"I am certain there are other gentlemen of good character and sufficient wealth who would gladly offer for your hand, my lady." While perhaps of a rather unusual disposition, Lady Georgina was, nevertheless, a beautiful woman. Her auburn hair complemented her jade-green eyes and creamy white skin to perfection. Even the generous sprinkling of freckles across her nose only made her look more charming. And although she was of rather shorter stature than most women, she moved with an easy grace that would do credit to any gentleman wise enough to wed her.

"Without a dowry or any monetary or landed gain whatsoever?" A sad smile tinged her lips. "Most gentlemen of the *ton* would not make such a foolhardy decision. Only a vicar's son who held love above any other type of gain." She shook her head, tears glistening in her eyes. "If you told the *ton* gentlemen that their bride would bring nothing but the clothes she stood up in, one King Charles spaniel, and the animosity of the Marquess of Blackham, I do not think you would find them so disposed as to ask for my hand."

All Rob could do was bite his tongue to keep from shouting a resounding "no" at her. Every inch of him wanted to take her by the arms and shake her until she understood that she herself had value beyond any price her father might have set for her. "I think you would be surprised at the number of young gentlemen who would thumb their nose at your father and his money and beg for your hand."

She cocked her head, a smile turning up one side of her mouth in a most charming manner. "Are you perhaps one of those young gentlemen, my lord?"

Rob's jaw dropped, which made Lady Georgina dissolve into a fit of giggles. "No, of course not, my lady." Was the woman serious or was she trying to make a cake of him? Or was she trying to entrap him into a declaration? He spoke the first words that came to mind. "I'd be in the suds if I ever mentioned such a scheme to your brother."

Lady Georgina sniffed, though the smile still played around her lips. "I was given to believe Jemmy thought very highly of you. I somehow doubt he would object to your suit. However, I am actually wondering now if he has concocted a plan to have you kidnap me to keep me from marrying Lord Travers." Her smile turned to a glare. "It's just the sort of harebrained scheme the two of you would come up with."

More and more perturbed at his friend's sister, Rob drew himself up to his full six foot two. That often gave both men and women pause. What an opinion she must have of him to think him agreeable to kidnapping a young woman. "I assure you, madam, I have concocted no scheme with your brother. He wrote to me asking for an idea of how to prevent the wedding, but we have not put any such plan into action." The words were scarcely out of his mouth when he thought better of them. Would Brack do something so dimwitted as to hire men to kidnap his sister to keep her from a man such as Travers? In a similar situation, Rob had to admit, he himself might be desperate enough to enact such a deed. So if he prevented the kidnapping, might he be thwarting his friend's plans?

"In that case, Lord St. Just, I insist you hire a carriage for myself, Clara, and Lulu so that we can continue our journey." The lady nodded to her maid, who arose, gathering the dog's leash. "I will take full responsibility for our welfare until we reach Blackham Castle. When we arrive I will make certain my father learns of your assistance and rewards you accordingly."

Rob clenched his jaw until that annoying tic in his left cheek began to jump. "I will require no such 'reward,' Lady Georgina. A gentleman of good repute does not seek reward for doing what is considered to be his duty as an honorable man."

Still, it struck him as unwise to send her onward to her father's estate. It could very well lead her into danger or doom her to a disastrous marriage. And might indeed thwart the plans and wishes of the friend who'd been a steadfast part of his life for more than ten years. That reason, more than the others, gave him pause. If he unwittingly foiled Brack's plans, he'd never forgive himself.

Decision reached. Now to inform the damsel who didn't even think she was in distress.

"I fear I cannot, in good conscience, allow you to willingly march into danger, Lady Georgina. I have a duty to your brother to keep you safe until such time as he can advise me of his plans for your welfare." Carefully, trying not to give away his actions, Rob backed toward the doorway. He wasn't completely certain what the lady was capable of, but he'd wager that she'd try to bash him over the head with the poker if given the opportunity. Another step and he bumped into the cabin door. "Your brother wrote to me asking for my assistance; therefore I must render it."

"And I am telling you the only assistance I require is in continuing our journey to Blackham." Her green eyes flashed like emeralds on fire.

"On that point, my lady, I fear we must disagree. I will pen a brief note to Brack, informing him of the change in plan—"

"Aha!" Lady Georgina stepped toward him, an accusing finger pointed at his chest. "I knew the two of you had concocted a plan."

"Your brother may have done. If so, I will take full responsibility for spoiling it." He grinned at the outraged woman, her cheeks redder than a hot poker. "But I believe he will agree my idea is the better one, or at least safer under the circumstances. Because if your brother didn't have you kidnapped, I would very much like to find out who did. Before you fall into their hands again."

"My brother?" Lady Georgina stopped as if she'd walked into a wall, her face ashen. "You think Jemmy arranged to kidnap me?"

"We'll know when we receive a letter from him in a week or so." Taking advantage of her shocked state, Rob turned the key in the lock then withdrew it, leaving the door ajar. "I'll write to him this instant, tell him our plans to sail to Cornwall, and ask him to come fetch you, your maid, and your dog *post haste*." With nimble feet, Rob slipped through the door and shut it with a bang just as Lady Georgina slammed her hand against the smooth teak panel.

"Wretch! I give you my oath I will make you regret this."

Grinning ear to ear, Rob pocketed the key and headed down the passageway. Regret an adventure? Not likely. He'd not had anything exciting happen to him since he and Brack had returned from their Grand Tour. As he hurried to the other stateroom that he used as an office, his excitement built. This would be a lark to end all larks. He sat down at the desk, grabbed a pen and commenced shaving away bits of the quill in short, excited strokes.

The grand scrape he and Brack had found themselves embroiled in when they'd visited Milan came to mind, and he laughed out loud. The old Italian gentleman had never known about the harmless dalliance with his daughter, thanks to Brack's quick thinking and Rob's own ability to look completely innocent no matter how guilty he might be. The memory of the exhilaration of pounding down the winding, cobbled streets of the city in the dark of night overtook him, and he could actually smell the damp streets, hear the *slap, slap* of their shoes hitting the pavement.

Rob paused, allowing his eyes to close so he could see the bright, dark eyes of the pretty, black-haired signorina . . . who suddenly had auburn hair and green eyes. He jerked back to the present, confused as to how his memory could have shifted from the delightful Angelina to the prickly Lady Georgina Kirkpatrick. Two more different women could not be found in the wide world. Best attend to his real business. He raised the quill to begin the letter to Brack only to discover the nib now a tiny stub, the table littered with flecks of quill.

Blowing out a breath, Rob retrieved another pen, carefully mended it, then drew the inkpot to him and pulled a sheet of foolscap from the drawer.

My dear Brack,

Rob stared at the words. How was he to phrase this vital message? Obviously he should first assure his friend of his sister's well-being. He scribbled furiously for some minutes, then re-read it, muttering under his breath.

Rather abrupt, but, dash it, there was no gradual way to relate such a thing. Besides, if Brack himself was behind the escapade, Rob should, out of decency, apologize for frustrating it.

Another bout of hasty scratching as his pen flew over the paper, scarcely pausing to dip the nib in the inkpot. There. That should explain the reasons for his actions clearly enough.

Mother would love having another woman's company. She'd been so alone ever since Grandfather's death two years ago. A companion, even for the week or so it would take Brack to make the journey, would do her good. Although . . .

Blast. He couldn't fit this last bit of advice above his signature, so he added a post script, then perused the missive once more.

It would serve.

Rob folded the short note and sealed it with a drop of wax. Lady Georgina had mentioned her brother was still in Buckinghamshire at Hunter's Cross. He scribbled the direction, tossed the pen on the table, and bounded out of the room. Once on deck he called for Cartwright.

"Aye, Captain?"

"I take it Barnes, Ayers, and Chapman have returned with the required parts?" By the position of the sun, it was high time.

"Aye. I fetched 'em back with the equipment not long ago. They're stowing the parts away down below. Are we settin' sail now, Captain?" Cartwright sounded eager for home. So was Rob.

"Not quite yet." Rob gazed at the harbor, the shadows shifting as the sun began her descent into the west. "Call the crew on deck. We've got one more thing to do before we sail. I need you to post this letter, quick as you can once we get ashore, then meet us on the beach just there." He pointed to a large rock jutting out of the sand near The Ships Inn. "Be quick, so you don't miss all the fun."

"Aye, Captain." Cartwright tucked the letter into his jacket and headed toward the passageway calling, "Barnes, Ayers, Chapman. Look lively, lads. Captain needs you on deck."

Rob gazed at the shoreline, pinching his lip as he contemplated how in blue blazes he was going to find Lady Georgina's carriage to retrieve her trunks. It had occurred to him, as soon as he decided to take her with him, that the woman would be more amenable to such a journey if she had her clothing and things with her. The rub was finding his way to her father's carriage. He could ask her if she could give him a landmark, but he feared she would either say nothing or quite too much—and none of it helpful. He must think about it logically. There wasn't much time if they were to make the evening tide.

"Here we are, Captain." Ayers, Barnes, and Chapman ran up from belowdecks, Cartwright bringing up the rear.

"We're never shoving off yet, are we, Captain?" Ayers, the helmsman, glanced over the railing at the water.

"Not quite yet." The crew was seasoned, holdovers from his father's and, in the case of Barnes, his grandfather's day as captain. Despite Rob's relative youth, they respected him and responded well to his commands. "We've one more chore before we sail. We need to discover where Lady Georgina's carriage is so that we may gather her trunks for the voyage."

"Beggin' your pardon, Captain, but who is Lady Georgina?" Ayers and Chapman exchanged a quick glance.

Rob had already thought about how to handle this without the risk of compromising the lady. God knew he was skating close to the edge with this one. "An old friend of my family who needs assistance. She'll be accompanying us to St. Just to visit my mother."

"How did she lose her carriage, Captain?" Chapman's

frown was a portent of questions to come. Best give the exact truth and nothing more.

"She didn't lose it, but rather fled from it." The puzzled faces before him made Rob hurry on. "The lady claims she was kidnapped by some ruffians bent on God knows what kind of mischief. Fortunately, she, her maid, and her dog managed to escape, and, by great good fortune, she found me, before they recaptured her."

"Kidnapped?" Ayers looked aghast.

"Lord have mercy." Chapman looked around, as if expecting the villains to appear. "Do you want us to help you capture the blackguards?"

"No, Chapman, I don't think—"

"We're with you, Captain." Barnes cut him off. "They should be made to pay for doing such a terrible thing." He smacked his fist into his hand.

"Quiet, men. We do not have time to act as avengers for Lady Georgina. We can, however, cock a snook at her kidnappers by taking her trunks from underneath their very noses."

Wide grins spread across all their faces, Chapman elbowing Barnes in the ribs and laughing outright. "That would be a good 'un, Captain."

"Aye, we're with you on that one, Captain."

Breathing a sigh of relief, Rob herded his men toward the railing beneath which the small boat was tied. "Once we reach the shore, Cartwright will post a letter from me to the lady's brother, informing him of the circumstances and that she has decided to visit my mother in Cornwall. Now to the task of finding her carriage."

"But that carriage could be anywhere in Portsmouth, Captain." That protest came from Barnes, likely thinking of the miles he'd have to walk.

"That is why we are fortunate that I have a plan. Go on down with you."

The men swarmed down the ladder, and, when they had all settled in the boat, Rob cast off." Chapman manned the oars to take them into shore.

"Once Cartwright has returned from posting my letter, we will go to the spot where I met Lady Georgina. From that point, we will each take a street and run the length of it looking for the carriage with the Blackham crest of a black lion rampant. If you find it, go back to the end of the street where you started and look for me. I'll wait for each of you to report before we move on to another set of streets. Pay special attention to inns where the carriage may have stopped."

"The lady didn't see the name of the inn?" Barnes's shaggy eyebrows almost touched his nose.

"She claims she was fleeing the kidnappers, Barnes. I daresay she was not interested in names, only in escaping. I cannot chastise the lady for not paying attention under such circumstances." Rob shook his head, wondering if Lady Georgina had indeed noted a name or anything else helpful. He'd wager she had, despite her desperation to escape. Blast it, he should have at least tried to ask her.

"Aye, Captain. Some women are quite scatterbrained even when they're not being pursued." Chapman gave a huge pull on the oars, and the boat grounded. "Believe me, my Betty is one of the worst. Never can tell me straight what she's done all day."

Nodding and grumbling about the flighty nature of women, the crew climbed out of the boat and stood ready for him to command. If they couldn't find Lord Blackham's carriage and retrieve Lady Georgina's things, it would likely be a miserable voyage for all concerned, as the lady would then have only the clothes she stood up in. But so be it. The tide would begin going out in an hour. If they didn't find her belongings, Lady Georgina could wear sailcloth for all he cared.

The tide waited for no woman—with clothes or without.

Chapter Six

Georgie's half boots thumped loudly on the wooden flooring as she paced back and forth in the cabin, fuming. From the window to the door and back, in the past hour she'd likely worn a groove in the planks. Drat the man for imprisoning her in here. She rattled the door for the twentieth time since the marquess had sneaked out. Lord, the man was terribly stubborn.

"It's still not opening, my lady." Clara stared at her from the comfort of the captain's chair. "Not until his lordship returns with the key."

A retort on the tip of her tongue, Georgie opened her mouth, then huffed a sigh and closed it. Much as she hated to admit it, her maid was correct. Georgie wasn't going to get the dratted door open save with the key. She'd rattled the latch until it should have fallen to pieces. Then she'd pounded on the door, but apparently there was no longer anyone onboard. In desperation, she'd even tried to pry the nails out of the hinges with a knife she'd found, but to no avail. That door wasn't budging. She had to give the marquess credit. The ship was very well built.

"Then I'll simply have to find another way out of this cabin and off this ship." Georgie strode back to the porthole that looked out over the water and to the beach.

This stretch of land and water had become so well-known to her, she could see it in detail if she closed her eyes. There were three gigantic casks sitting in the sand directly across from her. Holding brandy or rum, most likely. Not that they were labeled as such, but Georgie had always imagined casks that transported spirits would need to be huge. Beside them were two square boxes covered by a tan oilcloth. She'd no idea what might be in them. A young sailor sat on the sand next to the casks, his back propped against the boxes, his feet dangerously close to the water that lapped at the shore. Because the lad hadn't moved since Georgie first spied him, perhaps an hour ago now, she assumed he must be asleep in the orange glow of the sun that was beginning to set. She certainly hoped the lad's captain didn't find him thus and pitch him into the cold water of the harbor.

She forced her attention from the sleeping sailor back to the porthole itself, her final possible means of escape. The round glass pane opened out into the cool air. That, however, wasn't the problem.

"Do you think either of us could fit through this opening, Clara?"

The maid eyed her from where she sat. "You might be able to shove Lulu through the likes of that. Though I don't know what good that would do you."

Georgie sighed and shrugged. Still, it was their only hope. She stuck her head through the porthole and peered down. Drat. "Apparently, it wouldn't do us any good even if we could squeeze through. There's a drop of only about twenty feet but the water looks very icy."

Withdrawing from the opening, she crossed her arms over her chest and resumed pacing. "I've actually attempted something like this once before. Father had locked me and my brother in our rooms at Blackham. My room there had a sheer drop of about thirty feet, and the walls held no purchase, just pockmarked stone. Just as unforgiving as the smooth side of this ship."

"Did you manage to get out, my lady?" Clara cocked her head, apparently interested now.

Georgie nodded. "Well, my brother did. We twisted the bedsheets from both our beds to make a rope, and Jemmy slid down it, stole a horse, and headed to London." It had been most exciting. But of course, she hadn't been the one dangling from a rope in a high wind. And wouldn't be this time either. "Unfortunately, now there is only a single pair of sheets on the bed, and neither of us could slither through that porthole even if we stripped down to our chemises and covered ourselves in grease."

Clara blanched. "I should say not."

"And I couldn't do it, even if I did fit, because I'd have to drop into the water, and, as I never learned to swim, I absolutely cannot do that." Georgie clenched her teeth and made a growling sound that brought Lulu's head up. Seeing no threat, Lulu settled down once more. "Drat Lord St. Just. Why couldn't he simply have agreed to help us return to Blackham Castle, as any normal gentleman would have done? We'd be on our way home this instant." She commenced pacing again, shaking her head at the jackanapes. "Do you know what this means, Clara? Do you?"

The maid shook her head.

"It means, if Lord St. Just takes us with him, he will quite likely confound any hope of my marrying Lord Travers." Why couldn't the man have let well enough alone and put them in a hired carriage hours ago?

"I was thinking that very thing, my lady." Clara looked away. "There's nothing we can do about that, is there? There's no way off this ship, I'm thinking."

"Not unless we can transform ourselves into the bodies of twelve-year-old girls who can swim in the next few minutes." Georgie paced to her chair and plopped down in it. Disgust with their helpless state left a bitter taste in her mouth.

"I'm that sorry, my lady."

Waving away the well-meant sympathy, Georgie sighed and tried to think of something more encouraging. "Well, I must say I am not truly sorry I won't be marrying Lord Travers."

Clara's brows shot up.

Laughing, Georgie relaxed and her spirits rose a tiny bit. "You know I am not fond of the man in any way and never have been. A more lewd gentleman I've never met. Even Lord Fernley had more to recommend him."

At her feet Lulu awoke and stretched, then sat looking up at Georgie hopefully, tail wagging.

"All right, my girl. You may save the pitiful looks." She lifted Lulu into her lap and stroked the soft fur. "What does concern me a great deal is how Father will take the news." She slid her hand down Lulu's glistening fur, rubbing her gently. Such attentions usually had a calming effect on both her and Lulu. "I quite fear he'll disown me again. He said as much in December when he informed me of the match. And he swore that if he did cast me off again, it would be for good."

Gripping the chair arms, Clara leaned toward her. "What will you do, my lady?"

Hugging Lulu, Georgie lay her head on the sweet dog. "I don't know, honestly. I seriously doubt Isaac's sister will accept me back into her household." Not that Georgie wished to return to that dreadful situation. Her late husband's sister had taken her parents and, reluctantly, Georgie, in after his death. The woman had made Georgie's life a merry hell until her friend Charlotte had encouraged Georgie to stay with her. "And now that Charlotte, Fanny, and Elizabeth are all married and increasing, I don't feel that I should impose on them."

"Surely your brother will take you in, my lady." Clara's hopeful tone smote Georgie's heart.

"I know he and Elizabeth will offer, but Father still controls my brother's purse strings and will continue to do so until August, when Jemmy inherits from my mother's settlement. Until then we must all walk on eggshells and hope Elizabeth will produce Jemmy's heir. Then I doubt Father would deny him anything as they are naming the child after him."

"But it's only January now. August is such a very long time away." The dawning realization that she might soon be without employment turned Clara's countenance glum.

Georgie slumped in the chair and clutched Lulu tighter. "I know. If only I could marry—a gentleman who was not Lord Travers. But I have no means to go to London this Season and little hope of a gentleman's taking me with no dowry." She couldn't do a lot of things, but there was one thing she could do. Taking Lulu's face into her hands, she spoke earnestly to her beloved pet. "If that door opens, Lulu, and Lord St. Just appears, bite him."

Twenty minutes after Rob had sent his men to find the Blackham carriage, he stood peering at his pocket watch. The tide had already begun to turn. None of his men had reported back to him so far. The afternoon sun was sliding down the sky, sinking into the west at an alarming rate. The sailors knew if they didn't return soon they would miss the evening tide and have to remain in the harbor until the next opportunity to sail presented itself, more than twelve hours later. And even if they managed to succeed in retrieving Lady Georgina's trunks, her kidnappers would likely still be scouring the city and the harbor for the lady. Not a good time to be anchored just offshore and a prime target.

It would also give Lady Georgina too much time to devise a way to escape the ship.

Brack had related several of her exploits when she was a girl still in the schoolroom. The most vivid of these tales involved her attempt to visit a tenant farmer's wife who'd taken ill. When her father had forbidden the visit, lest the girl fall ill as well, Lady Georgina had found a truly unorthodox way of getting to the home. She had disguised herself as a groom and ridden on the back of a carriage heading in the general vicinity of the tenant's house. Once near enough she'd jumped off the moving carriage and walked the rest of the way to tend to the ailing woman.

Rob shook his head. The lady was as adventurous as any man of his acquaintance. Not a totally ladylike trait, but he for one wouldn't hold that against her. If the lady hadn't been so set against him, they might have had a lark of their own together.

Discovering himself grinning like a fool, Rob cleared his throat, put on a more sober countenance, and turned back toward the street he'd sent Cartwright down. Lady Georgina's penchant for adventures might yet bring them to grief.

"My lord."

Rob whirled around to find Chapman sprinting toward him. Puffing like a winded horse, the sailor slid to a halt in front of him, narrowly missing a stack of crates.

"I found it, my lord." Chapman bent over, sucking in air by the lungful. "Three streets over, near the water, at The Ship's Arms Tavern."

"Excellent work, Chapman. There'll be an extra crown in your wages this quarter." Rob clapped the man on his back. "You are sure it's the Marquess of Blackham's carriage?"

"Yes, milord. Shiny black lacquer, gold trim, and a lion"—Chapman stood up, his arms raised, fingers splayed out like claws—"up on his hind legs, ready to fight."

Chuckling at the man's amateur theatrics, Rob nodded and scanned the street., "We'll wait for the others to return, then we're off to The Ship's Arms."

A few minutes and Barnes came into view.

"What ho, Barnes." Rob motioned the men toward him.

"Didn't find a thing, Captain." Sounding disgusted, Barnes shifted uneasily on his feet.

"But Chapman has. Just along there, at The Ship's Arms Tavern, lies our prize. We just have to wait for the others—"

"Captain!" Ayers and Cartwright popped around the corner together and jogged toward them. "Nothing down that way, Captain." Ayers pointed back along the street they'd come from. "Cartwright and I met up at the ends of our streets. They came together at a point."

"But no carriage on either street, Captain." Cartwright's lips were pursed, his brows lowered.

"Not to worry, Cartwright. Chapman found it at The Ship's Arms Tavern." He gazed at the excited faces surrounding him. "Are we ready then to take back her ladyship's belongings?"

"Aye, Captain." Barnes straightened and nodded, his gaze fully on Rob.

Ayers nodded too and grabbed a baling hook off a nearby bale of cotton. "Aye, Captain."

"That we are, my lord. What would you have us do?" Chapman still gulped air, but his resolute face didn't waver.

"Give me a moment." Rob adjusted his hat, thinking furiously. "Let me see where it is. Chapman, you lead the way." They all trotted briskly down the street. Rob had visited that particular tavern several times when he'd been in port. Unfortunately, now he needed a plan, preferably one that might actually work. How could he steal away Lady Georgina's luggage without the kidnappers any the wiser? At least not until they'd set sail. It would do none of them any good if they were caught in the act and would be even worse if the kidnappers managed to follow them back to the ship—and Lady Georgina.

"There it is, Captain." Chapman pointed to a serviceable establishment across the street from them that teemed with custom.

"Wait." Rob stopped short and backed them up, taking them instead into a noisome alleyway across from the inn that stank of manure and molasses. From this vantage point he could better assess the situation. Slowly he stuck his head around the corner of a clapboard building.

The shiny black carriage stood gleaming in the court-yard, its horses nowhere in sight. Why hadn't it been moved to the stable area?

"Why has the carriage been left unattended, but the horses have been taken inside?"

"What do you mean, Captain?" Barnes cocked his head.

"If a carriage comes into an inn and the passengers are staying the night, the horses are put in the stable and the carriage is put back behind it, to make way for other rigs. However, this carriage"—Rob gestured to the Marquess of Blackham's equipage—"is sitting right there, for all to see. Why?"

His men looked blankly at him.

"Because it's being used as bait." Rob lowered his voice, though, by the surprised expressions, the others hadn't thought of that. "Whoever kidnapped Lady Georgina is hoping she'll send someone for her trunks, or even better, she'll try to take them herself. So they've made it look easy. I assure you, it won't be. We won't be able to retrieve the carriage itself." Not that he'd ever entertained that notion. "But the trunks are right there, just calling for someone to snatch them." One sat in a compartment beneath the rear of the conveyance; the other was strapped to the rear where a groom usually rode. Though both trunks were small, there was no way to determine how heavy they were. Rob and his men would have to make the best of it.

"It's going to take some doing to get those trunks away, Captain. Might even run into some trouble." Ayers ran his hand along the hook, as though itching to use it.

"That we may, Ayers, but we won't court it. Let it come to us." Rob drew back around the corner and squatted down, his back to the planks of the building that faced the street. Although none were in evidence, he assumed there were guards watching that carriage very carefully. If he and his men were not to be found out, they must tread softly. Or better yet, create a diversion.

Rob peered around the area, noting anything that could possibly be of use to him, when his gaze fell on a young lad, not more than twelve, dressed in serviceable clothing, though it had seen better days. The boy was sitting atop a barrel that had been left just adjacent to the inn yard, tying a square knot in a bit of rope, passing the time. Likely a cabin boy or had been. The lad could tie a decent knot; he'd give him that. The question was, could he do more than that.

"We need a diversion."

Ayers raised his hook, but Rob hastily waved that away. "Not from you, Ayers." He put his hand over the hook and pushed it away. "I'm going to create a commotion that will distract these hidden watchers, draw them into the ruse, and, while that is occupying their attention, you will all run in there, grab the trunks, and head back to the ship. First, I'm going to enlist the help of that young lad over there." He loved it when plans fell seamlessly into place, and, if this did, he'd have bested whomever the kidnapper was and had a famous lark into the bargain. "Gather close, gentlemen. . . ."

Several minutes later Rob rose, adjusted his coat and hat, and strode purposefully from around the corner of the building, which happened to be a warehouse. He wished for a walking stick to complete the ensemble of the gentleman he was impersonating, but what he had would have to do. Assuming his best lordly air, he strode between the barrels and boxes that littered the street as if inspecting his cargo, until he halted in front of the lad tying the knots, who'd progressed to the half hitch. Rob's back was to the carriage and hopefully to its guards as well. "How'd you like to earn half a crown, lad?"

The boy, who up close looked no more than ten years of age, stared at him, his china-blue eyes narrowing suspiciously. "You'd best move along, guv'na. I don't take kindly to coves like you what wanna take a toss with lads like me. Neither does me da. He's a carpenter on a big ship—the *Nantucket* she's called—an he'll plant you a facer for sure when he comes along."

Heat flushed Rob's face as the gist of the lad's accusation registered. Dear Lord, just the sort of diversion he didn't need. "No, my lad, you misunderstood." He took a deep breath and lowered his voice. "I'm rescuing a maiden in distress, and I need your help."

The boy glanced from one side of the yard to the other. "Don't see no maiden."

"She's not actually here." The lad was a mite sharper than he looked. "Rather I'm rescuing her trunks for her, the ones on that black carriage there in the yard."

The boy peered around Rob, who shifted subtly so the guards wouldn't see the boy's interest. "My men need to rescue those trunks without anyone seeing them do it, so I need you to make a scene . . . like in a play. You've seen a play before?"

"Oh, aye, in Drury Lane." Bobbing his head fiercely, the lad looked interested in Rob's request for the first time. "There was lots of talking at first, but in the end, the men fought with swords and died. I liked that part."

"Well, then, do you think you could do something like that? Something that will draw the attention of the men who are guarding that carriage away from it? That will allow my sailors to nip in and grab the lady's trunks."

"I don't see no men." The suspicion was back in the boy's face.

"They've very cleverly hidden themselves, just out of sight. Likely in the inn. What do you say, lad?" The sun was quickly heading for the west. The tide was heading out to sea. He needed action, and he needed it now.

The boy's eyes brightened. "Are we going to fight with swords?"

"Unfortunately, no. However, you are going to play the wonderful part of a thief. Do you think you can do that?"

"A thief?" The doubt in his voice made Rob sigh with impatience.

"You will need to be a good runner. Are you a good runner?" Rob pulled his purse from his jacket pocket and poured coins into his palm, then slid them into a pocket, leaving a half a crown in the leather pouch.

The boy's bug-eyed gaze never left the pouch, though he nodded.

"Good. Then I want you to snatch this purse from me and run, first around me, then over to the carriage. Open the door, scoot through the carriage and out the other door. I'm going to act like I'm chasing you, but once you get through the carriage, run for your life, because I'm going to send the guards after you. And you don't want them to catch you under any circumstances." Rob nodded gravely, and the lad blinked. "Are you with me?"

A slight nod, and the boy set his rope aside.

"Good lad. Thanks for your help." Rob tensed, but held the pouch loosely in his hand and whispered, "Go."

In that instant, the boy leaped from the barrel, taking the pouch lightly from Rob's fingers as he went.

"Stop, thief!" Rob yelled in his best Drury Lane voice as

he pursued the lad toward the carriage. Stirrings inside the inn told him he'd been correct.

The boy headed toward the waiting carriage, yanked the door open, and jumped in. Rob slowed just a bit. He didn't want to get too close to capturing the lad. Not that he thought he could. "Stop that boy!" He continued to call out, directing his cries toward the inn. "Someone help me!" Rob climbed into the carriage as the boy jumped out the other side, hit the sandy ground, and took off running. "Come back here, you jackanapes!"

"What are you doing, my lord?" A deep gravelly voice behind him made Rob swing around to face a tall man with a flattened nose.

"What does it look like I'm doing? I am trying to retrieve my belongings, and you and your partner are going to help me." Rob jumped to the ground as a second burly fellow came up to the carriage. "Both of you, chase that urchin down and bring him back here to me."

The man took a step back, looking around almost comically, as if to see who Rob was addressing. "Yes, you there. Tall fellow. That boy stole my purse. Go after him this instant."

"I ain't allowed to—"

"I do not care what you are not allowed to do or by whom. You will pursue that thief, or you will answer for what he stole." Puffing out his chest, Rob tried to make his voice as supercilious as possible. "Now!"

"What's goin' on, Bill?" The second man looked suspiciously at both Rob and Bill.

"This cove got his purse snatched."

"Both of you, stop talking and follow that thief. I will send my servant for the watch, and they will deal with this urchin, if you will move your arses and go find the little rotter. You're letting him get away." Taking the men by the arms, Rob shoved both in the direction the lad had gone.

With reluctant glares at Rob, the men finally trotted down the street in the direction the lad had gone, but Rob had no fear he'd be caught.

Immediately, Chapman and Ayers scrambled toward the carriage and grabbed the trunk stowed beneath while Barnes and Cartwright removed the straps that secured the chest to the rear. To cover this activity, Rob sauntered over to the innkeeper of The Ship's Arms, who stood in the doorway shaking his head, a tankard he was polishing in his hand.

"Have you ever seen the like, sir?" Rob scowled at the man and gestured to the vanishing guards. "A thief takes my purse, and no one will assist me. What has Portsmouth come to, I say."

"It's a real shame, my lord. I never would have pegged Jim Carpenter's boy for a thief. Jim's been a carpenter for nigh on twenty years. Crews with the *Nantucket* and keeps a good eye on his lad. Had him waiting at the captain's table this past year." The innkeeper shook his head. "Jim'll tan his hide proper, make no mistake of that. Be lucky if the lad don't lose his job."

Gritting his teeth, Rob clenched his fist. This wouldn't do. Not by half. "Mr. Harriman, I believe it is?"

The innkeeper nodded, though his eyebrows rose just a fraction.

"I've been in your tavern a time or two. I'm asking you not to tell the lad's father he stole my purse. He didn't steal it."

Confusion crept over the man's face. "But, beggin' your pardon, milord, you just said—"

"I know." Rob blew out a breath. Dash it, he was no good at subterfuge. He glanced back at the carriage, but his men had gone, thank goodness. "I must confess, I was playing a jest on the servants of a friend of mine. So I told the lad to take my purse and gave him the money in it. So he absolutely did not steal anything."

"You did, my lord?" Harriman gave Rob a wary look, but returned to polishing the pewter tankard.

"I'm of a fanciful nature, Mr. Harriman. Pray don't mention it to Mr. Carpenter. I wouldn't want to get the lad in trouble." Rob fished out another half crown and pressed it into the innkeeper's palm.

"Thank you, my lord." The coin disappeared, and the innkeeper's face lit with a smile. "No, my lord, I'll say nothing of it to Jim Carpenter. You have my word. Can I do anything else for your lordship?"

"No, thank you. I'm meeting my friend in a short while. I'll let you know if we require anything then."

Mr. Harriman turned away, still smiling, and Rob heaved a sigh of relief. If he could just get back to the ship without running into Bill or his chum, they'd be sailing in no time, and the danger would finally be past.

An inch of brandy remained in the bottle when Travers sank his chin onto his chest and drifted into an uneasy doze. His men should have caught Lady Georgina and her maid by this time. Tanner might not be the brightest star in the sky, nor Norris—not Norris, it was Morris—but they were like hounds to the scent when they were set to pursue a quarry. Shouldn't have taken them this long, though. Should've sent Cole. A human bloodhound that one.

"My lord." Crawford gripped his shoulder, and Travers came upright with a snort.

"What's the news? Where's Lady Georgina?" He peered around the dimming room. Sun must be going down. How long had he slept? Shaking his head to brush away the brandy's fog, and failing, he instead grabbed the cup and downed the bit of spirits left in it. Not enough by far.

"Where is the lady, Crawford? Has Tanner not returned with her yet?"

The valet shrunk back toward the door. "He returned some time ago, but had no one with him."

"Damnation!" Travers slammed the glass down on the table, and it shattered into a spray of fine shards. "They've done nothing right the whole blasted day." He shook his hand, glass fragments and blood flying. "Serve them right if I gave them all the sack."

Crawford ran for the bedchamber and returned with a wet washing cloth and began to sweep the shards together.

"Did you speak to Cole?"

The valet looked up, eyes wide and wary. "Who, me, my lord?"

"No, the blasted Lord Mayor of London," Travers roared. Why did he only employ imbeciles? He dropped his gaze to the cut on his hand, blood welling up in a bright red bead that grew larger. Fishing in his pocket, he put his hand to his mouth and sucked the blood in, then spat it into his handkerchief.

"Should I fetch a surgeon, my lord?" Careful not to cut himself, Crawford gathered the sharp glass into the wet cloth and shook the contents into the fireplace.

Travers gazed at his hand. One piece of the glass had slashed it rather deeply, and the cut ached. He nodded and waved Crawford toward the door. "Did you speak to Cole? Did the woman or her maid attempt to retrieve their belongings?"

Crawford stopped as if stabbed in the back. Slowly he turned toward his master, his face unusually pasty. "Mr. Cole wasn't sure, my lord. If it was the lady or her maid . . . or someone else."

"Someone else who did what? Stop speaking in riddles, man." Travers was through with his servants. Tomorrow he'd sack the lot and begin again.

Crawford had managed to open the door. Now he darted his gaze from his master to the hallway beyond the chamber. "Who took the trunks, my lord."

"What?" The pressure behind Travers's eyeballs rose until he expected them to pop out of their sockets. "Someone took the trunks?" His voice hit a crescendo that rattled the glass in the window.

"Yes, my lord. I'll just fetch the surgeon now." Crawford bolted out the door, slamming it so hard in his haste that it rebounded into the room.

Too shocked to move, Travers clenched his jaws, his fists, his toes in his boots in an attempt not to bellow out his rage that the one way he had to track Lady Georgina had been lost. *All was not lost, all was not lost.* If he kept telling himself that often enough, it might make it true.

He still had the cargo from Mr. Sturgehill to think about. The whole reason he was here in this Godforsaken port to begin with and not snug at his primary estate in Essex. But Sturgehill, God rot him, had insisted Travers pick up the goods from this run himself. Maybe he didn't trust Cole after the last time. His servant had apparently lost his edge when it came to sharp dealing. Still, once Travers married Lady Georgina, he'd no longer have to rely on the proceeds from his smuggling venture. He could pay off his debts and start anew. With his wife's money. All he had to do was hold on a little bit longer.

Slowly he exhaled, straightened his jacket, and wrapped the bloody handkerchief around his hand. Nothing had gone right today. Finally, he strode out of the chamber, leaning to one side. He pelted down the staircase, going so fast he missed the bottom step and fell into the wall, bounced his shoulder off the newel-post, and careened into the innkeeper, who had emerged from the kitchen at the worst possible moment. Luckily, Mr. Harriman had nothing more in his hands than a pewter tankard.

"Beg pardon, my lord." The man righted himself and bobbed his head. "Are you in need of something?"

He was in dire need of Lady Georgina, but he could hardly say that. "I need my man Cole. Is he still with the carriage, blast him, or has he dragged himself in here to hide in your taproom?" Travers whirled around, casting his gaze over the establishment in search of the man who had allowed his prisoner to escape him not once but twice today.

"I believe Mr. Cole has bedded down above the stable, my lord. He and your other servants secured the carriage and horses and retired rather abruptly."

"Hiding," Travers growled. Now his blasted hand was beginning to hurt fiercely. "Ought to go sack the lot of them."

"Begging your pardon, my lord, but I'm sure your friend meant no harm." Mr. Harriman set the mug down.

"My friend?" The innkeeper must have been sampling his own wares. "I have no friends with me at the moment."

"Perhaps he's just come to town and recognized your equipage, then. He said he was playing a prank on your servants."

Narrowing his eyes, Travers softened his voice. "What joke was that, if I may ask?"

Mr. Harriman proved quite loquacious. A veritable fount of indispensable knowledge. By the time he finished the tale about the supposed "friend's" exploits, Crawford had returned with the surgeon.

"Take him to my chamber, please, Crawford. I'll be there directly." Travers fished in his pocket and drew out a shilling. "Did my friend give you his name, Mr. Harriman? I confess I have several who would play such a jest."

"I'm sorry, my lord, but he did not give it."

Damn. Just his luck. He started to put the shilling back in his pocket, when Mr. Harriman spoke up again.

"However, he did remind me that he's been in the tavern a time or two. And I recollect now who he is."

Travers stared at the man, the coin falling from his fingers. "Who?"

Harriman caught the coin neatly. "Lord St. Just, my lord. The Marquess of St. Just of Cornwall."

Chapter Seven

Sunk down into her now uncomfortable seat, Georgie kept trying to keep her eyes open despite the almost constant pull to close them and drift off into a much-needed sleep. Determined not to give in to the weakness, she opened her eyes wide, staring hard at Lulu curled up at her feet. Perhaps she should follow Lulu's example and take her rest when it came to her. Clara had managed to find a comfortable enough position to doze off. A gentle snore emerged from her from time to time, attesting to the maid's exhaustion.

Still, Georgie forsook sleep, wanting to keep herself alert and prepared for the moment when Lord St. Just returned. Oh, but she longed to escape this ship, though she'd be going God knew where. She *had* to try. Her presence alone with his lordship and his crew, even with the chaperonage of her maid, could spell disaster for her reputation if word of this voyage got out. What St. Just was playing at she didn't know, but make no mistake, when he finally reappeared she'd ring a peal over his head so loud he'd think a bell clapper had been struck. She'd make him forget all about this outlandish scheme to sail all the way to Cornwall with her. If she and Clara could evade him, then make a run for it, perhaps they could find an inn in which to spend the night. In the morning she could send word to her father to come rescue her.

Not the best of plans considering that she didn't really want her father to know anything whatsoever about this escapade. But it was the best she could come up with on such short notice. Unfortunately, it all hinged on getting off this dratted ship.

Thudding feet and shouting voices brought her instantly alert. Jumping up from the chair, she winced at the sharp pain in her back and narrowly missed Lulu, who had also risen and was stretching herself right beneath her feet.

"Please be careful, Lulu. You don't want me to step on your paw, do you?" Untangling herself, Georgie stepped away from the King Charles spaniel and hurried to the door. She pressed her ear against it and listened.

"What's going on, my lady?" Clara had sat up and was rubbing her eyes.

"Shhh, I'm trying to find out." The door panel was thick enough that what Georgie could hear sounded like the quacking sounds of someone in distress. And of course the actual words were too indistinct to make out. Drat. "I assume this activity means Lord St. Just has returned to the ship, although I have no way to be certain. For all I know we've been beset by pirates attempting to steal the ship."

"My lady!" Clara looked scandalized. "Don't borrow trouble. We're in a tight enough fix as it is."

Without warning, the ship bobbed violently. Caught off guard, Georgie stumbled backward into the bed behind her. The back of her knees caught the edge of the bunk, and she sat down hard. She grabbed the railing that ran around the bunk, pulling herself upright. Excellent idea to have something to help keep a sleeping person in bed if the ship took a notion to pitch like this. And the person most likely occupying this bed every night was . . .

A flurry of heat shot through her, as if she'd suddenly

stepped into the blazing sun of a summer's day. Not that merely sitting on a gentleman's bed was improper, especially if he wasn't present. Or maybe it was improper. She certainly felt wicked all of a sudden. Shuddering, she leaped to her feet. "Something is happening." More than she cared to admit, too. She hurried to the porthole and gasped.

The sandy beaches of Portsmouth were speeding by her, as though the ship had put up its sails and . . . "Drat the man!" Oh, but she longed to be able to curse him properly. "He's set sail with us."

"He does seem to have given us no options." Clara sniffed, her eyes beginning to moisten. "And all our belongings back in the carriage." A tear slid down her cheek. "I shudder to think what your gown will look like when he introduces you to his mother."

"That is the very least of my worries now, Clara. Although, as you are my lady's maid, I suppose it is only right that it be your first concern." She patted the maid's shoulder. "We will devise a way to make him pay for this affront as well."

A key grated in the lock. Lulu growled and stalked toward it, the fur on her back rising straight up.

"Not yet, Lulu." Georgie gathered the leash. "Don't bite him quite yet."

Her dog stopped advancing on the door; however, the growling did not abate. Better be safe. She gathered Lulu into her arms. "I'll give you the signal."

The cabin door swung open, revealing Lord St. Just, an impossibly broad grin on his face. "Wait until I tell you what my men and I just did."

"You don't have to tell me, my lord. I already know." Georgie glared at him and held Lulu tighter. The little animal was shaking, and Georgie was sure if she loosened her grip Lulu would launch herself at the unwary marquess. Serve him right too.

"You do?" He frowned and cocked his head, which made him look like a puzzled puppy. Lulu looked just like that whenever she was unhappy. But what did he have to be unhappy about? He was the one who had kidnapped her.

"You have set sail, my lord, with me and my maid aboard against our wills. Many sensible people call that kidnapping." She'd always known this man was a pirate. In fact, she'd told her brother so. She handed Lulu to Clara before the dog could leap out of her arms and tear at his lordship's throat. If anyone was going to attack the marquess, it would be Georgie herself. Plant him a facer and see how he liked being set upon.

"Oh." The impossible man was all smiles again. "Yes, we had to put out or miss the evening tide." His grin had returned, showing many straight, white teeth. "But we did manage to steal your trunks, Lady Georgina. If you will consider yourself abducted again, at least rejoice in the fact that you will have clean linen throughout the ordeal."

Georgie blinked. What an unusually thoughtful gesture from Lord St. Just. The man deserved credit for that at least. And since they had already set sail, there was likely no going back. She'd have to make the best of a bad bargain and pray that it all came to rights eventually. If Folger and the other servants were still alive, and she certainly hoped they were, they would likely inform her father of her abduction as soon as they could reach Blackham Castle. Of course, they would have no idea where she'd been taken so he certainly would wonder where she was. She'd have to worry about that later. "Thank you, my lord. That was very . . . thoughtful of you."

St. Just's smile threatened to crack his face in two. "My utmost pleasure, my lady." He stepped aside, allowing her to precede him into the passageway. "My mate has taken both trunks to your cabin. Well, it will be your cabin as soon as Ayers finishes removing my belongings from it. I usually use it as an office, and it has become quite cluttered. He is now elevating it to the status of stateroom fit for a lady."

St. Just's grin was intolerably infectious, especially when he was being maddeningly charming—as he was now. She supposed this charming, boyish demeanor and desire to help others, no matter how misguided, was what had endeared him to her brother. In her experience, Jemmy was seldom if ever wrong about people. Of course, there was a first time for everything.

"Thank you. That is very kind." She managed to clip the words without biting her tongue. "This way?" She inclined her head toward the darker recesses of the passageway. Silly goose, of course they wouldn't go back toward deck. What had come over her?

"Yes, just there, on the opposite side from my cabin." His gray eyes bright, he indicated for her to go ahead of him through the cramped space.

Something in his voice—she had no idea what—made her stomach drop. True, that could be attributed to the swaying of the vessel, although it was not nearly as rough as she had believed it would be. She'd never been on a ship before, so she didn't know what it was supposed to feel like. Still, she must keep her mind on her task, which was . . . What was it she was attempting to do?

Despite the cold weather outdoors, here, inside, was quite warm, making her head all a muddle. As she was no longer actively trying to escape, Georgie didn't quite know what her purpose should be now. The present goal, she supposed, was to settle into her cabin and devise a letter to be posted to her father as soon as they reached Cornwall, explaining everything and asking his forgiveness for being kidnapped in the first place. Although how he could blame her for what had happened she certainly didn't know. Still, she didn't doubt he would. At least it would give her something to do.

Doing anything was always better than simply staring at the walls, waiting for something to happen.

With a nod, though she now couldn't fathom what she was agreeing to, Georgie stepped cautiously toward the door he'd indicated, indeed identical to his. "Thank you, my—"

Without warning, the ship pitched violently to the left.

Georgie shrieked, flailing out for some sort of purchase. She'd have fetched up hard against the wall had it not been for St. Just, snaking his arms around her just in time.

"Steady, my lady." Effortlessly, he engulfed her in an embrace that was strong, and safe, and warm. Her back lay fully against an iron-hard chest, her head cupped in the cradle of his shoulder.

She'd not actually realized how tall he was nor how solid his arms and chest were. For the briefest of moments she relaxed against him, indulged in allowing herself to imagine he was Isaac, with his strong arms holding her, making her feel safe and loved once more. Oh, but she had sorely missed that close, intimate contact this past year, no, almost two years now. How she missed him still.

She shook her head—she refused to go down that path of misery again. Isaac would never come back to her, would never hold her again, never kiss her. The sweet memory of his love she would keep forever, but nothing else. Sadly, the only arms allowed to embrace her now were those of Lord Travers.

Frightful thought. For the briefest moment she clung closer to Lord St. Just, as if he could shield her from her fate, but that was silly. She had willingly agreed to marry Lord Travers in exchange for her father's good will. A steep price to be sure; still she was prepared to pay it. If only Travers were not quite so abhorrent. If only St. Just were not so devilishly good-looking . . .

With a gasp, she pulled away from Lord St. Just. She could not allow herself to dally with his lordship on board this ship or any place else. And certainly not right outside her bedchamber. Retreating until her back bumped into the door, she held out a hand as if she were fending off the gentleman. "Thank you, my lord."

"I do apologize. The Channel is quite choppy this time of year." He still held onto her arm, and she was actually glad of it. She was so muddled by the bobbing and twisting ship—and by his touch on her arm—she had not paused to consider just how uncomfortable this journey that she did not want to take was actually going to be. Or how she might tolerate the voyage at all. Some people, she had been told, managed quite well, with few ill effects. Others, however, struggled with devastating sickness. Hopefully, she would be the former type of passenger.

A growl behind her turned into a whimper. Poor Lulu. "Give her to me, Clara. I daresay she is not happy to be pitched about either."

Lulu yipped again, as if in agreement. She struggled in Georgie's arms until Georgie was obliged to set the dog on the floor. "No biting yet, Lulu," Georgie whispered. "I'll give you the signal if I think it's warranted."

With a snuffle that turned into a low growl, Lulu sat down and stared at Lord St. Just's black Hessians, teeth bared and at the ready.

"I think she'll calm now, my lord. If we can only settle comfortably into our accommodations, I think we will all feel better." Although, despite her words, Georgie had begun to feel distinctly unwell.

The ship chose that moment to pitch violently. Georgie would have been thrown to the floor had St. Just not put out an arm to steady her.

"As I said, the Channel is never a treat, even in good weather, but in January or February, well"—the wretch grinned as the ship rolled the other way—"it's been known to turn the most fearless captain back to shore."

Georgie might have returned his outrageous grin had her stomach not chosen that moment to make itself known. The roiling of the waves was nothing compared to the rumbling from within.

Shooting a stricken look at Clara, Georgie motioned her toward the door. Clara darted forward and opened it.

Attempting to maintain her dignity even though she wanted nothing more than to breach protocol and cast up her crumpets here and now, Georgie walked slowly up the passageway.

"If you do not mind, my lord"—the maid grabbed Georgie's arm and guided her toward the doorway—"I will see to Lady Georgina." Clara's face puckered as she pulled her mistress into the chamber. "I'll send for one of your men if we have need of anything." Clara hurried in and shut the door sharply as Georgie sank down into a chair and gripped the arms until her knuckles turned white.

Drat it, she would not succumb to this inconvenient weakness. Staring steadfastly at the table in front of her, Georgie willed herself to hold on. Her stomach, however, was past caring about embarrassment. She took a deep breath, fighting the awful sensation in her stomach, hoping that would help steady her. To no avail. "Oh, Clara. The chamber pot, quickly."

Rob started as the maid slammed the door in his face, then tried to repress a grin, but the haughty Lady Georgina was about to be brought very low. The muffled groan and the stricken words, "The chamber pot, quickly," told him he would get revenge on the lady through no effort of his own.

Poor lady. He understood all too well the misery she'd be feeling presently. Sobering, he rapped on the door. "Are you all right, Lady Georgina?"

Another, louder groan issued forth from within.

"Can I get you something? Some tea and toast, perhaps?"

The unpleasant retching sounds that ensued made him pity the lady heartily. He'd had his own stint with seasickness when he'd first begun sailing with his grandfather. An episode Rob had never forgotten, though he'd been a lad of ten at the time. Once he'd gotten his sea legs under him, he'd been fine. Until then, he'd wished for a swift death. So he sympathized with the lady, although he couldn't help but believe the gods were exacting some sort of vengeance on his behalf. "My lady? Do you require anything?"

The door jerked open, and Clara thrust a rather disgusting chamber pot into his hands. "If you'd like to be of use, my lord, kindly dispose of that and bring me several more empty ones." She glared at him, and all thoughts of vengeance vanished. He truly didn't wish Lady Georgina ill. "And the less said about food and drink, the better, although"—Clara again fixed him with an icy stare—"a bite of food and drink for me wouldn't come amiss. I'll be tending to her day and night by the looks of it."

"I will be sure to see to it, Clara." Nodding deferentially, Rob tried not to wince at the stench wafting up from the chamber pot. "I'll also send a mate to swab down the cabin and help you with anything either you or Lady Georgina requires." Holding the repulsive pot as far away from his nose as possible, he turned toward deck, then back to the maid. "It may sound cruel, but once the initial sickness is over, the best remedy will be for her to eat some hard biscuit and drink ginger tea. All sailors swear by it to cure seasickness." He lowered his voice. "Also, tell her to lie still and let her body go with the ship."

The piercing look Clara shot at him could have skewered a weaker man, had it been a weapon. She held his gaze a full minute, then nodded and shut the door.

Rob ran nimbly up the stairs to the deck, where the brisk, cold wind scoured away the reek in moments. "Clean this up, Ayers." He snagged the first lad he saw and thrust the pot at him. "Find as many more as you can throughout the ship and take them to the lady's chamber, along with a mop and bucket. You'll see to their comfort and do whatever Miss Clara instructs you to do."

"Very good, Captain." Ayers wrinkled his nose, but dutifully trotted off toward the bow of the ship.

Rob turned toward the galley. For runs of a shorter duration, he usually brought no more than a three-man crew, plus himself. This time, however, as it was January, and the Channel presented even more of a challenge than usual, he'd brought along Barnes, to help cook as well as tend the ship when necessary. Rob popped his head into the galley and found the older man with a kettle on the stove and a bowl of potatoes on his lap.

Stabbing a sharp knife into one potato to draw it from the bowl, Barnes looked it over with a keen eye before commencing to peel it. When he noticed Rob in the doorway, he tried to rise, but was waved back into his chair. "Don't let me disturb you getting on with dinner, Barnes."

"You're not disturbing me none, Captain." The older man paused, knife in one hand, half-peeled potato in the other. "There's not much time, so I thought a nice bit of beefsteak, roasted potatoes, and a ragout of vegetables would serve us right enough."

"Very good. I wanted to remind you we'll have one extra mouth to feed tonight. Be sure we have ample provisions for her."

"Not two mouths, Captain?" Barnes's eyebrows rose ever so slightly.

"One only. And no, I'm not trying to starve one of our guests. Miss . . ." Blast, he needed to find out the wretched maid's surname so he and the men could address the woman properly. "Lady Georgina's maid is tending her mistress, who has a touch"—God he hoped it would not be a severe case—"of seasickness. Before you serve me and the men, you will take her meal to the cabin." Rob gazed about the galley and seized a canister. "For now, please brew a weak ginger tea for the lady and ready some of these biscuits for her as soon as possible."

"Aye, Captain." Barnes dropped the potato and knife into the bowl, set them on the table, and lit the stove.

As he made his way back on deck, Rob reluctantly came to two realizations. First, that he hated to see any lady suffer—even if she might deserve the tiniest bit of it—and so he would attempt to help Lady Georgina overcome her mal de mer as quickly as possible. The other was that, having held Lady Georgina in his arms, although it had been a brief embrace, he could and would attest that she was a pleasant armful and much, much too high above the likes of Lord Travers. In those circumstances, Rob would have to act.

Standing in the bow of the *Justine*, sailing into the dark, windy night, Rob vowed to do everything within his power to keep Lady Georgina Kirkpatrick out of Travers's clutches. "So help me God."

Quite likely he would need all the help he could get.

Chapter Eight

Perusing the most recent copy of the *Times*, the Marquess of Blackham sipped his third cup of tea, taken without milk but with plenty of sugar. Breakfast was his least favorite meal, although using the time taken to inform himself about events in the world beyond East Sussex made the waste more palatable. He'd just turned to the back page when Quick, his unflappable butler, rushed into the room.

"My lord." The elderly butler puffed the words out, his eyes as wide as a skittish horse.

"What the devil's the matter with you, Quick?" Blackham folded the paper and tossed it on the table. "You're white as a ghost."

"It's Folger, my lord." Quick still fought to catch his breath. He must have run all the way from the front door.

"Yes, he was supposed to arrive this morning with Lady Georgina." Consulting his pocket watch, the marquess raised his eyebrows. "He made damn fine time, although I trust my equipage did not suffer for it."

"That's just it, my lord. Folger's arrived, but without the carriage." The butler swallowed hard. "Or Lady Georgina."

Blackham's brows lowered almost to his nose. "Bring Folger here this instant," he barked.

"He is here, your lordship." Quick scurried through the doorway and immediately John Folger stepped into the room.

Had the man not been announced, Blackham would have scarcely recognized his coachman. The man looked as though he'd recently slept in the road. His jacket and pants had bits of dirt and dead leaves sticking to them and his boots were caked with mud. A lump the size of a pigeon's egg puffed the skin above his left eye. "What the devil's happened to you, Folger? And where are my carriage and my daughter?"

Folger winced, as if steeling himself for a blow. "Begging your pardon, my lord, but I'm afraid I don't know."

The hackles on the back of Blackham's neck bristled. "What do you mean you don't know, Folger? You were entrusted with the care of both, so I would think it would be in your best interest to know where both of them were every minute of the day."

"I was, your lordship." The coachman gripped and twisted the hat in his hands, although the brim had already been broken. "Until yesterday when we pulled into The Running Horse in Leatherhead. I'd gone into the woods to use the necessary when two fellows attacked me. Hit me over the head and I knew nothing until I came to this morning, tied up in the woods behind the inn. The two outriders and the groom were there beside me. Said the same thing happened to them."

"Pah." Blackham threw down his napkin and rose. "Worthless, the lot of you." He strode from the room shaking his head. "You should never have been alone. That way no one could accost you."

"But my lord." Folger had followed him at a trot. "A man doesn't take another man with him when he goes to take a piss."

"He wouldn't need to stand there and hold it for you, man. Just guard your back to make sure you didn't get waylaid." Blackham hurried into his office, making for the huge black walnut captain's table he used as a desk. "Are the others in pursuit of the villains?"

Folger stopped, then backed up a step. "No, my lord. We asked at the inn this morning but all they could tell us was that the carriage left after about fifteen minutes with a fresh team. One of the ostlers did say he thought your carriage headed south out of the yard but was busy and didn't pay much attention." The coachman cleared his throat. "As we had no idea where the carriage or Lady Georgina might be, we thought it best to come here and raise the alarm."

"Raise the alarm?" Blackham stared at the man, wishing it were permissible to whip servants. "The time to raise an alarm was at the inn as soon as you came to and realized my property was missing. You have been utterly useless to me, Folger. Consider yourself sacked."

"Sacked, my lord?" The disbelief in Folger's voice irritated the marquess to no end. Any other servant in his employ would have expected such an action automatically.

"And without a reference. I'll expect you to be off the property by noon." Blackham slid into his chair and reached for his box of pens.

"But my lord—"

"Had you been this persistent at The Running Horse, Folger, I might not be bereft of my carriage and child at this moment." The marquess drew a sheet of creamy paper to him. "That is all, Folger."

A sigh followed by a shuffling of boots on the carpet told Blackham the coachman had gone. Good riddance. Now to find out what had really happened to Georgina and his carriage at The Running Horse. Of course, this must be another scheme by his youngest daughter to avoid the match he'd made for her. She'd run off and married out of hand before. No reason not to believe she'd done it again. And if she had, there was likely only one person who knew about it.

Dipping the pen in the inkpot, Blackham narrowed his eyes and glaring at the paper as though he had the intended recipient before him, began to write.

The splash of waves hitting the side of the ship near her head dragged Georgie out of the fitful doze she'd finally fallen into around dawn. The fierce movements of the ship had caused her to be violently and disgustingly ill throughout the night. Casting up one's accounts had to be the most wretched feeling. She hated it more than anything—even worse than cats—and now she was to be captive on a bounding ship for an untold number of days, doing the very thing she despised most of all. If she didn't already hate Lord St. Just for ruining her reconciliation with her father, she would detest him for visiting this plague upon her. She sat up in the bed and was immediately sorry. "Ohhh." Her stomach roiled yet again. "If I live, I vow on Lucy's grave I will have his guts for garters. Even if they are not a fashionable color."

"Beg pardon, my lady?" Clara appeared at her side immediately, wiping her face with a cool cloth. It didn't really help Georgie feel better, but being fussed over soothed her soul a little. "Who is Lucy? Your mother?"

"No. Ohhh." Georgie clutched her stomach. "She was Lulu's great-grandmother. Oh, drat. Do you know any really awful curses, Clara? I want to curse Lord St. Just for doing this to me, but I don't know anything truly bad to call him."

"You mustn't think such things, my lady. They'll only make you feel worse." Wiping her brow, Clara *tsk-tsked* under her breath. "Does that feel better?"

"No, it does not." Georgie crossed her arms over her stomach again. "And since I am positive I cannot feel worse, I will chance the cursing all the same. Oh, dear. The pot, Clara. Quickly."

In the moments that followed, the painful and slow death of St. Just was the sole image that gave Georgie any solace. Never would she ever forgive the man for torturing her like this. Finally, she eased herself back onto the bed, exhausted. "This must be how the medieval saints felt when put to the rack." She breathed slowly, praying for her insides to settle. "I do believe, Clara, we might have fared better with the kidnappers after all."

"I doubt that, my lady." Trying to stifle a yawn, Clara took the chamber pot to the door and set it outside for Ayers to deal with. "They might just as well as not have taken you on a ship too. They took us directly to the docks, if you remember."

"It could not possibly be worse than this." Gingerly, Georgie turned on her side. When nothing untoward seemed imminent, she sighed slowly and sank onto the pillow. "At least they likely would not have abandoned me as Lord St. Just has done."

"Abandoned you?" Shutting the door with a loud bang that made Georgie wince, Clara returned to her side, her face like a thundercloud about to pour down rain. "How can you say he's abandoned you? Far from it, let me tell you. Quite a nuisance he's made of himself, if you ask me. Knocking on the door all hours of the night, asking how you were faring. He's been ever so helpful with suggestions for when you're well enough to take tea and toast."

"Ugh." Georgie made a face and shuddered. Her stomach sent out its own loud protest. "He's trying to kill me, although I may very well die before he accomplishes it."

"I asked him about that, my lady, when you were so ill in the middle of the night. He assured me that this illness would pass and more quickly than you would ever believe. He said to tell you that no one ever died of seasickness."

Glaring at the traitorous maid, Georgie swallowed down her rising gorge. The thought of any food whatsoever made her stomach clench painfully. "Perhaps I shall have to die then, just to prove him wrong."

"I can assure you, my lady, you are not in the least dying. At least your speech seems to be rather lively for someone with one foot in this world and one in the next." Clara stifled another tremendous yawn. "You sound much stronger than you did last night. Lord St. Just says if you'll just take a bit of tea and toast . . ."

"Traitor," Georgie hissed through clenched teeth. The mere words "tea and toast" made her want to retch again. "I cannot believe my own maid would plot my murder right in front of me."

"Believe me, my lady, you'll take more killing than this." Clara dropped down in the chair beside the bed. "Can I do anything more for you?"

"Other than stopping the ship or putting me out of my misery, no." Closing her eyes, Georgie concentrated on scenes of meadows with birds and butterflies amid a sea of violets. Oh, not a sea. She needed something more stationary—a carpet of violets, that would work. Carpets did not move, save when you beat them. Yes, violets. And Isaac.

Just as she was drifting off, the ship heaved up and down so violently Georgie bounced in the bed. Her eyes flew open and panic seized her; she expected to see water pouring in from somewhere. However, the cabin remained intact, thank heavens. Her innards, unfortunately, were making their presence known again.

A glance at her maid showed Clara still asleep, hand pillowed on her cheek. How the woman could sleep through such an upheaval, Georgie could not fathom. Thank goodness this sickness hadn't affected her maid or Georgie would have been in even direr straits than now. She'd try to allow her to sleep a little while longer, though Georgie, of course, had little control over matters having to do with her stomach at the moment.

A whimper from below brought Georgie's head up. "Lulu? Is that you?"

The little dog's sweet tricolored face popped up at the side of her bed, her silky paws resting on the edge of the bunk, and she barked.

"Shhh." Georgie glanced at Clara, but the maid hadn't stirred. "Don't wake her. She needs her rest." Stroking the soft head she sighed. "Can you jump up here?" She patted the covers beside her. "Perhaps your company will make me feel better."

Lulu's head disappeared, then she sailed up onto the bed, landing directly on Georgie's stomach. Lulu slid onto the bed where she sat panting and smiling.

"Oof." Pain stabbed Georgie, bringing tears to her eyes. "Oh, Lulu. What have you done to me?"

A sharp knock at the door brought Clara awake with a snort. "What?" She looked around as if trying to recognize her surroundings. Her gaze found Georgie, and she jumped up. "I'm so sorry, my lady. I was so tired I must have dozed off."

The knock was repeated, more insistently this time, followed immediately by St. Just calling, "Lady Georgina?"

Holding her aching stomach, Georgie shook her head. "Please don't let him see me like this."

Nodding, Clara made for the door, but before she reached the middle of the cabin, it opened revealing St. Just, bearing a tray with a bowl and a cup on it. A mischievous smile lit his face. "I see you are awake, my lady." As if invited, he stepped briskly into the cabin.

"Oh, no, my lord." Swiftly, Clara moved in front of him, barring further entry. "You cannot come in here." The maid held up a finger as she paused to yawn. "It would ruin Lady Georgina's reputation."

St. Just eyed the sleepy woman, then trained his gaze on Georgie. "I won't tell if you won't."

Raising her head to upbraid his insolence, Georgie caught a whiff of the hot soup he carried, and her protest turned to a groan. She clenched her teeth and screwed her eyes shut, willing her body to behave. If she cast up her accounts in front of the marquess she would die of shame. Dying might just be her best option in any case.

He set the tray on the table and turned to Clara. "I've dealt with seasickness before. Leave the lady's care to me, and I'll have her shipshape in no time."

"I cannot do that, my lord—" The maid stopped, a huge yawn interrupting her objection.

"You'll be asleep as soon as I leave the room, Clara. Then who will be left to tend to Lady Georgina? The dog?"

Lulu bared her teeth at him.

"Her name is Lulu," Georgie managed to say before dropping her head back onto the pillow, exhausted.

"Well, neither Lulu nor Clara can take care of you at the moment." Jaw set, he glared at Clara. "Go to the small cabin just down the passageway that is usually used for storage. Chapman has made up a bed of sorts for you there. All the crew is on deck, so no one will disturb you. Get some sleep." He turned a thoughtful eye on Georgie. "In the meantime, I will see to Lady Georgina."

Opening her mouth, hopefully to object to this scandalous proposal, Clara locked eyes with St. Just. Her shoulders sagged, and, with a fleeting, apologetic glance at Georgie, she fled the chamber.

Chuckling, St. Just settled himself into the chair. "I have that effect on servants when I deem it necessary." He looked her over, concern showing in his gray eyes. "And this is necessary." He pulled the chair closer to the bunk, settled back, and gave her the piercing look she assumed he'd given Clara. "So, my lady, what shall I do with you?"

* * *

Ten o'clock in the morning was hardly the time for brandy, but Travers simply couldn't help himself. He'd spent the best part of the night cursing his fate, St. Just, Lord Blackham, and Lady Georgina herself. In between curses he'd drunk glass after glass of the inn's middling vintage, which explained why his head had been thumping with horrible regularity this morning ever since he woke. After an hour of groaning, he'd finally called for more of the vile stuff, and a little hair of the dog had calmed his head to a dull throbbing.

"Crawford!" Oh, God. A white-hot sizzle of pain shot through his head, threatening to pop out his eyeballs. Curse St. Just most of all.

He'd been livid when Mr. Harriman had told him the name of the gentleman who had orchestrated the theft of Georgina's trunks. A name vaguely familiar to Travers, belonging to one of the dozens of gentlemen of the *ton* to whom he'd been introduced over the years—the image of a tall, lean man with oddly bright gray eyes appeared in his mind's eye—but not an intimate by any means. So definitely not a friend playing a joke. Much more likely a friend of his betrothed who was assisting her in fleeing and therefore knew where she was hiding.

Had he been at home he could simply have looked the chap up in a copy of *Debrett's*, but he'd not find such a volume at this establishment. Cole and Brown had denied any knowledge of the man beyond this encounter, although their description of him had coincided with Travers's own recollection of his appearance.

As the surgeon had dressed the cuts on his hand, he'd done the only thing he could think to do and sent his men out to scour the waterfront establishments searching for anyone who knew or knew of the marquess. Was he a local landowner? If so, the retrieval of Georgina might be easier than expected.

The surgeon's parting instructions had been rest and the liberal application of spirits. This advice Travers had taken to heart, perhaps a trifle too well in fact, for he'd passed out before the men had returned. Steeling himself against the pain, Travers shouted again. "Crawford."

The parlor door opened, revealing Crawford standing hesitantly, somewhat like a deer sensing danger but compelled to enter an open meadow all the same. He carried a jug of steaming water by way of peace offering. "Good morning, my lord."

Despite the hushed tones of the valet's voice, a searing, agonizing bolt shot from one temple to the other. Clenching his teeth against the pain until it passed, Travers hunched over the table, glaring at the man. "For the love of God, Crawford, be quiet." He breathed deeply, and the ache receded. "Where are Cole and the others? Did they find St. Just or Lady Georgina?"

The valet set the washing water on the stand. "They returned around midnight with news, my lord. Should I fetch them here?"

"News?" Travers sat up so quickly his head snapped back, sending waves of misery through his skull. "What news?" he whispered.

"I believe you should speak with Mr. Cole for the exact details, my lord, but I gathered they located Lord St. Just."

Squeezing his head between his hands, Travers tried to speak forcefully, though it came out a groan instead. "Send Cole to me now."

Crawford scurried out.

Gingerly, Travers made his way the six steps to the wash basin and upended the jug over his head. Warm water cascaded over his hair and face, soothing him a little. He would tear the head from the marquess's body with his own two hands, if only he could stop his own from pounding.

Using his sleeve to wipe his face, he shuffled back to the table and eased into the chair. Where the devil was Cole?

At last a hesitant knock sounded on the door.

"Come."

Cole presented himself, hat in hand, looking chastened and frightened. As he should.

"Tell me that you found St. Just."

Shifting from one foot to the other, looking as if he would bolt from the room any second, the big man bit his lip and said, "I did and I didn't, my lord."

The dull thumping in Travers's head had returned, more insistent than before. "You did or you didn't find him, Cole. It has to be one or the other."

"Beggin' your pardon, milord. We searched all along the waterfront, stopping at every inn and tavern we thought a gentleman might put up in."

"And sampled the wares at each one, I'll wager." Travers stopped glowering at the man long enough to eye the bottle of brandy. Another drop would taste good, no doubt. Reluctantly, he turned his attention back to Cole. He needed to gather his wits and concentrate on the man's tale.

"Well, a pint here and there makes for easier talk."

The man was probably right. "Continue."

"Morris even went into the town proper, as far as Cherry Street, but none of us could find a sign of St. Just."

"So you didn't find him." Why must this dimwit act as if he didn't know he hadn't found the man?

"Not then, my lord." Cole's voice took on an eager tone. "But on the way back here, Morris runs into an old chum, and they gets to talkin' and come to find out, the chum works on the waterfront for a ship that was moored directly next to one called *Justine*, out of Penwith, Cornwall, owned by Lord St. Just."

"The man has a ship moored near here?" Travers would never have thought of such a thing, but it played rather nicely into his hands. He and his men could storm the ship and recover Lady Georgina, or if she wasn't there, brandish weapons and make the marquess tell them where she was hiding.

Cole edged back a step. "Not exactly, milord. Morris's friend took us to the place where the ship was supposed to be, but it had gone. Sailed on the evening tide."

Travers's mouth dropped open. "And you waited until now to tell me?" He pounded the table until his hand hurt. This was simply too much bad luck for one man to have. Grinding his teeth, he tasted blood.

"I didn't think it mattered, milord." By this time, Cole had backed to the door and bumped into it. "If he was already gone."

"Get out." If the man didn't leave, Travers might throttle him here and now.

Cole apparently saw the threat in his eyes and shot out the door, slamming it behind him.

"Crawford!"

"Yes, my lord?" The valet emerged slowly from the parlor.

"I need you to dress me before you go out." After last night's indulgence, Travers was rather disgusting at the moment, if truth be told. He required a bath, fresh shave, fresh linen, and his best blue superfine suit.

"Out, my lord?"

"Yes, I need you to first call at The Harbor's Heart to see if Mr. Sturgehill has left word for me of his arrival. Then, check about passage for both of us to Cornwall. You cannot reserve us places yet, as we must await word from Mr. Sturgehill. Then come back here and pack up everything. We must be ready to leave the instant my venture with him is complete."

"Very good, my lord." Crawford turned toward the

dressing room, then spun back around. "But where are we going in Cornwall, my lord?"

"Penwith. And Crawford, inform Cole he will be leading the others on horseback to that same area in Cornwall. They are to pack their things and be on the road within the hour." With hard riding and a bit of luck the men would already be in place near St. Just when Travers arrived on the ship.

"Yes, my lord." The valet hurried out.

Travers leaned forward and poured the final inch of brandy into his glass. He'd be damned if he let St. Just steal his bride away. Unless Blackham had already broken the contract. This whole scheme had been launched with that very contingency in mind. He prayed to God it had not come to pass.

Draining the last dregs from his glass, Travers weighed the wisdom of writing to the marquess to find out the lay of the land, so to speak. Of course, if Blackham had suddenly taken him in dislike, there was nothing to be done. The lady's father would simply tell him that the offer of Lady Georgina had been withdrawn, and that would be that. Meanwhile, if he wrote simply to inquire about the plans for the coming wedding, might he not draw attention to his insecurities regarding the marriage? Blackham could see that either as a sign of weakness or disrespect and call off the wedding.

Gazing at the empty glass sourly, Travers shook his head. Too great a chance to take. He would proceed with his original plan: get Lady Georgina into his bed, preferably with witnesses, and secure her as his wife shortly afterward. The end was all that mattered, no matter how he accomplished it.

Chapter Nine

As far as sick rooms went, Lady Georgina's wasn't actually as foul as some Rob had had occasion to visit. Despite her fatigue, Clara had kept her mistress as clean as possible and the room tidy. Still, a small cabin tended to retain odors. So getting the lady on her feet and out of the malodorous room would certainly speed her recovery. Being on deck, where the wind, though cold, was fresh, would make a world of difference to Lady Georgina. But in order to get her there, he would have to coax her to eat something. Therein lay the challenge.

"Lady Georgina." With steadfastly closed eyes, the lady lay mute, although he'd swear she was not asleep. Stealthily, he poked his finger into her shoulder. "Lady Georgina."

That drew a mumbled response he couldn't quite hear. "I beg your pardon?"

She sighed and whispered a bit louder, "Please, go away."

Shaking his head, Rob grabbed the cup from the tray he'd brought, the spicy steam wafting into the air. "I'm afraid I cannot do that. I have taken you on as my charge, you see, willingly or not, so I am bound to see you safely to St. Just or my honor is forfeit. You would not wish that, would you, Lady Georgina?"

Dead silence.

Well, he supposed it only natural she felt some ill will against him at this point. "Whatever your feelings for me, I am in charge of your welfare, which includes attempting to cure you of your seasickness. To do that you must eat."

"No." Scowling at him, she shook her head vehemently. "If I eat that I shall be violently ill." She clamped her lips shut and stared at him, defiant.

"You may be a bit queasy at first, but once we get the tea down, the ginger will take effect, and you'll feel much better. This has been a sovereign remedy for mal de mer for generations of sailors." Perhaps a bit of a distraction would help. "Did you know that Admiral Nelson also suffered from seasickness? All his life. Still, during his entire career he fought it and died a hero despite the affliction."

"I assure you, I do not intend to make a career of the sea, my lord."

Rob chuckled and slipped his arm beneath her shoulders.

She stiffened. "What are you doing?"

"Moving you into a sitting position so you can drink the tea without drowning in it." He pulled her up, careful not to spill the tea, until she sat more or less erect. A tempting armful in more ways than one.

"I said 'no,' my lord, and I meant it." Staring directly into his face, she drew her lips inward.

More spirited now. A very good sign. "I also had a bout with seasickness when I was a lad." He eased his arm from behind her to free his hand. "I was perhaps ten at the time, and I reacted the same as you. Nothing my grandfather said would convince me to drink this tea." Grasping the handle with one hand, he tested the temperature with the other, to make sure it had cooled sufficiently. "But my grandfather had a remedy for such stubbornness." He lifted the cup before her eyes. "Would you prefer to take a sip of your own accord, or shall I demonstrate my grandfather's method?"

If the daggers in her gaze had been real, he'd have been a dead man.

She clamped her lips shut tight.

Very well. Lady's choice, then.

Without warning, Rob seized her nose, pinched it shut, and waited.

Lady Georgina's eyes widened, and she batted at his hand, making it hard not to spill the hot tea on her. "My lady, you are going to make me scald you if you keep this up."

She opened her lips a crack, letting out a squawk before shutting them a second before he could bring the cup to her lips. The dog started its infernal barking, bumping against his boots as if trying to knock him off his pins. This might be the closest to a cell in Bedlam that he'd ever been.

Disregarding the animal, he moved the cup close to her mouth. She couldn't hold out much longer without breathing. She had spirit, he'd give her that. Her face had taken on a bright red hue before she opened her mouth at last, gasping for breath.

Nimbly, Rob slipped the edge of the cup to her lips and poured.

Coughing, she almost choked, but got a good swallow down.

He released her nose and held the cup out to her. "Would you care to try the next one on your own?"

"Wretch." She wiped at her face with the sleeve of her white nightgown, frilly lace at sleeves and neck. The elegance of the garment suited her, somehow. Not surprisingly, she took the cup from him.

"One swallow down, one to go before we advance to the broth." A good sign that the first sip of tea was staying put. Distractions were good, and came in many different forms. He nodded, waited a moment, but when she didn't move, he reached for the cup once more.

The lady snatched it out of his reach and took a tiny sip. "Are you satisfied with tormenting me, my lord?"

"I am pleased to see you are assisting with your recovery— What is that dog doing?" He peered down at the bit of fluff trying to worry his good leather boots.

"She is protecting me from unscrupulous gentlemen who would take advantage of a lady when she is obviously suffering and incapacitated with a dire illness." Frowning, Lady Georgina took another small sip, without his prodding this time.

Excellent.

"Well, she is attempting to ruin my best pair of Hessians. Will you call her off before I am forced to interfere in a manner similarly unpleasant?"

Another look of delightful malice from the expressive green eyes, then Lady Georgina called to the animal. "Lulu, go sit in the corner. I'll tell you if I need you to"—she stopped abruptly and glanced at him—"assist me further."

Amazingly, the dog seemed to understand her mistress completely, for she trotted to the corner and lay down, muzzle on outstretched paws. What an extraordinary woman.

"And now, my lady, the broth if you please?" He plucked the cup out of her hand and swiftly substituted a bowl of chicken broth instead.

Wrinkling her nose, Lady Georgina curled her lips up. "Are you always such a bully to your captives, Lord St. Just? I must confess I did not suspect this side of your character when we met at Lyttlefield Park last autumn."

"As I recall, Lady Georgina, at that time you were not attempting to sail the Channel in the dead of winter."

"Neither would I be doing so at this moment, Lord St. Just, had you not kidnapped me."

"I thought I was rescuing you, my lady." He couldn't suppress a grin. The woman was charmingly diverting.

"That may be your version of the events. However, I have

a different perspective." She sniffed the bowl of soup and made a face. "I asked you to take me to Blackham Castle, but instead you are taking me to Cornwall when I do not wish to go there." She raised her chin triumphantly. "I believe that may be the very definition of kidnapping."

Rob nodded to the bowl. "The broth, my lady?"

Another withering look, but she raised the spoon to her lips and sipped. Her eyes widened. "It's very good."

A huge smile spread across Rob's face. Their first battle met, and they had both come out victors. "I'm glad you like it. Barnes does certain dishes I prefer very well, but in order to accomplish that, he first had to learn to make a good broth."

She took another, larger sip.

"And for the pièce de résistance"—he grabbed a napkin he'd kept hidden in his pocket—"a biscuit." Unwrapping it with a flourish, he held up a piece of hard, round bread.

"What is that?" She seemed to shrink back in the bed, as though the biscuit might attack her.

"Hardtack, made from flour and water only, baked for over an hour in the oven." He banged it on the tray, making the teacup dance. "It's called that for a reason. It is also the third part of my grandfather's remedy." He held it before her face, and she swallowed hard. "Care to try it?"

She eyed him coolly. "Do I have a choice?"

"Not really. Especially if you wish to feel well enough to go up on deck. It's cold, I'll grant you, but the breeze is crisp, and the smell of the salt air will cleanse your soul."

Her eyes changed from sharp and wary to wide and inquisitive. "You have a great fondness for the sea, do you not, St. Just?"

"I admit I do." Fondness? Lord, so much more than that. "All my life I have loved the sense of freedom she offers. The wide-open skies, the infinite water. Staring out to sea knowing you alone are in charge of your own destiny. The sense of adventure you feel standing at the bow at the break of day watching a new dawn burst into life as the spray stings your face. Riding slow and easy into a sunset that turns every color imaginable." The life he'd truly been meant to live, save for the accident of his birth. "Had the duties of the marquessate not been my lot in life, I'd have been a sailor. Then I'd never have to leave her." Distractions did come in many forms. He nodded to the biscuit. "Try a bite."

Eying the hardtack, Lady Georgina sighed, then raised her eyebrows. "How did your grandfather propose getting this down a reluctant patient?" The humor in her voice made his spirits unaccountably soar.

"Do you wish a demonstration?"

"I do not." Raising the hard bread to her mouth, the lady nibbled it and curled her lips. "It's very dry."

"That's the secret to it. The dryness settles the stomach. I don't know why; it just does." He took the half-eaten bowl of broth, and, after she'd managed a couple of small bites of the hardtack, he whisked that away too, laying it next to the bowl on the tray. "That is quite enough for the moment. Too much will simply set you back." He rose, well-satisfied with his charge. The lady might be stubborn, but she wasn't unreasonable. Surprisingly witty, which had been a boon. And very beautiful with her hair mussed and unruly against the pillow.

Where had that come from? Heat rose in Rob's cheeks at the random thought. The inappropriateness of his being there suddenly dawned on him. Had he just compromised this woman? He grabbed the tray and started for the door. "I'll tell Clara that you are feeling a good deal better. When you've rested for a bit, I'll tell her you may dress and come up on deck."

"That sounds an excellent plan." Yawning, Lady Georgina slid down between the sheets and smiled at him.

His cock surged up with a sudden desire stronger than any Rob had ever known before. He needed to leave and now, before he did something stupid, like ravish his charge here and now.

"Thank you very much, my lord." She turned eyes of liquid emerald on him. "You have been most kind . . . for a kidnapper."

Rob burst out laughing at the unexpected and less than sterling compliment, his disturbing mood broken, thank God. Lady Georgina was as unpredictable as she was beautiful. A dangerous combination, were a man's heart in jeopardy. "I will do my best to continue that kindness, my lady." He opened the door, and a whimper came from the corner. "What's that noise?"

"Oh, Lulu." Lady Georgina peered over the bed toward the little dog, now on her feet. She barked shrilly and darted toward the door. "My lord, would you take her on deck to a place she can do her necessary? The poor thing hasn't had the chance in hours."

"Of course." Rob set the dishes back on the table. He'd attend to them later. "Come here, Lulu." He bent to pick her up, only to be met with bared teeth and a growl. "Lulu, I am only trying to help you."

"Lulu, come here."

The animal trotted over to the bunk and put two paws on the edge, panting and seeming to laugh into her mistress's face. Lady Georgina bent toward her and whispered something in her ear. When she leaned back, the dog dropped to the floor and walked sedately to Rob's side and sat, looking up at him as if to say, "Can we get on with this?"

"She'll be fine now. I told her not to bite you as you were helping us now."

Rob glanced from the now amenable animal to the lady. "And she understood you?"

"She seems to have, don't you think?"

Well, the lady had a point. Lulu appeared to be resigned to accepting his help. At least he hoped so. Gingerly, he stooped and picked her up. She put up no fuss whatsoever. Very odd. With one last dubious glance at Lady Georgina, Rob left the cabin, more puzzled than ever by the woman. As he carried Lulu up the passageway toward the fresh sea air, he shook his head.

"Now, I don't know if you understand everyone or just Lady Georgina, but I'll tell you anyway, Lulu. I believe I'm beginning to like your mistress more and more."

They reached the deck, and the crisp air hit his face. Bracing. With a laugh of pure delight, he lifted one of Lulu's long, fringed ears and whispered, "Just don't tell her I said that."

The sun was well up by the time Georgie awoke a second time. Immediately, she sensed a difference in her body. The dreadful queasy feeling had gone, leaving her rested and alert. Her stomach was rather sore, but considering what she'd been through, that seemed nothing. When she remembered the horrors of the night before . . . *No, don't dwell on that.* She snuggled under the covers, stretching and relaxing. Though loathe to do it, she would have to give Lord St. Just credit. He'd known what he was talking about as far as curing mal de mer. Or his grandfather did. That didn't matter. What did was the confidence stealing through her that she could finally manage a venture out on the deck.

Clara had not put in an appearance. Poor thing must still be sleeping. Well, let her sleep. Lord knew she deserved it after the night she'd spent. Georgie was perfectly capable of dressing herself if she had to. If she could find her front-closing stays, that was. Cautiously, she sat up in bed. No difference, thank goodness. She swung her legs over the side of the bunk and managed to stand. The ship was cooperating, finally. That dreadful pitching had ceased, and she seemed to be gliding along as easy as you please. Or else Georgie was simply getting used to the motion. Either way, it was a godsend.

Surprisingly, it took her an age to dress herself, even though she put on her simplest gown, the blue wool with the large flounce at the bottom. The buttons kept slipping out of her grasp, though eventually she managed to make herself presentable. She twitched her skirts this way and that, wanting them to hang just so. When had she become so dependent on Clara? She used to dress herself of necessity when she lived with her sister-in-law, Mrs. Robinson. Georgie shuddered and quickly wound her hair into a low knot on the back of her head. She never wanted to go back to those unhappy days under her sister-in-law's rule. She must make certain she did not incur her father's wrath because of this unfortunate episode. When they arrived at St. Just, she would write him and explain everything and reassure him that she still intended to marry Lord Travers.

A pang shot through her, somewhat sharper than usual, when the idea of her marriage arose. She would so have liked to marry someone for whom she had a fond regard, but she had already married the love of her life. Life would never be the same no matter who she married. He would never be Isaac, so did it really matter who he was? Still, the idea of marrying someone she could laugh with, or tease, or enjoy a spirited war of words with, tugged at her heart. Despite her illness earlier, she'd quite enjoyed the little tussle of wills with Lord St. Just. Lord Travers did not strike her as a man with whom one could have such an encounter. From what she'd learned of him, he would have sent a servant to tend her. Or left her to her own devices, in which case she'd still likely be retching in the bed.

Shaking her head, Georgie determinedly grabbed the cup of cold tea and took a sip, then nibbled a little more of the peculiar hard biscuit. Both went down well and sat comfortably within. Perhaps she might be able to manage something a little more substantial for dinner tonight. From her memory of the cook's broth earlier, dinner promised to be a treat.

Humming a merry little dance tune from one of the parties at Lyttlefield Park, she slipped on her blue pelisse and marched out of the room, at last ready to brave a turn on deck.

She made her way up the passageway, which brought her onto the main deck of the *Justine*. The sun had hidden itself behind a bank of fluffy clouds, but the wind, as St. Just had promised, had tempered a bit and brought the clean smell of salt spray into her nostrils. She breathed deeply, the smell of the salt air bracing. The gray Channel water seemed endless, and thankfully calm. Scarcely a ripple marred the surface.

Georgie looked about for Lord St. Just, finally spying him at the bow of the ship, gazing westward into the glimmering light of the hidden sun. Plucking up her skirts, she carefully made her way toward him. When she got closer, she could make out Lulu roaming around in the bow as well, sniffing everything, though she stayed close to St. Just. He'd apparently made one conquest, which brought a smile to her lips. Despite her misgivings about the marquess, and she still had several, she was happy Lulu had befriended him.

Suddenly, a brilliant ray of sunlight streaked through a chink in the clouds. It drenched the entire bow with bright light, including St. Just, glinting off his dark, curly hair, accentuating the excellent cut of his jacket. The rising wind had flung back the jacket's front panels, revealing the trim figure he presented, tall of stature, wide of shoulder, narrow of waist and hip. Like the Greek statues in the gardens at home, but brought to vivid life. Although with rather more clothes on, thank goodness. Or not.

Georgie gasped and jerked her gaze away from him as the wicked thought took root in her mind and stubbornly refused to leave. What would Lord St. Just look like nude? What a totally inappropriate thing to think! What was wrong with her? She'd not had any such carnal thoughts since Isaac had died. Not even at Charlotte's house parties, where her widow friends had actively encouraged her to flirt with the gentlemen, had she remotely entertained such ideas.

She stole a glance back at the object of her dubious desire. He'd not seen her yet and was still looking out to sea, a look of intense satisfaction on his face. She had barely scraped an acquaintance with the man before he'd kidnapped her. And trusted him only as much as she must, although after his well-meant ministrations earlier, she probably should trust him a bit more. Still, that didn't explain why she should wonder about the man in a state of complete undress.

Really, she must shake off such fanciful and disturbing thoughts. With a determined step, Georgie hurried toward the lone figure. Before she got close to him, he turned, as though he had sensed her coming, greeting her with a broad smile.

"Lady Georgina. How wonderful to see you up and about and looking so well." His gray eyes twinkled in the sunlight. "I see my grandfather's remedy has worked its miracle yet again."

"Yes, my lord. It seems to have done." She returned his smile, her heart beating faster than usual. Obviously, she'd walked too quickly from the cabin. After her ordeal she must take things more slowly. "Lulu seems to be taking to life aboard ship very well. Thank you for looking after her."

"My pleasure. She's a spirited little thing. Once we came to an accord, we have gotten along famously." He gazed firmly at Lulu, then offered Georgie his arm. "Would you care to see the best view on the ship?"

An unexpected trembling seized her, her hands growing cold, and her throat suddenly tight. This was nonsense. There was nothing in the man's request to make her come over so queer. She must get hold of herself. Nodding, she wound her hand through the crook of his elbow. In spite of the chilly temperature and brisk breeze, she noticed a steady warmth where their bodies touched. A disturbingly pleasant warmth, in fact. Make small talk and ignore everything else. "What kind of ship is this, my lord?"

"A schooner my grandfather purchased twenty-odd years ago, just after he bought the tin mining company. He believed it would be a canny investment given the remoteness of Cornwall. His acumen has been proven time and again over the years." Lord St. Just had maneuvered them almost to the very front of the ship. "I'll wager that's a sight you've never seen before, have you?"

She gazed out over the vast sea of gray water, and her mouth dropped open. Truly, she had never seen anything like it in her life. The ship cut the calm waters almost silently as they bounded forward, the *shush, shush* of the water against the side the only sound. No land as far as she could see in any direction, only the sea stretching endlessly onward, always moving, always changing. Straight ahead grayish-pink clouds lowered almost close enough to touch the water in a lover's kiss.

Abruptly, Georgie became extremely aware of Lord St. Just's body so close to hers, their arms entwined, giving off enough heat that her pelisse was scarcely necessary. Dear Lord, more inappropriate thoughts about the marquess. This would never do if they were to be onboard together for some days. However, she had no earthly idea how to stop such notions.

Lulu barked, putting her paws up on the side.

St. Just's long silence suddenly struck her. He'd asked her a question ages ago. What was it? "Oh, no, my lord. I have never in my life seen such an awe-inspiring sight."

A sharp gust of wind made her stagger into her companion's side. The jolt was like a lightning strike, sizzling through her veins from her hair—which might indeed be standing on end—to her curling toes. She could do nothing but cling to him as the ship dipped and a splash of spray cascaded over the bow rail, spattering them with cold seawater. "Let's get you back to the safety of the mast. The wind's picked up rather quickly, which means the waves will likely do the same. We wouldn't want you drenched and catching a chill." He grinned and reversed their course. "Not when you've just begun to enjoy sailing."

"Of course." Swiftly, she stepped away from him and moved toward the towering timber in the center of the ship. "Come, Lulu."

The ship dipped violently forward, and a giant wave of water cascaded over the bow.

Georgie shrieked and grabbed St. Just's arms again.

"I've got you." He grabbed her about the waist, his strong arms anchoring her to his rock-hard chest, and she relaxed against him.

Frantic barking drew her attention to Lulu, drenched by the huge wave.

"Oh, Lulu! Come here." Georgie bent down and beckoned to the dog.

The ship pitched forward again. Georgie lost her footing on the slippery planks and tumbled to the deck.

"Careful, my lady." With St. Just's help, she staggered to her feet, righting herself just as Lulu slid forward and disappeared over the side into the merciless waters of the Channel.

Chapter Ten

"Lulu!" Lady Georgina screamed—a sound as piercing as any bosun's call Rob had ever heard—and began fighting to get out of his embrace.

"Lulu! Oh, dear God." Clawing at his arms, she twisted to and fro until she suddenly threw herself against him with full force. Catching him off guard, she broke free of his hold and staggered toward the rail, still shrieking. "Lulu."

"Georgina." Rob darted after her, afraid she'd jump overboard to try to save the animal. "Come back. She's gone."

The drenched deck pitched again, and his feet went out from under him. He hit the planks and slid toward the bow, fetching up against the rail with a force that shuddered through his whole body. Shaking his head, he picked himself up and ran to the bow where Georgina stood, still screaming and sobbing.

"Lulu. Oh, please, please, help her." She turned miserable eyes on him, heavy with tears that poured down her cheeks. "Can't you save her? Turn the ship around? We can't just let her drown."

"I'm sorry, my—"

"No!" She slammed her fist into his chest with enough force to make him stumble backward. "You do not get to be sorry. You have to save her. You brought us on this ship."

Her eyes flashed green sparks in the setting sun. "She's your responsibility. Save her."

Over Georgina's shoulder he could just make out the tiny head, still valiantly swimming toward the stern of the vanishing ship. Impossible to lower a boat in time. The frigid water would claim her before they could get it to her.

Georgina searched his eyes, then dissolved into renewed tears at the hopelessness she found there. "No, no, no."

She laid her head on his chest, sobbing as though her heart had broken in two. Perhaps it had. Her tears scalded him through his wet shirt, searing him all the way to his soul.

Damn.

He wrenched her away from him. "Keep your eyes on her. Don't let her out of your sight."

Stunned, she swallowed hard, then nodded and quickly faced the sea and pointed. "There. There she is."

Rob dashed aft, calling for Chapman.

"Aye, Captain." The lad sprang up from nowhere.

"Haul to and lower the boat."

"Haul to, Captain? Why?" Confusion rent the boy's face.

"Man overboard." Rob raced to the starboard side. "Where is she?" he called to Georgina who had moved astern, tearing his jacket off over his head as he ran.

"There." Georgina pointed far to the stern, where the dog was almost swallowed by the waves.

"She?" Chapman looked at the lady, his frown deepening. "Who's gone overboard?"

"I have." Rob stepped onto the rail, balanced precariously long enough to say a swift prayer to St. Jude, then dove into the dark waters.

Freezing blackness engulfed him, the intense cold like a thousand needles of ice piercing every part of his body. The shock drove the air out of his lungs before he could stop it. Panicking, he fought to clear his head. Had to breathe.

Furiously kicking his feet, Rob sped toward the surface, lungs on fire for air he couldn't reach.

The light became brighter until he burst through the surface, gasping in a lungful of blessed, cold air. Panting to get as much into him as quickly as he could, he groaned when the frigid water registered once more on his body.

Move. He had to swim or freeze. Whipping his hair out of his face, he turned in a circle until he spotted the *Justine*, alarmingly far away. But the sails had dropped, bless Chapman. Christ, he couldn't just bob here in the water watching the ship. If he didn't start moving he'd freeze to a solid statue before he could reach the dog. Got to swim. Where was the wretched beast?

"Where is she?" he called to the lone figure on the stern.

"There." She pointed behind him.

He twisted toward what he hoped was the correct direction. With no land as point of reference, he could be swimming anywhere. The choppy water continued to push him up and down as he scanned the surface. Where was she? The waves shifted, and Rob caught sight of the little head, scarcely above the water, yet paddling furiously toward him.

"I'm coming, Lulu." He stretched out and began to swim toward her, all the while praying they had got the boat in the water by now. If the current didn't cooperate—and if they didn't have a great deal of luck—he and Lulu would freeze to death before Lady Georgina's eyes.

Georgie screamed again when Lord St. Just plunged off the railing of the ship into the murky, freezing water. Dear Lord, the fall alone should kill him.

Holding her breath, she peered at the spot where he had gone in, willing him to surface. Nothing. Nothing for so long. Her lungs ready to explode, she glanced over the waves, trying to catch a glimpse of Lulu. And there she was, doggedly paddling toward the *Justine*. *Good girl*. Although she wasn't swimming as swiftly as previously. Was she beginning to falter? Had Lord St. Just's heroic action been for naught?

Lungs aching, Georgie swung her attention back to where the marquess had dove in and praise God, there he was. His sleek, dark head had broken the surface. She gasped in a thankful breath. He lived—at least for now.

The figure in the water looked up at her. "Where is she?"

"There!" Georgie pointed behind him, to the small, struggling Lulu. Dear Lord, she looked so tiny in the vastness of the Channel. Even Lord St. Just looked insignificant against the stark, endless sea. Would he make it to Lulu in time?

As if in answer, St. Just stretched out on top of the water and began swimming vigorously toward Lulu. Powerful muscles in play as he crawled across the choppy waves, effortlessly. At least he made it look effortless. The poor man must be freezing. As was Lulu.

"Do something." She snagged one of the mates scurrying past her. "We have to help him."

"Aye, m'lady. We're putting the boat in now. Cartwright, you're the fastest on the oars. In you go. Pardon me." The man sprinted past her toward the small boat that had brought them to the *Justine* as the youngest of the sailors was climbing into it. "Pull with all your might, Mr. Cartwright."

"Aye, Mr. Ayers." The sailor's eyes were fixed ahead of him, and he gripped the oars. "Lower away."

Wiping tears from her eyes, Georgie ran back to the right side and peered over. St. Just's head was the only thing she could see. He turned around, as if searching for something.

Lulu. He couldn't see her because of the waves. She could see the dog not many yards away from him, but he suddenly started swimming in the opposite direction.

"No!" She screeched, climbing onto the rail, holding

onto a rope for dear life. "That way." She pointed frantically at Lulu. "Behind you."

He didn't hear her, for he continued on his same path, away from the little dog who had almost stopped paddling. No, no, no. "Lulu!"

Her shout must have carried all the way to the dog, because a muffled "yip" carried back to Georgie, and Lulu began paddling toward her voice once more. Even more miraculously, St. Just had seemed to hear that "yip" as well, for he reversed course and headed straight for Lulu.

"Lady Georgina!"

Clara's shocked voice startled Georgie so badly she almost toppled over into the water. Now that would have been a hobble. She clutched at the rope and turned toward the maid, blinking in the sunlight.

"What are you doing up there, my lady?" The maid's indignant voice sounded almost comical. "And where is Lulu?"

The small but distinct "yip" coming from behind him brought Rob's head up. He spun around and caught a glimpse of the struggling animal. There she was, thank heaven. "Hold on, Lulu." He spat water and wearily struck out toward her once more.

Lulu must have seen him as well, for she paddled toward him faster, with frantic strokes, whimpering constantly.

Poor thing was likely almost done in.

He was almost done in if it came to that. Despite his vigorous swimming, the cold had penetrated his skin, sucking the heat from his body at an alarming rate. He could no longer feel his fingers or feet, though the latter kept pumping of their own accord, despite the fact that his boots now seemed made of lead. If the crew hadn't gotten the boat in the water by now, neither he nor Lulu would live to tell the tale.

The rough waters parted, and Lulu slammed into his

face, whimpering and shivering. He stopped swimming and gathered her into his arms, relief and joy unexpectedly coursing through him. "I've got you. You're going to be all right."

Lulu licked his face, the warmth of her tongue heating his frigid skin for only an instant, but that spark spread throughout him. "Thank you. And you're welcome. Now let's get back to my ship."

Glancing all about, he finally located the *Justine*, stopped in the water, thank God. Even better, the boat was in the water as well, coming toward them at a fair clip, but much too far away for his liking. It would be a close thing. Lethargy had already begun to steal over him. He wanted nothing more than to simply stop struggling and let the boat come to them. Shivering uncontrollably, he clutched Lulu to his chest. She was so cold and wet she could give him no spark of warmth to help him along. God, but he was cold. Closing his eyes he tried to imagine a blazing fire with toasty blankets all around him, a hot grog in his hand.

"Yip."

A splash brought him out of his dangerous daydream to find Lulu had leaped out of his slack arms into the water again, and was swimming briskly for the boat that suddenly loomed much closer. Shaking his head to dispel the deadly vision that had tried to lull him into a stupor and possibly death, Rob forced himself to follow the animal and struck out again.

"Captain!" The welcome shout sounded closer than he expected. The light had truly begun to go, the rowboat a huge black shape closing on them fast. He pushed himself to overtake Lulu. He'd have to lift her into the boat, then try to pull himself in as well. An arduous operation that was going to be, given his frozen and exhausted state.

Finally close enough, Rob grabbed Lulu's collar and took a moment to tuck her under his arm securely. The boat was heading straight for them. Cartwright had begun to slow its progress. This would be the agonizing part, simply waiting in the frigid water for help to arrive.

Shivering violently, Rob began to pray.

"Get down from that railing, my lady, or you'll end up in the water too." Clara's no-nonsense tone penetrated Georgie's fear-laden brain and she grasped the rope tighter and jumped to the deck.

"I'm quite all right, Clara." She swung back around, her gaze going directly to the boat, thankfully now almost to Lord St. Just.

"Who went into the water?" Peering over the railing, Clara gasped. "That's not his lordship?"

"Yes, it is. He went in to save Lulu."

"Lulu!" The color drained from Clara's face, leaving it a pasty white.

"She got washed overboard. But it looks as though he's got to her. And the boat is almost to them now." Georgie grasped the rail, pushing at it as though she had oars and could help speed the little boat.

"Cartwright's a good man with a strong back." Beside her, Ayers spoke up, his gaze on her hands. "He'll have the captain and your dog back here before you know it." He narrowed his eyes. "That water's powerful cold, though."

The pit of Georgie's stomach churned.

As though he'd suddenly thought of something, the sailor bolted past her for the passageway, calling, "Mr. Barnes!"

Shaking off her fear, Georgie hurried to the farthest part of the stern to catch a better glimpse of the boat in the deepening twilight. "Do you see him?" she asked the only crew member remaining on deck.

"Aye." The lad pointed. "There. Mr. Cartwright's on him now."

"Oh, thank God!" Georgie flew to the railing, Clara right behind her. "Where is he? Oh, there. There."

Muffled barking ensued as Lord St. Just clasped Lulu around her middle like a huge wriggling sausage and heaved her over into the boat. With Cartwright's assistance, St. Just crawled into the boat as well and sat huddled in the bottom, Lulu in his arms, as the sailor reversed their course and headed back to the *Justine*, the boat fairly flying toward the ship. After pulling alongside, Cartwright swarmed up the ladder, and he and the others slowly raised the boat until Lord St. Just and an excitedly barking Lulu came into sight.

Crying with a fierce joy, Georgie scrambled toward them, slipping on the wet planking and ignoring everything but the sight of the two drenched and shivering creatures crouched on the bottom of the boat. "Lulu! Oh, Lulu." She snatched the shaking animal up out of St. Just's arms, clutching her wet little body to her chest.

Lulu whimpered and buried her very cold nose into Georgie's neck. Goose flesh rose all along her spine, but cold had never felt so good to her. She ripped open her pelisse and shoved the dog against her gown, wrapping her in the warm woolen folds of the coat, totally disregarding the ruin of both garments. What did she care about that? Lulu was safe.

And cold. The water that had streamed off Lulu now soaked into Georgie, and she shivered. "Goodness, you are like a block of ice, Lulu." Perhaps the deck, even colder now the sun had all but set, was not the best place for her to make a fuss over the little dog. They should retire to the cabin where she could dry Lulu off and make certain she had taken no other hurt. But first she must thank their champion. "I want to thank you, my lord—"

The sight of St. Just, slumped in the bottom of the boat, unmoving, sent a pang of fear coursing through Georgie.

Dear God, don't let him die. She thrust Lulu into Clara's arms. "Take her below."

Clara nodded, grasping the wiggling Lulu, and hurried toward the passageway.

"Is he dead?" Georgie sent a frantic glance at Ayers, who had run up with a blanket that he was now tucking around his captain. She bent swiftly over St. Just's still form, dread in her heart.

"I don't think so, my lady." The doubt, both in Ayers's voice and eyes, sent Georgie into a panic. Almost afraid to touch St. Just, she laid her hand lightly on his shoulder. His thin shirt was plastered to shockingly cold flesh, face glowing ghostly pale in the early twilight. She choked back a sob. "My lord?"

No response at all.

Blinking away tears, Georgie shook him gently at first, then harder until finally he groaned and opened his eyes.

"Lulu?" His hoarse voice cracked, and he coughed deep in his chest.

"Thank God, Captain." Ayers staggered in relief as St. Just sat up in the boat.

"She's fine. Here, let me help you." Georgie put her hand under St. Just's arm, and between them she and Ayers got him out of the boat, steered him to a bench and sat him down.

Shaking his head, he waved her away. "Tired. Just need a rest."

"Captain, are you all right?" Cartwright and Chapman ran up to him, their faces pinched and anxious, more blankets in their hands.

"Fine." St. Just hung his head, as if too weary to raise it.

"He needs to warm up." Georgie couldn't stand by and do nothing. The marquess looked all in. She could not leave him until she knew he was safe.

"Aye, he does." Ayers stood St. Just up again, drew the sodden blanket away, and pulled his shirt over his head.

"What are you doing?" Stunned at the sight of the man's bare chest, Georgie stood rooted to the deck. A sense of impropriety warred with anger that they would deliberately expose a freezing man to the elements. "Are you mad?"

"No, my lady." Ayers's hands were busy at St. Just's fall now. "We've got to get the wet clothes off him or he'll freeze for sure."

Good gracious! Before the sailor could say or do anything further, Georgie pulled off her pelisse and draped it around St. Just's front. That should provide some warmth and somewhat preserve decency. Even better . . . "Perhaps he can make it to his cabin. Wouldn't that be best?"

"Can you walk, Captain?"

The marquess swayed, took a step, and stumbled. He shook his head. "No strength in my legs." He sat down hard on the bench, and Ayers succeeded in stripping his breeches down to his boots. "Get the blankets around his back, Chapman. Cartwright, help me with his boots."

Draping thick wool covers around St. Just, Chapman tucked them in as best he could, given that her blue pelisse still covered his front. The boots finally thumped to the deck, and Ayers stripped St. Just's stockings and trousers completely away.

"Another blanket, Chapman." The lad took off at a run.

"Can someone go get him some hot tea, for goodness sake?" The violent shivering that wracked the marquess scared Georgie more than she wanted to admit. "We've got to get him warmed up. You fetch the tea and I'll stay with him."

"Barnes is supposed to be boiling the water. I'll see what's taking him so long. Cartwright, go check our course and, when Chapman returns, start to hoist the sails. You'll be all right with the captain, my lady?"

Nodding, Georgie sat beside St. Just, who pulled the blankets around himself closer, still shivering. "Are you sure you can't make it to your cabin, my lord? You'll be much warmer and recover quicker."

Shuddering so hard the bench vibrated, he shook his head.

This was madness. She had to do something to get him warm. Like Lulu. To the devil with propriety, then. He'd saved her dog. Now she'd help him as best she could.

St. Just had hunched over, not moving.

"I'm going to try to keep you warm, my lord. Keep the cold off you until you can make it to your cabin."

"T-t-thank y-you." He sat straight up, looking around in confusion. "Wh-what do you pr-propose to do?" Trying to pull the blankets around his shoulders better, he glanced down and spied the small blue coat covering his front. "What is this?"

"My pelisse, but it's not nearly large enough and it's rather wet from where I tried to dry Lulu off." There simply wasn't enough material in it. But what else could she use to help keep him warm?

The only other thing on deck that was warm, of course. It had worked with Lulu, so it would work with him. And as it was only for a short period, Society did not need to know.

She slid closer to St. Just, turning so she faced him. Her leg pressed up against his, and he moved back, not understanding. "Lord St. Just, stay still please."

At that his brows furrowed a bit.

"You need to get warm before you freeze to death or catch a severe chill or something much worse than that. Now stay still." Georgie managed to press next to him again, then, without warning, she tossed the sodden pelisse to the deck, grasped him around the waist, and pulled him directly against her chest.

The incredible cold sucked her breath right out of her

lungs. This was like embracing a block of ice from her father's ice house. Her shocked gasp filled her ears.

Or perhaps he had gasped; she couldn't tell. But St. Just had stiffened and gone still at her embrace, save for an occasional shiver. Now he was attempting to pull away. But she wasn't having any of that. "Be still," she hissed. "The least you can do is allow me to keep you warm until more blankets and hot tea arrive."

"Well, if it's the least I can do." His ragged voice held a touch of his normal, arrogant humor that usually irritated her so much. At the sound of it now, however, she rejoiced deep in her heart. Surely he wouldn't speak like that if he were dying.

His arms came around her, pressing him against her even more firmly. Soaked chest to soaked chest, so that every muscle of his hard body seemed to touch her.

Georgie gasped again, but not from the cold. Heat burst through her, as though the sun had miraculously reappeared, shining as intensely as on a midsummer's day. Slowly she pulled back and gazed into his eyes, more black than gray now, with a fierceness in them that stirred her in places deep within. Places that hadn't been touched in a very long time.

"Here you are, Captain." Ayers appeared from nowhere, holding out a blanket that he draped over St. Just's shoulders.

Startled out of that heated moment, Georgie pushed away from St. Just and jumped to her feet. Cold exploded across her wet chest, distracting her from the mortification of being caught in such an inappropriate embrace. Not that it was wrong to attempt to save someone's life, but it must have looked exceedingly . . . intimate. Had been extremely intimate.

Clutching her arms across her sodden clothing, Georgie backed away as Chapman arrived, a steaming mug of hot tea in each hand. "Here, Captain, my lady." He thrust one at her, which she just managed to grab before the sailor turned to St. Just. "Have a sip, my lord. Get yourself around this, and you'll be right as rain."

St. Just nodded, taking the cup in both hands and seeming to savor the warmth. He took a huge swallow and groaned. "God, that's good." He peered up at Georgie with an impish grin. "Very good indeed. Thank you."

Cheeks heating despite the cold wind sweeping across the deck, Georgie backed away another step, heart beating like a galloping horse, her gaze still locked with St. Just's. What was happening to her?

Rather than risk staying to find out, she turned on her heel and fled to the relative safety of her cabin. As she'd known all along, one should never trust a pirate.

Chapter Eleven

Trembling as though she'd been in the water too, which anyone might assume looking at her dampened state, Georgie reached her cabin and fought to calm herself before she entered. She mustn't let Clara suspect anything had happened. Not that anything had happened, actually, although clasping a naked, wet man to one's bosom as though he were one's hope of heaven might be considered something. No. She slowed her breathing, trying to calm her heart, which had gone from a steady beat to a fluttering tempo to a fast *boom, boom, boom* like a drum someone was banging with a huge mallet. Act calmly and everything would be fine. She abandoned the untasted mug of tea on the floor beside the door for one of the sailors to find. If she tried to drink something this moment she'd choke.

She opened the door, and Lulu bounded off the bed, running to her feet and leaping up on her. Another wave of relief coursed through Georgie. "Lulu. Oh, Lulu." She gathered her dog into her arms, burying her face in the animal's fur, thanking God again for her survival. Whatever she might be unsure about, her gratitude to St. Just for rescuing Lulu was not in doubt. She clasped Lulu to her, squeezing her tight.

Lulu yipped and wiggled to be put down. She seemed to

be suffering no ill effects whatsoever from her dip in the frigid water. "She doesn't even feel cold, Clara."

"Her thick fur helped a good bit, I think." Clara shook out a hefty piece of toweling and draped it over the back of the chair. "She was cold enough when I brought her here, but I've been drying her off ever since, and she seems fine. Is Lord St. Just doing well, also?"

Georgie started, then berated herself. If she didn't want to appear guilty she must not jump like a deer when someone spoke his name. "He appeared to have taken no hurt that I could tell, although at first I believed him dead. He was so still and pale. I don't know what I would have done . . ." Her throat thickened, cutting off any further speech.

"He's that heroic, I'll give it to him, my lady." The maid grabbed up the piece of linen again. "There's not many would jump into the Channel to save a dog. Here, let me dry you off before you catch the croup. Lulu's got you wet enough you look almost like you went into the sea."

Continuing to cluck over her mistress, Clara draped the fabric against Georgie's chest. "Let's get you out of these wet things and into a warm—" The maid ceased both rubbing and speaking. "How did your back get soaked, my lady?"

Georgie cringed and drew the toweling closer around her. "Uhhh . . ."

A loud knocking at the door saved her from further inquisition. "Will you see who that is, Clara?"

The disgruntled maid marched to the door and pulled it open.

Georgie continued to rub herself briskly with the linen. She'd had no idea she'd gotten this wet when she'd pressed herself against St. Just. Unconsciously she closed her eyes to better remember the feeling of his body against hers.

Clara shut the door.

"Who was it?"

"One of the sailors, my lady. Returning this."

Opening her eyes, Georgie found Clara staring at her accusingly, her mouth pursed and brows lowered.

Georgie's damp blue pelisse dangled from her hand.

Drat it. She'd forgotten she'd wrapped it around St. Just. How did she explain that? Perhaps, in this case, honesty was the only option. "I gave it to Lord St. Just."

"He's taken to wearing women's fashions, now, has he?" Clara's gimlet eye didn't waver.

"He was freezing before my eyes, Clara. What was I supposed to do?"

"Well, I must admit, your disrobing before him probably warmed him better than any blanket."

"Clara!" Heat tinged Georgie's cheeks. Taking the pelisse off hadn't warmed him nearly as well as her embrace of his naked body had. "You act as though I stripped down to my chemise, which I assure you I did not."

"And so how did the back of your dress become wet? *Something* has soaked it through."

Unable to devise a rational response, Georgie resorted to simple denial. "I have no idea. I'm certain I do not know what you are talking about."

"Lady Georgina." The maid's face fell into somber lines. "I understand that you were grateful to his lordship for rescuing Lulu. There's not many would do such a thing. But to then allow the man liberties as part of that gratitude—"

"I did no such thing." Georgie fanned her hot face with her hand. That wasn't how it had been at all. Not really. "He was shivering, and the sailors went to get blankets and hot tea, but they took so long, and he seemed to be worsening. I couldn't stand there and watch him hurting and do nothing, could I? I just couldn't." Plopping down into the chair, she put her face in her hands. Even if there had been nothing untoward in her gesture, if word of it ever got out, her reputation would likely suffer.

"It might have been harmless, my lady. But it may not

have looked so." Clara shook her head sadly. "Here, stand up.
I need to get those wet things off you before you take a chill."

Silently, Georgie complied, standing like a statue as
Clara stripped the sodden clothing from her body. Her attitude toward St. Just had gone from disdain and loathing this
morning to admiration and compassion in the span of a few
short hours. The possibility that those feelings would continue to change, or perhaps grow, gave her pause. She'd not
thought of enjoying passion with a man in a very long time.
When contemplating marriage with Lord Travers, neither
passion nor even affection had ever crossed her mind. That
union would be based on duty to her family alone. She had
already experienced the perfect love of a husband in Isaac
Kirkpatrick. In accepting her father's choice of husband, she
had understood that her lot in life from now on would not
include that deep abiding love that had made her marriage
a heaven.

Only now she'd discovered similar stirrings for another man.

Clara dropped a fresh, warm nightgown over Georgie's
head, and she pulled it down over her body, smoothing it
with her hands.

What might it be like for his hands to touch her like this?

She jumped when another hand brushed her neck, an
eerie chill racing down her spine.

"Did I shock you, my lady?" Clara busied herself with
smoothing down the collar of Georgie's nightgown.

"Yes, you did, rather," Georgie said, moving away from
the maid to sit at the table. Her legs were suddenly not
steady at all. If St. Just had experienced anything like the
heat and desire that had poured through her body when they
clung together on the icy deck, shouldn't she at least consider the possibility of him as a suitor? Their first few
meetings had not been auspicious by any means, especially
the one in this cabin yesterday afternoon. However, he had

more than made up for those shortcomings by rescuing Lulu. At this very moment Georgie could have been prostrate on the bed, weeping for the loss of her beloved pet, had it not been for St. Just.

Of course, Lulu would never have gone over the side if his lordship had not spirited them away to his ship, but that was neither here nor there. The point now was that he'd risked his life, and very nearly lost it, saving the animal.

And he'd been so solicitous about her health this morning, making certain she was cared for and received the proper treatment. Although his methods, and the enjoyment he seemed to derive from them, left much to be desired from the man.

Georgie sighed. Lord St. Just could be seen either as her savior or her tormenter, depending on how you chose to look at him. As always when she had a problem to solve, she worried her bottom lip with her teeth. Somehow that always seemed to help her arrive at the best solution. And the dilemma of how she truly felt about Lord St. Just was a thorny one that might require more than that for her to chew on. A royal banquet might not even be enough to allow her to disentangle the difficulty posed by this particular marquess.

Tucked into his bunk under half a foot of blankets—each of his men had gladly contributed one from their own bunks—Rob finally ceased to shiver. It had taken him seemingly forever to remove the one remaining article of his clothing. He'd been shaking so hard he thought he'd never shed his sopping small clothes.

For the first time he cursed his refusal to bring Lovell with him. Rob never did when sailing, finding freedom from his valet part of the adventure of the sea. Well, that decision might just cost him his favorite pair of boots. The

seawater had soaked into them, and Rob had no idea how
Lovell would care for them. They sat over in the corner
where Chapman had thrown them when they'd finally
brought him down to his cabin. When he got up, in a month
or two perhaps, he'd set them upright and hope the valet
could salvage them when he got home. Meanwhile he'd
have to wear the spare pair he kept on the ship, though they
didn't feel as good as the others.

Turning onto his back, quite a chore under all this
weight, Rob cautiously brought his arm out from beneath
the covers and settled it behind his head, his favorite position for sleep. The cabin had warmed remarkably after
Ayers had stoked the stove, so Rob could relax and drift off
to some much-needed sleep.

The trouble was, despite all that exertion in the water and
the cold that had exhausted him even more, he wasn't sleepy
in the least. All thought of sleep had fled the moment Lady
Georgina had pressed her body against his. At that moment,
he'd thought himself dreaming some erotic fantasy that was
a precursor to death. Would have continued to believe it had
it not been for the hard evidence of her coat tossed onto the
deck and retrieved by one of the sailors. If the coat was real,
then surely all the rest was as well.

He closed his eyes so he could better live that moment
again when her breasts had first rubbed against him. Even
through the layers of clothing and stays, the sensation had
been so sensual his nearly frozen cock had stirred to life. As
it was again now, simply remembering her warm and soft in
his arms.

God. He blew out an exasperated breath and pounded
his forehead with his fist. The lady was his best friend's
youngest sister. Brack would hang him from his own yardarm
if he even suspected Rob had had carnal thoughts about her.
He had to think of something else, something not amorous
at all. Why was his mind a blank, save for the image of Lady

Georgina in her blue dress, the fabric sticking to her chest and arms where she'd grasped Lulu. And him. Rob groaned. This was going from bad to worse.

He stared at the low ceiling of his cabin, searching for some problem there that could claim his attention, but absolutely nothing presented itself. They were heading once again for the Cornwall coast; the waters had calmed somewhat, so likely the lady wouldn't be ill again. A fortunate circumstance, despite the removal of a perfectly good reason for him to visit Georgina.

Damn. He'd inadvertently slipped and called her by her first name earlier, when for one agonizing moment he'd believed she'd been about to jump over the rail after the animal. Not an unforgiveable sin . . . However, he mustn't slip up and call her that without being invited to use her first name. Society frowned upon gentlemen who did not abide by that rule. He hoped she had been too distraught at the time for it to register. If not, he was sure he would hear about it in a matter of hours.

"Grrrr." His stomach rumbled loudly. No wonder. He'd had breakfast and precious little else all day. The cup of tea Ayers had brought had been delicious, but Rob could do with something a bit more substantial. In fact, a full meal would not come amiss, now that he thought of it. He consulted his pocket watch on the table beside the bed. Lucky thing he carried it in his jacket rather than his breeches, or it would have been lost to him like his boots. The hands stood at ten minutes past seven o'clock. No wonder he was ravenous and not at all sleepy. The warm bed might be inviting, but he wouldn't linger here. Not alone. The thrill of his adventure had left a definite ache in his groin he'd love to appease.

The image of Lady Georgina lying in his bed, naked, her marvelous red hair fanned out over his pillows, made him catch his breath. His cock sprang to attention as well, eagerly bumping against the sheet. God, this would never do. Why had he become infatuated with this woman? Other than the fact that she was beautiful, witty, and strong. Rob groaned. Such thoughts would surely lead to madness.

Hastily pushing back the mountain of covers, Rob sat up and swung his legs over the side of the bed, wincing as he did so. His vigorous kicking in the water had made his calves sore. Still, hunger outweighed that insignificant pain. He stood, grabbed his breeches, and pulled them on, tucking his shirt carelessly into the waistband.

He'd roust Barnes from whatever he was currently attending to and send him to the galley with instructions to fix a meal of grand proportions. Rob's mouth watered as he thought of beefsteak, seared quickly so the juices ran freely when cut into. In the past, Barnes had created a marvelous cream sauce for vegetables, rich and filling. Over green beans and carrots it would be splendid. Rounded out with a potato and leek pie, this would be a dinner to savor.

So why eat alone?

The voice inside his head whispered seductively. He could invite Lady Georgina to dine with him. Such an invitation was only polite, and he could make sure she had suffered no ill effects from the cold. From that cold embrace that had flamed roaring hot. At least it had to him. He had no idea whether she had felt anything other than discomfort. She'd certainly left hurriedly as soon as Ayers had appeared with the blanket. She might very well have returned to her cabin and retired for the night, thinking nothing further of Rob.

At that point in his musings he almost abandoned the idea of inviting her to dinner. But he was her host, or kidnapper as she would put it, and as such should make the gesture. He'd speak to Barnes about the dinner, then visit her cabin to ask if she cared to dine with him. Glancing down at his disheveled appearance, he swiftly revised that notion. He'd get one of the men to take her a note. That would give him time to repair his appearance and properly prepare for her company, should she deign to give it. And he truly hoped she would.

When had life become so fraught with uncertainties? That was easy. Ever since Lady Georgina Kirkpatrick had run into him. Would life ever be the same again? Rob smiled and opened the door. God, he hoped not.

Chapter Twelve

The remains of a loaf of fresh bread and crumbles of what had been a hunk of light, white cheese lay on the table between Georgie and Clara. As the dinner hour had approached, with no notion of food forthcoming, Clara had ventured to the galley and returned with what would have to suffice for the evening's meal. The maid had been complaining ever since. "I'm sure the cook and the rest of them are attending to his lordship, but that's no reason to let the other passengers starve."

Georgie leaned back in her chair, stifling a burp. "Well, I for one am quite sated. Bread and cheese is as good as a feast if one is hungry enough." She snatched another crumb of the soft, nutty-flavored cheese. "This is delightful. I wish I knew what it was exactly. Something local to St. Just's home, I assume." She tossed the piece to Lulu, who snapped it up. "There you are, my girl. We'll have better rations in the morning."

Lulu yipped, then turned around in the corner before lying down, curled into a ball on the piece of toweling Clara had dried before the fire.

"Well, it's good enough, I'll grant you, but a little meat to go with it would not have been amiss." Clara tore off a wedge of the dark bread and used it to wipe up tiny morsels of the cheese from the plate. "Something to drink would have been even nicer."

"If you call for Ayers, I'm sure he will accommodate us." Georgie stretched and yawned. The combination of the stress of today's excitement plus the comforting food had left her yearning for her bed. She had half hoped to see St. Just again before retiring, a whim that she understood, though wanted to deny. The man had likely taken to his bed and was fast asleep. She would follow suit shortly.

The close proximity of those two thoughts brought warmth to her cheeks. She must stop this silliness about Lord St. Just. She'd never given the man a second thought before yesterday. Once she was back on dry land and on her way to Blackham, she would forget all about him in the bustle surrounding her wedding. In the excitement of the day, she'd completely forgotten about Lord Travers, and he was the man she was going to marry. It should be far easier to forget a man she would never see, never speak to, never have contact with again. An inkling, lurking in the back of her mind, however, said she would never forget the Marquess of St. Just, if she lived to be a hundred years old.

A sharp rap on the door startled her, and brought Clara out of her chair and Lulu to her feet, growling. "Who is that?" the maid whispered to Georgie.

"If you open the door you'll find out sooner, I'm sure, Clara." Georgie tried to act aloof, all the while her heart raced and her blood sang in her veins. It wouldn't be St. Just, but one of his men come to check on them. Clara could then ask him for some wine, perhaps. Georgie would like a glass of Madeira at the moment.

With a withering glance at her, Clara opened the door a crack. A low murmur of voices ensued, and Georgie slumped back in her seat, disappointment stealing through her. Fool that she was, she'd hoped again to find St. Just at the door. She hoped Clara secured a full bottle for them.

For perhaps the second time in her life, spirits would be required to get through the night.

The maid shut the door and turned toward Georgie, her eyes mere suspicious slits.

"Are they bringing the wine?" Georgie held out her hand to Lulu, but the dog settled back on her spot once more. Even Lulu had abandoned her this evening.

"Yes, Mr. Ayers said they'd be bringing my supper to me shortly, including wine."

How exceedingly odd. Georgie raised her eyebrows. "Am I being punished and sent to bed without my supper then?"

Clara held out a folded piece of paper. "I suspect this will explain everything, my lady."

Perplexed, Georgie took the note and unfolded it.

> *My dear Lady Georgina,*
>   *May I request the pleasure of your company at dinner this evening? The table will be laid in my cabin at half eight, if that is convenient.*
>
>   *Yr ob't servant,*
>   *St. Just*
>
> *Post Scriptum—Please do come*

Excitement welled up in her; a rush of delight spread a smile over her lips that she could not deny.

"Well, I suppose you are not to go hungry after all?"

"I am to dine with Lord St. Just at half-past eight. Good Lord, what is the time?" Snatching up her jewel case, she hunted through it until she found her watch and breathed a relieved sigh. It was only half-past seven. Time enough to become presentable to the marquess.

"What gown should I wear, Clara?" The blue she'd worn

earlier was out of the question, of course. "I was thinking the green with the lace overlay. You always say it—"

"Deepens your eyes, yes. It does." Working swiftly, Clara had removed the nightgown and was rummaging for another pair of stays. "So are you now friends with Lord St. Just? This morning you wanted nothing more than to push him out the door."

"At one point I wanted to push him off the ship, but having more or less done that, I find I am more pleased with the marquess now than then. He did rescue Lulu at the very real risk of his life. The least I can do is act cordially toward him." Stays in place, Georgie ducked her head as the maid drew her gown over her head.

"You had best not act too cordially toward him. It's very easy to become overly attracted to gentlemen who do you some heroic service." Clara sniffed as she tied the gown closed. "I've seen such things happen before, my lady. The next thing you know you'll be looking into his eyes and he'll be taking you into his arms, and who knows where it will lead."

Hastily, Georgie stepped away from Clara. The woman had come much too close to the truth to let her see her face. Instead Georgie bent her head over her jewel box, searching for the emerald earrings she always wore with this particular dress. Clara was likely right about the possibility of mistaking gratitude for a more intimate emotion. However, that would not keep Georgie from dining with the marquess this evening. She was on her guard, and forewarned was forearmed, so they said.

"What are you looking for, my lady?"

Hoping her cheeks had sufficiently cooled, Georgie raised her head. "My emerald earrings. I can't seem to find them."

"You mean the ones you already laid out there on the table?" Pointing to the square-cut earrings with the tear-drop pearl pendants, Clara shook her head and handed them to Georgie. "You need to keep your wits about you, Lady Georgina. That's all I'm saying. Your father instructed me to look out for you."

"I understand your concern, Clara." Georgie slid the heavy earrings into her ears. "I promise to return unscathed, although I do hope to enjoy Lord St. Just's company. He is really quite jovial when he is not trying to pour tea down one's throat."

"Just see that he does not try to do anything else. You are as good as a married woman again, my lady." The maid nodded her head vigorously as she pulled Georgie's gloves over her fingers. "Lord Travers is waiting for you, and likely frantic if your father or brother have found out our predicament and passed that information on to him."

That was unfortunately true. At the end of her journey lay Lord Travers and a marriage ceremony she'd begun to dread even more deeply. Before this . . . adventure, she'd reconciled herself to marrying the earl, for the sake of her father. Now her sensibilities had shifted, her duty to herself weighing as much as that to the family. If Lord St. Just had affixed his interest on her, that was. This could very well be a bag of moonshine she'd concocted, as Clara had said, after the marquess had been so heroic.

"I cannot help if Lord Travers is frantic or not. I have no way at present to inform him of my situation, nor do I think it wise to do so. We shall wait and see what happens when we reach Cornwall." Georgie picked up her best silk shawl and wrapped it around her shoulders. "In the meantime, I propose to enjoy the company of Lulu's rescuer. I hope you enjoy your dinner as well, Clara."

With an aplomb she was feeling not at all, Georgie swept out of her cabin and up the passageway the few steps to Lord St. Just's. Even though Clara might be correct Georgie intended to find out for herself if the moonshine had some substance to it this once.

* * *

Adjusting his cravat for the sixth time, Rob jumped when the firm knock sounded on the door. Lord, he'd better get himself in hand and quickly. He didn't want to make a cake of himself in front of Lady Georgina, although hope of avoiding that was waning faster with each second that passed. Straightening himself to his full six foot, two inches calmed him, steadied his hands as he strode to the door, and, forcing what he hoped would be taken for a cheerful smile, opened it.

The words of welcome he'd meant to say died on his tongue at the sight of Lady Georgina. The woman he'd last seen dripping wet, hair straggling about her shoulders, had been replaced with a vision of loveliness. The pale green gown became her both in color and in its simple style. Her complexion, like cream and roses, seemed to glow in the candlelight while her glorious red hair, again simply done but elegant, framed her beautiful face magnificently.

Smiling sweetly, she looked at him expectantly for a moment, eyebrows delicately raised.

Tongue-tied like the fool he'd hoped not to become, Rob could only stare at her, unable to form a single word.

"Thank you so much, Lord St. Just, for your kind invitation to dine. I had hoped you were not feeling any ill effects from your earlier adventure." She peered at him closely. "The cold water hasn't made you lose the power of speech, has it? That would be distinctly inconvenient, especially for a ship's captain. You couldn't give orders, you know."

Laughter cleared his brain, thank God, and Rob bowed, himself again. "Not at all, Lady Georgina. As you can see, I have that faculty fully in hand. Welcome, and thank you for agreeing to dine with me." He ushered her into the cabin that had been transformed, as much as possible by two sailors and himself, into an elegant salon. "Would you like some Madeira?"

"Oh, yes, please. My goodness." She stepped inside the doorway and stopped. "It's as bright as day."

Ayers and Cartwright had gathered every candle, lamp, and lantern on board—save the ones in the galley, where Barnes insisted he needed light to cook—and set them all about the cabin. The light they gave off did indeed make the room glow as though the sun shone inside.

"The better to see your beauty, my lady." Rob closed the door, and she headed toward the table, already laid with the rather plain tableware he kept on the ship. He hated that it wasn't more elegant, but he'd never seen the need for anything more serviceable on board. As soon as they made landfall, he'd remedy that. Even if he never had cause to use the china and crystal again, he'd be ready to entertain in future.

"I would have thought it the better to see our dinner." She chuckled softly and let her shawl slip from her shoulders. "I had no idea you were so well equipped for entertaining, my lord. This looks fit for the Prince Regent himself."

"I doubt you'd ever find Prinny on this ship, but I thank you. Will you be seated?" Rob pulled out the chair opposite his, and she lowered herself onto it, her back straight, the sweep of her neck tantalizingly close to him. The sweet smell of roses wafted up from her, intensified by the heat of the candles, making it hard for him to concentrate on anything other than her.

Wine, he'd offered her wine. He hurried to the sea chest that did double duty as sideboard and poured them both glasses of the deep amber Madeira. This should steady him. "Here you are. I hope you like the vintage. I prefer the smoky and fruity flavors, with just a hint of sweetness."

"It sounds delicious." She sipped, and a smile crossed her lips. "Yes, that is nice. An excellent choice." Another sip and she put the glass on the table and looked directly at him, her green eyes penetrating him like a knife. "I did want to thank you again, my lord, for saving Lulu. It was a kind and brave thing to do for a woman you scarcely know."

Rob relaxed, suddenly very much at ease with Lady Georgina. He sauntered to his chair and sat. "You are welcome, my lady. I admit I had second thoughts about it, but what honorable man could stand by and watch your heart break?"

She grasped her wine again and looked away. "Lulu means a great deal to me, my lord. The one thing in my father's house that has some affection for me."

"I could tell you were very fond of her." He sipped his wine, unsure how to proceed. "One thing that decided me was the fear you would jump in after her yourself."

That brought the lady's head up, her eyes wide. She moved restlessly in her chair. "I confess, I did think of it. But I cannot swim, and it would have done neither of us any good to have both of us drown."

"Ah." He'd been right about her desperation. And was grateful she'd not acted on it, or the day might have gone quite differently.

"Was that why you called me by my first name?" Her frank stare held no censure, just simple curiosity.

Still, he ducked his head. "Umm, well, yes." He was doing this badly, damn it. "I thought if I called you by your name perhaps it would startle you enough to stop you from going over the side. And it was much quicker to say when time was of the essence." Steeling himself, he looked her in the face, ready for a dressing down of epic proportions.

To his astonishment, she beamed at him. "How clever of you. It did make me pause, long enough to realize I couldn't help her."

"I am glad then that I did so, but I assure you, I will not

do so again, Lady Georgina. I would not be so familiar with you without your permission."

"But you have it, my lord. After what you did, I would be honored for you to call me Georgina, or really Georgie." She smiled a bright, charming smile that would captivate a hermit. "That is what all my friends call me."

Almost speechless again at this unexpected boon, Rob cleared his throat and sat straighter in his chair. "If I am considered one of those lucky few, my lady, I will be honored to address you as such." He took a sip of the wine and charged forward. "I would be honored also if you would call me Rob. It's short for Robin, which I have never liked, but is apparently the name that has to be continued in the Kerr family by some sort of royal decree having to do with the creation of the marquessate in 1622. All firstborn sons must bear it, I fear."

Her eyes lit up, and she laughed. "I will be delighted to call you Rob, although I think Robin a perfectly fine name."

"You wouldn't if even your friends made fun of you at various points in your life about being Robin Hood."

"Oh, dear." Georgie laughed even harder. "I'm so sorry, Rob. I suppose that was dreadful. Do forgive me."

"Of course. Your brother and I became great friends because he was one of the few chaps I met at school who didn't mention that at all." Brack had been a very good friend indeed. Rob only hoped running away with his sister didn't put an end to that friendship. When he finally met with Brack, at St. Just in a week or so, he'd explain why it had seemed the best plan to take Georgie with him.

Gazing at the beautiful woman across the table, surrounded by candlelight, with the memory of their encounter on the deck so fresh he could still feel her pressed up against him, he feared he might end up having to explain more to Brack than just absconding with his sister.

The door opened, and dinner arrived in a stream of

steaming dishes carried by Barnes, Ayers, and Chapman. They quickly laid them on the table, Barnes arranging each one just so, before bowing and leaving, shooting Rob furtive glances as though they expected he would devour the lady along with the food. Did he actually look as obvious as that? Lord, he hoped not. Not that he had any intention of ravishing the lady, though the experience would be magnificent if it occurred.

Enough. He rose and served Georgie some of the beef and vegetables before his imagination ran completely away with him.

Over dinner they chatted amicably about several different subjects, nothing even close to hinting about that interlude on deck. Perhaps she hadn't experienced the same soul-stirring attraction to him as he had to her. But she should have felt something, shouldn't she? A worry guarded behind her eyes made him hope so.

"This is something that I have sorely missed these last two years," Georgie said, as she licked the last crumbs of her gooseberry tartlet off the fork.

"Gooseberry tarts?" Rob slid the plate that still contained two of the little tarts toward her. "Please help yourself. If your cook requires the recipe, I shall have Barnes write it out for you directly."

"Not the tarts, although they were lovely. I must tell Barnes so." She put her fork down on the plate and took a long sip of wine. "No, I meant having dinner alone with a man, with my husband, Mr. Isaac Kirkpatrick."

Rob sat back, his fingers gripping the stem of his glass. "I see. I beg your pardon, Georgina. You have my most sincere condolences."

"Thank you." She smiled, but it was a mere raising of the corners of her lips. No warmth behind it. "It is interesting how you miss a person in stages. At least I did. At first, I could not take it in that he was gone. I'd look up each time someone entered a room, convinced it would be him."

"I would think that natural." Rob did not wish to hear this confession, but would not stop her. Perhaps she needed to think about her husband after the eventful day she'd had.

"I suppose so, but it hurt abominably to hope and have that hope dashed every day." Tears glistened in her eyes. "By the time that stage had passed, I had met the other widowed ladies of my circle, which was comforting. Still, I missed my husband terribly. I missed bringing him tea in the study, or walking hand in hand in the evenings, down by the river in the village where we lived." She glanced at Rob, that sad smile again on her lips. "I still miss sitting across from him at dinner. We would talk about what we had done that day, or what had bloomed in the garden, or what had gone on in the village. Simple things that formed the basis of our life together."

"You loved him very much."

"I did. I truly did." She wiped a tear that had welled up out of her eyes. "He was the kindest, most thoughtful, most loving person I have ever met. I fear I shall never love another man as I did him." Looking into his eyes, she swallowed, and paused. "So why should I even try? Why not appease my father and have some peace between us if my marriage to Lord Travers will accomplish such a thing?"

Moved by her deep sorrow, Rob took her hand in his. "Because you deserve whatever happiness you can carve out of your life, my dear. No one can take the place of your husband in your heart." Rob stared at her hand. "But there are other gentlemen who are kind, and thoughtful, and loving. They may not be Mr. Kirkpatrick, but they are decent men who would try their best to make you happy for the rest of your life. If you can, give them the chance to do so."

Nodding her head, Georgie slipped her hand from his. "Thank you, Rob. You are very kind."

Their eyes met, a timeless moment in which he could have drowned a second time that day, this time in the green depths that drew him closer to her. Even closer as he leaned toward her, toward the red lips he wanted desperately to kiss, toward the slim body he longed to hold once more, if only to comfort her, to take away her pain.

She stopped breathing as she gazed at him, searching his face for something only she could determine. Then, with a sigh, she drew back and stood. "I believe I have had quite enough adventures for one day, Rob." Her happy smile had returned. "Thank you once more for a lovely dinner and for being Lulu's rescuer."

"It has truly been my pleasure, Georgina."

"Georgina?" She stiffened and gave him an arch look.

"Georgie." He laughed and stood. "May I escort you to your cabin?"

Nodding, she drew her shawl back over her shoulders and took his arm. "Yes. You must protect me from the ravening hordes of . . . What do you have hordes of on a ship?"

Laughing, Rob opened the door. "I am sorry to disappoint, but there are no hordes, ravening or otherwise, on this ship, my dear. I must confess I asked to escort you simply to spend another moment or two in your excellent company." He stopped outside her chamber door and disengaged her arm, though he kept hold of her hand. "I enjoyed our dinner immensely. Thank you for a lovely evening." He bent toward her, close enough to hear her light gasp. It shot a bolt of hope through his heart as he lifted her hand and kissed it. "Good night."

With a slight bow, Rob turned back to his cabin, treading softly enough that he heard her door open. Hand on his door latch, he glanced back at her. Their gazes met for a heated second that stole his breath, then she was gone. For now.

Chapter Thirteen

"The morning post for you, my lord."

Jemmy, Lord Brack, took a swallow of coffee in the breakfast room just as Lord Lathbury's excellent butler placed a silver salver with two letters on it before him.

"Thank you, Smythe." Jemmy raised his eyebrows at his wife, sitting across the table from him. He waited for the servant to leave, then leaned across the table. "Do you know what that means, my dear?"

Elizabeth, Lady Brack, put a small piece of ham in her mouth and chewed vigorously. Once she swallowed, she smiled at her husband. "I suppose it may mean that you are an amazingly clever gentleman, and all your friends follow your every movement so they may consult you on their personal affairs as well as affairs of state."

Jemmy laughed and picked up the first letter. "I was going to say it meant everyone had discovered where we are. I had quite looked forward to enjoying the solitude here in Buckinghamshire, just the two of us alone. But I see by the seal this letter is from Father, one of the few people who knew we were here for the wedding."

"I would hardly say being with a houseful of wedding guests qualifies as alone, my love." She placed her napkin beside her plate and caught his gaze. "Alone would give us much more time together." Her voice had changed to sultry tones. "Together as we were earlier this morning."

"My dear." Jemmy set the letter down and leaned closer. Since the beginning of her pregnancy, his wife had become even more amorous, especially in the mornings. Not that he was complaining at all. "Are you feeling fatigued, perhaps? Shall I escort you back to our chamber and tuck you into bed? I promise to attend to your *every* need."

Laughing, Elizabeth sipped her tea, her dark eyes promising that she would take him up on his offer. "I think I can manage until you've read your letters, my love. If you don't dawdle."

Eagerly, Jemmy grasped the top letter, heavy cream-colored paper he had recognized on sight, and turned it over, popping the black seal. "I do dread opening this. Missives from Father never bring good news."

"What ill tiding could he have, my love? He is more than pleased with our marriage now, and with the son I may bear you. Georgie has been a model daughter. What else could be wrong?" She grasped Jemmy's hands, arresting his opening the blasted letter and sending a wave of desire throughout his body.

Confound it, Father could very well wait. He must tend to his wife's—and his own—needs immediately. "Elizabeth, why don't we—"

"I simply wanted to say, don't borrow trouble, my dear. Believe me, it will take up residence soon enough on its own." She settled back in her chair, loosening her grip on his hands.

Breathing deeply, to calm himself and refrain from ravishing his wife here on his host's breakfast table, Jemmy relaxed back in his chair. "I do not tell you enough how much I love you, Elizabeth." He grasped her hands afresh and raised them to his lips. Their warmth made him tingle.

"You show me how much every chance you get." Her eyes twinkled. "As I said. Earlier this morning."

Jemmy groaned as his cock bumped against his breeches, insistent even after their thorough and passionate encounter just after dawn this morning. That vigorous lovemaking probably accounted for his increased appetite just now. He'd been ravenous when he'd come down to breakfast. And still was. "I hope to do so every day—several times every day— for the rest of our lives." Memory of their tangled sheets this morning spurred him on. "So now, why don't you allow me to escort you back upstairs?"

Elizabeth tapped the letter with one long, elegant finger. "Your father before pleasure, my dear. What does his letter say?"

Groaning, Jemmy unfolded the thick paper and began to read the severe strokes made by his father's pen, always pressed deeply into the stationery.

Brack,

I wish to inform you that I have, this instant, been told by Folger, my coachman, that my carriage was overtaken at The Running Horse Inn in Leatherhead, and Georgina and her maid were abducted. Folger insists that he, my groom, and two outriders were accosted, bound and gagged, and left in the woods behind the inn. They were not discovered until the following morning, half frozen, although once they were freed and restored they returned to Blackham immediately with the tale. From your sister I have not heard a word.

In light of these events, I must assume that Georgina, with her unfortunate history of headstrong behavior, has taken it into her head, once again, to disobey me and elope with some new, inappropriate man. If you have communication with

her, inform her that I will make good on my promise
to cut her off from the family, and treat her as
though she were dead and without a farthing.

Yrs,
Blackham

Alarm growing as he read the missive, Jemmy raised his stricken face to Elizabeth.

A puzzled frown on her countenance was turning to an expression of concern. She stopped with her teacup poised inches before her lips. "Jemmy, what is the matter? Is it your father? You look as though you've seen a ghost."

Jemmy's heart thumped painfully inside his chest as he expelled the breath he'd been holding while he read his father's ghastly letter. "My dear, Georgie is missing."

Elizabeth's cup rattled into its saucer. "Georgie missing? She can't be missing. She left here three days ago."

"She has apparently not arrived at Blackham as was expected. Father tells me his coachman told him Georgie and Clara were abducted at an inn in Leatherhead." The hearty breakfast he'd just finished had turned to lead in his stomach. "Father assumes she has eloped with someone yet again. If you know anything about her meeting a man, please tell me, my love. My fear for her grows by the minute."

Shaking her head, Elizabeth looked aghast. "She told me nothing, Jemmy, I swear. Not a word." His wife's face had paled, and he raced around the table to put his arm around her. "Perhaps she is simply trying to delay her return to your father's estate and her wedding to Lord Travers. You know she was most unhappy with the match."

Gripping Elizabeth's arm, Jemmy helped her rise. "I do not think so, my love. The carriage was actually stolen, apparently. That does not sound as though she was merely trying to delay her return. Something else is afoot here. But come, you should seek your bed. This shock cannot be good for the child. Georgie has ever had a wild streak in her, and her schemes have almost always come aright in the end." He clenched his jaw. Wait until he found Georgie. She wouldn't sit down for a week at least.

Wracking his brain for some clue, some hint from his sister that she had decided to elope *again*, Jemmy stared at the breakfast table, remembering the last time he'd seen Georgina there. She had been disillusioned but resigned to the marriage with Travers. She wouldn't have spoken of such a bold move to him certainly, but might have perhaps . . . A completely new idea arose. "Might she have gone to one of her widow friends?"

"My dear, we are all still here." Elizabeth shook her head. "She would hardly go to Charlotte's home while she was not in residence."

"But she resided at Lyttlefield Park for some time last autumn. Perhaps—"

"No, Jemmy." Elizabeth silenced his protest emphatically. "Lyttlefield has been closed since Charlotte's wedding last month." Her hand tightened on his, and she bit her lip. "I pray nothing untoward has befallen Georgie."

He squeezed his wife's hand. In her condition she should not worry about anything. "I'm certain it has not. We simply have not thought this through. Are there other places she might go?"

Frowning, Elizabeth shook her head. "Jane is still here and, in any case, has only Lord Theale's townhouse as her residence. Georgie would not go there after Fanny's tale of his treachery. And as for Maria, well . . ."

His wife gave him a speaking look. Another of their widow friends had caused a tremendous scene at a house party last October, and actually eloped with one of the guests. Again, not someone Georgina would have gone to, even under duress.

Worry lines appeared around Elizabeth's eyes. "Jemmy, what if she has truly been abducted?"

"I doubt that very much, my dear." He patted her hands. "Father made no mention of any sort of a ransom demand. And the country is very settled. No highwaymen about as they were last century."

All the same, a tickle of unease twitched the hairs on the back of his neck. Still, he wouldn't alarm his wife unduly.

"Do not fret, love." Jemmy smoothed out the wrinkles in her brow. "I am certain there is a good explanation for this behavior. Georgie is well-known within the family for possessing an endless supply of those. Meanwhile, I shall write to Father and tell him I will go to Byfleet and see if I can discover anything of her whereabouts there. My sister will feel the sting of a cane on her derriere if this is some lark she is attempting on her own." Despite his carefree words, however, Jemmy's heart skipped a beat at the thought of Georgie in actual danger.

"Who is your other letter from?" Elizabeth nodded at the remaining piece of folded stationery. Quite different paper, foolscap in fact, the direction splotched and the seal half broken.

"Let me see. I don't think it's from Georgie—Oh, good show. It's from Rob." Jemmy popped the remaining piece of red sealing wax off the letter with such force he sent it flying up into the air. "Please be seated, my love. I don't want you to fatigue yourself. I'll be just a moment reading this."

"I had no idea a letter from Lord St. Just would be deemed so exciting." Smiling at last, Elizabeth sat back in the chair and took a sip of tea.

"His letters do not always elicit such a reaction, I assure you," Jemmy said, settling back into his chair and unfolding the page. "But I wrote to him some time ago with the request to help me think of some way to stop Georgie from wedding Travers."

"Lord St. Just has knowledge of such schemes to jilt a man?" Delicate eyebrows raised, Elizabeth set her cup back into its saucer. "I shudder to think what escapades the gentleman has engaged in."

"Why will women think ill of Rob?" Jemmy said absently, smoothing out the page with his friend's message. "First Georgie calls him a pirate, and now you, my own wife, is deeming him unsavory." Raising his head, he tried to look sternly at Elizabeth, but failed miserably. "I will have you know, my best friend is . . ." Pausing, he stared at the opening lines of the letter, reading them again. And again.

"Your friend is what, my love?"

"A pirate!" Jemmy crushed the sheet of paper in his fist.

"What?" Elizabeth jerked toward him.

"A blackguard."

"Jemmy!" Her eyes were like blue saucers.

"A fatherless cur." By God, he couldn't think of anything bad enough to call the scoundrel.

That had brought his wife to her feet. "Jemmy, for goodness sakes, what has he done?"

"He's taken Georgie."

"What? No." Elizabeth sank back into her chair. "But why? He's your friend, Jemmy. Why would he do such a thing?"

"All I can think is that he's run mad." Mad as a hatter. That was the only explanation Jemmy could muster.

"What does he say?"

Prying his fingers from around the crumpled paper, he thrust it at Elizabeth. "You read it. I cannot . . ." He couldn't believe it. As though someone had ripped out his very soul, the betrayal left a gaping hole in him. Rob had kidnapped

Georgina. God have mercy on his soul when Jemmy laid hands on him.

With shaking hands, Elizabeth seized the letter and read it aloud.

Dear Brack,
 I must inform you that I have your sister,
Lady Georgina, with me on the Justine *currently*
anchored at Portsmouth Point. I will be setting sail
with her on the evening tide bound for St. Just
Castle in Cornwall.

Elizabeth's voice faltered, her gaze straying from the startling words to Jemmy's face.

How could Rob do such a thing and then calmly write to Jemmy about it? He must be mad.

"Shall I read more?" Her face pale, Elizabeth nevertheless spoke calmly.

"Please. I could get no further." Jemmy slumped in his chair and covered his face, expecting he knew not what.

I am taking this drastic course of action because
the lady claims she was kidnapped on the road
and brought to Portsmouth against her will.

"What?" Bolting upright again, Jemmy snatched the paper from his wife's hands. Elizabeth sat back in her chair, her mouth open, though no sound came out.

If this abduction was part of your own plan to
thwart the lady's upcoming nuptials, I do beg
your pardon.

"He thinks I had my sister kidnapped?" Jemmy jerked up in his chair. Good God, his friend had indeed run mad.

"Hush, Jemmy. Let me finish." Elizabeth's hands shook as she continued.

> *But as I have no way to ascertain your involvement in these actions, I believe I must intervene to assure myself of the lady's continued good health and welfare.*
>
> *Therefore, I am sailing back to St. Just this instant with Lady Georgina, her maid, and her dog. They will be safe at my estate with my mother, where we will await your arrival to fetch the lady to your home.*
>
> > *Yr obdt servant and friend,*
> > *St. Just*
>
> *Post Scriptum*
> *You might consider hiring a ship from Portsmouth to bring you to Cornwall. The sea journey is much shorter, if somewhat more treacherous this time of year. The overland trip is safer but cannot be accomplished in comfort in under eight days.*

The astonishing words left Jemmy bereft of speech. The whole situation was fantastical to the point that he wondered if he'd seen something similar in a Drury Lane drama.

The door to the breakfast room opened, and Matthew and Fanny, now Lord and Lady Lathbury, sauntered in, their arms around each other's waists, their gazes locked on each other's.

"Oh, Jemmy, Elizabeth." Fanny had to drag herself away from her new husband's regard. "We didn't think anyone else would still be breakfasting." She glanced from one to the other. "Is there something the matter?"

"That's an understatement," Jemmy grumbled.

Fanny sat in the chair next to her friend. "My dear, what is it?"

Elizabeth looked inquiringly at her husband, and he shrugged.

"You must tell them. I fear I need to concentrate on controlling my temper, lest I kill the man when next we meet."

His wife's eyebrows shot into a high arch. "Jemmy! You can't mean that. Why would you kill your best friend? He's an honorable man, isn't he?"

"He may be an honorable man, but if word of this scrape gets out in the *ton*, Georgie's reputation will be dashed. She'll be given the cut direct, pure and simple. Do you not recall what happened to Lady Sarah Leacock?"

Lady Sarah had fallen from her horse while out riding in the country with her cousin when a thunderstorm had blown up unexpectedly. The two had taken shelter and spent the night together in an abandoned barn. When they were discovered the next day, despite Sarah's tearful explanations, the *ton*'s tongues had wagged until Sarah's reputation lay in tatters. The puns on her name alone had been enough to send the rest of the family into seclusion. The cousin had not wanted to marry her, which had made it even worse, although he'd eventually been coerced into the marriage for the sake of Sarah's younger sisters.

The deep red that arose in Elizabeth's cheeks said she remembered. "Oh, well, yes. I suppose I see what you mean."

"I remember Lady Sarah's scandal, but pray do tell me about Georgie." Fanny took Elizabeth's hand in hers. "You cannot leave us in such suspense."

"It is all too strange for me to tell it right." She nodded toward the crumpled letter on the table. "Jemmy just received this letter from Lord St. Just . . ." Elizabeth managed to relate the contents of the letter with her usual calm efficiency, although Jemmy became more and more incensed with every word she uttered. When she finally finished the tale, he jumped up, running his hand around the back of his neck where the muscles had tightened abominably during the retelling. Damn it, he must do something and now.

"Do you think Georgie has simply eloped again? With St. Just this time?" Fanny looked hopefully from Elizabeth to Jemmy.

"My father suggested that very thing." Unable to remain still, Jemmy paced around the long, polished mahogany table. "He didn't name St. Just, of course, but his first thought was that she had disobeyed him once again."

"Well, then." Fanny leaned back in the chair, a gloating smile on her face. "I know it is rather out of hand, however, St. Just is quite the eligible *parti*. And a much better choice for Georgie than the one your father picked." She turned a warm gaze on her husband. "Mistakes should be rectified."

"Fanny is correct, my love." Elizabeth rose and came toward Jemmy, staying his frantic pacing. "Georgie may simply have chosen her own husband in her own . . . eccentric way."

Jemmy grasped her hands as though they were a lifeline. "I grant you the episode is not unlike others my sister has arranged in the past. Still, something does not seem quite right."

"Might she have confided it to Charlotte?" Fanny glanced about the room. "Haven't she and Nash come down yet?"

"Not since we've been here." Elizabeth smiled. "I believe they may be 'resting.'"

Jemmy raised an eyebrow, and Matthew laughed. "Married men take their 'rest' when they can." His gaze darted to his wife, and his eyes darkened. "As often as they can."

A blush darkened the pink in Fanny's cheeks, and Jemmy chuckled. He and Elizabeth had certainly seen very little of their host and hostess during the day since the wedding two weeks before.

"I will talk to Charlotte. However, I do not think Georgie was planning any such thing. In fact, St. Just's letter doesn't mention an elopement." Elizabeth leaned against Jemmy, setting his pulse to racing, despite his concern for Georgie. "Instead, it says he expects Jemmy to retrieve his sister from Cornwall."

"Definitely not the response one would expect from a prospective husband." Lathbury frowned. Apparently at least one other person thought the contents of the letter did not involve an elopement.

"Besides, if Georgie did intend to run off with anyone, it wouldn't be St. Just." The more Jemmy thought about it, the less likely that solution seemed.

"Why do you say that, Brack?" Lathbury headed to the warming pans on the sideboard and began to fill a plate. He glanced at his guests and shrugged. "One must keep up one's strength if one is to pursue a woman across half the country."

"My reason to doubt she is with St. Just voluntarily is her dislike of the gentleman." Jemmy followed Lathbury to the sideboard and picked up a plate.

"Jemmy! You've had your breakfast already." This reproof likely had more to do with the fact that Elizabeth could eat but little in the mornings than with an actual concern that he indulged too much at table.

"Lathbury is correct, my dear," he said, heaping piles of ham and roast beef on his plate. "We gentlemen must keep up our strength if we are to follow the troublemakers and discover why Rob has kidnapped Georgie."

"More tea, please, Thomas." Elizabeth nodded to the footman, who set off immediately. "So, if Georgie hasn't eloped with Lord St. Just, why was she in Portsmouth? In his letter he states she was kidnapped on the way to Blackham and diverted to the south. If that is true, then St. Just is actually saving her from the clutches of . . ." Elizabeth threw up her hands. "Who would want to kidnap Georgie?"

"That is quite the question, my dear. And one I will be asking myself all along the road to Portsmouth." Jemmy sat down to his heaping plate, his appetite restored now that he once again had a plan to follow. He'd pursue Georgie and Rob, catch up to them in Cornwall, and then set about thrashing the man who had compromised his sister. "Care to join me, Lathbury? I could use some company on the journey, and perhaps a second when I encounter St. Just."

With a sidewise glance at his wife, Lathbury shook his head, regret written on his features. "Afraid I can't oblige you, Brack. I am newly married, if you remember. And if you don't, my wife will remind you."

Jemmy chuckled. "Of course. Your duties lie elsewhere at present." His own duty to Elizabeth would be sorely tried by the coming absence of at least some weeks. He considered himself still on his bridal tour—and likely would until their child appeared. "I will make do alone."

"I will accompany you, my dear." Pouring milk into her tea, Elizabeth spoke up.

"You will do nothing of the kind." Jemmy attempted to glare at his wife, only to find her lovely blue eyes trained on him like a hunter's on its prey. "Your interesting condition, my dear."

"My interesting condition does not preclude my riding in a carriage. If it did, we would be imposing on Fanny and Matthew until the end of July."

Jemmy trod on the thinnest ice imaginable. "Still, you should only ride as far as London, my love. You do not want to overtax the child."

"This early in the process there should be no 'taxing' of the child. In fact, St. Just suggests we make most of the journey by sea, as it is a faster route than overland. And I am an excellent sailor." Elizabeth set her jaw. "It is settled. I shall accompany you to find Georgie. I am certain she will need another woman's comfort when we do find her."

With a sigh of resignation, Jemmy nodded. He hadn't known his wife for very long; however, when she set her jaw about something, he might as well keep his breath to cool his porridge. "As you will, my dear." He turned to Lathbury. "When can our carriage be readied? Apparently we are for Portsmouth." He smiled at his wife, all along wondering, when they found Georgie and St. Just, which one he would strangle first?

Ensconced behind his massive, captain's table, the Marquess of Blackham picked up the next letter from a tall stack of morning correspondence and paused. Brack had written back much more quickly than usual. That could bode interesting news. If anyone knew the whereabouts of his youngest daughter, it was his eldest son.

Thick as thieves they were, ever since Georgina's birth, no matter how hard he'd tried to break their affection. Allegiance to one particular brother or sister was not to be encouraged in his household. Only allegiance to the family as a single entity was acceptable. If they favored one another too much, they would eventually put the welfare of one above that of the Cross family. That would not do at all.

Using his penknife with skill born of long practice, he carefully lifted the red wax seal and unfolded the letter.

Father,
I received your letter regarding Georgina and
wish to assure you that she has come to no harm.

See. He could depend upon it. Brack would know what the chit was up to. The marquess scowled as he continued reading.

I have learned from my friend, Lord St. Just, that
my sister was kidnapped on her way to Blackham
Castle and taken to Portsmouth.

The marquess's eyebrows shot up. Kidnapped? What a bag of moonshine. Brack was as noddy-headed as they came if he thought his sister had been kidnapped. Oh, no. She'd gone and run off with a man other than the one she was supposed to wed, just like before. Well, she'd better hope her nest was better feathered this time than last, because he would wash his hands of her completely. He glanced back at the letter, disgust pulling his mouth askew.

She managed, by great good luck, to escape her captors and ran into Lord St. Just. In order to keep her safe from her abductors, he is taking her to Cornwall, to his primary estate where she will be under his protection and the chaperonage of his mother, Lady St. Just.

"Cornwall!" Lord Blackham tossed the letter onto the table and leaned back in his chair. Of all the idiotic things to have happen. How did Georgina manage to get herself constantly embroiled in such bizarre doings? Of course, she could simply be eloping with St. Just, but why go all the way to Cornwall? The girl was of age and a widow to boot. Any clergyman could have performed the nuptials in Portsmouth, although her contract to wed Travers might have been deemed an impediment. Still, could there be some truth in Brack's statement?

But then who would want to kidnap his daughter? Did they believe he would pay to ransom her? Hah. More fools they. Travers might be so foolish, or Brack, but not him. He grabbed the letter up again.

I will leave this instant, with Elizabeth, for Portsmouth. St. Just suggests a sea voyage will be more expeditious than an overland journey, so we will secure passage as quickly as may be and follow

them to Cornwall. Once there I shall take charge
of Georgie, procure a conveyance, and bring her
swiftly back to Blackham.

Inform Lord Travers of this matter at your
discretion. However, I fear when he learns of this
turn of events he may wish to withdraw from his
suit—which may in the end be a blessing.

I will write you as soon as my sister is secure.

> *Yr ob't son,*
> *Brack*

Lord Blackham tossed the letter down again, scowling. Brack didn't deceive him for a moment. Having gained some favor with him, his heir had tried to persuade him to call off the arrangement with Lord Travers for Georgina, citing her dislike of the gentleman and her desire to marry for love. Pah. Blackham narrowed his eyes to mere slits. Love matches were the absolute bane of Polite Society these days.

Marriages in the upper classes had always been, heretofore, affairs of business contracted by the sensible parents of the couple to best benefit the families involved. A business transaction, no more, no less. If affection ensued—as with his second marriage—then that could be considered a boon. He stared at the small polished quartz statue of an owl that always sat on his desk and sighed. His late wife, Louisa, had given it to him during their first year of marriage. Athena's owl she called it, to remind him of the value of wisdom. Quite a remarkable woman.

Shaking off the chill that had unaccountably settled on him like a cloak, Blackham pulled a sheet of stationery toward him. With short, precise strokes he mended the pen, then dipped it in the silver standish. Brack was a simpleton if he thought his father didn't see what had actually happened. Georgina had taken Travers in dislike and had persuaded her gullible brother to aid her in her scheme to be rid of her betrothed. They had concocted this ploy with Brack's friend in order to take the girl out of her father's reach and hopefully thwart the marriage.

If true, then they had seriously misplayed their hand. Once the deal with the duke's son had fallen through, Travers had held claim to Georgie, before her marriage to that thieving Kirkpatrick. As a man of his word, Blackham would see to it that justice was served, with a vengeance. He had promised Georgina to Lord Travers, by God, and he would deliver her to him.

Putting his pen to the paper, he swiftly but exactly framed a letter to the steward at his estate in Somerset.

> *Buckley,*
>   *Events have transpired to thwart me in my purpose. To which I instruct you to raise a group of men—tenants, footmen, grooms, day laborers— to ride to Cornwall, to the estate of the Marquess of St. Just with the express purpose of securing my daughter, Lady Georgina, who was taken there against her will, and my wishes, by ruffians. Any men who agree to assist me will be handsomely compensated. This is a grave and secret matter that I trust to your discretion. Furthermore, no one is to know about this journey, including my son, Lord Brack.*

Blackham signed the letter, sanded it, and sent for a running footman. When the man arrived, he stood before Blackham, eyes trained straight ahead. A good man to have on your side. Well-trained. Blackham insisted on that in his servants. "George, you will take the fastest horse in my stable, Dobson will tell you which one, and you will ride as swiftly as the animal will take you. You are going all the way to Somerset to deliver this letter directly into the hands of my steward, Mr. Buckley. When you are sufficiently recovered, return home." He stared hard into George's eyes, while the footman still stared straight ahead, until at last the man blinked. "Do not fail me, George." He held out the letter until the servant took it. "Do not fail!"

George's eyes widened, but he straightened his shoulders and grasped the missive. "I will not, milord."

Blackham waved him away and pulled out the next letter from his pile. If Georgina was a willing participant in this debacle, he would drag her from Cornwall to Blackham Castle where he would lock her in her room and literally throw the key away.

Chapter Fourteen

The sun shone brilliantly on the craggy coast of St. Just as the *Justine* sailed into a small inlet early on the morning of their fourth day at sea. Georgie stood on deck, Lulu clasped securely under one arm, dazzled by the bright light shimmering off the waves of the blue water. After the extremely rocky start to the voyage, yesterday had been calm sailing indeed. She and the marquess had enjoyed each other's company on deck and again at dinner, making Georgie almost wish the journey would never end. That, sadly, was not to be.

They seemed to be making for a sheltered part of the cove where she could just make out a landing at the foot of towering rock cliffs. At the top of the cliff to her left, massive rock structures jutted out of the ground, soaring straight into the sky. On the other side sat a massive, gray stone castle that looked to be carved out of the cliff itself.

"Castle St. Just, my lady."

Rob's voice in her ear made her jump and Lulu bark.

"Do not tell me you brought me all this way just to frighten me to death before I can see it properly, my lord." She cut her eyes toward him, trying to look severe, but laughing instead. She'd laughed quite a lot with Rob in the past couple of days.

"Never." He stared up at his home. "It is rather impressive, wouldn't you say?"

"Are you trying to impress me?"

"Perhaps."

The deep timbre of his voice sent a pleasant thrill down her spine. In their few short days together, Rob had become a true friend whose company she enjoyed immensely. They teased each other constantly, very much like she and her brother did, although the thoughts she increasingly had about Rob were anything but sisterly. She must make the most of her remaining time with him, before Jemmy arrived to take her back to Blackham. To Lord Travers.

"We're coming about to drop anchor, Captain," Ayers called out from the ship's wheel.

"Excuse me, my dear." Rob ran to help Cartwright pull in the sails.

As the breeze dropped, cut off by the high crags, the vessel slowed, rocking gently from side to side, until it settled to a halt several hundred feet from the shore. A small boat started toward them, the men in it rowing enthusiastically.

All about her, sailors bustled to and fro, securing lines, furling the sails, clearing the deck in anticipation of going ashore. Chapman appeared from belowdecks carrying her trunks.

"Ready to go ashore, my lady?" Rob had returned to her side.

"Yes, please." She had become used to the shifting deck under her feet, but she'd be truly grateful for a floor that didn't move.

"You'll be the first one in the boat."

Lulu barked and bared her teeth.

"The first two in the boat then." Rob petted the spaniel's head, narrowly avoiding a nip.

"Behave, Lulu. He saved your life." She smiled at him

and tucked the dog more securely under her arm. "Lord St. Just is a friend now, remember."

Lulu sneezed and shook her head, then sighed.

Rob grinned. "I think I'll still beware the dog for a while longer. Now let's get you on shore."

The short boat ride was followed by a longer trek, via a pony trap, up a steep, winding road that gave a magnificent and terrifying view of the rocky beach below. Fresh salt breezes were temperate today, making Georgie fling back her head and drink in the clean air. Not that it was different from the air she'd been breathing on the ship but being on solid land again somehow made it better. The air, the wild terrain, the sheer beauty of this place, so completely different from any place she'd ever imagined, created in her a feeling of happiness she'd not experienced in a very long time. Perhaps not since Isaac had died. She'd never believed she could be that happy again, but in the right place, with the right man . . .

Rob sat next to her, looking ahead up the road. His clean profile accentuated his straight nose and high cheekbones, the strong jaw even now set determinedly, although about what she had no idea. Unless it was how he was going to explain her presence to his mother.

Her stomach dropped as though she were back on the ship. With everything that had happened in the past days, she'd quite forgotten about this important part of the journey. Making a good impression on older women was of utmost importance. They could make your life miserable, because they'd taken you in dislike for some imagined slight, or delightful simply because you'd pleased them in some way without your knowledge. Meeting Lady St. Just would be even more important because . . .

Secret thoughts Georgie steadfastly refused to put a

name to swirled around her head, but she shooed them away. Being introduced to someone's mother was an important step in furthering any acquaintance. She and Rob were friends, nothing more. They could be nothing more unless she wished to break once and for all with her father. Sometimes life simply wasn't fair. Not that she hadn't known that before.

The trap finally came to a halt in front of the huge, gray stone castle, its entry door painted a bright blue. Looking upward, which was impossible not to do, Georgie squinted against the sun to see the castellated battlements high above her head. Taller by far than those of Blackham Castle, although the black stone of her family's dwelling was probably more intimidating than the paler gray here. Still, this was an impressive display of strength.

"What do you think?" Rob held out his hand to help her down.

"I was wondering why there isn't a moat." She smiled and grasped his hand, always frightfully aware of his touch ever since their encounter on the ship.

Rob laughed and twined her arm in his, as though it were the most natural thing in the world.

No, she could not think that. Not when she had to keep her wits about her to meet his—

"Mother, may I present Lady Georgina Kirkpatrick? She is Brack's sister." Rob fairly beamed as he looked from the tall, elegant woman with dark hair and a sweet face, impeccably dressed in burgundy silk, to her. "Lady Georgina, my mother, the Marchioness of St. Just."

"My lady." Georgie curtsied as low as she could without toppling over on the loose gravel underfoot. "It is such a pleasure to meet you."

"And I you, my dear, although I must say you are quite an *unexpected* pleasure." She raised her delicate eyebrows. "Do you have something to tell me, St. Just?"

Rob winced. "Yes, I do, Mamma, although not necessarily what you might think. Come." He took his mother's arm on his left without giving up Georgie on his right. "Shall we give Lady Georgina tea before we put her on the rack?"

"You must excuse my son, Lady Georgina. He has always had a flair for the dramatic." Lady St. Just gazed up at Rob, a hint of humor in her eyes.

"I have noted that tendency in him myself, my lady."

Rob squeezed her arm in the crook of his.

Smothering a laugh, Georgie continued in her sweetest tones. "He could have been a credible highwayman or pirate in many a Drury Lane drama."

"Indeed?" The marchioness shot Georgie a look that quelled any desire for further levity. "I insist you tell me what has happened, St. Just. Is Lady Georgina in any sort of trouble? Fleeing the authorities, perhaps?"

Georgie shuddered, her steps slowing until Rob had to pull her over the threshold. Now she had gone and done the very thing she had wanted to avoid. What must Lady St. Just think of her?

"Don't fret, Georgie," Rob whispered in her ear. He'd relinquished his mother's arm, and the lady had vanished into the interior of the house. "She is simply dying to know what all of this is about. I promise you, she's going to love you."

A silent butler took their coats.

"But she believes I'm a criminal, escaped from Bow Street or Newgate. Or perhaps even Bedlam." How horrible for his mother to think such things of her. Of course Georgie's presence here was unexpected to say the least. What other explanation could the woman expect?

"Well, you are rather well dressed to be an escapee of any of those establishments, I assure you."

Looking down at her attire, Georgie had to admit he was correct. She'd worn the best gown she'd brought, a blue velvet with delicate white Van Dyke lace points at collar and hem. Scarcely the clothing an inmate of Bedlam, or any other institution would wear. "Then why would your mother say—"

"Shhh." Rob gathered her arm again. "Let me suggest that the parent from whom I take my sense of the dramatic is my mother."

"Oh." Georgie digested that statement as Rob led her further into the house, up a flight of stone stairs, to the first floor drawing room where tea had been laid. The marchioness sat in a chair large as a throne, a cheerful fire behind her.

"Welcome, my dear." Lady St. Just rose and embraced the startled Georgie. "Please be seated. How do you like your tea?"

"Milk and sugar please." Perching on the edge of the sofa, Georgie smiled and accepted the cup, although it might choke her to take a sip. Rob was not helping her nervousness any, by staying silent and eating one slim sandwich after another.

When his mother had finished pouring for herself and Rob, she sat back, sipped, and said, "Now, Robin, if you please. Explain why Lady Georgina is here currently sipping my best blend of Assam and congou."

"I told you she would be fine, Lady Georgina." Rob stopped eating his fourth sandwich to beam at her. "She only calls me St. Just when she's annoyed with me."

"And I shall switch back to that moniker for the rest of the day if you do not tell me—"

"I was kidnapped, my lady." Georgie could stand it no more.

"By my son?"

"Yes, but that was later."

His mother turned to stare at him, her eyes narrow slits. "Robin, for the love of all that is holy . . ."

Raising his hand, Rob finished his sandwich and sipped a mouthful of tea.

If the man didn't say something this minute, Georgie

would take up the pretty china teapot and break it over his addlepated head.

"All right, Mamma. I promise you, this is actually what happened."

The next three quarters of an hour was spent describing that day in Portsmouth and the past several days on board the *Justine*. Lady St. Just's facial expressions as she listened to the tale convinced Georgie that Rob was correct about where his dramatic nature originated.

At the end of their story, his mother sighed, shook her head, and raised her cold tea only to find it all gone. "Robin, ring for more tea, please. I feel as though I have been on this journey with you and must keep up my strength. My dear"—she turned to Georgie—"I am so sorry this happened to you, although had it not I fear we would never have met. And that would be a shame." The marchioness rose as did Georgie. "Would you like to retire to your room to rest? I have put you in the green room, which overlooks the boxwood maze."

"Uh, Mamma, I think you should put Lady Georgina in the blue room." A hesitation in Rob's voice brought Georgie's attention back to him.

"The blue room? Truly?" Lady St. Just seemed unusually startled at the suggestion.

"It has such a lovely view of the cove and the ocean beyond." Fidgeting with his teacup, Rob finally set it down and came over to them. "I'd planned to ask you to arrange that, but we were talking, and I never got the chance to speak to you alone."

"Ah, well, we shall make it so. If that's what you wish, Robin." One last quizzical look from his mother, who seemed somehow more at ease.

"It is."

"Then, my lady"—Lady St. Just linked her arm in Georgie's—"there will be a slight delay while your room is readied. I will instruct the footmen to move your things and give any assistance necessary to your maid. In the meanwhile, you might like to take your spaniel, Lulu I think you said her name was, out to the maze. It is a lovely day, especially for early February. You should take advantage of it. I used to walk my pugs out there quite often." She paused. "I used to have several pugs, quite adorable little animals. The last one, Daisy, was so lonely when all the others died; when she passed on, I didn't replace her. Perhaps I should do so. Quite good companions, aren't they?"

"They are, my lady. I don't know what I would do without Lulu." Georgie smiled, unsure how they had gotten off on the subject of pugs. At least Lady St. Just liked dogs. That was one obstacle Georgie wouldn't need to overcome. Perhaps Lulu would prove a way to stay in the marchioness's good graces.

"Why don't you go on out to the maze, my dear? Robin can bring Lulu out to you."

"Thank you, my lady." Relieved at being given leave to go, Georgie curtsied and hurried from the room. The butler, not quite so silent this time, assisted her with her pelisse and showed her which door led to the maze. The sunlight, so bright earlier, had dimmed a little as the day progressed, but still shone cheerfully on the tall boxwoods. She must make sure not to get lost in there, although she assumed Rob could find her and rescue her again. That made her smile as she walked cautiously into the maze.

The sensation of being swallowed up by the trees on either side gave her a moment's concern, but her sense of adventure took over, and soon she was striding forward excitedly, turning first left, then right, until she came to a dead end. Perhaps it was designed that way, for there was a clever little stone bench set against the wall of trees, the perfect place to rest, or to step up and take one's bearings.

Climbing up swiftly, she peered over the tops of the hedges, looking for a glimpse of Rob.

"There you are."

Georgie whirled around, too fast as it turned out. She windmilled her arms to keep from falling off the bench.

With one giant step, Rob reached her, grasped her around the waist, and steadied her.

When she had her balance, she rapped him sharply on the shoulder and jumped down. "Why do you insist on sneaking up on me?"

"Because there's no fun in it otherwise." He laughed and whistled, and Lulu came sailing around the edge of the hedge. "I had no idea she would come to a whistle."

"Neither did I." Georgie crouched down to pet the dog. "Lulu, have you taken to Rob at last? He can whistle, and you'll come?"

Lulu yipped and took off after something rustling in the boxwoods.

"Well, I certainly hope she will," Rob said, helping Georgie to her feet, "because I for one do not wish to spend the night searching the maze for a dog. I'd do it," he added quickly. "I just wouldn't enjoy it very much."

"I can't say that I would either." Georgie smoothed her pelisse down as best she could. It was the same light blue one she'd put over Rob to keep him from freezing, and it had not been right ever since. Neither had she.

"So how do you find Castle St. Just?"

"Absolutely lovely, Rob." Not wanting to meet his gaze, she spread her arms and turned around. "Your castle is like something out of a fairy story. That is not always the case with castles, I'll have you know. I grew up in one that was more of a nightmare."

"And you'll go back there once your brother arrives? You'll marry Travers?"

The very thing she did not wish to think of. Not here, in

this beautiful place. Not with Rob so close. "I am betrothed to him, Rob." Summoning her courage, she turned to look at him. "I agreed to the marriage of my own free will. Not for love, no, but for my father and my family. When I disobeyed Father and broke from him to marry Isaac, I lost all connection with my brothers and sisters. My father forbade them from having any contact with me. He disowned me and vowed to treat me as if I were dead to him." Desperate to move, she paced around the tiny circle. "I could live with that censure while my husband was alive. He was all that I needed. But when he died, I lost everything. My family could not or would not take me in, so I had to beg to live with my sister-in-law who despised me because my marriage had cost her father his living. Isaac's father was our parish vicar, and when he married us, without Father's approval, he was turned out of the vicarage almost overnight."

"Georgie—"

"No, Rob." She blinked back tears she didn't want to fall. "You have to listen. You have to understand how it was. Mrs. Robinson took me in, out of common Christian charity, she said, but she treated me worse than any servant in my father's house. I wore my mourning clothes long after my period of mourning was officially over, not only because I still missed Isaac, but because I had no money for new clothes. My friend Elizabeth took pity on me and had some of her gowns made over to fit me, else I'd have been wearing those hideous dresses still." Rubbing away the tears that had insisted on falling, Georgie came back to stand in front of Rob. "So when my father sent for me and said he'd take me back if I agreed to marry Travers, I had no choice but to say yes. My mother's inheritance does not come to me until I am thirty. Do you know a gentleman who would wish to wait so long, who would take me with nothing to my name?"

He took her hands, which made her want to cry all the harder. "Georgina, they would line the streets of London if only you would say the word. And I would be at the head of the line."

"What?"

"Do you think your father would change his mind if someone else offered for your hand?" He grinned down at her like a lunatic. "Someone with more wealth and better social position than Travers could ever hope to have." Loosening his hands from hers, he stroked his thumb down her cheek, leaving a trail of fire in its wake. "Someone you would prefer to marry."

Scarcely able to make sense of his words, Georgie gasped as Rob tilted her face up to his and pressed his mouth to hers. As though the world around her had stopped, she knew only the touch of his lips and the fierce longing that their gentle touch awakened in her. She slid her hands up to cup his face, to keep them together as long as she possibly could.

He must have taken that as a signal, for he immediately deepened the kiss, his tongue stealing into her mouth, exploring her, tasting her, teasing her. Promising more if she wished it. A more secluded spot could not be found for a passionate tryst. And she did wish for more. But not quite yet.

With a sadness that was almost physical, she backed away and let him go.

To her surprise, he smiled as broadly as if she'd just given him the moon. "I shall write directly to your father, Georgie. I am an eligible parti with a good reputation. He should consider my suit."

"I am already betrothed, Rob." Oh, but she did not wish to get her hopes up. "Besides that, my father never changes his mind."

Grinning even more widely, Rob took her arm and whistled for Lulu. "I think we shall have to see about that."

Chapter Fifteen

The cramped cabin Jemmy had procured onboard the *Pegasus*, bound for Scotland, but stopping in Penzance, proved barely large enough for him and Elizabeth to stand up and turn around in, but as the saying went, beggars couldn't be choosers. They'd been lucky to find any vessel heading out this time of year, according to the captain Jemmy had contacted upon their arrival in Portsmouth. Thank God the journey would only take three days, plus another half-day's travel by coach from Penzance to St. Just. For what seemed like the thousandth time, he cursed Rob heartily for bringing them on this wretched journey.

"Are you ready, my dear?" He truly did not know how Elizabeth was managing to cope with the accommodations, but she seemed to be taking it all in stride. To look at her now, dressed for dinner in a lovely maroon gown with small puffed sleeves, hair swept on top of her head, her eyes sparkling in the light of the one candle, she might have just stepped out of their chamber at her parents' town home in London.

"I am." She grinned at him as she pulled her gloves on. "Such an adventure this is, my love. I am quite enjoying our little trip so far. If we find Georgie safe and sound at journey's end, I will count this one of the most remarkable exploits of my life."

Shaking his head, Jemmy took her arm and kissed her cheek. "I am glad you are finding our journey so much to your liking, Elizabeth. I pray, however, that such 'adventures' will come to us but rarely. I, for one, am extremely put out by the whole escapade. I still cannot fathom what Rob was thinking to bring Georgie off all the way to Cornwall."

"Please do not continue to let it upset you, my dear." Elizabeth patted his arm, and he opened the door that led directly onto the much more spacious dining room. The other five or six passengers and several officers were already assembled, although no one had sat down as yet.

"Lord Brack, I believe?" A young man in blue officer's garb bowed to him. "I am the *Pegasus*'s first officer, Mr. Benton. How do you do?"

"How do you do, sir." Jemmy turned to Elizabeth. "My dear, this is our first officer, Mr. Benton. May I present my wife, Lady Brack?" Jemmy's chest swelled whenever he introduced Elizabeth as his wife. He doubted that pride would ever go away.

"Lady Brack." Mr. Benton bowed to Elizabeth, a bit more elegantly than before. "I am delighted to meet you. Shall I introduce you to the other passengers? Most will be continuing on to Scotland, but there is one gentleman who, like you, will disembark at Penzance."

"That will be lovely, Mr. Benton." Elizabeth smiled serenely as the officer led them toward an older couple. Jemmy couldn't take his eyes off her. Not only beautiful, but his wife took everything in her stride as well. God, he was a lucky man.

Benton introduced them to Mr. and Mrs. Saunders, a banker and his wife relocating to Glasgow with their two young daughters, and to Mr. Jonathan Croft, a medical student on his way to Edinburgh by way of Glasgow. Several minutes of pleasant conversation ensued, Elizabeth and Mrs. Saunders speaking about the care of children while Jemmy and the two other gentlemen discovered a mutual enthusiasm for grouse shooting.

"You both will have the best time of it in Scotland," Jemmy declared, quite jealous of their proximity to the exceptional grouse moors in northern Scotland. "I visited relatives there several years ago and went shooting every day for a week. Peak of the season, of course, but truly magnificent sport."

Mr. Croft had just inquired about the best guns to use, when Mr. Benton reappeared at Jemmy's side.

"Pardon me, Lord Brack." Mr. Benton smiled and indicated a man standing at the sideboard speaking with another officer. "This is the gentleman I spoke to you about, who is also going to Penzance." He steered Jemmy to the other side of the room, where said gentleman was in deep conversation with the captain.

"No, I had not heard that the *Antoinette* had gone down," Captain Bryant said, his face grave. "The Channel can be treacherous this time of year."

"I'd been waiting for weeks for that cargo to arrive. Its loss was quite a blow. But then, I've had several such setbacks recently. I trust my luck is about to change, however." The brooding tone of the unknown man sent an odd chill down Jemmy's back.

"Excuse me, Captain, my lord." Mr. Benton nodded to Jemmy. "Here is the other gentleman who is traveling to Penzance. May I make Lord Brack known to you?"

The gentleman, attired in a well-cut gray jacket that had seen better days, whirled around to face them. "Brack?"

Jemmy's head reeled. "Lord Travers?"

"What are you doing here?" They spoke in unison, so

loudly all other conversation in the room ceased and heads turned.

Elizabeth quickly excused herself from Mrs. Saunders and hurried to Jemmy's side. "My dear, what is wrong?"

With great effort, Jemmy assumed his social manners. Much as he might wish to plant the man a facer, he had to act with civility, at least in public. "My dear, allow me to make known to you Lord Travers. Lady Georgina's betrothed."

Her eyes flew open wide, though she did not give any other sign of astonishment.

"My lord, allow me to present my wife, Lady Brack."

"A pleasure, I'm sure, my lady." The man mumbled so badly it was hard to make out his words.

"And for me, my lord." Elizabeth cut her eyes toward Jemmy, who shrugged. He could only think that Travers had discovered where his betrothed had gone and was in pursuit of her as he and Elizabeth were. The question was, how had Travers found out?

Before Jemmy could think how to frame the question, Captain Bryant moved to the head of the table. "Ladies and gentlemen, if you would take your seats for dinner, please?"

Due to the dictates of precedence, Travers was seated at the captain's right, Jemmy at his left, and Elizabeth on her husband's left. The rest of the company filled in with the officers around the table, Mrs. Saunders sandwiched between Mr. Benton and her husband at the other end of the table.

Dinner arrived, and for a while everyone applied themselves to the delicious white soup, roasted chicken, a veal pie, pickled beets, green beans in a cream sauce, and a splendid blancmange. Conversations lulled, though comments lauding the cook were heard throughout the dining room.

Sitting across the table, Travers glowered at Jemmy in between swallows of wine. Jemmy had no recollection of anything he'd personally done to the earl to merit such impudence. He'd spoken out against the match, but Travers could hardly know about that unless Father had told him. And how had the man learned of Georgie's flight to Cornwall?

The man's sullen face, with puffy, bruised-looking eyes and sunken cheeks, spoke of a life of dissipation. How in God's name had Father come up with this wastrel as a husband for Georgie?

"What takes you to Cornwall, my lord?" Captain Bryant's cheerful voice broke in on Jemmy's musings.

"My wife and I are visiting an old school friend for several weeks. He suggested the voyage as a speedier alternative to an overland journey." Jemmy eyed Travers, but the man gave no reaction to his words. He'd be a sharp card player that one.

The captain motioned for more wine. "And you, my lord?" He looked inquiringly at Travers. "What business brings you to Penzance?"

For a moment Jemmy thought Travers wouldn't answer. The silence lengthened as the earl stared menacingly at him.

The captain cleared his throat, obviously afraid he'd offended the peer. "I'm sorry, my lord. I didn't mean to pry." He turned to Elizabeth as a refuge. "My lady—"

"My wife." Travers drained his glass and set it on the damask tablecloth with a heavy thud.

Elizabeth jumped, and Jemmy stared at the man, thinking he'd not heard right. "Your wife, my lord?" What was the man implying? "Did you say your wife?"

"I did, sir, as you well know. More wine here." He fixed an ugly stare on one of the junior officers, and the man came at a trot with the carafe.

"I know nothing of a wife who belongs to you, my lord. Please enlighten us." This was odd behavior indeed.

"She's your sister, Brack. I should think you know her." Travers glared at him, a menacing stare filled with unrelenting animosity that put Jemmy immediately on guard.

Trying to avert a disaster at his table, Captain Bryant

charged in to change the subject. "Lady Brack, I believe I was told your late husband fought—"

"I do, Lord Travers." Jemmy wasn't about to let Travers's remark go unanswered. "But unless my father somehow forgot to inform me of the nuptials, she is not your wife." Glancing down the table, he winced. He'd tried to keep his voice down, but all eyes were focused on their end of the table.

"We are betrothed, the contracts signed and sealed. Just as good as wed in a court of law." Travers had sunk back in his seat, brows lowered until they appeared to touch his nose.

"I think not, my lord." The captain valiantly dove into the choppy waters. "A betrothal, while legally binding, is not considered a marriage."

"We'll see about that." Leering at Jemmy, the earl took another sip of his wine. "I intend to find her and to kill the cur who took her."

Squeezing Jemmy's hand, Elizabeth began to tremble, her face drawn and pale. She turned her frightened gaze on him, but he squeezed back, sending her strength as best he could. "Perhaps we should save this discussion for a private moment, Travers."

As if just noticing he had a very attentive audience, Travers shook himself, drained his glass, and rose. "If you will excuse me ladies, gentlemen." He bowed, strode away to his cabin, entered it, and slammed the door.

A clamor broke out at the table, everyone speaking at once and looking toward Jemmy for answers. He stared back at them, at a loss for words. He had no idea what Travers planned to do, although it certainly sounded like he intended to do more than just draw Rob's cork. His friend could be in actual danger from that blackguard.

Surreptitiously, Elizabeth fanned her face with her hand.

"Are you all right, my love?" Jemmy whispered in her ear.

"I would like to retire as well, my dear. I am feeling distinctly unwell."

Jemmy shot up out of his chair and assisted Elizabeth in rising. "My wife is fatigued after a very trying day. Do forgive us for leaving so early."

"Nonsense, my lord." The captain took Elizabeth's other arm and escorted her to their chamber door. "I hope your recovery is swift, Lady Brack. My lord, please call one of the officers if you or your wife requires assistance during the night."

"Thank you, Captain. I will inform you if my wife's health worsens." Opening the door, Jemmy helped Elizabeth across the threshold and shut the door. Allowing his worry to surface at last, Jemmy grasped Elizabeth's arm and compelled her to the tiny bunk and forced her to sit.

"Jemmy, what are you doing?" An eyebrow rose.

"Making certain you are not so distressed by this turn of events that you become ill, my love."

"Jemmy, I am fine." Drawing his hand to her lips, she kissed it, sending a shiver down his back. "I wanted to have a word with you, away from everyone who would have been asking questions immediately had I not been 'overcome.'"

"So you are well?" He gripped her hands. The thought of Elizabeth ill, or even worse, losing the child she carried, had been a constant worry since they had set out from Buckinghamshire.

"Truly I am. Now come, sit by me. It is the only place." She patted the bunk beside her. "I fear we shall get very little sleep tonight in this excuse for a bed."

"And for all the wrong reasons." Waggling his eyebrows, he sent her into a peal of laughter that she immediately tried to stifle.

"Hush. They will never believe I was overcome if you

make me laugh." She leaned on his side, laughing silently as she shook.

"Well, it's not as if you were tying your garter in public."

She gave his arm a squeeze. "Enough. I wanted to ask you what you make of the fact that Lord Travers is also heading for Cornwall. How did he get the information that she is there?"

"I assume Father informed him after reading my letter." Jemmy shook his head. Didn't his father know what Travers was capable of? Obviously not if he had agreed to Travers marrying Georgie in the first place. "So he is here and spoiling for a fight with Rob. I am afraid, however, that Travers will simply waylay Rob, which will leave Travers Georgie's only hope of avoiding scandal and ruin."

"There must be another way." Linking her arm in his, Elizabeth laid her head on his shoulder.

"Of course, there is. The easiest one imaginable. For Rob to marry Georgie." Jemmy slid his fingers around his cravat to loosen it and pulled it off.

"I thought you said she disliked him." Elizabeth yawned and snuggled closer.

"She does, or did." He paused in the act of unwinding the cravat. "But Rob can be the most persuasive and charming of fellows. I would not be surprised if he hasn't made her fall in love with him." Tossing the length of fabric onto the floor—there was absolutely no place else to put it—Jemmy stood and raised his wife to her feet. "Come love, let me undress you. It's a good thing we left our servants at home. We'd have had no room for them at all."

"Sometimes I wish only you would undress me at night." Stretching up on tiptoe, Elizabeth raised her arms so he could undo the buttons down her back.

"And why is that?" Jemmy slipped his hands around to cup her breasts and free them from her stays.

"For this very reason." She arched her back into him, and

he groaned. The next few days would be torture. The bed was simply too small for any kind of amorous activity. "Do you think Lord St. Just may have developed an affection for Georgie?"

"I have no idea, but I will tell you, I'd much rather she marry Rob than Travers. Even if I do need to speak a word in the marquess's ear, I know he is the better man."

"But will your father see it that way?" Elizabeth turned toward Jemmy, her breasts now temptingly close.

If he leaned toward her, he could brush against her. . . .

"Hand me my gown, please."

Groaning again, Jemmy complied, gritting his teeth and summoning his willpower.

"After our miracle marriage, I believe it is Georgie's turn." She climbed up and settled into the far side of the bunk, curving her back against the ship's wall. Patting the sheets invitingly, Elizabeth sighed, whisper soft. "Come to bed, my love. I am sure we will find a way to make do here."

Pulse racing, troubles forgotten, Jemmy stripped out of his breeches, coat, and shirt in an ungodly short period of time. He climbed into the bed and managed to pull Elizabeth into his arms. "I believe you are correct, my love. We will do just fine right here, and, pray God, Georgie and Rob will find a way around both Father and Lord Travers." He kissed Elizabeth, and heat rose all over him. "There is always a way."

Chapter Sixteen

The next few days were virtually a dream come true for Georgie.

She had dutifully sat down the next morning and written to her father about the mysterious kidnapping—neither she nor Rob nor Lady St. Just could come up with a plausible idea of who would have had her kidnapped and for what purpose—asking if he had any enemies or if a ransom note had been delivered to him.

Admitting that she had nothing to lose, she also suggested that given the time she'd spent alone on the ship with Lord St. Just, Lord Travers might not still wish to marry her. However, St. Just, having compromised her, was willing to marry her. She then touted Rob's bravery, his kindness, and his quick thinking in time of crisis. Then, to put things in terms her father might actually value, she gave him an idea of the wealth of the marquessate along with the designation of precedence accorded to the Marquess of St. Just, one well above Travers and slightly above his own.

With a prayer to the Almighty for her happiness, she'd signed and sealed the missive, gotten Rob to frank it, and sent it off in the daily post packet to Penzance. That unpleasantness done, she'd joined Rob as he'd gone about the many duties for which he was responsible for the continued prosperity of the estate.

The first morning after breakfast they had gone to the tin mine to deliver the urgently needed parts that had taken him to Portsmouth in the first place. She'd been fascinated by the mining operation, although she'd declined a closer look when Rob suggested she go partway down a shaft.

The next day he'd asked her to accompany him as he visited some of his tenants who were dairy farmers. The cows were in from pasture, making the workload somewhat more taxing now than during the summer months. A conscientious master he liked to check in on them every month or so. Georgie eagerly agreed to this visit and was fascinated as much by the tenants as the cows. This time Rob managed to persuade her to try her hand at milking. The hilarity that ensued had kept not only Rob but the tenants laughing for at least ten minutes as she tried and tried to squeeze the milk out. At last the cow had had enough and simply walked off, stepping on her half boot in the process. Her toes still ached, but then Rob complained that so did his sides from all the laughter.

This afternoon, instead of a local errand, he'd suggested he show her around the castle. She'd seen very little of it, in fact, beside her room, the breakfast and dining rooms, and of course, the maze. Since she'd arrived, they had been busy outside the castle walls, so perhaps it was time she saw more of the home in which Rob had grown up. Seeing his world had made her long even more to be a part of it, but she had reminded herself several times that her particular fairy story might not have the happy ending she wanted so badly.

They started in the foyer, with what turned into a history lesson about the Kerr family.

"These weapons and shields date back to the fifteenth century, when the Kerrs were just plain knights." He waved his hand at the swords, battle-axes, daggers, and lances positioned high up on the walls. "I'm positive they have been cleaned, but I daresay most of them have been dipped in blood at one time or the other." He raised his eyebrows in mock horror. "You aren't particularly squeamish about such things, are you?"

"Not particularly, no." Georgie laughed, but looked closer at the point of a broadsword hanging directly over her head. Was that a spot of rust or . . .

"I wouldn't stand so directly under that if I were you, my dear." Gently he took her arm and pulled her from beneath the weapon. "I do not know how long it's been hanging there, but if the fastening happened to come loose, well . . . a bit messy, don't you think? Best to be safe." He took her arm and looped it through the crook of his elbow. "Perhaps a less dangerous tour is in order. Let us go look at the library."

"Well, that certainly seems much safer." Sighing, Georgie accompanied him out of the foyer. "At least books cannot kill you."

"You wouldn't think so, would you."

"Rob!" She batted his arm. "You cannot convince me you have a deadly book in your library. What does it do? Are its pages treated with poison? Or does it explode when one reaches page two hundred seventy-six?"

"Perhaps I should peruse your library at Blackham. Do you have such volumes there?" The false eagerness in his face, laced with laughter behind his eyes, made her laugh as well.

"You wretch. No, we have no such books at Blackham. And I'll wager you have none such here at St. Just."

"And just what would you care to wager, my lady?" The humor in his face had died, replaced by a fiery passion. "A kiss?"

Although thrilled at the thought of kissing him again, Georgie schooled herself to caution. "You would hardly make such a wager if you didn't know for certain what books your library holds."

"Unless I am bluffing." His eyes darkened to black. "Do you think I am bluffing, Georgie?"

"I . . . I don't know." Lord, he had her so confused she could barely remember her name.

"Then let's find out, shall we?" He led her down the corridor to the rear of the castle, to a huge oak-paneled door that he opened. Beyond was a delightful room with a fireplace where a pleasant blaze crackled, a chaise and several comfortable-looking chairs, and masses of tall, polished wooden bookshelves filled with books of all descriptions. High atop the shelves, busts of stern-looking men peered down at them.

"Oh, but it's lovely." Georgie wandered toward the fire, holding out her hands to the friendly blaze. "A very cozy room despite those heads above us." She pointed to a bust of Cicero. "Not a place for murderous books at all. I believe you are bluffing."

"You think so?" Chuckling, he strolled over to one of the bookshelves and pulled out a black bound book, looking to be of quite some age. "Come look at this." He carried it to a nearby table and set it down.

In spite of herself, Georgie eased toward the table as if she truly expected the volume to burst into flame or explode. Once close enough, she read the title and looked at him, frowning. "*The Holy Bible*?"

"Yes, but a very special one." His eyes twinkled. "It belonged to an ancestor from the time of King Henry VIII. This particular Kerr was a cleric at Henry's court who had displeased the monarch and was awaiting execution in prison. Knowing King Henry's whims and his own precarious situation, he'd taken precautions just in case he should be imprisoned. He requested that his wife bring him his personal copy of the *Holy Bible*, this very one here, to be a comfort to him in his last hours. The request was granted, and the wife delivered the book to him. Later that night, the ancestor began praying, weeping and wailing, calling out to his jailors that he was being possessed by a demon."

"You are making this up, Rob." Georgie didn't know whether to laugh or be frightened.

"I assure you, I am not." The sincerity in his face convinced her, almost. "So the jailors ran into the jail cell, and by that time my ancestor was writhing on the floor. The two guards turned him over, and he rose up and stabbed them in the heart with this." Rob flipped the Bible open to reveal a narrow compartment carved out of the pages in which lay a long, narrow dagger.

"Dear Lord." Georgie gasped and stumbled back.

"The ancestor then replaced the knife in the Bible, closed the cell, pulled his hood up over his head, and walked out carrying the book. No one stopped him as they assumed he was a priest there to give last rites to the condemned man." The pride in his ancestor's clever plan resonated in Rob's voice. "He went home, gathered his wife, and they struck out for the most distant place they could find, which turned out to be Cornwall."

"It seems the entire family tree is fraught with actors of one kind or another." Narrowing her eyes at him, Georgie shook her head. "I am not quite sure this tale isn't a bag of moonshine." She ran a finger along the mass of cut pages and shuddered. "However, the book is, I grant you, a deadly tome."

A look of triumph flashed across his face as he gathered up the Bible and returned it to its place on the shelf. "And thereby I win my forfeit?" The dark look of desire was back in his eyes.

"Yes, you do, my lord." Tingling all over, Georgie raised her chin, and closed her eyes, anticipation of his warm mouth on hers filling her with an exquisite tension.

"Excellent." He grabbed her hand and pulled her toward the door.

Her eyes popped open. "What are you doing? Where are we going?"

"Somewhere more private." He turned down a corridor that led to a steep flight of steps.

"More private than a library?"

"Trust me." Squeezing her hand, he started up the dark stone staircase.

"Where are you taking me?" Panting to keep up with Rob's breakneck pace, Georgie pulled on his hand. "Slow down or you will kill me yet."

"You are made of sterner stuff than that, Georgie."

"You . . . can say that. . . . You're not even . . . breathing hard." How could he run up this steep staircase and not be winded at all? She'd danced entire evenings and never been this out of breath.

After what seemed an eternity, Rob flung open a door, and they stepped out into dull sunshine and a crisp, hard breeze. All about her was light and wide-open space as far as she could see. Her head spun. "Where are we?"

"The parapet."

At the top of the castle. Goodness. Georgie breathed heavily, but was still dazzled by the incredible view. To the back of the castle lay the boxwood maze and beyond that a forest, mostly black spires at this time of year. To her right was the crushed shell driveway that led toward the tiny parish of St. Just. And if she swung around the other way, she looked down on the top of the crags, the blue ocean just beyond, stretching onward seemingly forever. Breathtaking, even if she had no breath left to give.

"You can stand here and look straight down the cliff." Rob had ventured dangerously close to the very edge of the parapet, a short, raised ledge all that stood between him and a drop to his death.

"No, thank you." She licked her lips and swallowed hard. Heights always made her queasy. "Why don't you come back over here."

"But don't you want to see—"

"No." The man would try the patience of a saint. "Rob, please."

"I am perfectly fine, Georgie." He turned his back to the ocean, mere inches from the edge and that terrifying drop. If he stepped back, hit the back of his legs against the rim . . .

Hand over her mouth, she turned away, horrified at the thought of what would happen if he stepped back, even one step.

"Georgie." His voice sounded close to her ear, and she almost slumped with relief. He put his hand on her shoulder, and she flung herself into his arms.

"Oh, Rob. Please don't ever do that again." Clinging to him, head buried in his chest, she tried to control her sobs.

"Sweetheart, I am sorry. I had no idea heights affected you so." Slipping his arms around her, he pulled her tight against him. "They have never bothered me at all, so I don't really think about it. I've been running around up here since I was about six years old. I used to love to hang my head over the side and gaze down on everyone." He chuckled, and it rumbled in her ear. "I thought I was the king of the castle up here."

"You can just as well be king on the first floor," Georgie muttered into his jacket.

"Yes, my lady." Hugging her closer, he brushed his lips on the top of her head. "It will be as you command."

Relief flowing through her like a river, she sighed and rubbed her cheek on his comfortable chest. "Rob, would you tell me something?"

"Anything, my dear."

She raised her head to peer at him. "Was that story you

told me at Charlotte's party, about you and the smugglers, true, or were you simply trying to impress me?"

Laughing and shaking his head, he stepped back to look in her face. "My dear, I will never know what to expect from you. What made you think of that?"

"The view out to sea. I remembered you talked about stealing into and out of the cove at night, whenever there was a smuggling run. I should think that would be very tricky in the dark."

"Believe me, it is. And yes, during the war years, when I was much younger and wilder, I went out a time or two with the local smuggling ring." He gazed into the distance, a fond smile on his lips.

"Wilder?" Lord have mercy. How much wilder could the man have been and lived to tell the tale?

"Much. I wanted all the adventure I could find, and, this close to Land's End, smuggling was about all I could do to slake that thirst." Pointing out toward the cove, he continued eagerly. "We would sail out about an hour or so due south of here, meet up with a ship from France, load a part of their goods—usually brandy, but one time it was a lot of French silk—then sail it all back into the cove. I don't know how it traveled out of St. Just. I was never privy to how it was moved, but it kept many a family's larder well stocked and their homes in good repair."

"Do they go out still, your smugglers?" None of this surprised Georgie. Still, she did hope he was no longer a party to this criminal activity.

"No. The whole operation dried up after the war ended. No need for it when there was free trade once again between the two countries. Pity." His mouth drooped. "When we go down I'll show you the smugglers' tunnel that goes out from the castle to the harbor. My ancestors dabbled in the trade a bit more than I did."

"I told Jemmy I thought you wanted to become a pirate." Oh, yes, she'd known it all along. "I see I was right after all."

"A pirate?" Rob's laughter boomed out over the parapet, causing several seagulls perching on the stone wall to squawk and take flight. "I don't think I ever fancied myself that, although I can see a connection with the smuggling. They are both rather adventurous occupations." He grasped her hands and pulled her into his arms again. "But I am done with those sorts of adventures."

"Have you, truly?" Being in his arms made her hope with all her heart that was so.

"I have. The only adventure I crave now is you, Georgina." He kissed her brow, her ear, her cheek.

Fire licked through her veins, melting her insides just from that fleeting touch.

Cupping her head, he brought her mouth close. "And now I will claim my forfeit."

"Why did you bring me all the way up here to claim it?" Staring into pools of darkest gray, she thrilled to the very closeness of his body.

"Because here I am king of the castle, and I would make you my queen." He lowered his lips to hers, the sweet taste of him flooding her senses.

Overcome with the need to claim him, she grasped his head and pressed her lips against his, licking the seam with a soft dart of her tongue. Seeking to invade him.

A small sound of surprise, then his mouth opened wide, allowing her entry to plunder. Oh yes, she would be the pirate here, taking him prisoner. She swept in, exploring him inch by inch, until he captured her tongue, making her squeal as her body went up in flames.

She no longer had any doubt. This was the man she had been waiting for, the one she burned for with an intensity like none other. The man she wanted to share her life with for all the rest of time. The one she could trust with her life and with the lives of those she loved.

If only she could have him.

Reluctantly, she pulled herself out of Rob's arms and caught his startled look.

"What's wrong, sweetheart?" His puzzled frown cut her heart to its core.

"I can't . . . We can't . . . I am still legally betrothed to Lord Travers, Rob." Curse her father for ever persuading her to throw her life away like that. "I am bound by the contracts to marry him."

"Such things can be got around, my love." He came toward her, but she backed away.

"I don't think so. It's a binding contract that only my father can break." She ducked her head. "Which I am absolutely certain he will not do."

"There are other possibilities, Georgie." Rob inched toward her. "Perhaps I could persuade Lord Travers to rescind his offer."

"Huh. As soon persuade the moon down from the sky." She pulled the collar of her pelisse higher. "The wind is getting brisk. We should go back inside."

"We can last another moment." He had succeeded in getting close enough to her to catch hold of her arm. "I wish to have this settled, my dear." With a piercing gaze he stared into her eyes, compelling her to listen. "I declare to you, Georgina Kirkpatrick, I will not let you marry that cur. If it comes to it, I will challenge him to a duel and put a bullet in his black heart before I let that happen."

"You cannot do that, Rob." Panic rose in her, like a bird flushed out of a field.

"If I have to make a choice between allowing him to marry you or calling him out, I will meet him without hesitation." Grasping her shoulders, Rob kissed her again, an all-consuming possession of her mouth that left her knees weak. "You are mine, and by God, no one will take you from me."

Bewildered by that declaration, Georgie stared at him, unsure if she'd truly heard him aright.

"Georgie!"

The faint call brought her out of her reverie, and she shook her head. "Did you hear someone call my name?"

"Georgina!"

"Who in God's name is that?" Rob peered over the edge and swore.

"What is it?" Georgie inched over to the side of the parapet that looked out on the driveway to the front steps and gasped. "Oh, no."

Down on the graveled driveway, looking up at her with varying degrees of consternation, shock, or dismay, were Jemmy, Elizabeth, and Lord Travers.

Chapter Seventeen

Stunned to see her brother and Elizabeth so soon, and completely dumbfounded by Lord Travers's presence, Georgie could only stand for some moments, peering over the parapet and gripping Rob's arm. The dizzying sense of falling that usually overcame her when she looked down from any height had come upon her with a vengeance. Clutching Rob as though he were her only anchor, which at the moment he absolutely was, she straightened, trying her best to control the dread rising in her. "I didn't expect Jemmy to arrive so soon."

"When I wrote to him at Hunter's Cross, I suggested he sail from Portsmouth." Frowning, Rob led her from the edge of the parapet to the staircase door. "My only thought then was that it would be quicker for him to come and take you off my hands. I had no idea he would be here this quickly." Rob took Georgie's arm and turned her to face him. "I would never have done so had I any inkling—"

"I know you wouldn't have. At that moment I was simply a bit of trouble and bother you would have preferred not to have to deal with." Putting on what she hoped was a brave face, Georgie smiled. "In your place I might have done the exact same thing, hoping to get rid of me as soon as could be."

"Nothing could be farther from the truth now." That truth shone in his furrowed brow. "I had no idea Brack would bring Travers with him. According to the letter he sent me last month, he quite opposed the match."

"As he did just a week ago in Buckinghamshire." Shaking her head, Georgie patted his arm. "I believe there is something else afoot here, although I am quite at a loss to say what. Let us go down and beard them in their den. Or your den, rather. This is your property, after all."

Rob dropped a kiss on her brow, making her whole being warm despite the circumstances and the chilly late afternoon wind. "Once more unto the breach."

They descended the staircase at a much slower pace than they had ascended, for which Georgie was terribly grateful. She did not wish to take a tumble down the stone steps. Neither did she wish to greet her brother so quickly, and she was positively loathe to meet with Lord Travers. The only person awaiting her below who she was truly glad to see was Elizabeth. Her friend had always been so supportive of her; it would be good to have an ally at such a trying time.

The staircase opened onto the corridor near the library, and it took them some minutes to reach the foyer where a stern-faced Jemmy waited, slapping his gloves into his palm and drawing them through his fingers. A sign he was not pleased with her at all. Lord Travers stood a little to the side, his face dark and brooding, quite ominous, although of course he couldn't be happy to discover his betrothed cavorting on a parapet with another man.

Her gaze was drawn, thankfully, to Elizabeth, her friend's sweet face wearing a puckered frown. "Georgina. Oh, thank heavens."

Then Georgie was in her arms, a weight she hadn't realized she'd been carrying lifted from her by the woman's firm embrace.

"Georgie, we've been ever so worried. Are you well?" Elizabeth peered into her face, and Georgie nodded.

"I am, wonderfully well." She glanced first at her brother, still glowering, and then at Travers, who looked as though he'd bitten into an unripe persimmon. "Let us retire so I can tell you what happened."

Without another look at any of the men, she grasped Elizabeth's hand and led her down the corridor and into a small receiving room and shut the door.

"Oh, Georgie." Elizabeth hugged her again. "Tell me what happened. Lord St. Just's letter said you were kidnapped."

"That is true, my dear." She led her friend to a comfortable chaise where they sat, and Georgie took Elizabeth's hands. "The first kidnapping. But that is just the beginning of the tale."

The moment Georgie and Lady Brack left the room, Travers strode up to Rob, snarling, "You are a dead man, you cur." He drew his arm back, ready to draw Rob's cork, when Brack pushed Travers aside.

"You didn't need to stop him, Brack. I'd have—"

Brack's fist connected with Rob's jaw, snapping his head back as pain exploded along the left side of his face. He staggered back a step, as much out of surprise as pain. "What the devil are you playing about?" Moving his jaw, gingerly to be sure, but it would move, Rob kept a wary eye on both Travers and the man he'd called friend until about a minute ago.

"You'd best be glad I don't thrash you to a pulp or call you out, St. Just. Don't you realize you've probably ruined Georgie's reputation?" Brack shook his hand, wincing. His familiar face had transformed into a gargoyle's with enormous protruding eyes and snarling mouth. "Are you prepared to marry her?"

"What?"

"No!" Travers leaped forward, an ugly snarl on his lips. "She's my betrothed. No one's marrying her but me, understood?"

"You want to have a go, too?" Rob swung around to face the other menace.

As soon as Rob's attention was diverted, Brack grabbed him in a body hold. Fortunately, Rob had spent a summer in London being instructed at Jackson's Saloon. He easily fended the man off, then stripped off his jacket and put up his own bare knuckles. "Which one's it going to be? I don't rightly care, myself." Eyes shifting from one angry face to the other, Rob danced on his feet as he'd been taught. *Keep your wits about you. Outthink your opponent, and you'll win every time.* And by God, he'd had enough of this foolishness. "I can best you, Brack, as you so well know. Lord Travers I can likely dispatch in three blows, if I don't let fly and pull his cork but good on the first try."

Rob danced closer to Travers, who skittered backward until he bumped against the wall, just underneath the medieval knight's sword. Wouldn't it be wonderful for that blade to crash down on the old reprobate's head and end everyone's misery?

Swinging back around toward Brack, Rob raised his chin. "What's it going to be? Words or war?"

"Words for the moment, I suppose." The bleak look still hadn't left Brack's face. "But don't for a moment suppose that your affront to decency has been remedied. It has not. You compromised my sister."

"I did no such—" Rob lowered his voice, although the servants had certainly already gotten an ear and an eyeful. "I did no such thing. Come. Let us at least be uncivil in private." He led them to a small, scarcely used reception room near the foyer and shut the door. Close enough, however, to be able to call a footman and have the both of them escorted out of the house and off the property if necessary.

The small room, while sparsely furnished with a writing desk, chaise, and chair, had the added advantage of also containing a decanter of cognac and numerous glasses. Rob headed straight for it, poured himself a half a tumbler full with a remarkably steady hand, then nodded to Brack to take a glass. Having poured a hefty tot for his erstwhile friend, Rob sighed deeply and indicated for Travers to pick up a glass. Even if he despised the man, he'd summon the common decency to offer him a drink—before throwing him out.

Travers stared first at the glass, then at Rob, but his thirst apparently won out, and he grasped the heavy tumbler and held it out to Rob. Once they all had libations in hand, Rob put his back against the wall, crossed his arms over his chest, and said, "Now, do you want to hear the truth of the matter or not?"

Neither man he faced seemed ready to want to listen to anything. Brack paced, grumbling under his breath, and Travers clenched his jaw so tightly Rob frankly wondered how he managed to drink the brandy. Still, he did so with alarming regularity.

"The truth, as you wrote it to me in your own hand, is that you absconded with my sister against her will." Brack stepped forward, then thought better of it and took a gulp of the brandy instead. "How did you ever think to get away with this escapade, Rob?"

Well, thank God for small allowances. Jemmy was calling him Rob again. Perhaps all was not lost. "There was no escapade on my part, Brack, I swear. Lady Georgina literally ran into me on the streets of Portsmouth, claiming to have been kidnapped."

"So you wrote."

"So your sister will say, and her maid along with her, if you'll only ask her." Travers remained oddly silent, brooding about Georgie, perhaps. Well, let him fret all he wanted. The loathsome man would marry her when pigs flew with their tails forward. "I have tended to believe her because I had the devil's own time retrieving her trunks out from under the noses of the kidnappers."

"You found the ruffians who kidnapped Georgina? And you didn't tell anyone?" Jemmy stared at Rob as if he were a lunatic. "Why didn't you contact the authorities?"

"Look, Jemmy. I had to sail on the evening tide. There wasn't a lot of time to ask questions. I did what I thought best, which was bringing the lady with me rather than risk her falling back into those ruffians' hands on the way back to Blackham. I'd only a small crew with me on that trip." He looked at his friend, though he waited for an explosion from Travers any moment. That one had been almost suspiciously quiet throughout the interrogation.

"And nothing untoward occurred between you and Lady Georgina?" The tension in Jemmy's face eased a trifle. "Even if it didn't—"

"I assure you it did not."

"It had better not have." Travers spoke up for the first time since they had come into the room.

"I could scarcely take advantage of a woman who was being violently ill for most of the voyage. Not the sort of mood one wants to encounter when bent on ravishment." Jemmy and Travers didn't necessarily need to know that, in this case, Rob's definition of "most of the voyage" was much shorter than other people's.

"She was ill the whole time?" Suspicion written on his face, Jemmy cocked his head.

"Well, she finally made it up on deck, and her wretched little dog ended up going over the side." He had to tell Jemmy that much. Georgie would be sure to do so and praise Rob's rescue with every breath.

"Lulu?" Jemmy turned quite pale. "Lulu was . . . lost?"

"And found, thank goodness, or your sister would quite likely have drowned me. I didn't miss it by far in any case." Rob couldn't help but smile at the looks of astonishment on the gentlemen's faces. "I dove in after her and, by the grace of God, rescued her."

"More fool you, St. Just." Shaking his head, Travers smirked then downed his glass. "Got another dram?"

Silently, Rob poured, assured the irony of insulting a man in one breath and asking for a drink of his best cognac with the next was lost on Travers. It apparently wasn't lost on Jemmy, who was attempting not to choke on his brandy.

"So you see, she was perfectly well chaperoned by her maid, and I was frozen solid the last day or so of the journey. Completely incapacitated. Needn't worry at all about improprieties." Oh, but he'd probably spend an extra decade or two in purgatory for telling that single lie. "And of course, Lady Georgina has been under my mother's chaperonage and my protection since our arrival. Nothing untoward could be said about her."

Jemmy shook his head. "I don't know about that, Rob. All it will take is one murmured rumor that she was on that ship with you and your crew, and her reputation will be in ruins. The *ton* talks whether there is substance or not to the tale."

"The only way to stop such a thing from happening is for Lady Georgina to accompany me back to Blackham where we will be married at once." Travers nodded, as though the matter had been settled.

"Over my dead body." Rob slammed his glass down on the desk and lunged at Travers.

With difficulty, Jemmy managed to separate the two

men. "My sister will be returning with me and Lady Brack and no one else. In my father's absence, I am guardian over her and none other." He glared at Travers, who scowled, but backed down. A moment later Jemmy had turned a stern gaze on Rob. "Do you agree as well?"

"Of course. You are her brother." Rob glared at Travers briefly, then turned his attention back to Jemmy. "But I will give you notice that I intend to accompany you and put my suit forth before your father for Lady Georgina's hand."

"So you do wish to marry her?" Jemmy's features relaxed.

"What?" Travers's face darkened as his brows drew downward, his lips puckered into a grimace. "I am already betrothed to her."

"A mere formality." Waving the betrothal away like an unwanted dish at dinner, Rob couldn't refrain from goading the hateful man. "I do wish to marry her, Jemmy. And since minds can be changed, even the Marquess of Blackham's, I will live with that hope. Especially when he sees clearly that I am the better man." Rob looked Travers up and down, with an insolence he rarely used. "In so many ways."

With a maddened roar, Travers charged Rob, grabbing him around the waist and shoving him against the wall. "Not if you're a dead man." Drawing back his fist, Travers was about to let fly with a punishing blow when Rob ducked under his elbow, grabbing his arm as he spun him around.

"We'll see who's the dead man, Travers." Rob cocked his arm back and put his weight behind the blow, connecting to the earl's stomach with a solid punch.

"Ooof." Air rushed out of Travers, and the man slid to the floor, groaning.

"Joseph!" Rob pushed past the crumpled heap and strode to the door, pulling it open and bellowing again. "Joseph!"

"Yes, my lord." A strapping footman, over six feet tall, appeared in the doorway.

"Please take this heap of"—Rob gestured to the downed man—"clothing outside and make sure it leaves the property *post haste*."

"Of course, my lord." Grasping Travers under his arms, Joseph hauled him backward out of the room.

"Let go of me, you oaf." The faint but aggravated tones of the earl continued through the foyer, until they were cut off abruptly.

"Did your footman take retribution on Travers, do you think?" Jemmy had started toward the door.

"No, I believe my butler, Myers, simply shut the front door on them." Rob picked up the decanter. "More brandy?"

Chapter Eighteen

The afternoon and evening flew by for Georgie. She and Elizabeth talked and talked, trying to catch up. By the time Rob found them to tell them to dress for dinner, Georgie had confessed her strong affection for the Marquess of St. Just and the nascent hope that events would work out in their favor. "Being a daughter of the Cross family, I have no reason to hope that Father will break the contract with Lord Travers," she told Elizabeth as they made their way upstairs to their chambers. "But now knowing Rob as I do, I cannot help but hope. He has a way of making things happen that you do not expect."

At the door of the guest room, Elizabeth hugged her. "I hope and pray this comes out right for you, my dear. You so deserve your happy ending after all you have endured."

"Travers certainly could not be deemed a happy ending, could he? I mean, not unless one had a very odd sense of happiness, that is." Quite the opposite, in fact.

"I imagine so, dear."

"Here, let me allow you to dress. I will see you at dinner." Georgie gave her friend a hug and flitted down the corridor, suddenly certain everything would work out, although she had no idea how.

Dinner was lively, with much stimulating conversation,

mostly from Lady St. Just, who seemed happy with more unexpected company. Although Georgie tried her best to hold up her end of the conversation, she'd been placed at Rob's right, and that gentleman monopolized her as much as he could. He also distracted her terribly by holding her hand under cover of the tablecloth in between the courses. Nothing could be more disturbing than having a gentleman rub his thumb across your bare knuckles and not be able to react to it. Of course, she would never complain about such a thing, even if she could. His warm skin on hers kindled a blaze deep within, awakening appetites not meant for a dining room.

After an eternity of such exquisite torture, the marchioness rose, Elizabeth following suit. Georgie attempted to rise, but Rob would not let go of her hand.

"Rob," she whispered under her breath, all the while smiling and fiddling with her gloves as the other ladies filed out. "You must let go. They will think it peculiar if I stay with the gentlemen."

"Come with me," he whispered back. "I'll just escort your sister to the drawing room, Brack," he called to Jemmy as they hurried out of the room.

"What has gotten into you, Rob? What are you doing?"

He'd pulled her into the library, now very dimly lit by a single candelabra.

"You are not going to try to frighten me again with that murderous book, are you?" Really, Rob was too ripe and ready by half, as Jemmy used to say. Always kicking up a lark of some sort. "It will not work a second time, my dear."

Chuckling, he shook his head and shut the door. "No, my love. Far from it." Pulling her to him, he sank his mouth onto hers, stealing her breath away.

Wave after wave of pulsing pleasure flowed through her, heating her blood until every inch of her burned with need. Need for him. Pressing herself against him fully, she reveled in their closeness, in the rightness of their being together. She'd never believed anyone could make her as happy as Isaac had, but she'd been wrong. When Rob held her in his arms, she wanted nothing more in the world than to stay within their loving circle. Forever and ever, amen.

An urgent bumping, in the vicinity of her nether regions, brought her back to the dim library. Rob had maneuvered them so her back pressed against the wall, and he plastered himself against her, every inch touching from the top of her chest, across her breasts, to her stomach, her hips. The insistent prodding was definitely coming from him—and she could guess why. She didn't want to tell him this was hardly the time or the place for such antics, but his lips lingered on hers, so sweet . . . "Umm, Rob."

"Hmm?" Leaving her mouth, he slid his lips down the side of her neck, making shivers cascade down her spine. "Mmm."

"Mmm, yes, I know. But we really must stop." Oh, but she didn't want to.

"I know." He trailed his lips further down into the décolletage of her favorite dress.

Except the fichu had somehow gone missing, so he'd buried his face into the V of her breasts. Lord, but it had gotten extremely hot in here. Panting, and with a supreme effort, she pushed at his chest. "Rob, we must stop."

He sighed, the cool air of his breath wafting over, pebbling her skin where it touched. Then he took a step back. "I'm sorry. This has not gone quite to plan."

"I don't mind." She took his hands and smiled. "Most of our plans have managed to go awry, yet here we are." Wanting another kiss, she swayed toward him. She could tempt a saint if she put her mind to it, and Rob was certainly no saint, if that kiss was any indication. "Shall we try again?"

"Well, but I had something else in mind, Georgie." He

gazed deeply into her eyes, and she simply melted. "I need you to know I love you. Before anything else happens."

Heart beating so fast she had to gasp in air, Georgie beamed at him. "I love you too, Rob. More than anything in this world."

"You do? Truly?" Eyes black with desire, he raised her hands and kissed the palms, his tongue stealing out to touch her flesh.

She shivered at this intimate caress, and a deep yearning to enfold him, to take him into her body, to complete the ritual of love engulfed Georgie. He seemed eager, and so was she. What did anything else matter? "Yes, my love. And if you wish to do it here in the library, then we'd better hurry. I do not want Elizabeth, or your mother, or even worse, Jemmy barging in on us."

"That might be awkward, true." Rob squeezed her hands. "Still, I didn't want to rush through it. This will be a momentous occasion in our lives. I want us to savor it."

Dear, sweet man. But impractical as most men were. "That is lovely, my dear, but I fear if you want us to savor it, we will have to put it off. They will certainly come in search of us any moment."

"I cannot wait any longer, my love. I think we will have time." The love and longing in his face decided her.

"All right." She dropped his hands and turned her back to him. "Can you manage the laces?"

"What? Why would you want to do that?"

The surprise in his voice baffled her. "I don't want to ruin my favorite gown." Surely the man had undressed a woman before? An even more embarrassing thought occurred, and she grew still. "Rob, you're not a virgin, are you?"

"Georgie! What does that have to do with it?"

"I mean, it would not matter to me, my dear." She turned to him and grasped his hands again. "I have been married before. I know what to do."

His mouth twitched. "I assure you, I know what to do as well." He squeezed her hands tightly.

"Oh." She couldn't understand his hesitation, then. "So, we really should get on with it." She peered into the gloom at the door. "Someone could come in."

"That at least is true, so I will proceed." Rob's smile vanished as he went down on one knee, just like he was going to . . .

"Oh!" Startled, she tried to pull back, but he held on steadfastly to her hands.

"No, no. You are not getting away from me. Ever." Gazing deeply into her eyes, Rob took a deep breath. "Lady Georgina, it would be the greatest honor of my life if you would consent to marry me and become my wife. I have never felt for any other lady of my acquaintance what I feel when I see you. Which is that I want to spend the rest of my life making you the happiest of women." He bowed his head. "Will you, Georgie? Please, for God's sake, say yes. I don't think I can do this again."

"Yes, Rob. Yes, I will marry you." Joy erupted in her heart, so much happiness that she didn't know what to do. Should she kiss him? Should they shake hands? She wanted to jump up and down like she had done when she was a child, on the rare occasions when she had been taken out for a treat. This treat, however, would be hers forever.

Rob seemed to have no reservations. Slowly, he stood and pulled her to him. "May I now kiss the bride-to-be?"

"You may." She threw her arms around his neck and jumped into his arms.

Their lips met and held, their mouths melded perfectly together. As though they had always been meant to be as one. She wanted to drink in this moment, remember it just like this through the years.

Straightening as he eased her to the floor, Rob grinned widely at her. "Now that the proposal is over, we can turn to other, more interesting things this evening." He wiggled his eyebrows. "I believe you wanted to engage in a very different sort of activity a few minutes ago, my love."

Mortified, Georgie hid her face, wanting nothing more than to kill him.

"I am happy to oblige you, if you still desire to do so."

"Wretch." She pulled her hands from his. "You are enjoying my discomfiture far too much to be a proper gentleman."

"I don't think you agreed to marry me because I am a proper gentleman. You agreed because I am a pirate, who is willing to take his stolen booty when he can get it." Bending swiftly, he scooped her up over his shoulder and spun her around in a circle.

"Rob." Laughing so hard she hurt, Georgie beat him lightly on his back. "Unhand me, pirate."

"Your wish is ever my command, my lady." He stopped and carefully set her down. "Demand of me what you will."

"That I will do, this minute." She smoothed out her skirts, though they would probably never be the same again, and held out her hand to him. "Come with me to tell the others."

Grasping her hand, he led her to the door, but turned before opening it. "I will gladly break the news to my mother, your sister-in-law, and even your brother. I leave you, however, to tell Lulu by yourself."

Deliriously happy, Georgie sat primly next to Rob on the comfortable sofa in the drawing room, the fire burning merrily, candles aglow all over the room. She couldn't help stealing sideways glances at him and, every so often, surreptitiously squeezing the hand that rested so conveniently next to her on the cushion.

"The largest problem they face is the blasted contract Father signed with Travers." Jemmy continued to pace around the drawing room, more than an hour after Georgie and Rob had entered to announce their betrothal. Her brother had wished them happy, but had seemed anxious ever since. "I'm not really certain such a thing can be broken. We'll need to consult a solicitor at the earliest possible moment."

"The bulk of our family affairs are overseen by Harcourt and Stokes in London," Lady St. Just offered. "We had a local solicitor in Penzance, but he died several years ago, and I have had no reason to need one since. Until now, perhaps." Peering at Georgie, she pursed her lips. "Lady Georgina has brought a new element of excitement to the family, to be sure. I wager we shall not need to worry about boredom ever again in St. Just."

"As I said to her earlier, she's the only adventure I now crave." Rob grasped Georgie's hand in both of his. "There's a reason for that, you know."

"Can they not simply be married here in St. Just?" Lowering her teacup, Elizabeth turned to her husband. "Georgie is past her majority and a widow. Even if settlements were signed, they only provided for her dowry and any children they might have."

"Unfortunately, Father was much wilier this time." Georgie sighed. She'd outwitted him once; she'd not be able to do so the same way again. "When I first came out, Father was busy with my other sisters' marriages, and so I had no impediment to falling in love with Isaac, until he asked for my hand and was refused. We discussed running away to Scotland, but Mr. Kirkpatrick was a clergyman and adamant about our being married in the Church of England. So we devised a plan to try to wait until I reached the age of one and twenty, after which we could, of course, marry without Father's consent."

"Three years is a terribly long time to have to wait, never knowing if your father would find a suitor of whom he approved." Elizabeth shook her head. "You must have been always on tenterhooks."

"It wasn't exactly three years, thank goodness, although Isaac and I were still not happy about it, of course. Fortunately, we did have an ally. My second year out Father was obsessed with arranging a marriage between me and the heir of the Duke of Carford. I had nothing against Lord Wrothby, except I did not love him. He too had placed his affections elsewhere, with a Miss Draper, and so was well willing to help me stall the proceedings. Eventually, Wrothby simply refused to agree to the match, and so Father and the duke had to end their negotiations." Georgie grinned at Elizabeth. "Father was so angry he agreed to the next gentleman who asked for me. Which turned out to be Lord Travers. And this is where luck and my birthday came in to save us."

"Your birthday?" Rob blinked. "How did your birthday come into this?"

"I was born in late July, you see. So when I had my come out, I was almost nineteen already. By the time Father had been disappointed by the duke, I was only a few months away from being twenty and one. I asked Father to allow me to finish my Season before thinking about marriage, and surprisingly he agreed. Likely because I did not put up a fuss about marrying Lord Travers." She wrinkled her nose. "But of course I never entertained that possibility for a moment. My birthday came, and the next day Isaac and I slipped away to the parish church and were married, as legal as you please."

"The vicar had read the banns in the marquess's own parish?" Eyebrows raised, Lady St. Just nodded to Georgie. "Your late husband came from bold stock, I see."

"Well, not quite that bold, my lady." Georgie smiled at the woman she prayed would be her new mother-in-law. "I'd saved money for over two years, mostly from my clothing allowance here and there." She leaned toward the marchioness, confidentially. "I did not have a proper new bonnet until my wedding. But I managed to save enough to send Isaac to London for a special license."

"Well done, my love." Rob kissed her knuckles. This time he refused to relinquish her hand at all, which would bring no complaint from her.

"And I almost missed the wedding because Rob here did not wish to leave Italy." With a mock glare at his friend, Jemmy helped himself to another cup of tea. "I returned to Blackham the morning of the wedding, then had to sneak off without letting on to Father at all where I was going. I don't believe he knows, to this day, that I attended."

"Is she the reason you dragged me away from Naples a full month early?" Frowning at her brother, Rob seemed to forget her presence beside him.

"She is."

Rob turned to her, mischief in his eyes. "Then you are forgiven, Brack. You should have told me at the time. I've been blaming you these last few years for the missed opportunities."

Pretending innocence, Georgie cocked her head. "Opportunities to do what, my dear?"

Her question caught him just as he was swallowing a mouthful of tea. Choking sounds erupted as her betrothed fought to keep his countenance. Finally the tea went down, although Rob was red in the face. "You will be the death of me yet, my dear. And opportunities to see more of the Italian countryside, of course."

"Of course," she murmured, smothering a smile.

"We have gone very far afield from the question at hand, Georgie." Elizabeth broke in. "What has your father done this time to ensure you go through with the marriage to Travers?"

Georgie sobered. Life could never be light for very long.

"Back in December, when Father sent for me, he told me that if he were to take me back into the family again, I had to sign a contract stating that I undertook the marriage of my own free will and would abide by the terms Father set forth." With a shrug, she looked away. "I had nowhere else to go. Charlotte was getting married, so I could not stay at her house any longer. To give myself a place to live and food to eat, I signed it."

"That was hardly a matter of free will, Georgie." Rob's face had darkened. "A choice of starving in a hedgerow or marrying a despicable man is no choice of free will at all."

"Still, her signature is on it. Father could contest any marriage performed in all of England." Scowling, Jemmy took a sip of his tea and made a face. "I'm sorry, but I let it get cold."

"I'll ring for more." The marchioness pulled a bellpull at her elbow. "Then simply don't get married in England." She looked expectantly at her son. "Go to Gretna Green. From what I hear, it is the fashionable place for elopements these days."

"It is also likely three weeks or more journey from here by carriage, Mamma." Rob sat rubbing his lip. "And the obvious place for us to go. Both Travers and Blackham will have their men hounding us the entire way. It's too much of a risk." He stood and strode to the sideboard. "I beg your pardon, ladies, but I fear I need something stronger than tea at the moment."

"But we don't need to go to Gretna Green, do we?" Georgie twisted around, looking from her brother to Rob. "We could be married anywhere as long as it's on Scottish soil. Isn't that right?"

"Yes, that is true." Decanter in hand, Rob paused. "Where in Scotland doesn't matter at all."

"Couldn't we sail up . . . up . . ." What on earth was the water on that side of the country called?

"The Irish Sea?" Rob's brows dipped, and he hastily poured his drink. "Well, it is considerably closer than traveling by carriage, but I will tell you, the sea is a great deal rougher than what we experienced on the way here from Portsmouth." Taking a long sip, he swallowed and sighed. "It would make those waves seem like a calm day. It's at least a day, maybe two days longer trip as well."

Georgie shuddered. That first day and night aboard the *Justine* had been nightmarish. To have to endure that horrible sickness for a lengthier time would be close to torture. But it would allow her and Rob to marry. "I'll do it." She rose and went to him. "I don't care that I'll be ill. As long as we get to Scotland and can be married, I will do it." She looked up at him and tried to smile. "You just have to make sure I survive 'til the end of the voyage."

"Where will you put in, Rob?" Jemmy came over and grabbed a glass.

"Portpatrick would be the closest port. About a five days' voyage with decent wind. We'll stay there for a day or two after the wedding, then return. In all, perhaps a little less a fortnight's journey." Gazing at Georgie, Rob ran his thumb down her cheek. "I'll make certain you survive, love. Trust me."

"Georgie may trust you, Rob, but I'm afraid I don't." Jemmy raised his glass. "I'm coming with you."

"What?" Both Georgie and Rob turned their heads to stare at her brother.

"You won't be married until the trip back, so I will be accompanying you as your chaperone. Or would you rather we go to Blackham and attempt to get Father's blessing?" Jemmy's smile would have made an alligator proud. "Rob has already gone a fair way to compromising you. I won't have him go any further."

"Do you forget, dear brother, that I am not some innocent little virgin? I was married a good deal longer than you have been." If Jemmy went with them, she and Rob would have no opportunity to anticipate the wedding. From the frustrated look on his face, Rob was having the exact same thought.

"And until you are married again, dear sister, you will remain as chaste as the virgin you once were." To her consternation the stubborn look her father always got—furrowed brow, pinched nose, poked-out lip—now appeared on Jemmy's face. The Cross family was certainly her cross to bear.

"Very well." She smirked at her brother. "Remember it was your choice when I cast up my accounts all over you."

Chapter Nineteen

Lulu at her feet, Georgie sat contentedly in her nightgown, brushing her bright, auburn hair a hundred strokes before the mirror, thinking of Rob's proposal and the life they could have together here at the castle. "It's rather like a fairy story really, Lulu," she confided to her companion. "The handsome prince sweeps the poor, downtrodden girl off her feet and brings her to his ancestral estate to live happily ever after." She switched hands and continued brushing on the other side. "Well, I'm not particularly downtrodden, nor actually poor at the moment, although that will soon be true. Still, he did sweep me off my feet there in the library. I'd say that counts, wouldn't you?"

Lulu growled, then yipped.

"I don't know how you can disapprove. The gentleman saved your life, you recall. I am willing to overlook a great deal of his shortcomings because of that one action." Georgie set the brush down and picked up her cream pot. "Not that he has many, you know."

Rubbing lavender-scented cream into her hands, she remembered the touch of his lips there on her palm, on her mouth, on her breasts. A shiver of longing raced down her spine. It had been so long since she'd had a man in her bed. Would it be strange, being intimate with someone other than Isaac? Her hand rubbing slowed. She had not stopped to consider that. She'd simply been enjoying the hot, flushed way Rob made her feel again. If it weren't such a private conversation, she'd ask Elizabeth how it had been for her. But of course, her friend wouldn't want to speak of it because the man she'd be talking about was Georgie's brother. Had Georgie known any of this would happen, she'd have asked Fanny while she was in Buckinghamshire. Fanny would tell her bluntly, and follow it up with advice on the subject, most likely.

Still, less than a week from now she'd know from her own experience. She trusted Rob with her life. If he'd wanted to make his proposal memorable, then certainly he'd find a way to make their nuptial night just as unforgettable. "He has been one to make an impression from the beginning, don't you agree, Lulu?"

Her pet yawned and snorted, then presented herself for her nightly good-night caress. Georgie obliged her, petting her head and silky ears, then scratching under her chin. Lulu replied with a lick to Georgie's hand, then trotted resolutely into the dressing room. Georgie had seen to a bed for her there with cushions. Lulu had not complained about the accommodations, for which Georgie was very grateful.

Sighing contentedly, she gazed around the magnificent chamber the marchioness had assigned to her. Rather grand for her own tastes, but perhaps, as Lady St. Just had intimated, they did not have many visitors this far away along the wild Cornish coast and wished to impress.

That thought brought Georgie up out of her chair. She padded over to the large window that overlooked the ocean and pulled back the heavy drapes. Chill air assailed her, even through the panes of glass. Still, she pressed her ear against the cold windowpane. Faintly the crash of waves against the rocks at the base of the crags could be heard even this far away. Day after tomorrow they would be out on that wild ocean, with even worse to come when they reached the Irish Sea. With a shudder she turned away and drew the drapes. She trusted Rob, but thoughts of the violently pitching ship made her queasy right here on dry land. She couldn't think about that right now. It was the only way for them to be married.

Forcing her thoughts away from the journey to come, Georgie made her way back to the massive four-poster bed that occupied the corner of the room nearest the fireplace and next to an oak door. She had tried that door earlier, thinking it led to a servant's chamber, but it had been locked with no key in the keyhole. A mystery she'd have to ask Rob about.

The magnificent bed, though it held no mystery, did instill a sense of awe in her. Never had she seen a bed so large. Three or perhaps four people could sleep comfortably in it. Spread with a burgundy silk velvet cover with a bold floral design, and matching curtains, the bed looked like a ceremonial dais for some huge monarch like Henry VIII. Not her choice, but she would be content to burrow under those covers. Despite the warmth of the fire, the room was chilly, and her nightgown was thin.

She shrugged off her robe, mounted the three steps up to the bed, and flung back the cover and sheet. Running her hand across the smooth expanse, she smiled. Clara had done her work well with the warming pan. Quickly Georgie jumped in, burrowing beneath the heavy covering and pulling it up to her chin, nice and cozy. Even cozier with two, but that wouldn't be for some days yet. Pity she could never bring herself to pull the curtains around her bed. The bedcurtains would help keep her warm, she knew, but the idea of being entombed gave her the shivers every time she even thought of it. She'd create her own little cocoon of warmth shortly. Slowly, Georgie relaxed, refusing to think

of the challenges she and Rob still faced. Instead she
imagined Rob with several little children, some auburn-
haired, some dark, running through the maze on a brilliant
summer's day, trying to catch her as she sped for the bench
at the dead end. Only the dead end turned into a door.
Laughing, Georgie opened it and slipped through and
was gone.

The creak of a real door must have dragged Georgie back
from her dream of frolicking in the maze. Groggy with
sleep, she listened for the click of Lulu's claws on the un-
carpeted portions of the floor, but no such sound filtered
through her dazed senses. A low *shushing* of shoes sliding
across carpet instead. Clara? Why would she be here in the
middle of the night? Why would anyone be here . . . ?

Rob. Georgie snapped wide-awake, not moving, but
breathing quickly and shallowly. He had come to anticipate
the wedding night. What must she do? Surely he must think
she desired to after her blunder in the library. Just thinking
about that misunderstanding right now made her want to
cover her head to hide her humiliation. Not because she
hadn't wished to be intimate with him, but because she had
made such a mistake at such a time. So did she want to do
it now?

With everything so unsettled regarding Lord Travers and
her betrothal to him, she just wasn't certain it would be
wise. In the very heated moment it had been one thing; now
that she was being rational, perhaps it would be best to put
off the moment. Savor it, as Rob had suggested. Although
he hadn't been talking about savoring that particular
moment. Still, he would likely indulge her on the matter.
They'd be married in five days, and then the waiting would
be over.

The bed dipped as Rob slid between the sheets. She'd forgotten what it was like to have someone sleep beside her, hold her as they snuggled together. Perhaps it wouldn't be too much temptation if they did that for a while. Smiling, she stretched. "I heard you come in. I know why you are here, and I want to as well, but I think we must wait until this unpleasantness with Lord Travers is past. We will be married soon, so a little restraint should be possible." She turned over toward him. "However, that doesn't mean we can't enjoy each other in other ways."

"The only way I plan to enjoy myself tonight, my lady, is between your legs."

The ugly, rasping voice told Georgie exactly who had crawled into her bed. The stench of alcohol merely confirmed that the odious Lord Travers had somehow managed to sneak his way into the castle and find his way into her room. Not for long. She drew in breath to scream the alarm, but a rough hand clamped down over her mouth, stifling her voice and almost cutting off her air.

"Oh, no, my lady. You're not sounding an alarm until I'm certain it's me and no one else you'll be marrying. Once I spill my seed in you, St. Just won't want you anymore. Won't want to live with the possibility that his heir is actually mine." He pushed his hand harder onto her mouth as he shifted his weight, fumbling with her gown under the covers.

God, she could not let this happen. Pushing her gown back down with one hand, she slapped at his with the other.

"Stop that thrashing, or I'll do more than stop your mouth. I've got big hands, my lady." He chuckled, and her skin crawled. "Hands that can give you pleasure or bring you pain. Or stop your breath until you swoon, real ladylike."

Georgie froze. She had to have her wits about her if she were to get out of this without being ravished. Slowly, she breathed in. She must wait her chance.

"It won't be the first time I've been in a lady who didn't know what had happened until I was all done. Fine for me, not so much pleasure for her." He'd rucked her nightgown up again and proceeded to fumble around his hips.

Unfortunately, she knew very well what that meant. What could she do to stop him from violating her that would also stop him from shutting off her air? He'd trapped one of her hands beneath his body, but he also had to keep one of his hands on her mouth. So they were more or less evenly matched. Breathing slowly and calmly, she tried to take as much air in as she could. At the same time, she stealthily slid her usable hand down between her legs. If he couldn't get through to her nether parts, he couldn't hurt her.

Suddenly, he lunged on top of her, his hard member pushing against her fingers then sliding upward. As he moved, something cool and squishy landed against her hand. Isaac had called them his jewels. They were indeed priceless. Clamping her fingers around Travers's soft flesh, Georgie gave a mighty squeeze.

Travers sat bolt upright, screaming in a loud, high-pitched voice.

"Help! Help!" The moment his hand left her mouth, she screeched aloud, almost as loudly as her attacker. With a mighty shove, she pushed him out of the bed. She couldn't see him bumping down the steps, but the thudding of his head told her he'd hit at least one.

Wild barking erupted from the vicinity of the dressing room.

"Lulu, attack, attack. Give no quarter!"

Furious growling turned into yips and tearing cloth.

Georgie dove for the candle on the bedside table, struck the tender, and lit the wick just as Travers's screams renewed in volume. She lifted the light over the other side of the bed to find Lulu growling, her teeth sunk into the backside of

Travers's breeches as, still screeching, he attempted to crawl away.

"Oh, no, my lord. You will face the music in full force." Leaning down, Georgie grabbed the chamber pot from beneath the bed, lifted it high, and brought it down with all the might she could muster on top of the earl's head. It shattered into a thousand tiny shards, drenching the man as he lay prostrate on the floor.

The door to the corridor burst open. Rob and Jemmy raced into the room, the candle in Rob's hand flickering as they tried to look everywhere at once.

"Georgie!" Her brother glanced from the body on the floor to her, his face blank and pale.

"Georgie!" Rob started toward her, only to be met by the still growling Lulu. She'd relinquished Travers's breeches, although around the tear in the seat Georgie spied a red stain spreading.

"Lulu, stop. Come." Georgie sat up on the side of the bed, wiping her eyes with shaking hands. The past few minutes had been a blur of terror she still couldn't quite comprehend.

Lulu sailed up the stairs onto the cover and sat beside her mistress.

Georgie wrapped her arms around the spaniel and dissolved into tears.

"My love, are you hurt?" Rob tried to make his way to her, but Lulu bared her teeth at him, and he stopped. "If he hurt you . . ."

"No, he didn't have a chance to."

"What happened, Georgie?" Jemmy had made his way to the bed.

"I don't quite know." She sniffed and let go of Lulu. All she wanted was Rob's arms around her. "I was asleep, and I woke up when someone got into the bed with me." She used her sleeve to wipe her eyes. "At first I thought it was y . . . you, Rob."

"What?" Jemmy rounded on his friend, fist clenched. "Why would she think you would come into her bed-chamber, St. Just?"

"Jemmy, if you don't stop that I'll tell Lulu to bite you." Opening her arms to Rob, Georgie sent a silent plea.

He darted forward, disregarding both dog and brother, and swept her up in his arms. Cradling her, he carried her to a chair, and sat, Lulu at their feet. "Shh. It will be all right. I've got you now. No one will harm you, ever again. I swear it on my life."

She burrowed deeper into his embrace, resting her head on his neck, safe at last. Slowly her heart began to calm.

"Georgie." Dropping into a chair next to them, Jemmy peered at her, concern in his face. "Can you please tell us what happened? Travers managed to sneak into your room?" He frowned at Rob. "How is that possible?"

"My first thought is that someone let him in, but I've always considered my servants loyal." Rob's tone was grim. "So I pray that is not the case. I will make inquiries to see if that avenue is unfounded. And there is another, very plausi-ble explanation. The smugglers' tunnel."

"A smugglers' tunnel?" Jemmy blinked. "You really were a pirate?"

"Not until I stole your sister's heart away, I wasn't." Rob kissed her head.

"Rob was about to show the tunnel to me when we dis-covered you and Elizabeth and Lord Travers had arrived. Where is it, Rob?"

"In the larder, behind a false panel. It slopes directly down to the bottom of the cliff. There's a hidden entrance there where the smugglers would bring the goods."

"How would Travers know about that?" Peering at the unmoving earl, Jemmy frowned.

"He probably plied one of the old timers with drink until he talked about the good old smuggling days and learned about it that way."

"But how did Travers know what room I was in?" An even better question than how he'd gotten into the castle.

Rob shrugged. "I have no idea. Perhaps he bribed a servant? We have several who live in the village and come in to work during the day. An extra coin would be quite tempting to some of the poorest. We shall try to pry that out of Travers when he awakens."

Georgie looked over at the downed peer. He hadn't moved a muscle. "Do you think he's dead?"

"Dead? Who is dead?" Elizabeth rounded the corner of the doorway, her dressing gown flying out behind her, and stopped short. "Oh, dear Lord. Is Lord Travers dead?" She wrinkled her nose. "What is that odor? It smells like—"

"A chamber pot." Georgie raised her head. "I hit him with mine." She turned back to Rob, tears trickling again. "I am so sorry, Rob. I'm afraid I shattered it on Lord Travers's head, so I hope your mother was not very f-fond of that particular p-pot."

Gathering her back to his chest, Rob shushed her again. So comforting to be crooned to that way. He made her feel so warm and loved. She never wanted to leave him.

"I'm certain she will be happy to give it to such a worthy cause."

"Georgie." Elizabeth had turned her attention on her friend again. "What is going on—Oh!"

Groaning, Lord Travers stirred for the first time since Georgie had hit him, then sank back to the floor.

Elizabeth skittered away, and Jemmy hurried to her side. "Stay here out of the way, my dear." He motioned Rob toward the fallen man. "I believe we have a bit of rubbish that needs throwing out, St. Just."

Much to Georgie's dismay, Rob deposited her in the chair. "Stay there, sweetheart. This won't take long at all."

"How is it you two come to still be dressed?" With a glare of suspicion, Elizabeth narrowed her eyes at Jemmy. "It is the middle of the night, you know."

"Nothing suspicious, Lady Brack, I assure you." Rob grinned at her. "After you and the other ladies retired, Jem and I sat to more brandy and reminisced about our Grand Tour travels. We were just coming up the stairs when we heard Georgie cry out." He glanced down at Travers. "A good thing we are dressed. We have work to do."

"What should we do with him?" Jemmy bent over the earl, then rose swiftly. He clamped a handkerchief over his nose. "That must have been an excellent knock, Georgie. He's only moved that once, though he is alive."

"More's the pity." Rob went to stand over the body, black fury in his face. "I say we toss him off the parapet. It would make our lives so much easier, don't you think?"

"Don't be so bloodthirsty, pirate." Shivering, Georgie sat up in the chair. She wrapped her arms around her chest, trying to get warm. The fire, though close, couldn't take away her chill tonight. Only Rob could do that.

"My dear." Speeding over to her, Elizabeth stripped her own robe from her and pulled it around Georgie's shoulders. "It must have been a terrible shock." She looked up expectantly at Jemmy. "Can you tell me, my love, what did happen?"

"By some foul means, yet to be determined, Travers entered the castle after most of us had gone to bed, got into Georgie's bed, and attempted to accost her." Gingerly, Jemmy leaned over and rolled the earl over on his back. The fall of his trousers fell open, exposing his nether regions, his member shrunk away to nothing and his thingamabobs red and swollen.

"Dear Lord." Jemmy reared back as Rob leaned closer.

"Oh, dear." Georgie and Elizabeth quickly hid their faces in each other's necks.

"Georgie, what . . . happened?" Rob stood as well, looking rather pale.

"He was trying to ravish me. He had his hand over my mouth, threatening to suffocate me if I moved or tried to scream." She pulled Elizabeth's robe tighter around her. "So I managed to put my hand down between my legs, to keep him away. And when he lunged at me, his . . . member slid up onto my wrist and his . . . jewels landed in my hand, so I gave them a hard squeeze." She demonstrated, making her hand into a fist. "Like I was squishing a ripe peach."

Both men groaned and looked away. Jemmy bent at the waist, as if he were in pain, while Rob walked stiffly away, cutting his eyes toward Georgie and shaking his head.

"For goodness sake, Jemmy." Elizabeth spoke sharply. She'd raised her head to discover Lord Travers still immodestly unclothed. "Make him decent, if you please."

"I'm glad I'm only Georgie's brother," Jemmy said, stooping to button up the unfortunate man. "You're going to be married to her shortly. I'd watch my step if I were you."

"Can we please just get him out of my home?" Taking charge again, Rob grabbed Travers under the right arm and motioned to Jemmy to follow suit with the left.

"You will refrain from tossing him off the roof or out the window, won't you, my dear?" Georgie called as they headed for the door.

"I promise to restrain myself as much as possible," Rob called as they dragged the still unconscious earl from her chamber. "When we're done, I'll wake a maid to come clean up the mess."

"Elizabeth, can you light our way?" With both hands occupied, Jemmy nodded to the candle she'd set on the bedside table.

"Will you be all right left alone, my dear?" Sweet that Elizabeth would worry more about her than about her own husband falling down the stairs in the dark.

"I will be fine. I have my guard dog here with me, don't I, Lulu?"

Lulu yipped and stood, as though longing for another fight.

"Then I will leave you for a short while only. I shall light them down, then return to you."

Shaking her head, Georgie rose and handed Elizabeth back her robe. "You need your rest. Go back to bed, and take your husband with you." The only one Georgie would want in her bed tonight was Rob, and that was impossible given the circumstances. "Good night."

As Georgie headed for the door to shut it, she met Rob's gaze in the uncertain light. The longing in his face exactly matched the longing in her heart. She sighed and gave him a small smile that he returned before he vanished into the dark corridor.

They had to wait this time. But not for very much longer.

Chapter Twenty

"I believe I could have slept the clock around after last night's excitements. Would you pass me the strawberry jam, Elizabeth?" Slathering butter on a piece of toast, Georgie looked expectantly at Elizabeth.

"Why didn't you, my dear? You certainly deserved to keep to your bed much later than this." Elizabeth handed her the pretty-cut crystal jelly dish, fashioned like a shell.

"I really had thought I wouldn't awaken until well after noon, since I don't believe my eyes closed again until almost dawn." Even then she'd fallen into a fitful sleep, starting up at imagined noises until exhaustion had claimed her for a little while. "However, I found myself awake and alert at eight o'clock, my stomach very noisily demanding food. So I rang for Clara, and here I am."

"You should rest today, my dear. Gather your strength for the coming journey."

Eying her half-eaten toast, and imagining the rough seas ahead, Georgie slid the bread and jam back onto her plate. She needed to find a way to distract herself from thinking about their voyage. At least at mealtimes. "Perhaps I shall nap this afternoon. I do want to speak to Rob, but I've not seen him this morning."

"My son is currently in the kitchen questioning the

servants about some intruder who appears to have accosted you last night, Lady Georgina." Lady St. Just sailed into the breakfast room in a swirl of cerulean-blue silk. "Good morning, ladies."

"Good morning, Lady St. Just."

"Good morning, my lady."

"As I predicted, we shall not be in need of any other type of excitement now that Lady Georgina has come to stay." The lady sat at the end of the long table nearest Georgie and Elizabeth. "I trust you were not injured in any way, my dear. Rob assures me you acquitted yourself rather handily in thwarting the villain." Nestling a napkin in her lap, Lady St. Just apparently ignored the strangled expression on Elizabeth's face and Georgie's choked-back laugh.

When she could compose herself, Georgie reached for her abandoned eggcup and tapped smartly on the shell. Appetite restored. Lady St. Just would provide a wonderful distraction. "Thank you, my lady. I believe I did go a far way toward helping with his apprehension." She looked up from her methodical cracking of her egg. "I fear I did use some unorthodox weaponry, so in the process one of your chamber pots was destroyed. I don't know if your son mentioned it or not."

The marchioness stirred her tea, round and round, her eyes mere slits. "He did not. One raises one's children to be forthcoming; however, I warn you, Lady Georgina, that does not mean you always reap what you sow. When Robin returns from the kitchen, I shall speak to him about the chamber pot without delay."

Good Lord. The last thing Georgie had meant to do was to get Rob in the suds. She hit the egg a glancing blow that took the top clean off. It sailed across the table, onto Elizabeth's plate.

Wide blue eyes met hers. The utter shock on Elizabeth's face only made it worse.

Georgie bit her lip trying to smother the laugh that would not be stopped. She whooped, laughing so long and so loudly that tears came to her eyes. When finally she calmed enough to gasp in a breath, the laughter continued, not only from Elizabeth, but also from the marchioness herself. Georgie looked up in astonishment.

"Oh, my dear. I see you prefer golf to tennis then. Well played, indeed." Lady St. Just touched the napkin to the sides of her eyes. "No wonder my son is enchanted with you. You would have the Prince Regent himself in an apoplexy."

"Who is having an apoplexy, Mamma?" Rob strode into the breakfast room on the tail end of his mother's comment. Looking about the room as if expecting to see someone prostrate, he frowned. "What is going on?"

That sent them all into another peal of laughter, Georgie holding her sides as her eyes streamed. "My dear, you have come at the exact worst time to get any sense out of us." Breathing hard to stop her giggles, which then brought on a fit of hiccoughs, she stared fixedly at Rob and held her breath. This often worked when she got the dratted nuisance.

Still frowning, Rob sat down beside her and laid his napkin in his lap. "I do not see what is so funny about having an apoplexy."

They burst out again, laughing even harder. Poor Rob. He must think himself the butt of the jest. Now he was sitting back, eying her coldly, his arms tightly crossed over his chest. "Georgina, please tell me what is going on. I have news about Travers, and here you sit, laughing like lunatics." He trained his stare on his mother. "Even you, Mamma. I am surprised."

"Do not be, Robin. I still have a sense of humor, despite my decrepit appearance."

The marchioness was an extremely handsome woman, scarcely touched by age, save a tinge of silver in her dark hair. Neither could her face or skin give away her years. Rob, of course, must have heard this all before.

"If you looked any younger or lovelier, Mamma, the villagers would suspect you of witchcraft or perhaps assume you had found a fountain of youth somewhere in the smugglers' tunnel." He managed to shake off his brief fit of pique and smiled at them. "Good morning, ladies. Please forgive my lack of greeting earlier, but I was so completely startled by your conversation, which I still do not understand, that I neglected to give you my greeting. Please accept it now."

"Good morning, my lord." Elizabeth had sobered quicker than the other ladies.

"Good morning, Robin." His mother's glance was sterner. Perhaps she was about to inquire about the dratted chamber pot he hadn't mentioned.

Taking matters into her own hands before things could get any more out of hand, Georgie smiled brightly at him and grasped his arm. "Good morning, my dear. We have been conversing about a great many very interesting things this morning." She cast her mind back, trying to retrieve anything that did not hint at their hilarity. "Such as golf."

Elizabeth sputtered and dropped her napkin over the incriminating bit of egg.

"Why, my love? Do you play?"

Lady St. Just raised one delicate eyebrow. "Apparently only at the breakfast table."

In the mayhem that ensued, Rob gathered bits and pieces of the story, laughing himself finally at the mad circumstances that had led to Georgie's display of golfing and his own unwitting part in the farce.

"I will admit, my life has had not one quiet moment since I met Lady Georgina." Rob took her hand and kissed it. "But I would not change one moment of it. Well"—he stopped and seemed to consider—"I admit I would change having to leap into icy cold water, if I could. Although I would then have missed a terribly efficient method of warming oneself up." His eyes twinkled at Georgie, and the heat rose in her cheeks. "You must demonstrate it again, my dear."

"Speaking of our first journey"—she tried to shift the subject from that terribly intimate moment—"when will we begin our next voyage together, Rob? I recall last time we had to hurry to catch the evening tide. Will we leave in the evening again?"

"Not this time. After breakfast Jem and I will go to the harbor and make ready the ship. I've sent round to the crew, so they will be arriving shortly." He looked up as Jemmy entered. "Just the man I wanted to see. Will you come down to the ship with me? There is much to do if we are to leave tomorrow morning." He smiled at Georgie. "That is when the tide should be running right."

"It's been a few years since I sailed, other than this short journey, but I hope I can be of some service to you, Rob." Jemmy settled into the chair beside Elizabeth. "You are not too fatigued this morning, my dear? You had a very late night. Perhaps you should go lie down, and I shall bring you a tray."

Georgie got the feeling her sister-in-law was rolling her eyes inwardly. Elizabeth already had two children from her previous marriage, so carrying a child was nothing new to her. She'd confided to Georgie that sometimes Jemmy managed to be too solicitous toward her. "I wish to be thought capable of more than just carrying this child," had been Elizabeth's sentiment when they'd been at Fanny's wedding. Perhaps that was why Elizabeth had insisted on accompanying Jemmy to Cornwall. Well, good for Elizabeth. What was life without a bit of adventure?

"My lord." Myers entered the breakfast room and bowed, a trifle of concern showing in his otherwise inscrutable face.

As a rule, butlers were unflappable. Her father's butler at the castle would likely have borne burning at the stake with the same enduring calm with which he had answered his master's door for the past thirty years. Something was up.

"Yes, Myers?"

"There are several liveried servants at the front door demanding to be shown to Lady Georgina."

Georgie sat up at attention. "Travers's men?"

Rob shrugged, but rose. "They could very well be. Having not succeeded last evening, he may have decided to try brute force. I told you, Jem, we should have settled his hash while we had the chance."

Tossing his napkin onto the table, Jemmy bounded up, his face all frowns. "Dash it, Rob, you can't just kill a peer."

"I could have if you'd let me. There's no other way to have satisfaction of him, save a duel." Rob looked thoughtful. "That is an idea. A nice, permanent solution. God knows we don't want word of what he did to get out."

"Well, if your butler is right, you may get your chance sooner rather than later."

"True. Summon all the footmen, grooms, coachmen, and gardeners, Myers. Have them assemble in the kitchen and await my instructions. Come on, Brack." His smoky gray eyes shone with excitement. "Let's go see how many of these fellows we can number to our accounts in the next half an hour."

"I'm coming too." On her feet before she could get the sentence out, Georgie wrapped her long, China silk shawl around her shoulders like armor. "I am the cause of all this ruckus. I should at least be there to cheer you on to victory."

"And I will accompany Georgie, Jemmy." Elizabeth had risen as well, her face set. "My support for her has been the reason for my entire journey. I will not fail her now." She held up a finger, not allowing her husband to rebut her statement. "And I will not allow myself to miss this encounter for the wide world." Lady St. Just stood and stared at her son, as if daring him to make her stay behind.

Rob took one look at the three women and shook his head. "We don't know who we are fighting yet, although Travers's servants seem the logical conclusion. Come with me." Rob led them through the corridor, down the front stairs to the castle's main door. "In any case, your safety is paramount, my dear." He'd managed to stay beside Georgie and now spoke directly in her ear. "If this turns against us, you are to retreat to the larder. After last night's intrusion, I instructed Joseph to take you, Lady Brack, and my mother to safety in Penzance, at the home of a friend of mine, Captain Martin. Ask him, on my behalf, to take you back to London. It won't be an easy journey, but it will likely keep you out of the hands of Travers."

"And what should I do then?" she hissed back, angrier than she'd ever been at him. "Do you plan to meet us in London?"

He avoided her eyes.

Just so. "As I thought. So my answer is no."

"Georgie." He pulled her to the side of the entry hall. "I am trying to keep you safe, my love. If something should happen to me . . ."

"If something happens to you, I will be here with you." Her words blazed forth, spoken directly from her heart. "By your side as though I were your wife in truth, instead of just in promise. Because if something happened to you, I would not want to go on. Again. It would be too cruel. You would not do that to me, Rob."

"You will be the death of me yet." He sighed and pulled her into his arms. "All right. Stay here. Let me go with your brother and find out who these liveried servants are and what they want with you. Then we will know better what we can and cannot do."

She nodded gravely and gave his hand a squeeze. "I will be waiting here for your return."

"I love you, Georgina." He pressed his lips fiercely to hers. "Be ready," he said, then strode to the massive oak door, and nodded.

Myers straightened his jacket, raised his chin, and opened the door.

Although Rob had steeled himself for a sizeable group of men, he had expected them to be locals who Travers might have hired for a day, merely for intimidation. If that were the case, he and Brack and the castle servants could likely withstand any onslaught they mounted. Some hired men might even think better of going up against their marquess, and slink off home when no one was looking. What Rob was not prepared for was the sea of men—there had to be at least fifty, strangers every one—standing like an invading army, their leaders in front dressed in black jackets with gold braid and buttons.

"Dear God." Brack had come up beside him at the doorway, his face gone pale.

"They certainly aren't what I expected," Rob whispered. "Especially not from Travers."

"They're not Travers's men."

"What? How do you know that?" Rob stole another glance at his friend, who had clenched his jaw so tightly the tendons had popped into clear relief.

"Because I know these servants." Raw anger flashed across Brack's face. The kind that flamed white-hot until it burnt itself out.

"Then whose men are they?"

"My father's."

Rob started, but checked himself. The marquess was living up to his reputation. "What are they doing here?"

"I'm about to find out. Wait here a moment. Let me see if I can get them to disburse." Jemmy straightened his back and marched down the front steps, like a general about to address the troops.

To hell with waiting. This was his home, and by Christ he was going to be the one to defend it. Rob dashed down the stairs, on his friend's heels.

"Mr. Buckley, isn't it?" Brack seemed unconcerned with anything save having remembered the man's name. "From my father's estate in Somerset."

"Yes, my lord." The tall, bulky steward, flanked by two even larger footman in livery, eyed him coolly.

"You are somewhat far from home, Buckley. This is the estate of the Marquess of St. Just. What is the meaning of this"—Brack looked out at the sea of unfriendly faces armed with a variety of weaponry—"assemblage?"

"Begging your pardon, my lord, but his lordship, your father, has instructed me to find Lady Georgina, who he suspected had been taken here against her will, and return her to Blackham Castle."

"But as you can see, I am here now and have things well in hand. I have spoken with Lady Georgina, and the entire episode was a misunderstanding." The commanding edge to Jem's voice and his stern visage was credible, nothing at all like his usual boyish demeanor. Good show, that.

"Your father gave me specific instructions, my lord." The steward reached into his jacket pocket and withdrew a letter. "I am to travel here, to St. Just, recover the lady from the bandits who stole her, and return her." He offered the paper to Jem. "I was also instructed to do so without informing you."

Jem tore the letter open, swiftly read the lines, then curled the missive in his fist. "I have written to my father that I would take care of this matter." He glared at Buckley. "You can stand these men down, if you please. I will see to it that the lady reaches Blackham Castle with all haste."

"I beg your pardon, again, my lord." The man's stance, however, was anything but conciliatory.

Restraining himself from throttling the man was the greatest feat of self-control Rob had ever accomplished.

"But I take my orders from the marquess, as I always have. Please have Lady Georgina brought out with her maid and her trunks. Her father insists we make the best possible time."

"Over my bleached bones." To hell with restraint. He pushed his way in front of Jemmy. "The lady is no longer of your concern. She is now betrothed to me and will remain here, with her brother, until such time as we can have the banns read and be married." See what they made of that.

Buckley looked taken aback, then his eyes narrowed. "The lady is betrothed to Lord Travers and will be taken to her father. I will request, civilly, that you bring Lady Georgina to me or step out of the way so we"—he nodded to the two huge footmen, towering over him—"can fetch her out here."

Drawing himself up straight, jaw firm, Rob planted his feet, transforming into every inch the marquess he'd been since the age of five. "You stand on the property of the Marquess of St. Just. Neither you nor your master has any authority here nor over any of the inhabitants of Castle St. Just. If they wish to seek sanctuary here under my protection, then they are entitled to it by my decree, given this date, this instant. Anyone"—he gazed out over the sea of angry faces—"who tries to oppose that edict will be treated as a hostile with the intent of overthrowing the marquessate. Anyone caught doing so can be held as committing treason against the Crown, as the title was created by the King's grace in 1622." Rob prayed to God none of these men knew the law. "Those persons will thereby be subject to the punishment for treason, which is death."

Immediately a low rumbling went up throughout the gathering. Feet shuffled, and the mood of the crowd changed from belligerent to cautious. They might have come prepared for a fight, but not at the cost of their lives. At the far edge the multitude seemed to fan out, as though some men had decided to leave. Had he pulled off the greatest bluff of his life?

Buckley turned to the crowd and spoke to one man. At once, a murmur rippled through the mob.

"What do you think?" Rob glanced at Jemmy.

The steward turned back to them and raised his hand. "Forward!"

"I think they're more afraid of Father than of you or the Crown."

The horde surged toward the castle.

"Damn." Rob leaped back, dragging Jemmy with him. Buckley swept up to him, and Rob let fly with the right hook he'd perfected at the boxing saloon in London. The steward went down like a tree felled in the woods. Jackson himself would have been proud.

Jemmy had acquitted himself well with one of the two liveried servants, but Rob and Jemmy couldn't fight this many unaided. Rob dropped back to the castle door, Jemmy at his side, ready to slip inside and bolt the door, when the doors burst open and the castle servants swarmed out, brandishing everything from soup pots to the ancient spit that Cook used to roast the traditional Christmas boar.

Grinning, Rob reversed course and waded into the fray. He grabbed up a fallen staff and swung it at the head of the other liveried footman. The man ducked, made a grab at the stick, and tried to jerk it out of Rob's hands. Rob let go, punched the man in the face, then grasped the pole once again and moved cheerfully on to his next victim.

What a glorious day to do battle.

Chapter Twenty-One

"Ouch." Rob shied back as Georgie tried to apply a cloth soaked in witch hazel to the bruised knuckles of his right hand. The skin was broken in several places, and the whole hand was swollen. Sitting on a small hassock drawn up next to a table spread with various medicinal paraphernalia Cook had supplied, he'd finally given himself over to Georgie's attempts to clean and dress the minor wounds.

"Hold still, please." She dabbed the medicine on relentlessly. "If you are going to act like a pirate, you should at least adopt a more stoic attitude to your treatment."

"I am not the only one wincing in pain, you know." He nodded to the other bodies that littered the chairs, sofas, and floor of the castle's largest drawing room, from which groans and yelps erupted at short intervals.

Shaking her head, Georgie surveyed the minor carnage brought about by the mercifully quick campaign on the castle steps some hours earlier. "You were lucky you weren't killed, Rob."

"We had the advantage of defending our home and our fair maiden." He picked up her hand and kissed it. "Everyone rose splendidly to the occasion. I think half the men were jubilant to actually fight for something they love." He squeezed her hand and gazed into her eyes until her cheeks heated like coals. "None of them went off to the war, including me, but we all long to demonstrate our willingness to sacrifice for the ones we love. It's a vital part of being a man."

"I cannot thank you enough for making the stand for me." Tossing the soiled rag onto the table, Georgie sighed and took up the bandage Cook had also supplied, winding it around Rob's hand. "I don't know what I would have done had they succeeded in taking me." Thoughts of her father's retribution had almost made her ill when she'd learned he'd sent his men to seize her and take her home.

"They would never have taken you, Georgie. I would never let anyone or anything harm you. Believe that." The strength of Rob's conviction warmed her heart.

"I do, my love." She stole a glance around the room, but everyone seemed occupied with the other wounded. Quickly, she dipped her head, kissing him with a fierceness that sprang from deep inside her. This was the man she would spend her life with, who she would stand with and die beside if necessary. Pray God it was not.

When she raised her head, Rob's eyes had a dazed look, and a lopsided smile was on his lips. "If that is how you are going to thank me for going into battle, I shall have to create a confrontation or invent a campaign on a regular basis."

"Wretch." She sat next to him, and he put his arm around her. "I will thank you a thousand times better if you *don't* go getting yourself into mischief. I want my husband unbruised and unbroken. So much better when all your parts are working."

"Don't worry, sweetheart. All the really important ones are." He waggled his eyebrows. "Care to find out how well they are working at the moment?"

"Rob." She leaned her head against his chest. "What are we going to do now?"

Sighing, he looked about the room.

The injured servants had mostly been seen to. Elizabeth and, surprisingly, Lady St. Just had worked alongside Cook and the housemaids to tend the cuts, gashes, bruises, and black eyes. Everyone was sore, but in rousing good spirits.

"We do exactly as we had planned. Tomorrow we sail to Scotland and get married, and then all of your father's machinations will be for naught. Buckley has set a guard before the door, but I'm betting he hasn't had time to discover the smugglers' tunnel. However, if Travers could find out about it, so will your father's steward. We must act quickly."

"Then why not leave today?" The quicker they were on their way, the sooner they could be married.

"Because, my love, neither the wind nor the tide is right. Trust me on this. We do not want to end up thrashing about on the ocean, going in the wrong direction." He kissed her temple, and peace washed over her. "We sail at dawn." He screwed up his mouth and frowned, though his eyes twinkled with mischief. "Dawn is a bit too early for me. I say we wait until after breakfast. Can't sail on an empty stomach, can we?"

"That is the only way I intend to sail." Georgie rose and held out her hand to him. "I must go tell Clara the journey is indeed still on. She'll need to commence packing. Come with me?"

"I will escort you to your chamber, then I must instruct Lovell to pack me as well before making sure we have provisions ready to take to the ship." Grinning, Rob wound her arm through his. "So many things to think about when one is eloping and evading two different parties trying to thwart one's efforts. Once we are married I think I will take to my bed for a week." He winked at her. "Care to join me there?"

"Oh, most assuredly, my love." Georgie returned his grin

as they headed into the corridor. "Although I suspect we will end up even more exhausted when that week is done."

"You'll want this traveling gown for tomorrow morning, my lady?" The fire crackled merrily in the grate as Clara busied herself helping Georgie prepare for bed.

"The brown? Yes, I believe that one will do. I don't wish to take too much with me, Clara. It will all have to be unpacked again when we return." Excitement washed through Georgie as she sat in front of the mirror, though she tried to restrain herself. This time next week she and Rob would be man and wife. Tingles spread from her innermost core all the way to her fingers and toes at the thought of her and Rob entwined in each other's arms, a tangle of sheets all around them.

"My lady?"

The maid's voice brought her out of her daydream. Clara stood before her holding out two day gowns. "Will these do? Or would you prefer the green brocade? That one might be warmer."

Lord, Georgie must keep her mind on her business. She resumed industriously brushing her hair. "I think those will do nicely. I won't want anything so formal onboard. My pelisse will suffice for warmth, or I can remain below-decks."

"Your pelisse is simply not what it used to be, my lady, if I must say so." Clara sniffed. "I've tried and tried to get the wrinkles out of it, but it's never been right ever since you got it wet. And the fur has become matted in places in the lining. If we were closer to a dressmaker, I'd say you needed to bespeak a new one."

"Well, that point is moot. We are not near a dressmaker, and we are technically still under siege, although Rob assured me at dinner that the few men remaining out there won't cause any trouble. Not to mention I will be at sea in a matter of hours." Georgie rose, wrapping her arms around her chest and going to peer out at the moonlit night. A little light bounced off the distant waves. Not long now until she was out there on the water once more. She shivered, and it had nothing to do with the cold.

"Very well, my lady. Did you need anything more to-night?"

"No, Clara, thank you. But I will need to be ready at first light, even though the marquess says we will breakfast first." She wrinkled her nose. "*He* will breakfast first and heartily, I hope, as there likely won't be much in the way of hot food on this voyage. Barnes has been spirited away by his wife and daughter to look after her toddler while she is attending to the birth of her next child."

"Hard to imagine Mr. Barnes looking after a babe." Shaking her head, Clara headed toward the dressing room.

"I suppose if it is your flesh and blood it becomes a different matter." Georgie had never taken care of children before, but if she and Rob were to have one . . . Her heart raced at the thought. Well, she'd likely act differently as well. God bless Mr. Barnes. Hopefully the man had laid in a goodly supply of hardtack for her before he left for more domestic duties.

"Likely it does, my lady." Clara opened the door to the dressing room as furious barking erupted.

"Lulu! Did you get shut up in there?" Georgie gathered the frenzied little dog to her, lifting her up and almost being licked to death in the process. "We have to be more careful, Clara." She rubbed Lulu under her chin. "Poor thing. You wanted your good-night rubbing, didn't you?" Kneeling down on the floor, Georgie set the spaniel down, then proceeded with her bedtime ritual of rubbing and chin scratching. "There you go, my dear."

Lulu snorted, then sauntered back into the dressing room.

"And who do you think will do that while we're away in Scotland, my lady?" Clara had picked up a pair of half boots and was polishing them industriously.

"We?" Rising, Georgie cocked her head one way, then the other. Clara had never declared her intention of accompanying them. "Did I say I was taking you? One chaperone on this trip will be one too many."

"Two is too few where you are concerned, my lady. You and his lordship need chaperoning." Clara gave the boot a vigorous swipe with the cloth. "I've seen the way he looks at you."

Chuckling, Georgie returned to her toilette table and picked up the brush. "I should hope he would look at me with a bit of fondness, Clara. We are getting married in a day or two."

"More than 'a bit of fondness,' to be sure, my lady."

That was nothing but true. The smoldering looks she'd caught him sending her whenever they were in the same room were almost indecent. Even married couples were expected to restrain their passion in public. The Marquess of St. Just, however, did not seem to care for that *ton* edict.

"Both you and my brother seem to forget that I am a widow, not some naïve, young virgin." Brushing her auburn hair as it curled around her hand, Georgie vividly recalled her wedding night with Isaac. An awkward, painful, and blessedly brief union. Of course, she had grown to love their passionate encounters, but that first one . . . "Thank goodness I am well past that stage of life."

"All the more reason you should be watched over, Lady Georgina." Clara set the shoes in the dressing room and shut the door, leaving a crack. "If you think you have nothing left to lose, no reason to guard the treasure chest."

Smothering a giggle, Georgie fought to maintain a somber countenance. "I promise to take that into consideration,

Clara. Truly I will." As much consideration as she would give a gnat. "So you don't need to accompany us."

"Huh. I wasn't born down a well, my lady. I'm coming with you, and that's that. Do you require anything else this evening?"

"Only that you take a nice long rest tonight. Sleep in in the morning, Clara. You deserve it."

Giving her a withering look, Clara marched out the door, poking her head back in for an instant. "I'll awaken you at six o'clock. Lord St. Just said we were to depart for the ship at eight."

Resisting the urge to stick her tongue out at the maid, Georgie resumed her brushing, sobering the instant the door closed. Despite her carefree façade, this whole business preyed upon her mind. She feared the worst from her father. Sending his servants to bring her back home, while it had not had dire consequences, still was an indication of his iron will to have her married as he directed once and for all. She could imagine to what lengths he would go, having been thwarted once, to assure himself it did not happen a second time. He was the most stubborn, inflexible, tenacious man she had ever met.

Of course, she was just like him in that respect. If she refused to marry Travers, there was nothing her father, Lord Travers, or the King of England could do about it. Well, the king could command her to do it, but it was very unlikely, given his circumstances. And the Prince Regent would likely take her side in the matter, as he'd detested his own marriage because he'd been forced to marry a lady he didn't love. If it came down to it, she would simply tear up the document she had signed in front of Travers and tell him to go hang.

A quiet knock brought Georgie out of her chair and sprinting to the door. "Yes? Who is it?" she whispered and leaned her ear against the panel.

Nothing. She pressed harder.

Louder knocking ensued, but not from the door to the corridor. She jerked back and looked at the door in the corner, near the fireplace. The door that had always been locked. Step by cautious step she crept to the doorway, then laid her hand on the latch and paused. Best be safe. She grabbed a poker from the fireplace and lifted the latch.

She raised the rod, her face screwed into the fiercest frown she could conjure, and the door swung wide, revealing a grinning Rob in a gray silk banyan that matched the color of his wide eyes, two glasses of wine in his hands.

"Rob! What are you doing here?" An inane question, given his dishabille and the lateness of the hour, but she was so flustered she couldn't think straight. She'd hoped he would come, but hadn't dared hope too much with her brother literally down the hall.

"I was going for a stroll and thought you might like to accompany me. The parapet is particularly lovely by moonlight." He handed her one of the glasses, bubbles rising steadily through the golden liquid. "Have some wine. It will help you relax."

"Why would you think I needed to relax?" She was strung tighter than a bowstring, and he knew it. Grasping the glass, she gasped in a breath.

"Because you were about to crack my noggin with that poker, if I don't miss my guess. After last night's visitor, I can't say I blame you, but"—he grabbed the poker, and she let go—"I do not think you want to use this on me. At least, not before we marry. Afterward, well, I will simply have to take my chances." He leaned the iron rod back against the fireplace. "I do love a resourceful woman."

"Oh, Rob." She laid her head on his chest, truly relaxing now. "I was hoping you would come here." She raised her head. "But how do you come here? I tried to open that door when I first arrived, but it was locked. I thought it might be a room for Clara to occupy, then we were told she should go to the upper floor. So where does that door lead?"

"To the marquess's suite of rooms of course." He sipped champagne, watching her.

"To your bedchamber?" Georgie frowned. "If your room connects to this one, then this must be . . ." Her mouth dropped open, and he had to grab the glass in her hand to keep it from spilling.

"The marchioness's suite, yes. My mother vacated it years ago when my father died. I moved into his chamber when I turned twenty-one and officially assumed the marquessate. And these rooms have been waiting ever since . . . for you."

"Oh." This magnificent room would be hers for as long as she lived. Right beside his.

"That is why I asked Mamma to put you in this suite of rooms." He smoothed a strand of hair away from Georgie's face. "I wanted you to become very familiar with them."

"But that first day you hadn't proposed to me yet." Had he been so certain of her answer even then?

He waved his hand. "Formality, only." He raised her hand to his lips. "Before we landed in the cove I knew I wanted only you as my marchioness."

Slipping her hand from his, she stepped back. "You seem to have been very sure of yourself. Almost cocky, one might say." She peered at him, pursing her lips. "What if I had said no?"

Giving her an arch look, he drained his glass, then plucked hers from her hand. With a devilish grin he set them on the bedside table. "Well, as you may recall, I can be particularly persuasive." He pulled her against his firm chest, harder now that only his robe and her gown separated them. Tipping her head back, he cupped it in his sure hands and stared deeply into her eyes. "As I recall you did say 'yes.' Isn't that right?"

"Yes." She scarcely breathed the word.

"And will you say 'yes' to me tonight?" His mouth hovered over hers, his breath warm and sweet against her cheek.

"Oh, yes." She urged her lips toward his, desperate for their touch.

He met her halfway, their mouths bumping awkwardly in their hurry. Then his tongue was in her mouth, greedily licking into her, drinking her in. She thirsted too, darting into him, tasting the sweet wine that made her hungry for more.

Pressing harder against him, she longed for them to be simply skin to skin, no barriers between them. She stepped back and, with one clean motion, pulled the tie of his belt. The gray silk slithered like quicksilver to the floor. There was a flash of smooth skin as the robe fell open, and he stood still, an air of expectancy about him.

"Finish unwrapping your package, my dear."

She could hardly wait. Grasping the soft, damasked fabric, she walked slowly around him, peeling the garment off him, revealing his beautiful body bit by bit, a powerful shoulder first, then muscular arm. She remembered well the strength of those arms holding her and shivered.

When she finally stood directly behind him, she gave a firm tug, and the robe came away, revealing the sleek muscles of his back. A low, hungry growl began deep in her throat. With a sure hand, she traced the deep crease of his spine all the way down to where his slender waist gave onto firm, small buttocks, reveling in the satiny feel of his skin. "You are beautiful, my love."

"And you have not yet come to the best parts."

Georgie couldn't help but smile, heat tinging her cheeks. She had no doubt his best would be spectacular. She slid her arms around his waist, hugging him to her, her breasts rubbing across his back, his bottom firmly nestled against her stomach.

A groan issued forth, and she released him, continuing around until she stood in front of him once more. His naked body reminded her strongly of the Greek statues in Lord Elgin's collection, the clean lines, the sharply defined muscles of his chest, the deep V of his hips that led the eye directly to his manhood. Which did not resemble the marble statues at all.

"I told you the best was yet to come."

Georgie jerked her gaze upward, her hands going to her hot cheeks. Had she been staring at him—down *there*—for very long? His entire body was magnificent, now that she could focus on his attributes above the waist: strong, broad shoulders, a well-defined smooth chest, and his stomach seemed etched in classic lines leading down to . . . There she was again, dragging her gaze back up to his laughing one.

"Look your fill, sweetheart." He ran his finger down her cheek. "Touch too, if you wish, although I would like to gaze on your lovely form as well."

"Of course." That was only fair. She untied the draw-string and began to slide her nightgown down over her shoulders, then slowed, suddenly shy. What if he did not like what he saw? Under no misapprehensions about her own physical appearance, she'd long ago accepted that she was not the ideal form for a woman. In addition to her red hair and freckles, which Rob had been kind enough not to mention at all, she did not have the pleasing curves that many women took for granted. Her breasts were undeniably small, her hips slim, and her skin, while pale, did not have the creamy glow she envied in others.

"May I help you with that?" He covered her hand with his and slowly pulled the gown down over one shoulder, then dipped his head to kiss the exposed flesh.

At the touch of his lips she began to tremble, her skin

pebbling, her nipples hardening to stiff points. Below, at her very core, she ached with need as she had not done for a very long time. *Please don't let him stop.*

He continued his kisses, traveling up her neck, behind her ear.

Low, keening sounds escaped from deep in her throat. Then her gown puddled about her feet, and she stood naked before him. Afraid at first to meet his gaze, she hung her head, waiting for some sign or sound from him. When none came, she slowly raised her chin to find his rapt attention fixed on her, frank admiration in his eyes. "Oh, my love, but you are glorious."

Flushed now, with relief and desire, she would have gone into his arms, but he resumed his kisses, scattering them across her chest. Suddenly, he drew one nipple into his mouth, laving it, then sucking on the tiny peak.

A bolt of desire streaked straight from that crest to her core, and she cried out, "Oh, dear God."

A piercing yelp sounded from the dressing room as Lulu, barking shrilly, darted out the doorway and headed straight for Rob.

"Lulu, no." Georgie pulled away and grabbed the spaniel before she could take a bite out of Rob. "I know you are trying to protect me, but this time it is not necessary." With an apologetic look at her beloved, Georgie carried the still wiggling and growling dog back to the dressing room. "Go to sleep, Lulu. I promise you all is well." After shutting the door, Georgie turned back to Rob, who had taken refuge on the bed. "She thought I needed protecting again."

"I hope she learns the difference between me and Lord Travers quickly, or Miss Lulu will be spending her nights locked in the dressing room." He lay relaxed on his side, head propped up on one hand, the other one rubbing the coverlet in invitation. "Care to join me?"

Still self-conscious, but not about to miss the offer,

Georgie walked swiftly to the bed, climbed the three steps, lay down facing him, then twisted around. "Oh, I forgot to blow out the candles."

"Leave them lighted." Beginning at her shoulder, he ran one finger down her arm, over her breast, along her side, and around her hip, coming to rest lightly on her thigh. "Who would not wish to see everything about you? How you look in the candlelight, with your hair glinting rubies here and here?" He stroked the locks of red that lay between them on the bed, then touched the russet thatch between her legs.

Georgie gasped, the heat within her rising throughout her body.

"I want to see that faint blush on your cheeks, when I caress you here." Covering her mound, he urged her to lie back, stroking gently, but firmly. "I want to see your face the moment I enter you for the first time. I want you to see me as well."

More eager than ever, she nodded as he swung himself overtop of her. Opening her legs wide, she slid her hands up his chest, needing to touch him, wanting to see all of him at this most intimate of moments. Breathing raggedly, she raised her head to stare as he guided his member to her opening and thrust forward.

Georgie hadn't quite expected the size nor the force of him. He stretched her wider than she'd have believed she could possibly accommodate, then filled her as he flowed forward, seemingly forever. She rocked back against the pillows, thrusting against him until he stopped, seated completely inside her. Panting, she looked into his eyes, touched his face as a look of wonder burst forth on it. A look she hoped was mirrored on hers.

"My love. Are you—"

"Shhh. I am fine. Show me more."

With a groan, he shifted his weight and began a slow, measured rhythm that fed the need within her.

Faster, she silently urged him, not wanting to wait for the completion that seemed almost within their grasp. She thrust her hips up, meeting him each time he plunged in. Almost there . . . She cried out sharply as she shattered around him, and shattered again when he strained hard against her, his own cry triumphant as he spilled his seed deep within her.

Immediately, he slumped over her, then rolled quickly to the side. They lay panting, matching each other breath for breath until finally her breathing slowed to normal. "Did you see everything you wished, my love?"

"Everything and more. And the best part is"—he rolled his head to stare at her, a smile curling his lips—"in a little while I'll be able to see it all again." His smile turned lecherous. "And again." He nuzzled her breast, bringing her nipple to attention. "We can't leave the poor little thing out all alone, can we? She needs someone to play with." He promptly sucked it into his mouth, making Georgie groan with pleasure.

It promised to be a long and passionate night.

Chapter Twenty-Two

The thin morning sunlight streaking through a chink in the curtains onto her face made Georgie turn over, reach for Rob, and encounter an empty bed. That brought her upright in the rumpled sheets with a vague remembrance of him kissing her as he left for his own chamber at dawn.

"No need to shock Clara with my presence," he'd whispered, "although I highly doubt she will remain ignorant of our tryst, given the state of the bedclothes."

Georgie lay back down, smiling as she pulled the covers up to her chin. A sense of peace and well-being stole through her, until she moved her hips. The soreness between her legs was a small price to pay, however. Her body would get used to the new activity, just as it had done years before when she and Isaac were first married.

Isaac. "Oh, my love." Although he had never been very far from her thoughts, somehow he'd been overshadowed by the new romance in her life. Given her very loving marriage and her almost inconsolable grief at Isaac's death, she was puzzled now at how she had fallen in love with Rob so quickly. Agreed to marry him and shared her body most eagerly with him. Should she have thought about Isaac more or about whether he would want her to marry again?

Perhaps this was the way mourning was supposed to end,

with a new beginning. She could remain a widow and true to Isaac's memory for the rest of her days, but what would that accomplish? Isaac was dead, but she was not. He had loved her enough that she was certain he would prefer her married and happy—pray God with children—rather than lonely and miserable, pining for him all her days.

She'd never even considered what Isaac would have thought about her marrying Travers, but that was because Travers would never have touched her heart. That marriage would have been done for family reasons alone, and Isaac would have understood that as well, though he'd likely not have approved of it because it would not have brought her happiness.

"You should be happy for me and Rob, my love." She spoke aloud to no one, although she knew quite well to whom she spoke. "He is a good man who loves me, not as you did, but still a true love. I can be happy with him and keep your memory close to my heart."

The feeling of peace blanketed her once more, and she drifted off until Clara roused her some time later, bearing a tray with tea and toast.

"Here you are, my lady. You're lying abed late, given the importance of the day." The maid set the tray on the bed and opened the curtains. "I'd have thought you'd be up and already dressed, champing at the bit, so to speak, to be gone."

"What time is it?" Georgie stretched, trying not to wince. "I hadn't even looked. Besides, Lord St. Just decided not to leave until after breakfast. It's surely not past eight already?"

"Nine and then some. Good thing your trunk is already aboard the ship. I'll get your traveling gown out. We'll have you washed and dressed in no time." Casting a critical eye over the bed, Clara cut her gaze at her mistress. "Seems like you had a restless night. I've never seen your bed so mussed before."

Georgie bit her lip. "As you say, it's an important day,

Clara. I tossed and turned most of the night thinking about this voyage."

"Looks like you twisted yourself right out of your nightgown, my lady." Clara stooped and retrieved the discarded garment from the floor.

Not knowing where to look, Georgie opted for the coverlet, seeing for herself how rumpled it appeared. "I must have gotten too warm and pulled it off during the night."

"I suspect you may have had help with it as well. Which is exactly why you need me to chaperone you during this journey to Scotland. You don't want to get yourself talked about, Lady Georgina."

"There is no one here to see or hear anything to talk about." Picking up the cup of tea, Georgie sipped it quickly. "Ugh, there's no sugar in it."

"It must have settled to the bottom. Give it a stir." Clara folded the gown over her arm. "You know as well as I do that houses have eyes and ears galore. It's when you think no one is around that everything gets noticed. Mark my words, if his lordship was here last night, someone knows it besides the two of you."

Making that pronouncement, Clara opened the door to the dressing room, and Lulu shot out, running around the room barking and sniffing. Clara nodded at the excited animal. "If that one could talk, I'm sure she'd tell a fine tale about last evening." Clara continued into the dressing room.

"Lulu, come." Georgie patted the bed next to her, and the little dog clambered up the steps and onto the bed. "Good girl." She lowered her voice. "You won't betray us, will you?"

Lulu yipped once, then bared her teeth.

Rubbing the dog under her chin, Georgie sighed. "We really must find a way for you and Rob to come to an accord."

A loud knocking at the door set Lulu off on another

round of frantic barking. "Shhh, Lulu. Clara, see who is at
the door, please."

Before the maid could return from the dressing room, the
door burst open.

Mindful of her total undress, Georgie dived beneath the
covers just as Jemmy strode in.

Lulu leaped off the bed, barking shrilly until she reached
Jemmy's boots. She sniffed cautiously, then stopped baying.

"Good morning, brother," Georgie called as he looked
around the room. "So nice of you to call before I completed
my toilette. I would rise, but I think we'd both be rather
embarrassed."

"You need to dress as soon as you can and present yourself downstairs, Georgie." Jemmy's curt command raised an
alarm in her.

Heart in her throat, Georgie sat up, clutching the covers
to her chest. "What has happened?"

He stared at her, his jaw clenched. "Father has arrived."

The formal drawing room on the first floor had been the
gathering place for all the family's after-dinner assemblies
since Georgie had arrived at St. Just. A pleasant room,
decorated in warm tones of rustic reds and browns, it had
been a favorite refuge for her each evening. Never, however,
had she approached any chamber with more apprehension
than now.

A sound like squawking geese met her before she could
even push the door open. Jemmy and Father, of course, ar-
guing so loudly she was surprised she hadn't heard them in
the upstairs corridor. Well, she was not afraid of Father, even
now. She had a right to happiness, and, if that made her
father unhappy, that was his choice. She would marry Rob,
and that was all there was to it.

Pushing the door open silently, she entered unobserved to

discover her father sitting in the high-backed chair usually reserved for Rob, as head of the household. That certainly boded ill, for her father would usurp every drop of power he could wrest from an opponent in any way he could. Jemmy stood in front of him, his face red, his hair sticking up as though he'd run his hand through it several times. To her brother's left, Rob sat in the chair his mother usually took. Upon seeing her enter, he rose and met her near the doorway.

"Good morning, Lady Georgina. I trust you slept well?" Love shone brilliantly in his eyes. Fortunately, his back at that point was to her father.

"Good morning, Lord St. Just," she replied in hushed tones. "I rested well, thank you." Not as well as when he'd been in her bed. "I am sorry for bringing this whirlwind down upon your household. I had no idea my father intended to come here."

"As well to have the final act play out now as later. As long as the outcome is our marriage, I care not if the ceremony occurs here or in Scotland or in the Antipodes." He took her hand. "If I have to move heaven and earth, I will do it to make you mine."

"Georgina." Her father's gruff voice rose above Jemmy's.

With a last desperate glance at Rob, Georgie composed her face and walked sedately, step by step, until she stood in front of the man. Her father hadn't changed an iota from the last time she'd seen him, almost a month ago. Not that she expected any change. He was the same stern monster from her childhood, ramrod straight and stricter than any moralist of the age. A man who gave no quarter, who never changed his mind. "Yes, Father?"

"What the devil have you been playing at? Brack insists that you did not run away yet again, with this popinjay"— he waved his hand at Rob, who grinned and straightened his jacket—"but were instead kidnapped on your way home. If that is true, which I very much doubt, inform me immediately who the kidnapper was, and I will see that he is caught and punished to the full extent of the law."

"Clara and I were indeed kidnapped on the post road at The Running Horse Inn in Leatherhead. They took us to Portsmouth, although I have no idea the reason why. Clara believed they wished to sell us as concubines to a sultan, but I tried to dissuade her from that."

Her father blinked at that, but it took more than a startling statement to turn him from his purpose. "Stuff and nonsense." The gruff tone held not a spark of sympathy for Georgie. "But who kidnapped you, Georgina? That is my question."

"I repeat, I have no idea, Father. They were not forthcoming with answers when I made that inquiry." Georgie tried to remember exactly what she had said to Odd Fellow in the clearing. "The odd-looking man who seemed to be the leader said he was working for his 'master,' but wouldn't tell me a name. However, he did say the man had planned the kidnapping well in advance and that he specifically wanted to kidnap me."

"And you believed him?"

"I had no reason not to. He was the one kidnapping me."

Her father stared at her until she squirmed. He always made her feel guilty, even when she was telling the truth. "You then miraculously escaped and, in a city you did not know, conveniently ran into this man, your brother's friend, who brought you here?"

Georgie shook her head. When stated baldly like that, it did sound farfetched. Yet it was all true. "That is the truth. I cannot change it because it sounds like a falsehood."

"Georgina"—her father rose—"you will have your maid pack your things so you can accompany me back to Blackham Castle where you will marry Lord Travers as you should have done long ere this. Brack"—he swung around on Jemmy, glaring at him, though Jemmy stood his ground—"I do not know whether you had a hand in this nefarious plot, but I give you warning. Interfere with your sister's marriage once more, and I will tie your affairs up so tight, you will not be able to take a breath without my overseeing it."

"No, Father." Trembling with rage, Georgie clenched her fists until her nails bit deeply into her palms.

"What did you say?" Father's head had snapped back around toward her, his eyes blazing.

"I said 'No,' Father. I will not go back to Blackham with you, and I will not marry Lord Travers." Time to show the man she had as much stubbornness in her as he had. She smiled at Rob and took his hand. "I intend to marry the man I love."

"Have you run mad?" Her father's thunderous frown might have frightened her another time, but, with Rob's hand firmly in hers, she cared nothing for the man's tempers.

"No, my lord." Rob stepped forward, towering over her father. "She has not. I wish your permission to marry Lady Georgina."

"Another lunatic." Father glared at Rob. "My daughter is already betrothed, St. Just. I would think you had been informed of that." He swung his attention to Georgie. "She signed a contract giving her consent to the marriage. I have it safe back at Blackham. So you will marry him, Georgina. Depend upon it."

"Did you know, Lord Blackham, two nights ago, Lord Travers stole into my house and attempted to ravish your daughter while she slept?" The tendons on Rob's neck were stretched so tight she could see the blood pulsing in his veins.

"Wouldn't you wish to lay claim to what was yours if your betrothed had run away with another man? I wondered when Travers would finally show some backbone. So Travers is actually here. Even better." Father smiled, and Georgie cringed. The sight of that mirthless grin always unnerved her. "We can have the wedding today."

"What?" Mouth hanging open, Georgie could not comprehend what her father was suggesting. "We cannot possibly do that. The banns have not been read."

"Yes, they have." Maintaining his frightening smile, her father pulled on his black leather gloves. "I had them read in our parish as soon as you left for Buckinghamshire so you could be married as soon as you returned. I have the sworn testament in my papers here. Any clergyman worth his salt will accept it if backed by the word of the Marquess of Blackham."

Recovering from the shock of that piece of news, Georgie steeled herself. She was made of stronger stuff than her father believed. "You may say what you will, Father, but the truth is this. I am above one and twenty years old, I am a widow, and I hereby revoke that contract you have put so much store in." She leaned in toward him, staring into his eyes, unblinking. "If need be I shall tear it into a thousand pieces and burn it in front of Lord Travers, but I will not marry the man."

To her horror, instead of flying into a rage, her father smiled again, and her stomach plummeted.

"I see that this whole affair has left you distraught, daughter." He turned to Jemmy, eyebrows raised. "Brack, Lord St. Just, you have just witnessed an outburst that I scarcely could credit to my well-behaved, docile daughter a month ago."

Georgie exchanged glances with Rob and Jemmy. Where was her father taking this line of reasoning?

"The stress of traveling to Buckinghamshire and that month of festivities must have strained her faculties. Thus this wild tale of kidnapping, her frivolous arguments, and now this dreadful outpouring of vitriol aimed at the man who has waited so patiently for her to keep her word to him." Father shook his head. "If she does not return to her normal, obedient self, I fear that, as her closest kinsman living, I shall have to resort to drastic measures to assure myself she will not do injury to herself or anyone else. Unfortunately, the only such place in all of London equipped for such care is the hospital at Bedlam." He patted Georgie's shoulder, the glee of victory in his eyes. "Do not worry, my dear. It might only take three or four months for you to regain your senses there."

Horror cascaded over her as though a bucket of the cold Channel water had been tossed at her. *Bedlam!* To even be threatened with incarceration in that, the most terrifying place in all of England, might send her into true madness. She stared into her father's merciless eyes, and hope waned.

"Father, you cannot do this." Jemmy darted forward as if to shield her from their father's threat. "Georgie is as sane as you or me, and I will attest to it in any court in the land."

Her father whirled around on his heir. "You will learn to speak when you are spoken to, puppy. Do not think, because I allowed your marriage against my better judgment, that I will allow your sister to rescind her word to Travers."

"Not even when St. Just is ten times the man Travers is? He has far greater wealth and is, in fact, a marquess with higher precedence than the earl." Her brother paused, as if considering well his next words. "In fact, I believe St. Just's precedence is actually higher than yours."

A hand on her arm startled Georgie, and she turned to Rob, who led her to a chair near the door. "Are you all right, my love?"

Staring helplessly at the red and brown Turkey carpet, Georgie wrung her hands, forcing herself to keep breathing. "He will do it, Rob. He will lock me away in that place until I agree to marry Travers." Tears spilled down her cheeks. "By that time I will likely not know the difference between one madhouse and the other."

"I swear to you on my soul, I will not allow him to do this to you." Though Rob's voice was low, the conviction in it rang true. "If I have to kill Travers and bring his head on a pike to your father's doorstep, I will do so before you set one foot over the threshold of that asylum."

"I can't . . . I can't let you do that, my love." She hung her head. Not even to save herself would she allow him to do something dishonorable. "They would hang you for such a deed. The man may be revolting, but he has committed no offense that warrants death."

"I'm not so certain about that. But perhaps there is another way." Cautiously, Rob looked at Jemmy, still railing against his father. "Your things are already on board the *Justine*, aren't they?"

"Yes." She looked at Rob, a glimmer of hope stealing into her.

"The moment you marry your father loses all power over you." He squeezed her shoulder. "Let us go then and get married."

Thrilling as the words were, they were only words unless she and Rob could make them truth. "How? Father will stop us."

"We wait for a distraction, then you slip out the door. I will wait a moment only, so it seems we did not leave together." He dropped his hand from her shoulder, leaving her bereft for a moment, then she steadied herself. "Meet me at the kitchen larder, and we'll be bound for Scotland with the morning tide."

"What is the meaning of this audience?" The drawing room door flew open, and Lady St. Just strode in, carrying herself as though she were the queen. Every inch the queen of her castle, she marched toward Georgie's father, eyes flashing with an unmitigated anger. "Why was I not informed of the Marquess of Blackham's arrival?" She stopped directly in front of Father, who amazingly seemed to shrink back.

"Go, now." Rob's whisper broke the spell, and Georgie scurried out the door, dearly wishing to see this battle of wills, but not at the cost of her happiness or sanity. She sped down the corridor to the kitchen steps at the back of the house. The servants used this staircase, but she didn't think they'd mind her presence here this once. Flying down the stairs, she made the final step, then turned a corner and almost ran into a maid carrying a coal scuttle.

"Oh, beg pardon, milady." The girl bobbed a curtsy then hurried on her way.

Gasping for breath, Georgie jogged along the corridor until she arrived at the door Rob had showed her just yesterday, the larder behind which the smugglers' tunnel lay. Now she must wait for Rob, for he hadn't told her how to navigate the tunnel, and she did not want to get lost and forfeit their chance to slip through her father's grasp.

She must wait and see who discovered her first: the ogre or the prince.

Chapter Twenty-Three

Closing the door quietly after Georgie's escape, Rob slipped forward, inwardly smiling at his mother's performance. He'd told her the moment the marquess had arrived, so she'd been aware of the man's presence all along. All she'd told him was to put the irate man in the drawing room and that she'd be along shortly. Well, Mamma did love to make an entrance. He just hoped she could distract Blackham long enough for him and Georgie to get onto the *Justine* and set sail.

"I am abjectly sorry, Lord Blackham, for my son's behavior."

Now that statement did not bode well. Rob inched up beside his friend.

Jemmy glanced at him and raised his eyebrows and whispered, "What is she doing?"

"Presenting a distraction, I profoundly hope." And nothing else.

Mamma smiled, her white teeth flashing, and Rob relaxed. That particular expression he'd seen many times before, always when Mamma was using her most dangerous wit. It told him she was indeed attempting to help with their escape. "He should have informed me immediately upon your arrival so I could have greeted you in accordance with all the honor you so richly deserve. I do hope you will forgive him and me."

Lord Blackham's mouth had dropped open slightly while she spoke. Either he wished to interrupt her or stood in awe of the woman so completely dominating the conversation. Rob certainly hoped it was the latter.

"I beg your pardon, madam, but have we been introduced?" Blackham's brows had furrowed into a deep V, his full attention on the lady.

"Why yes, we have, although it was an age ago. I suppose I have changed a little." She peered squarely down her nose at him. "You, however, are exactly as I remember you."

Blackham cocked his head, his eyes widening with recognition. "Were you Miss Stokely of High View in Kent? Viscount Bromley's daughter?"

"I was. I am flattered that you remember me, my lord." His mother's smile deepened, and Rob had to look away to bite back a laugh. She was relishing this to be sure. "You scarcely seemed to pay me any attention at all when I came out all those years ago."

"Oh, I assure you, my lady, I noticed you beyond a doubt." For once the marquess sounded sincere. "Such a beautiful and witty young lady was noticed by a great many gentlemen, as I recall. And you married extremely well, I see."

"I did. The Marquess of St. Just was the perfect gentleman. We had only a brief time together, but his legacy lives on in our son." She nodded toward Rob, who tried to look soberly at the marquess. "My son has also grown into a fine gentleman, one who would make his father extremely proud." She patted Rob on the shoulder as she moved toward her seat. "Leave now," she whispered sotto voce. "I think it interesting that our children have become great friends, do you not, my lord? Rob, ring for tea, please."

"Yes, Mamma." He strode to the bellpull, directly beside the door, Jemmy following after him.

"What are you doing? Where's Georgie gone?"

"She's waiting for me at the secret tunnel. Mamma is creating a diversion for your father so we can sail to Scotland as planned."

"I'm still going with you." Jemmy's face took on a wary look, and Rob sighed.

"You can't. If you leave now, your father will suspect what is going on, and we will never get away." Pleading silently for his friend to understand, Rob pulled the bell several times. "If you wish for your sister and me to wed, you must stay here and help create the diversion. Once our ship is away, there won't be anything your father can do." Rob pulled the tapestry pull yet again. "I am sorry, Mamma, but it does not seem to be working. Allow me to step into the corridor and summon Myers."

"Thank you, my dear." His mother met his eyes briefly, nodded, then turned back to Lord Blackham. "And I have heard that both your elder daughters married extremely well. How fortunate for your family. Now the elder is a duchess, I understand. . . ."

Rob opened the door, bent on a quick escape until Jemmy's hand fell heavily on his shoulder. "Jemmy, for God's sake," he hissed.

"*Bon chance*, my friend." The grip on his shoulder tightened. "Bring my sister back your marchioness or it will be between you and me."

Rob nodded. "Understood. Thank you."

A final thump on his shoulder, and Jemmy strode back into the room to join the conversation. "Emma was well married also, my lady, although not quite so high as Mary, a sore spot between the two to be sure."

Slipping out the door, Rob took off for the nearby servants' stairs. Running swiftly down them he cursed the timing that had made it necessary for them to wait until this morning to sail. Had they been able to leave yesterday, they'd have gotten away with Blackham none the wiser until he and Georgie had returned, man and wife. Still, if they could reach the *Justine* without detection, they could sail away and not look back. None of the others would reveal where they had gone, and, by the time Blackham realized they were missing, it would be too late to stop them. Traveling by carriage to Portpatrick would take the marquess weeks. If their luck held, they'd be married in five days. Then Georgie's father would be helpless.

He rounded the corner at the bottom of the stairs and started down the dim corridor toward the kitchens. The larder door was there on the left—but no Georgie. Skidding to a stop, Rob peered around. Had she made a wrong turn? If he had to go find her, they were never going to make it to the ship.

"Thank goodness, it's the prince."

Rob whirled around to find Georgie climbing out of a chest used to store pots. "What are you doing in there?" Then he shook his head. "Did you just call me a prince?"

"A figure of speech only. Here, give me your hand." She grasped it and carefully stepped out of the box. "I thought it wouldn't do for me to just stand around here, looking suspicious, so instead I hid and waited to see who appeared first, the prince or the ogre." Grinning widely at him, she handed him a large black cooking pot from a pile at the end of the chest. "Aren't you glad I dubbed you the prince? You're certainly not ogre-like in the least." She grasped another pot and deposited it in the chest. "Aren't you going to help me? This will go much quicker if you do."

He dropped the pot into the chest and pushed the top down. It crashed with a loud clatter that reverberated along the corridor. The distant chatter from the kitchen paused.

"Shhh. Rob, you'll give us away."

He grabbed her hand. "Come with me now if you want to marry me."

"Well, of course I do, but don't you think we should put the pots—"

"I have servants who will do that. We need to go before someone else comes along here." He pulled the larder door open and was met by complete darkness. "Damn. I forgot a candle. Wait here. Don't move." He raced back up the corridor to the staircase. The area was always dim, so they kept a candle burning in a sconce there. He lifted the entire sconce from its holder and raced back toward the larder door.

When he arrived, Georgie was bent over the open chest, apparently rearranging the pots to make room for more.

"Georgie!"

She jumped and straightened up, her hands stuck behind her. "You're back. That was rather quick of you."

"Come on." God knew he loved her, because he hadn't strangled her yet. He grabbed her hand again, then led them through the larder door and closed it with a sharp pull. "Watch your step." The steep wooden staircase led straight down to a large, cool room of rough stone where all the dry goods for the castle were stored. The torch flickered as he hurried along the curved wall toward a smooth patch of stone.

"It's getting colder." Georgie leaned closer, rubbing her arm against him.

"It'll get colder still as we go deeper, and the wind will be icy once we get outside." He raised her hand and kissed it. "I'm sorry you don't have your pelisse. You'll have to make do with whatever is on the ship, perhaps an old jacket of one of the sailors."

"I'll be fine as long as I'm with you." She smiled up at him, sending his heart racing. "I can always depend on you to find a way to keep me warm."

The image of them in bed, her naked beneath him as he covered her, made him pause as his shaft sprang to life, despite the cold.

"Is something wrong?"

"No. I'll explain later." Shaking his head to dispel the image, he ran his hand along the side of the smooth stone. There was a loud click, and the stone panel opened.

"Lord, it is colder here." Georgie peered into the dark opening. "What is this place?"

"Part of the smugglers' tunnel, but it also leads to the dungeon." Rob pulled the panel shut behind them and continued forward. The smooth stone beneath their feet sloped downward. Rob held the candle high to give them more light.

"You have a dungeon too?" The admiration in her voice made him chuckle.

"I promise you, it was here long before I was born. The castle dates back to the Middle Ages, when prisoners were held for ransom on a regular basis." They had reached another doorway, and Rob switched the candle to his left hand. With a mighty push, he thrust down the huge lever on the door, and it swung inward into the pitch black. "Hold my hand. Don't be afraid."

"Be afraid of what?" The alarm in Georgie's voice tugged at his heart.

"The smugglers had a rather crude sense of humor, it seems. And one a young boy could also appreciate." He stepped into the dungeon, and led her past cells with iron bars, now well rusted, running from the rock ceiling into the rock floor below. In the middle cell, a skeleton in the ragged remains of clothing gleamed white in the flickering light, its bony fingers wrapped around the iron bars.

"Oh, dear Lord." Her grip tightening on his arm, Georgie drew back against him.

"It's all right, my love. That's Gentleman John. Hello, John."

"John?" The horror in her eyes was pitiful to see. "You knew him?"

"Oh, no. He was here long before I was born." Lord, that didn't seem to help. "The story goes that the smugglers in my grandfather's day found the skeleton washed up out of the sand of the cove one day. They dug him out, put those clothes on him, then arranged him thus. Every time they brought the smuggled goods up from the ship, they'd talk to John. Say hello, ask him how his accommodations were, if his last meal was good."

"Rob, really." The frown on her face was better than the fear, but not by much. "You should have put a stop to that and had the poor man buried in a decent grave."

"And I will do so as soon as we return from Scotland. My word of honor." He held the torch high, throwing the skull into high relief. "We'll see you on the return journey, John." Rob bit his lip. He would probably go to hell for this. "Won't you speak a word to him, Georgie? This could be your only chance."

"I most certainly will not." She glared at Rob. "How disrespectful."

"Disrespectful to speak to a man? How is that?"

"He's dead, Rob."

"Then you should pay your respects."

That argument seemed to give her pause. She looked up at Rob, then back at John, and took a tentative step toward the skeleton. "I am very sorry about your demise, John. I hope you rest in peace."

"Why thank 'e, milady."

Georgie screamed and stumbled back into Rob, making the candle waver dangerously.

"I does appreciate your concern for me time in the afterlife." Rob could scarcely finish the sentence for laughing.

"Rob!" She punched his chest, and he laughed all the harder. "I should kill you here and now and leave you to be company for John. Serve you right. My heart is beating like a drummer pounding out quick time."

Smothering his laughter, Rob put his arm around her. "I'm sorry but it's the smuggler's initiation, love. You are truly one of the family, even if we're not yet married." He kissed the top of her head and got an elbow in his side for his pains. "Come, it's not much farther. See you later, John." They continued down the passageway, past another two empty cells, Georgie unusually quiet. "If it will make you feel any better, love, I will confess that when they introduced me to Gentleman John, I wet my breeches."

"You did?" She glanced up at him, her delectable mouth puckering in a smile.

"Yes, well, I was eight years old at the time, so you really shouldn't think the less of me." He guided her around an outcropping of rock. They'd passed out of the castle and were now descending toward the cove actually inside the cliff. "I remember my mother was not at all pleased with the escapade, and I was sent to bed without my supper for a week."

"Perhaps a bit severe for a young boy only seeking adventure." Georgie had taken his hand and laced their fingers together.

"Please remember that sentiment when you dole out my punishment this evening."

"You are no longer an eight-year-old boy, Rob."

"But I am still bent on adventure." He gazed into her lovely green eyes, longing to lower his mouth to hers. "The greatest one of my life."

"Wretch." The whispered word sounded more like a caress than an admonition. "I will take everything into consideration."

The tunnel had grown colder as it lightened until the candle was no longer necessary. Rob extinguished it and laid the sconce to the side of the tunnel, then doffed his jacket and pushed her arms through it. "It's going to be very cold, and the wind will try to blow you away."

"Rob—"

"Don't argue. I'll be fine. We have a fair amount of rough beach to cover. Can you make it?"

"I will."

"Good. Come on."

He seized her hand and pulled her out into the hazy sunshine, squinting in the light much brighter than that of the tunnel. The rocky terrain of the beach made even walking difficult, with great boulders jutting up out of the sand here and there, and scruffy sea grass poking up out of the crevices. Carefully, they picked their way across the short expanse to the dock that extended out into the cove. The chill wind whipping his shirt to and fro spurred Rob to run once they were on solid footing, their feet thumping loudly on the weathered boards until they reached the small boat. Briskly, Rob rowed them the short distance to the *Justine*.

"Welcome aboard, Captain. My lady." Ayers stood behind the ship's wheel, apparently awaiting their arrival. Rob had sent word to the crew yesterday to be ready to sail this morning. Now he hoped to God the tide was still with them.

"Is the crew assembled?"

"Aye, Captain. They're below, awaiting orders."

"Very good. Get ready to make way."

"Aye, Captain." The sailor ran to the gangway, calling, "Look alive, men. Captain's ready to make way."

Georgie huddled against him. "I suppose I should return your jacket and go below. That way neither of us will freeze." She struggled out of his blue superfine coat and immediately began to shiver.

"Come below. While the crew is making ready to sail, we'll find you something to keep you warm until I can be of service to you." He snagged her arm and pulled her to the gangway, just as the crew erupted out of it.

"Morning, Captain, my lady." Cartwright bobbed his head and headed toward the stern.

Right behind him came Chapman. "Morning, Captain, milady." He continued to the lines and began to pull them taut.

The last sailor to emerge, a lad of maybe twelve, looked at both of them, eyes wide. He mumbled, "Morning, Captain, Mrs. Captain," and fled to the rigging, pulling on ropes and releasing the sails.

"Mrs. Captain, is it?" Georgie smiled as she hurried below. "Somehow I like that better than 'milady.'"

"Then onboard the *Justine* you shall be 'Mrs. Captain,' as soon as I make an honest woman out of you." Rob led her to his cabin and began rummaging around in his chest, then in a drawer under his bunk. "Here we are." He pulled a dark blue coat from under his bunk. "I thought I remembered stowing this under here for emergencies. My old pea coat." He held the garment up proudly. Well used, the wool coat had faded spots and looked generally scruffy, but was also terribly warm. "Let's try this on you."

"Wouldn't you rather I stayed down here? I don't want to be under foot." Face pinched and drawn, Georgie had dropped into a chair.

"I know you must be tired, but you may have a better time of it up top, at least until we're well under way." He drew the coat around her shoulders. "This may not make you all the crack, however, it will keep you warm."

Georgie sighed and stood, putting her arms through the sleeves. She looked down at the sleeves, hanging well below her fingertips, and the jacket itself that almost came to her knees. "No crack at all to be sure." She set about rolling up the sleeves. "But if it must suffice until you are available, it must. How do I look?"

Altogether too fetching by half. "Exactly as Mrs. Captain should look."

She beamed at him. "Aye, aye, Captain."

Her bright eyes, sweet smile, and that oversized coat that somehow accentuated her lovely curves combined to turn his thoughts from getting under way to other more intimate pursuits. In one step he had her in his arms, his mouth pressed hard against hers, backing toward the bunk. This journey could turn out to be more pleasant than any other he'd taken aboard the *Justine*.

"Captain, we're about to raise the main staysail." Ayers's voice came from the corridor.

"I think you'd better go see to the raising of that sail." Pulling away from him, Georgie laughed as he frowned. "The raising of your mast must wait for later."

"Too late. It's already flying." Hopefully the cold would calm his shaft until he could resume this little interlude later. They had five whole days to themselves as they headed for Scotland.

"Come on up deck with me?"

"Aye, aye, Captain." Grinning, she sashayed by him, rubbing against his already aroused body in the tight quarters.

"Just remember those words when I get you alone tonight, Mrs. Captain."

Chapter Twenty-Four

Rob had taken the wheel so Ayers could help Chapman set the sails. Georgie stood to his right, watching the coastline as it shrank little by little from view. The sea had decided to aid them today, for the chop was less than usual so the ship glided along the water's surface without bouncing about. The air, however, was cold and damp, so much so that Rob shivered and longed for his own pea coat, currently in the care of his valet at the castle. At least he could be assured that Georgie was snug and warm.

The journey to Portpatrick should take them at most five days, less if the winds stayed in their favor. Once married, he might elect to remain in the small village for several days, simply to give Georgie a respite from sea travel. Certainly they could find sights to see and things to do. He glanced at the trim figure standing between him and the rail, her hair gleaming like fire in the sparse sunlight. Oh, yes. He could think of many things for them to do.

"I'll take the wheel now, Captain." Ayers had returned to relieve him. "We're well under way."

"Thank you, Ayers." Rob turned to go to Georgie, then turned back. "Ayers, who is the young lad you've got replacing Barnes? I didn't catch his name when we came on board."

"That's young Barnes, my lord. Barnes's eldest grandson. Sent him along yesterday morning since he himself couldn't join us. Says the lad's ready to start his official training."

Usually a lad going to sea began as a cabin boy, but perhaps Barnes was right. One learned a trade by doing it. "Very well, then. Make certain young Barnes knows what he's doing before he does it."

"Aye, Captain."

Hurrying to Georgie, Rob slowed before he reached her, then stole up behind her and slid his arms around her.

She must have heard him because she didn't jump with surprise. Instead she crossed her arms over his and leaned back against him.

"How are you doing so far, sweetheart?"

"Not too badly, but then the ship isn't acting like a bucking horse either." She clutched his arms tighter around her. "I am rather sorry we had to leave so hastily that I couldn't bring Clara with me. I hadn't thought before, but now I don't know what I will do if I become ill again."

"I will take care of you, my love. In sickness and in health, remember?" Kissing the top of her head, he breathed in the slight lavender scent that always clung to her hair. He would look forward to that delight for the rest of his life. He bent slightly so his mouth was directly beside her ear. "Besides, I have a new idea about how to distract you from becoming ill, Mrs. Captain. Can you guess what it is?"

"Hmmm." She snuggled her back into his front until he was positive she could feel his shaft bumping into her, even through the heavy pea coat. "I could guess, but I think it would be much more instructive if you showed it to me, Captain."

Growling and hoping Ayers didn't turn and see how quickly they were making for the gangway, Rob grabbed her hand and pulled her along, her laughter floating out over the open sea.

Once below, he swung her around until her back hit the side of the corridor, and he sunk his mouth onto hers, unable to wait another moment to taste her lips. He slipped between those lips and drank in the deliciously soft feeling of her cheeks and tongue. They needed to continue on to their cabin. It would not do at all for the crew to see them acting so absolutely wanton in broad daylight. With Herculean effort, he pulled away from her and seized her hand. "Hurry, before I explode, sweetheart. You will ruin me if I cannot have you in the next few moments."

They ran pell-mell down the corridor, shoving open his cabin door and slamming it shut. Let the men think what they would. All kinds of noises occurred on a ship.

Rob ripped his jacket open and buttons flew.

The pea coat had hit the floor with a soft plop, then Georgie's back was to him. "Buttons please."

Restraining himself from ripping the bodice open, he fumbled with the infernal buttons, a mercifully short row of them. He unlaced the stays as well, revealing her chemise and the exquisite slope of her neck. Burying his face in her nape, he kissed and nipped his way down her back, bringing squeals of delight that transformed into guttural moans by the time he'd pushed the garment completely off her shoulders. It slithered to the floor, and she stood naked and beautiful before him. Panting hard, he stopped and drank his fill of the sight of her.

A body blush crept up from her hips, spreading through her thicket of red curls, over her stomach, around her breasts—the peaks of her nipples furled into tight points—and finally up her neck to brighten her cheeks.

Rob fell to his knees, eyes staring at the tiny indentation in her stomach, then straying down to the ruby red jewel in

front of him. Sliding his hands up her thighs and around to
her bottom, he cupped the firm derriere and inexorably
urged her forward until her body met his eager mouth.

Breathing slowly and deeply, she rested her hands on his
head and gently pressed him forward.

He inhaled the special scent that was her, that was
woman, and had to fight bitterly the urge to take her here
and now. That would come later; this was now and just for
her. So he concentrated on where he touched her, how he
would pleasure her. A hesitant kiss on her mons turned into
a deep lick that drew a moan from her. He tried that again,
opening her legs just enough to allow him further access to
all of her most secret parts.

Her moans had intensified, becoming more guttural, and
her legs trembled, as though they could scarcely hold her up.

With his tongue he searched through her soft flesh for
the exactly right spot and pressed, then drew her into his
mouth and sucked.

She flew apart, crying out as her legs jerked beneath her.
Fisting her hands in his hair, she anchored herself as he did
it again. The tempest struck her more intensely this time for
she cried out louder and longer, straining against him
until she slumped, and he steadied her.

Still he needed to hurry if his own body's needs were to
be met. The urgency brought about by her cries had brought
him almost past the point of control. "Sweetheart? Are you
all right?"

Slowly she fought for balance, then straightened. "I don't
quite know." Unsteady, she staggered over to the bed and
dropped facedown on the bunk.

The sight of her uncovered bottom spread across his bed,
a waiting invitation if ever he'd seen one, sent a frenzy of
lust through Rob. He sprang to his feet, dragged his shirt
over his head, and unbuttoned his fall—to hell with the

boots—all in the time it took him to reach the bed. Bending over her, he whispered urgently in her ear. "Sweetheart, are you ready for me?" God knew he'd been ready for her for hours.

A sweet smile spread across her lips. "Oh, yes, Rob. Yes, my love." To convince him, she opened her legs wider. As if he needed convincing.

Mindful that he needed to be gentle despite his great need, Rob swept her legs open a little more, positioned himself, and pressed forward in a slow, deep slide that seated him firmly inside her. He held his breath, fought to hold on, willed himself not to spill his seed on the very first thrust.

"You feel so good, Rob. Ahh, do that again."

Her little moan undid him.

"My pleasure, love." He pumped hard and fast, letting himself go, pouring his essence into her as their cries echoed in the cabin.

Panting so hard he could scarcely breathe, Rob slid out and flopped down beside her, boneless and utterly spent. If someone attacked the ship at this moment he'd be of no earthly use to anyone. He'd just have to pray no one attacked.

Georgie turned over, then curled up beside him, her eyelids heavy. "Rob?"

"Yes, love?" He pulled a blanket up over them.

"I agree wholeheartedly with you."

"About what, sweetheart?"

"Your new idea of distracting me from being ill." She opened one emerald-green eye and smiled. "You are the most wonderful distraction, my love." Yawning, she burrowed her head into his shoulder. "Perhaps you can distract me again in a little while, even if I don't fall ill. It's probably better that way."

* * *

Grayish light filled the cabin the next morning, waking Rob from an exhausted sleep. Not that he'd have had it any other way. After dinner last night, cooked by Chapman and served by Ayers, he and Georgie had repaired to the bunk, sleep the furthest thing from their minds. At some point they had fallen asleep in each other's arms. Georgie slept still, her cheek pillowed on one hand.

The sweetest sight he'd ever awoken to. Her tousled hair spilled in bright waves over one satiny white shoulder and the mussed sheets, her mouth in a pink bow with her other hand curled beside it. He could watch her sleep for hours, although if he gazed on her much longer he'd wake her instead and see if making love in the morning light proved better or much better than making love in the night.

As though she'd heard his thoughts, she opened her eyes and stretched, one tender breast peeping out from under the covers, the rosy nipple seeming to beckon his mouth.

"Georgie?"

"Mmmm?" She snuggled closer to him, sliding her hand across his abdomen, making the skin there jump of its own accord.

Any restraint he might have had flew out the porthole. He slid down in the bed, pulling her toward him.

"Is it morning?" Her eyes remained closed, and he gently kissed the lids.

"Yes, barely, I think." Continuing his journey, he kissed her cheek, her nose, her chin, then back up to her rosebud mouth.

"Mmmm. What a wonderful way to begin breakfast." She opened her mouth to him, inviting him in.

He needed nothing more and thrust his tongue into her.

"Captain! Captain!"

Ayers's frightened voice cut through the fog of lust in

Rob's brain. He sat up in bed, shaking away the call of his body. "What's the matter?"

"A ship, Captain. A huge four-master pulling alongside us. They're hailing us."

"What in the—" Rob tore out of the bed, pulling on his shirt and breeches without thinking, struggling to thrust his feet into the tight Hessians.

"What's going on?" The sleepy calm had fled Georgie's face. She sat in the middle of the bed, her eyes two points of green in a sea of white.

"I've no idea. Stay in the cabin. Lock the door when I leave, and—" He ripped open a drawer in his desk and pulled out a pair of pistols. Checking to make sure they were loaded, he tucked one in his breeches and held the other out to her. "You ever fire a pistol before?"

She nodded, her gaze firmly fixed on the gun in his hand.

"Good." He thrust the loaded piece at her, grateful when she took it without protest. "I hope this is nothing, but I wouldn't wager a hot ha'penny on it." He grasped her to him, kissing her quick and hard, then ran out the cabin without a backward look. Had Travers staged a rescue attempt? How would the earl even have found out their plans? He'd not been seen since Rob and Jemmy had thrown him into the stable and bid the groom get him to his lodgings, wherever that was.

Running onto the deck, Rob immediately discovered they had turned into the wind. Searching the horizon for the enemy ship, Rob glanced to port and gasped. A fully rigged, four-masted barque had pulled within a dozen yards or so of them. At double her size, the enemy ship easily dwarfed the *Justine* and, with a long row of cannon pointed squarely at them, out-gunned them as well.

"Ahoy, *Justine*." A crew member, likely the first officer, hailed them from the bow of the ship.

"Why didn't you call me sooner?" Rob turned to Ayers, who stood beside him, ashen.

"They came up on us so fast, Captain, I scarcely had time to realize they wanted to detain us. They were well astern of us and just like that"—the sailor snapped his fingers—"they were pulling alongside and hailing us, guns drawn." Ayers pointed to the line of sailors on the other ship, muskets trained on them.

"Christ."

"Is it pirates?" Out of nowhere, Georgie appeared at Rob's elbow.

"I don't know." He frowned. "I told you to stay below."

"With a ship that large, I doubt my staying in the cabin would matter much." She pulled the pistol out of a pocket of the pea coat. "Besides, if I'm going to die, I'd rather do it by your side."

"No one is going to die." God he hoped he spoke the truth.

"They're sending a boat over, Captain." Chapman ran up, fear in his eyes.

"Steady, lad. We'll see what they want." Of course he knew quite well what or rather who they wanted. The question was who were "they"?

Silently, Rob, Georgie and the crew waited until the officer stood before them, the one who'd hailed them earlier.

"My lord, my lady." The man bowed. "I am Mr. Worthington, first officer on board the *Black Hart*. With the captain's compliments, my lord." He handed Rob a sheet of paper, folded and sealed in black wax.

Georgie grabbed Rob's arm and whispered, "That's my father's seal."

"And now we know for certain who it is that wants you back." Rob ripped the letter open and, holding it so Georgie could see it as well, read the spidery handwriting with growing anger.

Lord St. Just,

Captain McMorris on board my vessel the Black Hart has orders to fire upon your ship if you do not immediately relinquish Lady Georgina to him. She will be married to Lord Travers and no one else. Ignore me at your peril.

Blackham

Rob crushed the paper in a fist that shook. What kind of father would threaten his daughter's very life in order to get his own way?

"Do not comply with this demand, Rob." An insistent hand on his arm brought his focus back to Georgie's determined face. "If he wants me brought back alive, he will not act on this order whatever we do."

"I cannot take that chance, love, for your safety and that of my crew." Covering her hand with his, he squeezed it, then let go. As long as Georgie was safe, there was hope they could find a way to make this right. "Mr. Worthington—"

"Mr. Worthington, these terms are unacceptable." Georgie broke in, sending a glare of caution at Rob. "If my father wishes for my return, then I will return, but on this ship, not the *Black Hart*."

Flustered, Mr. Worthington looked from Georgie to Rob, then back at her, apparently at a loss about whom to address. "But Lord St. Just—"

"You will address me, if you please, Mr. Worthington." The green eyes flashed fire, and the first officer flinched.

"My lady, you cannot believe—"

"What I believe, sir, is that my father wishes my return, but will have no compunction, once I am on his ship, about opening fire on the *Justine*." Georgie's nose flared, and she clenched her fists. "Therefore, I will remain on this ship until we reach port. Tell Captain McMorris he can meet my terms or open fire. The choice is his." With a dismissive nod of her head, Georgie strode away from the awestruck officer toward the bow.

Rob was more than a little awestruck himself. She'd been calling him pirate all along, and yet Lady Georgina had just issued an ultimatum, without blinking, that would have done Blackbeard proud. She should be addressed not as Mrs. Captain but rather as Lady Pirate. "You heard the lady," he snapped at the dumbfounded Mr. Worthington. "Get back to your ship, and we'll bring the *Justine* about and head for home."

"Very good, my lord." A short bow, and Worthington turned and all but ran for the side of the ship.

Chuckling, Rob headed for the bow to compliment his lady pirate. She stood staring ahead at the open water, tears trickling down her cheeks. "My love, what's the matter? You were magnificent!" He caught her around the waist, lifted her, and spun her around.

"Oh, Rob, stop. Stop unless you wish me to cast up my accounts all over you."

Laughing, he slowed his mad twirling, setting her down gently. "You are a worthy opponent, my lady pirate. I would not wish to tangle with you on the high seas." He kissed her, letting his lips linger until hers stopped trembling. "In the bedroom, however, is another story."

"But we will never get that chance again, Rob." She wiped her eyes with the back of her hand. "My father will force me to marry Travers or resign me to the lunatics at Bedlam. He will never let us marry."

"My love, I will promise you this." Rob put his arms around her and drew her close to his chest. "I will move heaven and earth to have you as my wife. I will enlist the aid of every friend, relative, and acquaintance we have to prevent either of those things from happening." Leaning back, he stared straight into her glistening eyes. "Trust me, love."

She nodded and relaxed in his arms.

As Rob stared out over her head at the brightening day, his one solace was the knowledge that whatever power Lord Blackham wielded, there was one thing even he could not accomplish. He could not marry his daughter to a dead man. They should arrive back at St. Just at first light tomorrow. So there remained perhaps a day for Rob to come up with a plan to turn Blackham's black heart to their favor before Rob would have to go about the business of killing Lord Travers and consigning the blackguard to be company for Gentleman John.

After all these years, John deserved better.

Chapter Twenty-Five

As the cold dawn broke next morning, Rob and Georgie stood arm in arm on the bow of the *Justine* as it sailed into the cove. They had slept little, but had made love only once with a desperation that broke Georgie's heart. Perhaps their last moments of intimacy ever, and she'd not been able to savor them as she should for thinking that they were indeed the last. Instead, the rest of the time she'd lain in Rob's arms, breathing in the clean scent of him, mixed with the musky hints of their joining. Relishing the stroke of his fingers along her naked back, trying frantically to imprint the sensation into her memory, so she could call it to mind during the long, horrible years ahead without him.

Despite Rob's brave words, she simply could not foresee any outcome of the approaching meeting in which she and Rob would be allowed to be together. It was one thing to order about an officer who worked for her father. It was quite another to defy her father to his face without expecting retribution of the ghastliest sort. At worst she'd be locked up in the lunatic asylum; at best forced to marry Travers. Bleaker outcomes she could not imagine.

The *Justine* had stilled almost to a halt when Cartwright dropped the anchor and the crew readied the boat to take them to shore. Georgie gripped Rob's hand as he helped her in, dread filling her heart.

"Do not worry, sweetheart." Rob ran his thumb over the back of her hand. "I will make certain you marry no one but me."

Gazing up at him, she tried to speak words of comfort, but they choked her throat. So she smiled and laced their fingers together.

The crew lowered them over the side.

Time to face her fate.

When they reached the narrow dock, Rob helped her out and together they turned toward the shore, where a sea of faces awaited them. Georgie gasped and stopped. Had everyone come to witness the final battle of wills?

"Come, my love. Let's put our best foot forward." Rob started her moving again.

"I would if I thought it would do any good." The stern set of her father's face was familiar at least. Several of his liveried servants stood behind him, an impassive wall. Jemmy and Elizabeth stood to the side of Father, looking glum. To his left Lord Travers had made an appearance, apparently recovered from Georgie's brutal tactics. He'd apparently brought some of his men as well, a puny show of his strength next to her father's. She narrowed her eyes and glared at him. If Father forced this marriage, she vowed she'd make sure she wasn't the only one sorry about it. Even Lady St. Just was present, and interestingly one of the friendlier faces in the group. Georgie would have loved being her daughter-in-law.

"Georgie." Elizabeth rushed past Georgie's father, and Georgie flew into her arms. "Are you all right?"

"Yes, for the moment at least." She hugged her friend fiercely. "But not for much longer, I'm afraid."

Boney fingers clamped onto her wrist as her father hauled her out of Elizabeth's arms.

"You will not get away from me again, Georgina." Father released her, his mouth pursed as if touching her were the most distasteful thing he'd done in an age. "At least not before I dispose of you as I promised. Travers."

Limping slightly, Lord Travers shuffled over to them, his bloodshot eyes taking her in from top to bottom. "My lady, are you quite all right after your ordeal?"

"Thank you for your concern, my lord." Georgie stared him down. "But of what ordeal do you speak? The only thing to distress me recently was your unwanted attempt to ravish me, from which I have thankfully recovered, although"—she eyed the area of his fall very obviously—"I see you have not. If you continue to limp, I would suggest you consult one of the doctors in Harley Street. Perhaps they can put you to rights."

"Georgina!" Her father spun her around and slapped her across the mouth. "I will not tolerate insolence nor rudeness to your prospective husband."

Before she could raise her hand to her smarting cheek, Rob had appeared in front of her, pushing her behind him. Towering over her father, fists clenched, lips in a snarl, he looked like an avenging angel—and every inch her hero. "Lady Georgina has expressed neither insolence nor rudeness to me, my lord, and as I am her prospective husband—"

A roar of outrage erupted from Lord Travers, who hobbled toward Rob with an uneven gait. "You are not her prospective anything, St. Just. I have her father's oath and a promise, written in her own hand, swearing to marry me."

"And as that promise was elicited from her by coercion"—Rob swung his blistering gaze from her father to Travers—"and she has recently revoked her consent, it is no more valid than your claim to her hand. So, my lords, you will refrain from touching her again, either of you, in any capacity. I am not a man who suffers fools with any particular patience. And you are fools indeed if you believe I will allow any man, other than me, to lay hands on her."

"This is outrageous!" Her father's face had turned a ghastly shade of red. "My lady." He turned to Lady St. Just, standing serenely by, missing not a word. "Take your whelp in hand and instruct him that he has absolutely no authority over my daughter, nor shall he ever have. Perhaps he'll listen to his parent as he will not to his betters."

"I suspect, Blackham, that if he had been given instruction by his betters he would have heeded it. I have raised him to be respectful of those worthy of respect." Fixing her father with a steely eye, the marchioness stared at him unblinking until amazingly, he dropped his gaze. Without missing a beat, she turned to her son. "St. Just, you have laid claim to Lady Georgina's hand, even though it has already been given to another. Do you perhaps have a claim on her that her father has not yet discovered?"

Frowning, Georgie glanced at Rob. What was his mother talking about? He had no formal right to marry her, save that he loved her and she loved him. Unfortunately, a strong claim on her heart would hold less than no weight with her father. To her surprise, however, after a confused moment, Rob grinned broadly. What had she missed?

"I do have such a claim, Mother. No one knows of it yet, save Lady Georgina and I."

Everyone's gaze was now firmly fixed on Rob.

"What nonsense is this?" Blustering much more than usual, Father looked from Rob to his mother, and seemed to hesitate. "He has no right, no claim to my daughter whatsoever."

"Indeed I do have the better claim than Lord Travers, not only by having secured the lady's regard, but by virtue of circumstances that have recently arisen." He shifted his gaze to Georgie, mouthed "I love you" to her, and plowed firmly on. "I declare that I know for a fact that Lady Georgina is, at this moment, carrying my child."

Oh, dear Lord. Hanging her head to hide not only her hot cheeks but the murder certainly in her eyes, Georgie tried to ignore the gasps from all assembled and then the silence. Cautiously, she raised her head to find everyone's attention now on her.

"No! This cannot be true." Travers barged in between Rob and Father, his eyes almost starting from their sockets. "I was the first one in her bed. If she is with child, it is mine."

Outrage pouring through her, Georgie pushed past Rob and stalked up to Travers, who skidded to a stop. "You, my lord, are a liar."

Travers's mouth dropped open, though no sound of protest came out.

"You may have found your way into my bed by nefarious means, but merely lying in one does not cause a woman to have a child. And I can swear before God, you did not touch me in such a way that a child could be conceived. In fact"— she leaned toward him, and he swayed back—"I may have made sure that you can never produce a child." She held her hand up before his eyes and clenched her fist.

The earl shuddered and shuffled back.

"If that is the case, I am sorry." She didn't want to have been the cause of his line's dying out, certainly. But neither had she wanted him in her bed. "I did not mean to affect you thusly. But I did wish to save my virtue, and that was the only way for me to do so." Nodding her head, she found herself staring into the furious face of her father.

"You freely admit to this wanton behavior?" Father stared at her, disbelief plain on his face.

"I . . ." To admit this in public would be shameful beyond

belief. But if it was the only way for her and Rob to be together, then so be it. "Yes, yes it is true."

"I demand satisfaction." Barreling back up the dock, Lord Travers drew himself up to face Rob. Georgie believed he would punch her beloved in the face, but instead he ripped off one of his Yorkshire-tan gloves and threw it at Rob's feet. "Meet me now, sir, or else be known forever after as coward."

Leaning down to pick up the offending glove, Rob chuckled.

Why on earth would he laugh about such a serious challenge?

He snagged the scrap of leather and straightened. "It will be my pleasure, Travers, to put a ball through your black heart."

"Travers." Her father's frown said he did not approve of this turn of events. "Don't be a fool. He's trying to draw you out so he can kill you and marry my daughter."

"How can I not answer that slap, my lord?" Travers was stumping toward the end of the dock, moving toward the beach where several more men were milling around. "I've been waiting to bed Lady Georgina for nigh on five years. And St. Just has just told the world he's cuckolded me before I am even her husband. Cole." He called, and one of the men on the beach trotted toward him. "Bring me my set of dueling pistols."

The man nodded and headed toward one of the carriages sitting on the crushed shell road that led up to the castle.

"You carry dueling pistols with you all the time, Travers?" Rob had taken Georgie's arm as they and the rest of the company moved toward shore as well. "That speaks to your sense of preparedness at least. I suppose a man of your reputation never knows when he may be accosted by an irate husband."

"Rather disconcerting to have the shoe upon the other

foot now, is it not, Lord Travers?" Georgie spoke as sweetly as she could manage while biting back her fear. Under her voice she whispered to Rob, "You're not really going to duel with him, are you?"

The wretch laughed aloud and patted her arm. "Of course I'm going to duel with him. This is my God-given chance to get Travers out of our lives for good. You cannot marry a dead man."

"I know. So make certain he is the dead man and not you. Have you dueled before?"

"No, but I'm a good shot." He raised her hand for a kiss. "And I've got excellent motivation to succeed. Our future together."

They reached the hard-packed sand of the beach, still waiting for Travers's man to bring the weapons.

"Will you fight here?" She cast a doubtful look around. The beach was very rocky, not the best place if one needed sure footing.

"I'll suggest the front lawn instead." His cheerful confidence did not reassure her overmuch. This was a dangerous gamble, with stakes incredibly high for them. "The good thing about living so far removed in the country is that one does not have to go about trying to hide such things."

"Georgie, you must stop this." Elizabeth reached them as Travers's servant returned, a thin wooden box in his hands.

"I do not think I can, my dear." Her friend's worried countenance fed her own fears. "Rob assures me that—Oh, oh! There, that's him." She tugged on Rob's sleeve, Elizabeth completely forgotten. "That's Odd Fellow!" She pointed at Travers's servant as he handed his master the box of pistols. "Kidnapper! Kidnapper!"

Again all eyes turned to Georgie, but she paid them no mind. She ran forward to Travers's side, sticking an accusing finger in Odd Fellow's face. "You didn't think to see me again, did you, ruffian? Rob, Father, this is the man who abducted me, Clara, and Lulu. I know him well because of his very odd features. That's why I called him Odd Fellow to myself and Clara."

"What are you talking about now, Georgina?" Her father turned from speaking with Jemmy, frowning once again. "You are certainly proving more trouble than you are worth. How can you accuse Lord Travers's servant of abducting you? Why would he do such a thing?"

Grasping the pistol case, Travers jerked his head toward them, then back to the servant. "Go. Now," he hissed at him.

"Hold!" Rob shouted, striding forward. "Stay right where you are, sir."

The man stopped, his gaze shifting uncertainly between his master and Rob.

"I have no idea, Father," Georgie continued, "but I know that is him. All you need do is let Clara see him, and she will tell you as well."

"As can I, Lord Blackham." Eyes narrowed, Rob joined them. "That"—he pointed at the man, now trying to shield his face—"is one of the men who was guarding your carriage and Lady Georgina's trunks. I sent him off chasing after a boy to lure him away from the carriage, then my men and I secured her property and took it back to my ship."

"Travers!" Father bellowed so loudly the seagulls shrieked and fled the beach. "What is the meaning of this? Why are my daughter and St. Just claiming that your servant is the one who abducted Georgina in the first place?"

The earl shuffled over to them, his mouth smiling widely while his eyes shifted like a mouse in a trap. "My lord, I can explain."

"Good. Do so." Her father glared at the man until he squirmed.

"I was afraid, my lord . . . That is, I had heard rumors, you see, that your son did not look favorably on my match with Lady Georgina. And I remembered last time, when she ran off with Kirkpatrick, and slipped through my grasp at the very last moment." The conciliatory persona changed, Travers's voice becoming more peevish. "I couldn't let that happen again. I'd had to live it down the last time, that she jilted me for a vicar's son." He glared at Georgie, and she shrank back to grasp Rob's arm. "I wasn't about to do that a second time."

"I gave you no reason to suppose I would do anything of the kind this time." Indignant, Georgie glowered back at Travers.

"And yet there you stand on the arm of another man, once more, my lady."

Well, the man had a point, although, if he'd not interfered with her journey, none of them would be standing here right now. For the first time, she wanted to thank Lord Travers for something.

"So what had you planned to do to secure Lady Georgina's affections, Travers?" Beneath her fingers Rob's body went taut.

"We were to spend time together, to let her get to know me. The woman wouldn't even agree to speak to me before then." The petulant tone of his voice did him no credit, but Georgie couldn't help feeling a modicum of pity for the man. She had treated him rather badly, if you looked at everything that had occurred between them over the last five years.

"In an inn down by the docks in Portsmouth?" Rob's voice cut through her thoughts like a newly sharpened knife. "Without a chaperone, save her maid?"

"You had no more chaperone when you took her off," Travers shot back.

"But I didn't intend to ravish her against her will, as you so aptly demonstrated you did the other night."

"Enough!" Father put an end to the argument by pulling

Travers to the side. "You kidnapped my daughter because you doubted I would keep my word?"

Travers's mouth worked although nothing came out.

"Fool. You could have had her, her dowry, and in six years her mother's inheritance as well. I am known as a man who keeps his word, no matter what. You should have listened to *those* rumors before any other." Father glared at Travers, the tendons on his neck popping out like taut lines on a ship. "Not to mention the expense you have made me incur, due simply to your lack of faith in me. I had to pay for travel and lodging for my servants from Somerset to come rescue Georgina. And when I decided I must come to Cornwall to see to this debacle myself, I incurred another expense with my ship. Instead of shipping goods, it's been transporting me to this out of the way place." Father paced forward until he stood toe to toe with the earl. "Inconvenience me at your peril, Travers. I am not a man to take a slight lightly, especially one that costs me time and money."

"But my lord—"

Father raised his hand to Travers, effectively silencing him. "Let me assure you, I will refuse to ally myself with a man who has the poor judgment to mistrust my word. Even though the alternative"—he shifted his glare to Rob—"has little more to recommend his suit."

"I think you have misspoken yet again, Blackham." Lady St. Just's gaze beat down on Father until Georgie could swear her parent shrank backward. "My son has everything to recommend him. An old and prestigious title, wealth beyond Lord Travers's dreams, and the regard and affection of your daughter. I think all three of these things should be taken into consideration when bestowing your daughter's hand in marriage."

To her great surprise, Father gave Lady St. Just a thoughtful glance, then turned away from Travers to scrutinize Rob. "I take it you still wish to wed my daughter?"

"What are you saying, Lord Blackham?" Grasping her father's arm, the earl tried to turn him back toward him. "We have an accord, a signed agreement."

With a casual flip of his hand Father dismissed the man who had been his favored suitor for all these years. "Well, St. Just?"

Startled, Rob shot Georgie a glance and an impish grin. "Yes, my lord."

"You cannot renege on this marriage contract." The desperation in Travers's face and voice were making him reckless. "You promised me her dowry, and I have to have it, Blackham. My last investment sank to the bottom of the Channel a week ago, so I'm on the rocks, my lord. You gave me your word, so I was counting on Lady Georgina's dowry to see me through this lean time, don't you see?"

With an absolutely straight face, Father replied, "Then I believe you have miscounted, Travers. I agreed to align myself with you because five years ago your wealth was sound, your properties prosperous. I fear I neglected to rein-vestigate your financial standing when you renewed your suit. Apparently, I too have been the victim of rumors, ones that said you were still one of the wealthiest men in England. We might have saved ourselves a deal of trouble had I not done so."

The color had drained from Travers's face, and he re-mained speechless.

Father stopped, and put his hand on Rob's sleeve. "You are certain she's breeding already?"

A tinge of red invaded Rob's cheeks. "To the best of my ability, I believe so, my lord."

After a long stare that took in Georgie, Rob, and Rob's mother, Father nodded. "Very well. Be certain you do not disappoint me as others have done." Issuing a spectacular glower at Travers, Father sniffed and turned to Lady St. Just, to whom he bowed and offered his arm. "Would you do me the honor of allowing me to escort you, my lady?"

With a gracious nod, she laid her hand lightly on his sleeve. "I believe you will do after all, Blackham."

Unmoving, the stunned Lord Travers blinked several times, as if not quite certain what had just happened. Finally, he settled a grim look on Rob. "St. Just, you accepted my challenge. I want satisfaction!"

"With utmost pleasure, Travers." Rob moved so he was between Georgie and the earl. "I shall inform my second, who will contact yours. It may take them a while to reach us here in Cornwall, but I will be ready whenever you are." Rob bowed and turned his back, leading Georgie away from the befuddled lord.

"So you will still have to fight him?" Chills scurried down her spine. They were so very close to the happiness that remained just beyond their grasp.

"Our seconds will contact each other and attempt to settle the dispute." Raising her hand, he kissed it on the palm. "I suspect Travers will simply steal away, and no more will be heard of it. It would be very embarrassing for him if the reason for the challenge became public."

Pray God Rob spoke the truth.

"So that was all it took? Your father's given us his blessing?" Rob lowered his voice as they headed toward one of the carriages.

"Be careful you do not doubt it." She laughed, not truly believing it was real either. "You saw how quickly he turned on Travers." Grasping Rob's arm, she leaned into him, deliriously happy. "We are finally betrothed, although not for long, I hope."

"Unless you wish another voyage, or to travel to London by carriage over the next weeks to secure a special license, we must have the banns read in the parish church here." He caressed her cheek. "Will you mind waiting very much?"

"I suppose we will find ways to pass the time." Smiling, Georgie stopped as they crossed onto the shell road. Sliding her arms around his neck, she rose on tiptoe, her mouth hungry for his.

"Stop that this second."

Georgie jumped away from Rob as Jemmy came striding up to them, Elizabeth following in his wake.

"No intimate contact with my sister until after the wedding." His stern front did not disguise his glee. "I told you I would act as chaperone while you were on the voyage."

"But—" Both she and Rob tried to interrupt, but her brother droned on.

"As there is to be no voyage, but there will be a betrothal period, I intend to watch out for you and your reputation during the period between betrothal and marriage." Grinning as though he was enjoying himself immensely, her brother added one further admonition. "And I assure you, I have very sharp eyes."

Georgie punched him in the arm. "Jemmy! For goodness sake. After everything we've been through, can you not allow us even a kiss?" She looked longingly at Rob. "Not even one?"

"Considering," Rob chimed in, "as I just announced, we have already done much more than kiss, why not let us continue to anticipate our blissful wedding with an even more blissfully anticipated honeymoon?"

"I do believe, dearest, that you should make some slight allowance for Georgie and Rob." To the rescue as always, Elizabeth linked her arm through her husband's. "As you may remember, we shared much, much more than a kiss before we were married."

"Elizabeth." Jemmy sent an agonized look to his wife. "You are supposed to be supporting me in suppressing their urges before they are married."

"I refuse to be a hypocrite, my dear." Smiling sweetly at her husband, Elizabeth patted his arm. "As long as I remember that evening at the Harvest Festival, and the passageway between your room and Georgie's at Blackham Castle—"

"You stayed in my room at home, Elizabeth?" Even though no one else could hear her, Georgie still lowered her voice. Old habits died hard. "The one with the secret passage?"

"Yes, my dear. And we had the most marvelous evening—"

"Elizabeth." Jemmy tugged on her arm, heading up the path with a quicker than usual step. "Come. You have been standing for far too long."

"Yes, dear." The two of them moved toward the carriage.

Lingering just a moment behind, Georgie and Rob stood facing the *Justine* and open sea beyond. "A glorious morning, wouldn't you say, Captain?"

"I would indeed, Mrs. Captain." He took her in his arms before her brother could put up a protest. "My Lady Pirate, who has stolen my heart."

"Aye, Captain." She pressed her lips to his, for all the world to see. "Let us set sail on a new adventure."

Chapter Twenty-Six

A little over two weeks later, Georgie stood solemnly beside Rob before the altar in the Lady Chapel of the St. Just Parish Church. No one could have ever convinced her a month before that she would be so deliriously happy to be married again. It was as though the sun had decided to shine on her perpetually.

Because they chose to wait and have the banns read, Georgie and Rob were thrilled not only to receive letters of well wishes from her and Elizabeth's other friends, but also delighted when they insisted on coming all the way to Cornwall for the wedding. Although Georgie had argued that the week of bouncing in a carriage would not be wise considering their delicate conditions—Charlotte and Fanny were both, like Elizabeth, increasing—they were all adamant. Their other widow friend, Jane, who was not increasing, had agreed to ride with them to keep them company, and the journey sounded almost fête-like to Georgie.

Meanwhile, she and Elizabeth and Lady St. Just had not been idle. They had worked hard to plan a spectacular wedding breakfast in the large drawing room for Georgie and Rob, their guests, the local families, and friends. At the gathering after the ceremony, Georgie had met almost everyone in the parish, it seemed, before slipping off to talk and laugh with the members of the sadly depleted Widows' Club.

"I am the sole member left." The die-away, overly dramatic voice Jane used brought a smile to Georgie's face. "The members of the Widows' Club are now all happily wedded, even down to little Maria. She wrote to me not long ago, singing the praises of a blissful married life."

"All happily married except for you, Jane." Smiling archly at her sister-in-law, Fanny settled herself deeper into the chaise. "But then you said from the beginning that you would not marry again."

"As did you, my dear," Jane shot back.

"Well, Matthew finally convinced me that life without him would be the poorer indeed." Smiling widely and actually blushing, Fanny looked happier than Georgie had ever seen her. "He certainly was right, I must say." She leaned over and grasped Georgie's hand. "I'm confident you will find the same thing true with your Lord St. Just, Georgie."

"I am already convinced of that." Although she continued to smile, Georgie quieted as her thoughts flew back to the previous week, before her friends arrived, to the duel between Rob and Lord Travers.

They had believed all Travers's talk of the duel was bluster only, until a note had arrived requesting Rob name his second so the duel could take place while the earl was in Cornwall. Reluctantly, Rob had asked Jemmy, who had then met with Travers's second, a gentleman named Marsh, who had arrived recently from London at the request of the earl.

"I didn't quite know what to make of his statement, although it was rather to the point," Jemmy had told them that afternoon. "When I asked the usual question, 'What will it take to appease the earl?,' the man answered simply, 'Death.'"

Georgie's head had spun, and she'd slumped to the floor.

When she'd awakened, she'd clung to Rob, begging him not to go through with the challenge.

"I must do it, my love, or be branded a coward. And that is something I cannot have, for it would circulate through the *ton* at an astonishing rate. My honor is above reproach and must remain so." He'd kissed her and promised, "I will do my very best to return to you in one whole piece."

Two days later Rob had met Travers on the front lawn of St. Just Castle. Georgie had refused to watch, instead sitting in her dressing room, holding Lulu and praying, awaiting the dreaded gunfire. First one shot resounded, and she'd clutched Lulu until she yelped. An aeon seemed to pass before a second report had rung out. She had buried her face in Lulu's soft fur and cried, until Rob found her there.

"It's all right, sweetheart. It's all over, and I am none the worse for it."

She had launched herself into his arms, crying harder as Lulu had yipped at being dropped to the floor. "Oh, my love." She hugged him fiercely, never wanting to let him go. "I was so worried." A sudden dread crossed her mind, and she looked up. "And Lord Travers?"

Shaking his head, Rob stepped back. "It was the strangest thing. Travers seemed sober for a change and very much to the purpose. He spoke not a word to me or even to his second, just stood ready, in his place. Jemmy was elected to drop the handkerchief, and, when he did, nothing happened."

They had moved back into the marchioness's apartment, and Georgie had sat on the chair, puzzled. "What do you mean?"

"I had raised my weapon, but Travers did nothing. So I hesitated, wondering what he was playing at. Finally, he raised his weapon slowly, until it was aimed squarely at me, and I started to pull the trigger of my pistol, when he continued to move his weapon, raising it to the sky. All the while he stared me in the eyes."

"What was he doing?"

"I think he wanted me to kill him." Rob's gaze was distant. "Because he discharged his pistol into the air."

"I heard it." She had shuddered, knowing it could have been a deathblow to Rob.

"I waited a good long moment, contemplating doing exactly what I believed he wanted. You heard that he's truly in the suds?"

Georgie had shaken her head. She'd hardly given Travers a second thought since her betrothal to Rob.

"Jemmy received a letter from a friend of his in London, warning him to persuade your father to break your betrothal to the earl because he was in such grave financial difficulties. Apparently there is talk he might have to break the entailment." Rob looked away. "He might believe he'd be better off dead."

With growing horror, Georgie had grasped Rob's arm. "But you didn't . . . ?"

"No, I didn't." He had covered her hand with his. "Even if it was what he wished, I could not, in honor, kill a defenseless man."

Georgie had thrown herself into Rob's arms at that.

"What are you smiling at, my dear?" Elizabeth broke in on her reverie. "The wedding night to come?" She laughed. "At least Jemmy can devil you no more. You are well and truly married."

"Yes," Georgie agreed, her gaze lighting on Rob, laughing with Jemmy, Matthew, and Nash across the room. "Very well and truly."

Some time later, as the local guests were taking their leave, Rob snagged her hand and drew her up through the house toward her bedchamber.

"Are we beginning the honeymoon earlier than expected?"

she asked, squeezing his hand. It could not be soon enough for her. She'd missed having him in her bed these long weeks.

"Not exactly." He opened her door and whistled. Lulu barked and ran out into the corridor, panting excitedly. "This way."

He led them down to the first floor, then to the steep steps that wound up to the parapet, awash in afternoon sunlight. As they surveyed their domain, Lulu sitting happily at their feet between them, a sense of peace settled over Georgie that she had not experienced since Isaac had been alive. Perhaps this was a benediction from him, urging her to be happy for the rest of her life in this beautiful, wild place. With her wonderful pirate of a husband.

As if hearing her unspoken thought, Rob slipped his arm around her shoulders. "All of this will shortly be ours alone."

"Don't say such things, Rob." She smacked him lightly on his chest. "We want your mother alive and here for many, many years to come."

"Oh, I heartily agree, my love. But she will be leaving us shortly, for an undetermined amount of time."

Georgie cocked her head. "She will?"

"Your father has invited her for a visit to Blackham Castle, and she accepted." Rob reached over and put his finger beneath Georgie's chin to shut her mouth, which had dropped open.

"I don't know which is more startling, that my father asked her after all her very pointed barbs at him or that your mother accepted the invitation." She couldn't imagine the warfare to be waged by these two Tartars.

"I believe they have finally met their matches, as temperament goes, and are eager to wage that war with gusto. I have insisted that Jemmy and Elizabeth accompany them as chaperones, for propriety's sake. You know how warfare stimulates the appetites." Snaking his arms around her, Rob drew Georgie to him. "All of the appetites."

"Rob! You don't think . . ." Her *father* and *Lady St. Just*?

"All's fair in love and war, my sweet." He nuzzled her neck, sending chills down her spine.

"Then what about in surrender, Captain Pirate?" She molded herself against him, his rising interest making its presence known.

"My surrender to you or yours to me, Mrs. Captain?" Freeing her shoulder from her gown, he kissed his way over it, kindling a fire throughout her.

"I don't think that matters at all." Arching into him, her happiness was complete. "Not to a pirate."

Connect with
Us

Visit us online at
KensingtonBooks.com
to read more from your favorite authors, see books
by series, view reading group guides, and more.

for sneak peeks, chances to win books and prize packs,
and to share your thoughts with other readers.

**facebook.com/kensingtonpublishing
twitter.com/kensingtonbooks**

Tell us what you think!

To share your thoughts, submit a review,
or sign up for our eNewsletters, please visit:
KensingtonBooks.com/TellUs.